**Praise for**
***The Pumpkin Rollers***

"Elmer Kelton does not write 'Westerns.' He writes fine novels set in the West—like *The Pumpkin Rollers*. Here a reader meets flesh-and-blood people of an earlier time, in a story that will grab and hold you from the first to the last page."

—Dee Brown, author of the *New York Times* bestseller *Bury My Heart at Wounded Knee*

"A marvelous romantic western that will hold a reader's attention to the very end. Kelton is a wonderful storyteller who has won six Spur Awards. This book must surely climb to the top of his award-winning list."

—*Oklahoman* (Oklahoma City, OK)

"A big, brawling saga with enough action, character, suspense, history, rage, passion, and wisdom to please anybody who likes their bestsellers bold and relentless. This is his finest."

—E. J. Gorman, *Mystery Scene*

"A coming-of-age tale, Western style, and veteran genre-master Kelton handles the theme well. The key characters are all carefully and believably rendered....Fine reading."

—*Booklist*

"Flavored with the believable characters and historical authenticity that characterize Kelton's work....An especially compelling story."

—*Express-News Morning Edition* (San Antonio, TX)

"Elmer Kelton, winner of six Spur Awards, has done it again with his latest novel....A vivid and accurate depiction of how the West came of age during the exciting times of our nation's expanse."

—*American Cowboy*

"A marvelous coming-of-age novel that will captivate readers from any walk of life....No one writes better than Elmer Kelton, who is probably America's foremost novelist, and certainly one of this nation's treasures."

—Richard S. Wheeler, award-winning author of *Goldfield* and *Cashbox*

# THE PUMPKIN ROLLERS

## ELMER KELTON

A TOM DOHERTY ASSOCIATES BOOK
NEW YORK

This is a work of fiction. All the characters and events portrayed in this book are either products of the author's imagination or are used fictitiously.

THE PUMPKIN ROLLERS



Cover art by Howard Rogers

A Forge Book
Published by Tom Doherty Associates, Inc.
175 Fifth Avenue
New York, NY 10010

Forge® is a registered trademark of Tom Doherty Associates, Inc.

ISBN: 0-812-54399-8

First edition: March 1996
First mass market edition: April 1997

Printed in the United States of America

0 9 8 7 6 5 4 3 2 1

*To my three brothers and my sisters-in-law*
*who have stood beside them so long:*
*Myrle and Ann*
*Bill and Pat*
*Gene and Peggy*

# THE PUMPKIN ROLLERS

# ONE

Since about the time Andrew Jackson whipped the British at New Orleans two weeks after the War of 1812 had officially ended, it had been McLean family tradition to register births, marriages and deaths in a big leather-bound Bible. The Book was already a considerable repository of family history by the time James Wilton McLean's mother added his name in a studied hand a decade before the War of Northern Aggression.

After that, few occasions arose for his full name to be written down. His domino-playing father hung the nickname Trey upon him because he was the third-born son. It clung like an East Texas chigger.

It had become family tradition also that each son except for the firstborn would strike out on his own when he became old enough and big enough to whip his father. There was not room for more than one grown son to remain on the family's small blackland farm. That dubious privilege went to the oldest. Trey McLean was not certain he could whip Pap, and even less certain that he wanted to try.

So, turning his back on tradition, he said good-bye to his weeping mother and frowning father, venturing forth upon a wagon road that meandered off in a generally westward direction past the cotton gin and the gristmill, across the river and on toward that awesome, mysterious country most people simply called "out west." He wore a floppy farmer-boy hat that might have looked good on a scarecrow. The brown horse he rode matched his age and trailed four cows that would never be ten years old again. That was the sum of his accumulated wealth, earned laboring for neighbors when his father could spare him from the plow and the pitchfork, the cotton sack and the corn-heading knife.

Trey realized that four cows of such mature years offered at best a slow start toward a fortune, but a weak fence had allowed all to consort freely with a neighbor's black bull. In proper season he could expect his head count to double. He had been assured that somewhere to the west of Fort Worth he should find free grazing on land to which no one had yet established any legal claim.

He saw one potential complication. The Comanches and the Kiowas had not yielded to the army's insistence that they repair to the reservation. They were not ready to entrust their future welfare to Uncle Sam's bald-headed nephews who administered the Indian agency. But Trey had faith. Though he had been too young to fight for the Confederacy's lost cause, he had taken over the job of bringing wild meat to the family table while his oldest brother fought the war. He claimed he could knock the left eye out of a squirrel as far as he could see it wink. He figured Indians would have the good judgment to respect marksmanship and leave him and his livestock alone.

Besides, as slow as these cows walked, it was going to be a long while before they muddied their feet at the banks of the Brazos or the Colorado, or whatever other western watercourse he settled upon. The army's spokesmen kept promising they would soon force the wild tribes to yield.

The same people had vowed to bring the South to heel in a month.

Trey would not allow his high spirits to be dampened by concern about Indians anyway. He was too excited over the prospect of being truly free for the first time, responsible only for himself, adventuring into a new land where years of cotton had not yet wearied the soil and sapped it of strength. There, the newspapers claimed, the only limits to a man's prospects were his willingness to work and the size of his dream.

Trey had always been a hard worker, and his dream was as big as the cloudless sky under which he rode on this shining spring day.

Tied behind his saddle was the canvas war bag his brother had carried to Virginia and back. It remained in good shape except for two Yankee bullet holes, battlefield-mended in rough fashion. It contained a change of long-handled underwear, one homespun shirt and a pair of pants a little shorter than Trey's long legs. On his feet were the only boots he owned, homemade, bull-stout and hog-ugly, with a ten-dollar gold piece sewn into the top of one for emergencies. Hanging in two cotton sacks on either side of the saddle were flour, salt and coffee beans, a slab of fat bacon, a skillet and a can to boil coffee in. As for meat, he had no doubt he could live on the results of his marksmanship. That meant rabbit and squirrel now, perhaps venison and buffalo once he passed the heavily settled, heavily hunted East Texas settlements.

He had seventeen dollars Yankee in his pocket to meet whatever contingencies might arise. All in all, he felt he had a running start toward a career as a cattle baron.

His father did not share Trey's optimism. Pap had never taken into proper account that Trey was four years younger than his oldest brother and two years younger than the next. He had expected Trey to keep up with them in the amount of labor he could accomplish between daylight and dark. Thus, he had rarely acknowledged merit in his third-born son. A pattern of automatic criticism had become too deeply ingrained to change though Trey had grown to be the tallest and strongest of them all.

Trey had tried not to let his father's pessimism slow him, but at times the disparaging words burrowed beneath his confidence like a gopher undermining a cornerstone. He needed reassurance from time to time to shore up what Pap had undercut.

"You won't get fifty miles with them cows," Pap had declared. "They'll run off or get stole. You'll come draggin' back with the seat of your britches out and your belly thinkin' your throat's been cut."

"Bet you!" Trey had proven Pap's dire predictions wrong in the past, especially since he had finally outreached his brothers in length of leg and arm and hardness of muscle. He was determined to do it again.

And he did. He made it *seventy* miles before he lost the cows.

---

He was in an itch to hurry a lot of distance between himself and the black, gummy soil of the McLean homeplace, but he found there was a limit to how fast four long-aged cows would willingly travel, especially when their ribs were beginning to spring in their pregnancy. He carried a bullwhip on his saddle but did not like to use it. He had no wish to inflict pain upon his property. It seemed to do little good anyway. Like a mule, the cows had a way in their bovine stubbornness of rushing their hind legs a little when he pressed them, while their front legs kept going at the same stolid pace.

After a while he gave up the effort to hurry them and reconciled himself to spending the first night at the farm of Pap's brother, Uncle Matthew, eight miles up the wagon road.

Uncle Matthew was all right; he had often taken Trey's side when Pap had criticized him for one perceived shortcoming or another. But one could not take Uncle Matthew without accepting Aunt Maudie as well, and Aunt Maudie could talk until Trey's ears hurt. Uncle Matthew had taken refuge in deafness, though Trey had noted that he seemed to hear fairly well when he wanted to. His impairment was selective.

As Trey had feared, Aunt Maudie told him a hundred reasons why he should give up the foolish notion of going west and becoming a cattleman. She was firm in her conviction that herdsmen in general were indolent agents of Lucifer, while hardworking tillers of the soil were the meek God had chosen to inherit the earth. Besides, she said, it would be a hundred years before the country west of Fort Worth ever became anything other than a godless wilderness, and even a young man like Trey would never enjoy such a life span, especially out there where savage Comanches had free run. His life was likely to be as short as a dirt dauber's, she said.

Uncle Matthew said little in her presence, but next morning as he opened the gate to let the four cows out of his hay lot he took his old black pipe from his mouth and pointed west with the stem of it. "This was a raw country too when me and your pap put Tennessee behind us. We took ahold and made somethin' out of it. Now, you got the makin's to do better than him or me either one. You ain't got much to start with, so there ain't no way you can go but up. Do it, and make us proud."

Trey gathered up all the confidence he could muster. To prove his father wrong and his uncle right, he told himself he would ride through hell and out its far side.

He did not realize how short a trip it could be to hell. At the slow pace the cows set for him, it took about a week.

Trey had never known much about law or lawmen. Pap had always figured the less government there was, the better. That started with the county courthouse and held all the way to Washington City. Trey had only a nodding acquaintance with the local sheriff. An officer of the law always made him a little nervous, as if he had done something wrong that he didn't even know about but the officer did.

He had never been more than a few miles west of his Uncle Matthew's farm, so by noon of the second day he was among strangers in a strange country. By the end of a slow week he didn't even know the name of the county he was traversing. He stayed on or near the heaviest-traveled road that led west, and when he came to a fork where he couldn't tell the difference, he let the cows graze while he waited for somebody to come along and give him proper directions. He found most people friendly, inclined to tarry and jaw a spell.

He was not concerned, then, when a farmer rode up behind him in a buggy whose springs sagged under what must have been three hundred and fifty pounds of pure lard. The farmer's eyes were half hidden behind a roll of fat at the top of puffy cheeks that vibrated like pudding. He had the voice of a man speaking from the bottom of a well. "Where'd you come by these good cows, young fellow?"

Trey saw no reason not to tell him. On the contrary, he was proud of the fact. "Bought them with the savin's from my labor. I'm takin' them out west to start me a herd."

"No two of them seem to have the same brand."

"They come off of four different farms. I ain't figured out a brand of my own yet."

"You got any kin in this county? Any friends?"

"They're all sixty-seventy miles behind me. I don't know a soul around here."

He wondered why the farmer seemed pleased at that. Most folks tended to cluck in sympathy at the thought of his passing through a land of strangers, a pilgrim in the wilderness.

The farmer pointed. "You stay on this main road. You'll come to a fork a couple of miles farther on. Be sure and bear to the right. I expect you'd like to spend the night in town."

Trey hadn't so far. He had been managing about sundown each evening to find a farmhouse and somebody willing to let him pen his cows for the night. Most of them invited him to supper. In town they would want money for that. But he thanked the farmer anyway and watched the man put the large buggy horse into a long trot, laboring on ahead. He pitied the animal its heavy load.

The first sign of the town was the courthouse clock tower, standing taller than anything else on the horizon. He estimated that it was an hour to sundown and about that long to the edge of town. He could see a couple of people riding toward him, one on horseback and one in a buggy, but he thought little of it. He was used to meeting travelers along the road. After a time he recognized the farmer. The horsebacker was a stranger. He looked like a farmer too, about the same age as Pap. Not until he was near enough to address Trey without shouting did Trey notice the badge pinned to the man's shirt pocket. Immediately he felt that old welling-up of guilt, though he had nothing to feel guilty about.

The officer did not say "Hello" or "How do?" or any such pleasantry. He just rode a slow, thoughtful circle around the cows, which gladly took the opportunity to drop their heads into the grass and begin stuffing their paunches.

"I see four different brands here on four different cows. Where's *your* brand?" he demanded.

"Ain't decided on one yet."

"If you don't have your own brand, how do you know they're your cows?"

That seemed a foolish question to Trey. The officer probably knew more about plows than cows, this being cotton country. "By their marks and their colors and their general looks, same as I know people," Trey answered.

"You got any papers with you to prove ownership?"

A hard look in the lawman's narrowed eyes began to worry Trey. "There never was no papers. I just paid the money and got the cows."

The officer jerked his head toward the farmer in the buggy. "Mr. Lige Connors here, he says they're *his* cows."

"He may say so, but he's wrong."

The farmer leaned forward, making the buggy springs creak. His jowls shook. "You callin' me a liar, young fellow?"

Trey felt the stirrings of anxiety. "I'm sayin' you're mistaken."

The farmer pointed at the nearest cow. "They're mine, Micah. See that one with the twisted horn? I'd know that spotted hide if I seen it in a tan yard."

Anger coursed through Trey as he realized the farmer was flat-out trying to steal his cows. That was one sin. He was swearing false witness. That was two. Old Preacher Featherstone back home would have his work cut out for him, trying to pray this man back from the brink of perdition.

The sheriff declared gravely, "I'm takin' these cows into custody. And you too, young man. We take a mighty poor view around here of men who try to get off with other people's stock."

Even as Trey shouted, "They're my cows!" he saw the futility of it. In a wildly irrational moment he tried to put the cows into a run, but they had long since gotten past any fear of him. They moved two or three steps and dropped their heads into the grass again. They seemed willing allies to their own abduction.

The sheriff's voice was calm, as if he did this every day. "Now, son, I've got a pair of handcuffs here, but they got a way of gallin' a man's wrists. You can come along peaceful and help me drive these cows into town, or I can cuff you to my saddle and make you walk alongside me all the way. I ought to tell you, this old horse of mine is bad to kick."

"I can prove by my Uncle Matthew that these cows belong to me. I can prove it by my pa."

"They got paper to back up their word?" The sheriff waited for the answer, though he knew what it would be. "It'd come down to their statements against Mr. Connors's, and they're strangers here. Everybody in this county knows Lige Connors."

"I'll bet they do!"

The farmer was so jubilant over acquiring four cows without cost that he paid no notice to the implied insult.

The sheriff pointed toward town. "Them cows've got calves in them, so push them gentle, son. Have respect for other people's property."

---

The iron door clanged shut behind him with an impact that seemed to shake the stone jailhouse. The sound carried a brutal finality that sent shivers down Trey's spine. He had never seen the inside of a jailhouse before, much less the inside of a locked cell. He had accepted Pap's admonition that a man who stayed out of saloons, houses of ill repute and their like need never find himself in that kind of trouble. But his father had never had his cows coveted by a man to whom truth was a stranger.

Farmer Connors watched as the sheriff turned the key in the lock. "Son, mind tellin' me when them cows was bred? It'd be helpful to know when they'll be shellin' out their calves."

Trey's throat tightened with anger so that it hurt to speak. "How am I supposed to know, since you claim I stole them from you?"

The farmer's pudgy cheeks wobbled as he shook his head. "It's a disgrace the way the younger generation sass their elders. We've come into mean times." He turned toward the door. "I'll send a couple of boys to drive my cows on up to the house pens."

The sheriff jingled his ring of keys, wiggling one out of the lock. "You plannin' on filin' charges, Mr. Connors?"

The farmer's little eyes peered at Trey over puffed rolls of fat. "Naw, I reckon not. A night in the jailhouse'll probably teach him more than a month in the schoolhouse. You escort him to the county line in the mornin'. Make sure he understands we don't want to see him around here no more, nor hear no more of his sass."

The sheriff nodded quiet agreement.

After Connors waddled out, Trey declared, "You know he's lyin' about those cows, else he wouldn't have to ask me when they was with the bull."

"Sure, son, I know that."

"Then how come you to lock me up?"

"For your own safety. If I was to let you go now, you'd try to take them cows back and like as not get yourself shot. By tomorrow you'll have a cooler head. You'll see that you're lucky not to lose more than just four cows. They've already seen their best days anyhow."

"I worked long and hard to buy them cows."

"Figure it as the cost of education. Ain't nothin' comes free."

"Cows come free to a thief, and you're helpin' him."

"He's a power in this county. I need this job. Got a bad back, so I can't do heavy work no more." The sheriff's voice softened with sympathy. "I know how you feel, son, but don't think you been singled out. He's been pullin' this kind of stunt on travelin' folks for a long time."

"What need has he got for four piddlin' old cows? Ain't he already got enough?"

"For a man with an appetite like his, there *ain't* enough." The sheriff stopped at the door. "It'll be suppertime directly. If you'll promise to behave yourself, I'll let you eat with me and my family. Else you'll have to settle for beans in your cell."

"I've *been* behavin' myself. This trouble wasn't none of my doin'."

The cell's cot was hard and unfriendly, but Trey doubted he would get much sleep on it tonight even if it were a feather bed. He saw three fellow prisoners, all black and in other cells. It was not customary to put white prisoners with black unless crowding made it necessary, or unless there was a particular wish to humiliate the white ones—Yankees, for instance, who needed an occasional reminder that the South had taken a whipping but had not been beaten.

One of the prisoners ventured cautiously, "What you in here for, mister?"

"For ownin' some cows that somebody else wanted. Feller named Connors."

"Mr. Lige Connors? Lordy, mister, you're lucky he ain't had his field boss horsewhip you."

Another man spoke. "Mr. Connors hisself taken the horsewhip to me one time. All I done was tell him I come up a dollar short when he paid me for a job of work."

The first man said, "I heard him tell the sheriff to escort you out of the county. Was I you I couldn't get out fast enough, or far enough away oncet I was gone."

"But he robbed me. I worked a long time for those cows."

"You can find some godlier place and earn them over again. Better than havin' whip scars on your back, or be layin' wrapped up in a shroud."

It was good dark by the time the sheriff came back and escorted Trey downstairs to the family living quarters on the jail's ground floor. The lawman tried to lighten Trey's dark mood with an effort at humor. "My kids like to say that they've spent their whole lives in the county jail."

It was in Trey's mind that the sheriff ought to be living on the second floor instead of the first, but he did not think the officer would find much humor in such a remark. The more Trey thought about his cows, the less funny it was to him, too.

The sheriff took him out to a small back porch and pointed to a wooden railing covered by a one-by-twelve board. On it were a water bucket, a wash pan, a bar of lye soap and a towel.

Trey suspected by a hint of shame in the sheriff's wife's eyes that she knew what had happened. He need not waste his breath explaining. He counted five children and knew why the sheriff was anxious about his job. He guessed the youngest boy to be three or four. The oldest girl was probably fifteen or sixteen and eyeing him with a bold interest that brought warmth rising to Trey's cheeks. Back home they had a word for girls who looked at a man like that: *fast.*

Whatever fault Trey might find with the sheriff's devotion to truth and justice, he could not fault him in his choice of a helpmate. The sheriff's wife was a splendid cook. Trey suspected she had outdone herself tonight, perhaps trying to make up in small measure for the way her husband had treated him. He sensed through the meal that she was watching him, though whenever he looked at her she always glanced off in another direction. At length she said, "I'll tell you, Micah Bracken, there's a special hot corner in He . . . Hades, waitin' for Lige Connors. The wicked may prevail on earth, but in time they will be undone."

The sheriff gave her a critical look. "Not by us, and not by this young man. Blessed are the meek, for they shall inherit the earth."

Trey declared, "Not around this damned place they won't. Pardon me for the language, ma'am."

"Hardly the first time it has been heard in this house, and never for better cause." She stared accusingly at her husband.

"Eat your supper," the sheriff admonished his family. "And while you eat, be thankful you have it. If I ever lose this badge, we'll be lucky to have beans."

Trey expected a sleepless night in jail, and the night lived down to his expectations. The sheriff came up a while after daylight, bringing a meager breakfast to the black prisoners. He unlocked Trey's cell door. "You can come on down and eat with us again. Then I'll ride with you a ways."

Neither the sheriff nor Mrs. Bracken had much to say at the breakfast table. The tension hung between them like electricity in the air just before lightning strikes. Trey suspected they had argued after he left the supper table and that the bruised feelings had lingered all night. The children were quiet too, though the oldest girl stared at Trey in a way that made him wonder what would happen if they were left alone together for an hour or two. The thought was both scary and delicious.

Bracken pushed his chair back from the table. He left a cup still half-full of coffee. "If you're about done, we'll be saddlin' our horses and gettin' started."

Trey could have found a place for a couple more of Mrs. Bracken's tall biscuits, but he hurriedly swallowed what was left of his coffee. Mrs. Bracken said, "You come back by before you leave town. I'll sack up some vittles for you."

The sheriff frowned. Trey suspected he was calculating the cost of groceries.

Mrs. Bracken said defensively, "If you won't help this young man get his cattle back, the least you can do is spare him a little somethin' to eat while he travels. We ain't *that* poor."

"Thank you, ma'am," Trey said. "I'll be obliged to you for the vittles."

Trey had his horse saddled and was sitting on him while the sheriff still fiddled, getting the blanket straight. Finally ready, Bracken opened the gate and led his horse out of the corral. Trey followed.

"Whichaway?" the sheriff asked. "East or west?"

Trey had thought about it a lot during the long night. Heartsick over the loss of his cows, he wished he could just go back home. But in his imagination he could already hear the sarcasm in Pap's voice: "I told you. Serves you right, gettin' too big for your britches, takin' notions about risin' above your raisin'." And Trey had as good as promised Uncle Matthew that the next time they saw one another he would be on his way to success as a cattleman. To go east would be to concede defeat.

"West. That's the way I was headed."

"Good. There's a world of opportunity for an ambitious young man out there." It was also a fact that the majority who went west stayed west; they didn't come back. The last thing Bracken wanted was to see Trey McLean pass this way again.

At the edge of town they rode by a farm where several black men worked the fields with mules and moldboard plows, breaking ground for spring planting. In a set of wooden pens beside a big red barn he could see four cows, trying diligently to eat down a tall stack of hay by themselves. They were his cows.

The sheriff said, "Won't do you no good to be lookin'. Ain't nothin' over there but trial and tribulation."

They rode a long time without conversation. Trey had used his up yesterday, protesting the injustice imposed on him by Lige Connors's greed and Sheriff Bracken's dereliction of duty.

At length Bracken said, "Don't waste your time thinkin' about it."

"About what?"

"I can read your mind like a broadside for a mule sale. You're thinkin' about sneakin' back after dark and takin' your cows."

Trey would not deny it. "I wouldn't have to if the law did the job it's paid for."

"I know you don't think I'm much of a man, and even less of a sheriff. But you've seen my family. You can see why I can't afford to muddy the waters."

Trey doubted that Bracken would be much different even if he didn't have a family to feed. He had probably run from schoolyard bullies when he was six or seven and had never broken the habit.

Bracken said, "Men like Lige Connors generally pay up eventually. He'll pull that dodge on the wrong man and get his guts spilled all over the ground."

"Whoever does it will deserve a medal."

"Like as not I'll have to hang him. But I won't enjoy it."

Trey nursed his resentment. "You know this ain't fair."

"*Life* ain't fair. If it was, we'd all be born to a rich daddy. Them black boys workin' the fields yonder, they'd've been born white. It's like a poker game; you play the cards that's dealt you." Bracken reined up. "I've ridden with you far enough. If you know what's good for you, you won't stop ridin' 'til you've put a couple more counties behind you." He took a small tally book from his shirt pocket and scrawled in it with a stub pencil. He tore off the page and extended it toward Trey. "An old friend of mine runs a wagonyard in Fort Worth.

Maybe he can help you find a job. Pretty soon you can buy some more cows and go on out west like you figured." His eyes turned grave. "Come back thisaway, though, and time ain't all you'll lose."

Bracken extended his hand, but Trey made a point not to accept it. He touched his heels to the horse's sides and moved on. Resentment boiled in him. He struggled against a strong urge to go back in defiance of the sheriff.

Reason told him it was a bad idea. He had spent much of the night studying on a way to retrieve his cows, and the only thing he had come up with was just to ride in and take them. That was what Connors would expect, of course. He would give Trey about as much chance as a snowball on the Fourth of July.

Four cows weren't much, not enough for a man to die over, though men had. He could get more cows. What rankled him as much as the loss was the callous injustice of it. A man ought not to have to back off and accept treatment like that.

For now, though, he would. He had little choice unless he was willing to pay an exorbitant price for satisfaction. But Lige Connors owed him. Trey would tuck this bill away in his memory. Someday, if someone else didn't get Connors first, Trey would find a way to call in the chips, and that overweight gentleman would find those four old cows to be the highest-priced stock he had ever put his brand on.

# TWO

He skirted south of Dallas, for it was gaining a reputation as a cotton town and offered little to interest him. He had planted, plowed and picked enough cotton to clothe a small army. Fort Worth, though, had a boisterous reputation that appealed to the adventuresome side of his nature, tested but little so far in his life. The cattle trails from southern Texas passed through on their way north to the railroads at Abilene and Ellsworth, Kansas. West of there, bold Texans were pushing the frontier line farther out year by year, straining to burst free and overrun the buffalo range still claimed by Comanche and Kiowa. To reach that region had been his goal. It still was, though reaching it would be delayed somewhat, thanks to Lige Connors.

Fort Worth, perched above the Trinity, hardly presented an imposing sight. There had been talk for some years that a railroad was on its way, but so far nobody had turned a spade of dirt or cut a crosstie. The buildings were mostly of lumber or logs, long on utility and short on future, none rising far up from the ground. If everybody were to decide to leave tomorrow, the abandoned buildings would not amount to a great financial sacrifice.

The town had begun as an adjunct to a small military post and now clung to existence principally by servicing the needs of transient cattle outfits from spring into fall and as a supply center for venturesome land seekers who had established a toenail hold farther west. It had two chances at the trail-driving cowboys, once as they passed through going north toward the railroad and again as they passed through heading south toward home. Traveling in either direction, they were thirsty.

The modest village was poised on the verge of explosive growth, but at the moment it still justified the derisive name its Dallas competitors had hung on it: Panther City. They claimed the town was so quiet that a panther had been seen sleeping peacefully on its main street.

Trey was disappointed. From the stories he had heard, he had expected more. He did not even see a drowsy panther.

It struck him quickly that the opportunity for employment here was probably slight, judging by the little movement of foot, horseback and wagon traffic he could see on the dirt streets. He almost wished he had gone to Dallas instead. Cotton was more prosaic than cattle, but it put a lot of coin into circulation.

It appeared to him that along the street where he rode half the business houses were saloons. An aproned bartender stood beside the front door of one, eyeing him speculatively, probably hoping he was the vanguard of a bunch of cowboys. He doubted that he looked much like a cowboy. They were scarce over in East Texas; he had seen very few and had little to judge by.

A woman leaned from an upstairs window and waved a handkerchief at him as he looked up. He smiled back at her, thinking that it was a friendly town, even if it *was* quiet. He knew very well about her motivation. At the south edge of his hometown stood a two-story establishment that offered special services the respectable folks never spoke of. But in deference to the good ladies of the community the working girls conducted themselves discreetly and would never wave at a man from a window. At least not in the daytime.

He had no difficulty in finding the wagonyard, just a little west of the courthouse above the high bank of the river. Wagonyards were a necessity for any town big enough to have a name. There visitors from farms and ranches as well as travelers moving across country could leave their wagons and corral their horses and mules for a bait of hay or grain.

Trey took out the piece of paper the sheriff had given him, though he had memorized the name scrawled upon it: Abel Plunkett. A middle-aged man with a gray-salted mustache the size of a squirrel's tail stepped out of the big double barn door. "Lookin' for a place to put up your horse, young man? Fifty cents for yardage and all the grain he can eat without founderin' hisself."

At fifty cents a day that horse could eat up most of Trey's cash assets in a month. "Would you be Mr. Abel Plunkett?"

"Was the last time I looked." That huge mustache lifted at the corners as the stableman took pleasure in his own wit. He reminded Trey of Uncle Matthew. Trey was inclined to like him, just on the basis of that.

"Sheriff Micah Bracken told me to come and see you. Said you might know where I can find a job."

"Micah? He still wearin' a badge? I figured they'd probably have him in his own jail by now."

"Not yet." Trey left unstated his belief that that was where Bracken belonged. He did not know how strong the stableman's friendship might be.

Plunkett's eyebrows were bushy, in keeping with the mustache. They arched as he looked a hole through Trey. "I hope you wasn't a guest of his. You don't look like the jailbird type to me."

"I've always tried to stay out of trouble." Trey doubted that he could adequately explain the difficulty he had had with Lige Connors, not at least until the stableman knew him better. Most people wouldn't believe a man could so blatantly claim somebody else's cows and take them with the sanction of what passed for law.

Plunkett said, "I'm sorry, friend, but business is slow. It's a little early for the trail herds to start comin' through. Things'll bust open in another three or four weeks."

Trey wondered if seventeen dollars could be made to stretch for three or four weeks. He didn't count the ten-dollar gold piece in his boot; that was for a *real* emergency, like life or death.

"I'd work cheap 'til things start pickin' up. I'd work for grub, and I'd sleep under the shed."

He could tell that Plunkett was a figuring man; he could almost see him adding up the cost of meals in his head. "There *is* a right smart of cleanin' up and fixin' up that needs doin' around here before the rush starts. You look like you'd be no stranger to a pick and shovel or a hay fork."

"Growed up with them in my hands."

"Turn your horse into the corral with them others yonder. I'll board him and you. When the herds start comin', we'll talk about a fitten wage. Four bits a day, maybe six bits if you're doin' a good job."

At six bits a day it would take a long while to earn back the equivalent of four cows. But that was better than having no job at all. "I'm obliged, Mr. Plunkett."

He unsaddled the brown horse and picked an empty rack for his rigging, back under the shed where even a blowing rain was not likely to reach it. He had seen from the look of the country that rain was less common here than at home. Folks had told him that the farther west he ventured, the less rain he would see. It was the sort of thing a man had to consider if he intended someday to get into the cattle business. He wondered how he would be able to tell when he got just far enough west, but not too far.

Plunkett pointed him toward a steel cot. "You can roll out your soogans there. Now, if we have a real rush and there ain't enough cots to go around for all the customers, I'll expect you to sleep on the ground."

Trey had no quarrel with that. He had been sleeping on the ground or in somebody's haystack for most of the trip. Hay was softer than a cot, though less civilized.

Plunkett said, "Since you're here to work, we'd just as well get started. We got a dozen or so horses and mules to feed before we go to the house for supper."

Plunkett's wife was a shriveled-up little woman with a perpetual pinched expression as if she had just bitten into an apple and found half a worm. In contrast to Mrs. Bracken, she seemed less than pleased at the prospect of feeding an extra mouth. She carped at her husband while Trey busied himself washing face and hands on the back porch and tried not to overhear.

"You could at least've told me instead of bringin' him here right at suppertime. I swear, Abel Plunkett, you've got less consideration than just about any man I know."

"The boy's workin' without wages 'til business picks up. It ain't goin' to hurt you to fix for one more."

"That's savin' money for your wagonyard, but I don't expect any of it will find its way into my purse."

Embarrassed, Trey remained on the porch until Plunkett poked his head out the door. "Chuck's on. Wife's real tickled to have you."

"Much obliged, ma'am," Trey told her uneasily, hat in his hand. "I ain't one to eat very much."

"That's good," she said curtly, "because it ain't goin' to be much."

Plunkett bowed his head and thanked the Lord for the bounty on his table. Trey thought the prayer a little overdone for the warmed-over supper Mrs. Plunkett had laid out, but Plunkett sounded sincere. If the stableman was at all upset over his wife's objections to company, his appetite gave no indication. He refilled his china plate with roast and beans after putting away a generous first helping, and he finished off the meal by mixing butter and molasses in his plate, swabbing it up with cold biscuits. Trey ate modestly, hoping not to stretch a thin welcome to the breaking point. He carried his plate, cup and utensils to a washpan in the kitchen, as he had done at home.

Mrs. Plunkett seemed to thaw a little. "Somebody has taught you manners. That's more than I can say for most of the hostlers Mr. Plunkett has come draggin' in here."

"My mother's doin'."

"I wish your mother had hold of Mr. Plunkett."

For a place where business was slow, the wagonyard offered plenty of work. There were Plunkett's own horses and mules to be fed as well as those of whatever transient customers showed up, mostly farmers and ranchers in town shopping for staples. A couple of corrals had to be largely rebuilt; they looked as if a tornado had ripped through them.

Plunkett explained, "I kept a jack in here for a couple of months, breedin' him for mule colts. Fifty cowboys in town on a drunk can't tear up as much property as one jack tryin' to reach a mare in the next pen."

Then there was the shed roof to be patched as spring showers revealed where leaks had developed. Fortunately Trey had learned some jackleg carpentry skills on the homeplace and in helping the neighbors.

It was all right for a little while, working without drawing any pay, but it began to wear thin after a couple of weeks. Mrs. Plunkett's cooking was barely passable, nothing to compare with his mother's or Mrs. Bracken's. And though she no longer openly resented his showing up at the house three times a day, she usually started clearing the table while he was still eating. Supper was mainly the leavings from dinner, sometimes warmed briefly in the oven of her big wood range, sometimes not.

If the trail herds didn't show up pretty soon, Trey thought, he would be tempted to ride south and look for them.

He had been working with Plunkett a couple of weeks before he told about his experience with Lige Connors, and about Sheriff Bracken taking Connors's side.

Plunkett betrayed no surprise. "I sharecropped on Lige Connors's land for three years before I came on west. Ol' Lige was always lookin' for a way to beat a man out of what was rightly comin' to him. Sold our cotton and lied to me about the price. Made me use my own mules, then claimed they was his. I had to quit the county in the middle of the night to keep anything that was mine. But on my way out I gave him a taste of my knuckles to remember me by."

"I wish I'd done somethin' like that," Trey said.

"I was lucky to get away with it. You'd probably get thrashed within an inch of your life and then sent to the pen. It's cheaper in the long run to turn the other cheek." Plunkett mused. "Of course, a man ain't got but two cheeks. After that, the lid is off."

---

Trey thought he had seen a few scary-looking people back home, but a stranger who rode in from the south one day made all the others seem benign. Tall and gaunt, dressed in black from his derby hat to his swallowtail coat and dusty lace-up shoes, he looked like a preacher to Trey. Close up, Trey saw dark eyes sunk deeply into a black-bearded face. With an expression grim as the archangel of death, he gave Trey a severe, silent study before he stepped down from his horse and handed over his reins.

"Brush him down thoroughly," he ordered with the authority of an army officer. "Give him two quarts of oats. No more, no less. And don't pen him with any other horses. I will not have him bitten or kicked."

The man never asked what the charge would be. By the look of his black suit, he could afford it. Even if he couldn't, Trey would not want to argue with him. He felt a little cold as he watched the man take a roll from behind the cantle of his saddle and stride off toward a frame hotel.

"He wouldn't have any trouble convincin' *me* about hellfire and damnation," Trey told Plunkett. "Scariest-lookin' preacher I ever saw."

Plunkett's thick eyebrows seemed to bristle. "He's a lawman."

"I didn't see a badge."

"You don't have to see it to know it's there. You sense it. His kind can be as mean as the men they go after. They can kill you like a dog and never lose a minute's sleep over it."

Trey brushed the man's horse until he thought he looked fine, then brushed him again, just to be safe.

---

He had made up his mind that someday he would see Lige Connors again, this time in a situation more to his advantage than their last meeting. He did not expect to see the farmer quite so soon, however.

A customer leaving his horse at the stable mentioned that he had passed a small herd of cattle between Fort Worth and Dallas, moving westward. It obviously was not one of the herds the town had been waiting for; its direction of travel was wrong. And by his description these were East Texas-type cattle, not the longhorned and Mexican varieties which dominated the herds coming up from the south. But cattle were cattle, and Plunkett's spirits brightened.

"Probably somebody wantin' to throw his bunch in with a larger herd for the drive to Kansas," he commented. "Business is fixin' to pick up."

Trey saw the buggy coming up the street and knew by the way it sagged on its springs that it was carrying a heavier than average load. Not until Lige Connors hauled up on the reins did he realize who was so sorely taxing the black buggy horse.

Connors did not recognize Trey on first glance. "Here, young fellow," he said imperiously. "Unhitch my horse and give it a feed. Mind you, I will not be overcharged."

Trey gritted his teeth. "You already owe me for four cows."

Connors took a better look at him. Trey could see startled recognition and a flicker of uncertainty behind the fat that half hid the farmer's eyes. "Watch your tongue, young fellow, or I'll have you put back in jail where you belong. I'll not stand still for slander."

Plunkett spoke from behind Trey. "You're a long ways from home, Lige. You've got no pet sheriff in this town."

His face coloring, Connors stared past Trey. "Plunkett! What are you doin' here?"

"I belong here, and this wagonyard is mine. You go take your horse someplace else. I don't need none of your business."

Caught on his left foot, far from his base of power, Connors seemed inclined toward conciliation. "Now, Plunkett, I'm willin' to let the past be past, bygones be bygones."

"But I ain't. I got a nagsome memory. Now git, before I sic my dog on you."

Plunkett didn't have a dog, but Connors couldn't know that.

The farmer clenched his puffy fists. "You've gotten spoiled by too much prosperity, turnin' away good business. But there'll come a reckonin'. Pride goeth before a fall."

In a huff, Connors turned the buggy in the street and went back the way he had come, whipping the black horse into a stiff trot.

Plunkett said, "The old hypocrite starts spoutin' Scripture when things don't go his way. I'd like to be at the Pearly Gates when Saint Peter starts readin' it back to him." He added as an afterthought, "But I ain't in no hurry."

---

Trey became accustomed to farm families coming to town in their wagons to sell produce or to buy goods they could not raise or make for themselves. If they lived more than ten miles out, it was usually an overnight trip. Many could not afford or at least chose not to spend the dollar or two a hotel would charge. Plunkett had partitioned off a special sleeping section toward the back so the womenfolk at bedtime would not have to suffer the prying eyes of men or boys whose prurient curiosity outweighed their judgment. He would have taken a quirt to anyone he caught peeking through a knothole.

Trey thought little of it when a mule-drawn wagon with two women on the seat pulled up at the open front gate. A man who looked fortyish rode beside the wagon on a big, stout plow horse. A couple of boys in or nearing their teens perched where the tailgate should be, dangling their legs over the edge of the wagon bed. Trey walked out to greet the visitors. The man on the horse asked, "Is Mr. Plunkett anywheres about?"

"He's gone to see a man about a mule. I'll be glad to put your team and wagon away for you."

"Swampin' for him, are you?" The farmer's eyes suggested that Trey would do well to seek a higher station in life.

"Only 'til somethin' better comes my way. But as long as I'm here, I do the best job that I can."

"I wish all the young fellers today had that attitude."

"Your stock looks like it can stand some feed and water."

"So can my family. We'll be takin' care of that as soon as you can get us situated."

Trey raised his hands, silently offering to help the farmer's wife from the wagon. She shook her head and climbed down on her own, careful to hold her skirt tightly enough that she revealed no more than a glimpse of an ankle as she descended over the wheel. The effort was of little consequence; Trey had no interest in the ankles of middle-aged women.

The other woman's face was shaded by a slat bonnet, but he guessed her to be sixteen or seventeen, a daughter of the farm couple. Trey looked up uncertainly, not sure if he should offer to help her down in view of her mother's attitude. But she smiled and held out her hands. Trey took them with a little trepidation. He made it a point to look away from the flare of her skirt as she stepped down onto the wheel's wooden spokes.

"Thank you," she said in a voice that he thought must surely be meant for singing. "You are a gentleman."

His face warmed as he realized he still held her hands, though she was on the ground. "It's just part of the job I'm paid for." That was a bit of an exaggeration. Plunkett had not actually begun paying him except in food and a place to roll out his bedding.

The mother jerked her head at her daughter. She did not say anything; the sharpness of her eyes spoke for her.

He took hold of a mule's bridle and led it into the barn, drawing the wagon back to the sleeping area. One of the boys climbed up into the bed and handed down to his brother a basket and a wooden box covered with cloth. The second boy placed them on a rough wooden table Plunkett provided for his guests.

The father nodded amiably at Trey. "Join us, young feller? Womenfolks fried up some chicken for the trip."

Trey looked at the girl. Her eyes seconded the invitation. Then he looked at the mother. "No, thanks, already had my dinner. Mr. Plunkett generally keeps a pot of coffee on the stove in his office. I'll fetch it for you."

After feeding and watering the mules and the plow horse, Trey stood back where he could watch both the family and the front gate, in case other customers showed up. Mostly he looked at the girl. She had taken off her bonnet to reveal a delicately featured face that struck him as pretty, though a little burned by wind and sun during the long ride in from the farm. She had hair rolled up into a large, tight bun. He suspected it would fall far down her back if she released it. She was thin, almost skinny, as if she might not quite be through growing, though her eyes seemed those of a mature woman.

Once the farmer had put away some cold chicken and cold biscuits he turned moderately talkative. "Our name's Stark. Wife here is

Frieda. Boys are Luke and John. Daughter's Sarah."

Trey already had his hat off in deference. He nodded. "Mrs. Stark. Miss Sarah."

Sarah smiled.

The farmer said, "My name's Simon Stark. Takes us the better part of two days to get to town by wagon, so we don't come often. Left some more family behind to see after things."

Mrs. Stark said, "It'd be better if we never did come in. The big city gives young people all sorts of foolish notions." She glanced critically toward her sons.

"Yes, ma'am." Trey sensed that the remark was an oblique explanation of her chilly attitude. He tried to think what foolish notions Fort Worth had given him. Only one or two came to mind. They involved money, so he had not acted upon them.

When the family finished the meal, the two women put the leftovers back into the basket and box. Trey said, "Don't bother about the scraps. Mr. Plunkett has got a couple of hogs."

The Starks had not left much in the way of scraps, other than the chicken bones. Like his own mother, Mrs. Stark was probably a strong advocate of the adage to take only what you really want and eat all you take.

Stark said, "Please tell Mr. Plunkett the Starks are in town for the night. We'll go and start tendin' to our business."

When Plunkett returned, Trey relayed Stark's message. Plunkett's big mustache lifted at the corners, his eyes smiling. "Good folks. They farm north, on the road to Red River. Me and Simon have partnered to whip many a good domino player."

"Mrs. Stark don't seem to like me much."

"Or any other young man. Daughter Sarah's in full bloom, pretty near. Frieda's afraid somebody'll come along wantin' to pick flowers."

That evening Plunkett rounded up a couple of storekeeper friends and buckled down to a friendly game of dominoes with Simon Stark. Mrs. Stark sat upon a hide-bottomed straight chair and applied herself to some knitting she carried in a basket. But over her glasses she kept a wary eye on her two sons lest they stray out of her sight and become entrapped in the city's sinful snares.

Trey finished his stable chores and sat down to inspect the rifle he had brought from home. He found it dusty. It was difficult to keep anything clean in this barn, where horses and mules constantly stirred up the loose dirt and hay was always being transported in one direction or another. He took a cloth and a ramrod and set about cleaning the barrel.

The girl's voice startled him. "Good-lookin' rifle. Does it shoot straight?"

"It hits whatever I aim at."

"Every time?"

"*Almost* every time. Not much to shoot at here in town, though."

"You ought to come out our way if you want to practice shootin'. We've got coyotes, coons, all sorts of chicken-stealin' varmints."

"I guess your daddy's a good shot. And your brothers."

"Sure. Only I'm better than any of them except maybe Papa."

He looked up in disbelief. "You? What business has a girl got learnin' to shoot?"

"I can't go runnin' for Papa or the boys any old time somethin' gets amongst the chickens. I learned to shoot before I was this high." She held her hand flat at hip level.

He shook his head. "Where I come from, the womenfolks stay in the kitchen. They leave guns to the men."

She stiffened. "Well, you didn't come from where we do." She reached out and took the rifle from his hand. "You got a shell for this thing?"

The severity of her tone did not brook argument. He handed her a cartridge. She rammed it into the breech and walked to the back door of the barn. "Yonder, down next to the river. See that tin can?"

She brought the rifle to her shoulder, steadied it and squeezed the trigger. The explosion seemed to rock the barn. It set chickens out back to squawking and horses and mules to running in the open corral. Trey saw the tin can jump and go bouncing. White smoke curled around the muzzle of the rifle as she lowered it. She turned, grinning fiercely. "Where I come from, the menfolks stay with their plowin'. They know the women can take care of themselves."

Abel Plunkett hurried up, a startled look in his eyes. "Who got killed?"

Trey reached for the rifle, and the girl handed it to him. Chagrined, he said, "Me, I reckon. She sure shot me down."

Sarah Stark was still grinning as her mother and the domino players came to see what had happened. "If you ever come up our way, Mr. McLean, stop in and stay a spell. Us womenfolks'll teach you somethin' about shootin'."

# THREE

Trey had become acquainted with some of the town's sporting element. Though Plunkett did not approve of their ways, he had no qualms about accepting their business. He stabled their horses and kept their buggies in an open lot out back. On Sundays young bachelors would rent a carriage and take girls from the "line" for a ride along the river. Trey had no illusions about the innocence of their intentions.

He was not surprised, then, when a tall rancher came to town in a wagon and rented one of Plunkett's buggies. He came back down the street sharing the seat with a red-haired young woman from over in the district.

If Plunkett was inclined to make any sort of judgment, he kept it to himself. He said matter-of-factly, "That's Mead Overstreet. Got him a ranch out west, past Fort Griffin someplace. Lots of times he'll hire one of the sportin' girls to go back out there and stay with him 'til he's tired of her, or 'til she's had all that lonesome country she can stand."

"Looks like he needs to take him a wife."

"He likes variety. Time the weddin' bouquet wilted he'd be back here again chasin' after the girls."

Trey could see how Overstreet might cut quite a figure with the women. He stood straight as a ramrod and had as ruggedly handsome a face as Trey had ever seen. Trey found himself squaring his own shoulders, straightening his back. The first chance he got, he looked in a broken mirror that hung in the section of the barn where overnight visitors slept. He considered his chin too large, his nose not quite straight, his hands too big and awkward. He had a faint scar on his right cheekbone where a mule had once kicked him. Against Overstreet's good looks, he would be like a blackland plow horse competing with a Thoroughbred racer.

The little town was already stirring with anticipation days before the first herd appeared to the south, on the trail from Waco and Austin. Its approach had been reported by travelers who had passed it. Plunkett said, "I expect your four cows looked like a lot to you, but did you ever see a thousand or fifteen hundred, all in one bunch?"

"No, sir, nothin' like that."

"Some of the businessmen are ridin' out tomorrow to meet the herd and try to drum up trade. Most outfits hold their cattle at the edge of town while they lay in supplies and let the hands blow off their wages. I'll want you to go in my place."

The prospect set Trey's skin to prickling and aroused all manner of romantic images. He had seen a few cowboys visiting town from neighboring ranches, but he had not seen a real trail outfit.

The rancher Overstreet seemed to take a special interest in news about the trail herd. He asked Plunkett, "Anybody hear whose cattle they are?"

"Ivan Kerbow's. He's generally one of the first every season. Ivan don't let any grass grow under his feet."

Overstreet reacted to the name Kerbow as if a horse had stepped on his foot. "I'll be needin' my wagon quicker than I expected. I'll go see if the mercantile's got my supplies ready to load."

Watching him walk briskly up the street, Plunkett said, "That's odd. He generally spends a week or so in town, tryin' out all the girls."

"He doesn't act like he wants to see this Ivan Kerbow," Trey observed.

"Ivan's got a ranch in that same part of the country, but his business don't let him spend much time there. Him and Overstreet must've bumped heads."

Three black farmhands were loose-herding Lige Connors's cattle, some two hundred steers, a little way downriver. Connors had found accommodations elsewhere in town for himself and his horse, but the hands were camped outdoors, subsisting mostly on bacon and beans. They were in no danger of becoming as overweight as the man they worked for.

Connors joined the welcoming committee that met at the wagonyard the next morning, but he kept his distance from Plunkett and Trey. That suited Trey just fine.

He was surprised when three women showed up, two in a buggy, one riding sidesaddle. They flashed a lot of red silk and white lace that spoke of St. Louis, or maybe Chicago.

Plunkett made a sly smile. "If Mrs. Plunkett was to ask you any questions, you might forget you saw these pretty ladies."

By Trey's reckoning they were neither pretty nor ladies, but he supposed each man was entitled to his own definitions. He had been here long enough to begin reevaluating some of his own.

Plunkett handed him a couple of boxes of cigars. They were of fine stock from one of the saloons down the street. "Pass these out among the hands. Be sure to give the trail boss several. Wherever he puts up his horse, most of the hands will do the same."

Riding out toward the trail herd, Trey noticed that the dozen or so businessmen held aloof from the three women until they were past the edge of town. Then several crowded around the horse and the buggy, laughing and joking as if they had all known each other for years. He suspected that some had.

That fit with the general pattern he had observed in Fort Worth society. Tolerance was good for trade. Morality was one thing, business something else, and one should not stand in the way of the other. He had no quarrel with that philosophy. A man who could spare time to inquire deeply into the affairs of others did not have enough to do.

Connors invited one of the women to share the seat of his buggy, but she bluntly pointed out that it was already crowded. She rose several notches in Trey's estimation.

The balding operator of a mercantile establishment observed the cigar boxes tied to Trey's saddle. "You'll want to give several cigars to the chuck wagon cook. It'll smooth the way to gettin' us a good dinner."

Trey appreciated a man who had a practical turn of mind.

They met the chuck wagon first. It and the trailing "hoodlum" wagon had moved out well ahead of the herd and the dust. The cook was digging a fire pit to start preparing the noon meal. His Mexican swamper was busy with the teams. Trey thought it good politics to take over the shovel and finish the digging. The cook introduced himself as Zack Lynch. He was a skinny fellow of middle age who apparently did not eat much of his own fixings, or else he had a tapeworm that beat him to most of it. Uncle Matthew would say it took two of him to cast a shadow. His tobacco-stained mustache was large but no match for the heroic size of Abel Plunkett's.

The cook's pale blue eyes kept studying the three women even while he shook hands with the men. "Nice of you folks to deliver the merchandise out on the trail."

One of the women giggled. The other two pretended not to grasp what he meant.

Nudged by the mercantile man, Trey took half a dozen cigars

from a box and handed them to the cook. "Compliments of Abel Plunkett's wagonyard."

The cook was properly grateful. He bit off the end of one cigar and lighted it. "I generally don't fix very big at noontime, but for you folks I'll make an exception. You-all come back to the wagon with the first relief."

One of the businessmen owned a restaurant. "And while you're in town, Mr. Lynch, I'll be more than happy to reciprocate. It'll not cost you a thin dime."

Lynch rubbed his large nose, set off just a little to one side, victim of some past accident or indiscretion. "If I had a dime, it'd be a thin one."

Trey noticed that the man limped, one leg stiff. He was in all likelihood a stove-up cowboy no longer able to make a hand on horseback and so graduated to a kindred branch of the cattle trade that probably paid better anyway. Lynch gave one of his cigars to the Mexican, whom he addressed as Pancho. Trey thought that was generous of him, and properly democratic. Trey had passed up the Mexican but now gave both men an extra cigar apiece.

Connors remained at the chuck wagon. Trey feared the fat man might irritate the cook into spoiling dinner. The rest of the group rode on southward, toward a rising of dust. The trail was well marked from past years' traffic, though the grass was green and fresh. It would not long remain so as more and more herds passed over it, traveling northward.

The mercantile man told Trey the trail would widen gradually as the season wore on because drovers would keep pressing their cattle farther out on one side or the other, seeking fresh grass. "Cook told me the trail boss is Ivan Kerbow. He's an old hand at this. Makes a couple of trips a year up the trail. If you wish to learn the cattle trade, you'd be hard put to find a better teacher."

The thought set Trey's mind to racing. "You mean go up to Kansas with him?" He wondered if he really could. Pap had always told him he would never be able to do anything more ambitious than pick cotton.

"You are hardly becoming a rich man working for Abel Plunkett. Nor a fat one, for I have supped at his wife's table."

The cowboys riding at point and swing positions on the herd did not look as if they were becoming very rich, either. Though they were still on the early leg of the trip, their clothing bespoke poverty. Shirts were old and torn, britches patched and faded, boots worn and cracked.

"It'd be futile for a man to start with a new outfit," the merchant said. "He'd just ruin it on the trip. I don't sell them much on their way north, but a lot of them buy new outfits on their way back so they can go home in style."

Having no prior knowledge about trailing, Trey had assumed the herd would move in a compact mass. Instead, it was strung out like a ribbon, half a mile long and only a few animals wide. A point rider in front was followed by a long-legged red and white spotted steer which had a horn spread Trey thought could easily be four feet, maybe closer to five. He had seen nothing of its kind among the farmer stock with which he was familiar. The rest of the cattle trailed behind the lead steer, which had a bell around its neck, tolling gently to the steady stride.

Halfway down, the merchants came upon the trail boss. Most already knew him from past trips. He was tall and thin, his skin sun-burnished to a nut brown. In strong contrast, his weary eyes were a light gray. They looked benign behind a perpetual sun-squint, but Trey had a feeling they saw everything that moved, and much that did not. He sensed that Kerbow was not a man who smiled easily.

The mercantiler introduced Trey. "This young man is with Abel Plunkett's wagon yard. He is a farm lad, eager to learn about the cow business."

Ivan Kerbow's face had not felt a razor in two or three weeks. His whiskers were dark with patches of gray beginning to show, though some of that gray might have been trail dust. His eyes fastened on Trey like a clamp.

"First thing you'll need to learn is how to tell cows from steers. These are steers."

"I saw that."

"Next thing to learn is to always let them think they're doin' the opposite of what you want them to. Folks'll tell you the cow brute is a domesticated animal, but she and her kin are against you all the way."

A little ahead of them a steer broke from the bunch, made a half circle and started south in a dead run, its tail curled over its back. A cowboy spurred after it, swinging a rawhide reata. Trey watched wide-eyed, wondering how that loop could ever fit over such wide horns. It didn't. The cowboy dropped it down in front of the animal and picked up both forelegs with it, instantly jerking up the slack and taking a fast wrap around the big horn of his Mexican saddle. The steer plunged headlong, flipping over onto its back. It arose shakily to its feet, tossing its head in confusion.

Kerbow said, "There's what I'm talkin' about. That steer keeps tryin' to go back to the brush country. We'll consign him to the skillet in a day or two so he won't spoil the others."

The steer belligerently reentered the herd, chastened but not beaten. It limped a little from the rough treatment and offered the tips of its horns against any animal which dared crowd it.

Kerbow said, "I just wish Jarrett didn't enjoy it so much. He's got a rough way with the stock."

Trey was intrigued by the cowboy's prowess with the reata. He had never seen anybody handle a rope like that, though he had heard it could be done. This was a skill cowboys in South Texas had learned from the Mexican vaqueros. Most of the East Texas farmers of Trey's acquaintance handled their livestock with whips or prods. If they used a rope at all, they would draw up next to an animal and slip the loop by hand around neck or horns. He had never seen anyone throw it with much success.

After Kerbow drew away, Trey reined his brown horse up next to the cowboy's dun. "Mind tellin' me how you do that?"

The cowboy gave him an amused look. "It's not somethin' anybody can tell you. You have to learn by doin'." He extended his hand. "Jarrett Longacre."

Trey shook with him. "Trey McLean."

Amusement danced in Longacre's dark blue eyes. "How long since you left the cotton patch, farm boy?"

"About a month. I didn't know it showed."

"I can always tell a punkin' roller. You got cotton lint hangin' out both ears." Longacre's attention was drawn to the three women, who had attracted half a dozen young cowboys like watermelon draws flies. "I ought to've shaved this mornin'." His face had been a stranger to the razor long enough that the stubble was beginning to curl a bit. "I suppose there's more like them in town?"

"I haven't noticed." Trey *had* noticed, but he had held himself to distant observation. His seventeen dollars would evaporate like morning dew in that kind of company.

Longacre said, "Looks like you got a lot to learn besides how to handle a rope."

Trey gave him one of Plunkett's cigars. "You may be needin' a place to leave your horse while you visit Fort Worth."

Longacre frowned. "That the best you can do, swamp out a stable?"

"It's not forever. I'm just waitin' for somethin' better to turn up."

"Luck don't come lookin' for you. You've got to go out there and punch it up with a stick. Take some chances."

That ran counter to Pap's teachings. He had always said just being a farmer was gamble enough; a man should eliminate all other possible variables, devise detailed plans and stick to them like a cocklebur. But Longacre's philosophy appealed to Trey. His own leaving home and venturing west with only the vaguest notion of the future had been his personal declaration of independence from a well-ordered past. He liked the idea of keeping himself open to life's surprises, even if he was not always sure how well he could handle them.

He confided that it was his ambition to become a cattleman. "Bein' a trail driver might teach me what I need to know."

"Ain't much to bein' a trail driver. You let the boss and your horse do most of the thinkin'. The biggest hazards are gettin' bored and losin' sleep. I swear, you can lose six months of sleep in three months' time."

Trey remained beside Longacre for a while. He instinctively liked the cowboy, who seemed different from anyone he had known back home. Longacre showed him how he built a loop in the rawhide reata, how he held and swung it. He cast loops at the hind legs of nearby steers, almost always catching both feet. He avoided jerking up all the slack so the steers would kick loose without his throwing them down and taking the rope off by hand.

"A steer's hind feet can rearrange a man's teeth," he observed.

At length the trail boss and several of the merchants came up in a slow lope from farther back along the herd. Kerbow shouted, "You boys come on to dinner." The three women followed close behind, escorted by five or six eager young cowboys.

Half the hands remained with the herd while the others rode ahead to where the cook stood beside his chuck wagon, coffee cup in his hand. He had pots and Dutch ovens lined up near the campfire, the lids set back to reveal biscuits, fried steaks and red beans. The aroma set Trey's stomach to growling with hunger.

The lid that covered the front of the chuck box while the wagon was in motion had been swung down on a hinged leg to form a working counter for the cook. He had pulled out drawers to expose the tin plates, cups and utensils. Trey took a plate, knife and fork but caught a negative signal from the mercantile owner. "The working hands eat first," the man whispered. "Visitors come afterward."

Longacre said, "Better hurry up, farm boy, or it'll all be gone."

"Help yourself. I'll wait."

Trey caught an approving glance from the trail boss. Kerbow couldn't know that the merchant had saved Trey from breaching wagon-camp etiquette.

The cowboys would not hear of the women waiting. With a show of gallantry they filled the ladies' plates and fetched them coffee, pitching down a couple of bedrolls from the hoodlum wagon to serve in lieu of chairs. Longacre took a place beside the youngest of the women and immediately struck up conversation.

Kerbow watched with an air of slight disapproval. "What about you?" he said to Trey. "Don't you feel like makin' a fool of yourself?"

"I can't afford it."

"The rest can't either. Doesn't stop them from tryin'."

Connors had not waited. He was already finishing a plateful of food when the cowboys rode up, and he refilled it ahead of the women. Even as he ate, he introduced himself to the trail boss.

"Mr. Kerbow, I have business to discuss with you." His manner said his business was more important than anything else Kerbow might have to do at the moment, including the noon meal. Nevertheless, Kerbow filled his plate before he acknowledged Connors. His eyes clouded with caution.

Connors said, "I'm holdin' two hundred steers on grass. I'm willin' to sell them to you . . . at a fair price, of course."

"I'm not a buyer, sir. The cattle in this herd belong to a pool of ranchers. I've simply contracted to deliver them to the railroad and dispose of them at the best price I can get."

"Then perhaps I could arrange to add mine to the herd."

Kerbow said nothing.

Connors persisted. "My small bunch should not require any additional expense or labor on your part. Therefore I feel you can well afford to give me a special accommodation."

Kerbow's squinted eyes raked Connors with scorn. "Every man who has cattle in this herd gets treated equal." He turned away, dropped his empty plate in the cook's wreck pan and rode back toward the herd. Connors stared after him in red-faced frustration.

Trey decided that, if invited, he would willingly follow Kerbow to the rim of hell.

The merchants were ready to start for town after the chuck wagon meal. Trey wished he could stay and enjoy building an acquaintanceship with these dusty riders, most of them younger than himself. However, he would reach the wagonyard just in time to start feeding horses and mules. Perhaps now that the cattle drives had begun, Abel Plunkett would provide wages in addition to his wife's reluctant cooking. Trey left the remaining cigars with the cook, who said, "We'll camp at the edge of town by tomorrow. There'll always be coffee and beans."

"You're liable to see me," Trey said.

The vanguard of the herd reached Fort Worth the next morning. A sizeable number of local citizens went out to watch the cattle being spread loosely to graze while the cook began setting up camp. Though one outfit passing through would make only a minor contribution to local business, it was like the arrival of the first scissortail in spring—more important for what it represented than for what it was.

The black-suited lawman had visited the wagonyard a couple of times a day to see that his horse was properly cared for. Somberly he paid for his mount's keep on a daily basis and requested that Trey write a receipt for each fifty cents he yielded up, so he could be reimbursed by Bexar County. In this way Trey learned that his name was Gault, but he learned little else. He was uncomfortably aware that the man had studied him keenly, consulting a small book which he extracted from a shirt pocket. Plunkett told him that officers often carried notebooks containing handwritten descriptions of wanted men. The lawman's disappointed attitude indicated that he found no description matching Trey's appearance. He might have, had Trey obeyed his impulse to get even with Lige Connors.

Plunkett said, "You can bet your roll that he's expectin' somebody. He won't waste time with idle conversation. He'll shoot first and then say *howdy.*"

"I can't see him not givin' a man a fair chance. He looks too much like a preacher."

"His specialty is funerals, not sermons. A lawman can't afford to give fair chances. He wouldn't have to worry about savin' for his old age."

Just as the cowboys had broken into shifts to go to the chuck wagon for dinner, they divided up to come into town, leaving half in camp to watch the herd. Half a dozen brought their horses to the wagonyard. Trey did not see Jarrett Longacre among them. A towheaded rider said, "Jarrett'll get his turn tomorrow. This is *our* night to raise hell."

To Trey he looked too young to raise much hell. Perhaps in South Texas they started earlier.

Kerbow came to town a while after the first group of cowboys. Lige Connors ambushed him before he reached the wagonyard. Remaining out of Abel Plunkett's way, Connors waited across the street. After Kerbow put up his horse, Connors walked with him to a nearby saloon. Trey suspected yesterday's frustration had made the farmer more willing to negotiate.

Forking hay into a wooden rack for the horses, Trey was startled to discover the black-bearded Gault leaning on a fence inside a corral, quietly studying the cowboys and consulting his little book. Hair bristled on the back of Trey's neck.

It was spooky the way the man had materialized out of nowhere, like some dark ghost. Trey demanded, "Where'd you come from?"

Gault responded with a deep frown that told Trey to keep his mouth shut. He strode silently through the back door of the cavernous barn. Trey saw him go out the front and walk down the street. He shuddered, glad the man was gone. He would like nothing better than to see the lawman remove his horse from the stable and leave Fort Worth. But he had a feeling this was not going to happen, not yet a while. When Gault *did* depart, he would probably leave sorrow in his wake.

Trey went by the Plunkett house to tell the stableman's wife he would not be eating supper with her tonight. It would not have amounted to much anyway. One of her favorite night meals was cold corn bread crumbled and soaked in milk. She had not fixed enough at dinner to have anything left for night except some beans, which she would warm over. He remembered the cook's invitation and rode his brown horse out to the wagon camp.

The cook treated him as an old friend come to call. "Git down. Tie up and come get you some supper."

Only a couple of the cowboys were in camp, one a red-haired kid of eighteen or so named Scooter Willis, the other a smaller, younger boy named Johnny Fulton who seemed to look upon Scooter as a surrogate older brother. The rest were either in town or out with the herd, keeping the cattle from straying too far in their grazing. While Trey filled up on beef, beans and biscuits, Willis told him of their adventures coming up the trail from South Texas, the wild stampedes they had survived, the hazardous crossing of swollen rivers. Johnny nodded a solid endorsement to everything Scooter said.

The cook snorted. "You call them stampedes? Them steers wasn't hardly in a good trot. And you boys ain't seen a swollen river 'til you come to the Red when it's up on its hind legs. Them little old creeks we come across so far, hell, when I was your age I could've spit across the worst of them." He turned to Trey. "You can't believe half of what these green kids tell you. There ain't but two kinds of people in the world that lie worse than cowboys."

Willis poked Johnny with his elbow and winked. "One of them is wagon cooks. What's the other?"

Lynch gave him a look of mock reproach. "I was fixin' to say lawyers and horse traders. Ain't it time you two went to the herd and let the *workin'* men come to supper?" He watched the two cowboys untie their horses from a tree far enough out of camp that they would not stir dust into the food. "Brave boys, and foolish," Lynch said. "A man that sasses the cook is beggin' for raw meat and burnt beans."

Three other cowboys rode in after a bit. One was Jarrett Longacre. Trey arose from the bedroll he had been sitting on and extended his hand.

Longacre said jovially, "Evenin', farm boy. Ain't you got things turned around some, comin' out to this dry camp? Everybody here is bustin' his britches to go to town."

"I've been in town for a month. It ain't all that much."

The cook said, "If you cow chasers would listen to Trey, you could keep a lot more money in your pockets."

Longacre grinned. "You've just got too old to remember what money is for."

Lynch turned to Trey. "That's why cooks get paid better than ordinary cowboys. They have to put up with a lot of foolish talk."

"They'd probably pay you more if you'd wash your hands at least once a week," Longacre retorted.

Trey warmed himself in the glow of this good-natured bantering. He felt a contentment he had not known in a long time.

He did not sleep much until the wee hours, for the cowboys who had been first to town were reluctant to leave it. Just past two in the morning some came to the wagonyard for their horses, rousting Trey from the comfort of his cot. The rest did not show up until after daylight. Zack Lynch had warned him they would not be a pretty sight. He had to help a couple of them saddle their horses.

The next bunch came riding into town in the afternoon, taking the dirt street in a high lope, whooping and shouting and warning Fort Worth to get ready. Fort Worth showed little reaction. It had been ready all along, though a couple of horses tied to a rack in front of a saloon were spooked by the noise, broke their bridle reins and trotted away, heads and tails held high.

It would not take many hours to separate these young cowboys from whatever wages they carried in their pockets and send them back to camp sadder but probably no wiser. Plunkett said they would do the same thing over again when they reached Ellsworth and the railroad.

Trail boss Ivan Kerbow followed along behind the younger riders, holding his roan horse to a conservative pace befitting a man who was probably forty. Connors stepped out to meet him, remaining well clear of the wagonyard. Trey assumed by the hand motions and nodding of heads that Connors and Kerbow had come to an understanding. Connors turned away, and Kerbow came on across the street, leading the roan.

This time Trey was not taken so much by surprise when the lawman Gault suddenly appeared outside the corral, giving the riders a careful study. With him was a deputy city marshal whose face had become familiar, though Trey had never thought enough about him to ask his name.

As the punchers unsaddled their horses inside the corral, the bearded lawman sidled up to Trey. "That cowboy who was riding the dun . . . do you know his name?"

Trey answered "Jarrett Longacre" without thinking. Later, he would wish a thousand times he had pleaded ignorance. "Jarrett Longacre."

The lawman nodded grimly. "I thought as much." He motioned to the deputy, then drew a pistol from a holster high on his hip. The two men walked into the corral, Gault holding the pistol almost to arm's length. He stopped just past the gate. His voice was like a clap of thunder. "Jarrett Longacre! I have come for you!"

# FOUR

Longacre whirled. His hand dropped toward his own pistol, then stopped abruptly when he saw that Gault had the drop on him.

The lawman said grimly, "The rest of you, move away from him." He made a sidewise motion with the muzzle of the pistol. The cowboys stepped to one side or the other, powerless to help. Trey's skin prickled with fear for his friend.

Longacre said, "I don't know you, mister."

"It is not necessary that you do. I have been duly deputized by the county of Bexar to arrest you for murder. You can come peacefully or you may reach for your gun. If you choose to reach, may the Lord have mercy on your soul."

"It wasn't murder. It was a fair fight, and he started it."

"I only know that a man is dead. And so will you be if you do not surrender in the next five seconds."

Trey sensed that Longacre had no intention of surrendering, and he knew Gault would not hesitate to shoot.

The two lawmen had not stepped far into the corral. They stood within the plank gate's arc. Trey sucked in a deep breath and gave the gate a hard push. It slammed against Gault's shoulder. Startled, the lawman turned on one bootheel, by reflex swinging the muzzle of the pistol toward Trey.

Trey froze, expecting to be shot.

Longacre had seen Trey's move. His hand dropped quickly and came up with his pistol. Fire and smoke exploded from its muzzle. The report threw the horses into a blind, running panic. The dark-bearded lawman fell back hard, his weight pushing the gate toward Trey. Gault tried to level the pistol at Longacre but could not hold it steady.

With a gasp the lawman went down. His derby hat rolled in the sand.

The deputy made no attempt to draw his own weapon. Trembling, he raised his hands and beseeched Longacre, "Don't shoot me, boy. I didn't want to come in the first place." His face paled.

Tightly, Longacre said, "I got no cause. You better drop your gun on the ground and go."

The deputy complied, leaving the corral in a long trot. His boots thumped heavily on the board sidewalk as he fled down the street.

Trey and the cowboys were stunned by the suddenness of it all. Only Longacre and the trail boss moved at first. Longacre walked across the corral to look down on the lawman, whose eyes were rolling back. Gault's hands clutched the bleeding wound high in his chest, toward the left shoulder. Longacre picked up the lawman's pistol, which had never fired. Extending it toward the trail boss, he said plaintively, "I never figured on nothin' like this."

Ivan Kerbow gravely accepted the weapon. "You'd better throw your saddle on my roan. He's got more bottom to him than that dun you've been ridin'."

Longacre nodded woodenly. "Thanks. I'll head north for Gainesville, and then . . ."

"Don't say it," Kerbow interrupted. "The law can't make us tell what we don't know. Now, you'd best get started. That deputy is liable to come back with help."

Kerbow knelt and tore away the lawman's shirt to inspect the wound while Longacre saddled quickly. Trey opened a gate on the north side of the corral to let the cowboy head straight out for the river.

Longacre paused to lean down and extend his hand. "Thanks, farm boy. I won't forget what you done for me."

What Trey had done was help get a lawman shot. He felt his stomach turning. Any moment now everything in it would come up. He leaned on the gate, watching as Longacre rode for the bridge.

He lost sight of the cowboy then, for he was losing breakfast and dinner.

He heard the trail boss's voice before he felt the man's hand fall heavily upon his shoulder. "You've got a decision to make, and you don't have long to do it in."

"Decision?"

"Whether to stay here and take your chances with the law or to light a shuck like Jarrett did."

"I didn't do anything."

"Some might figure you as an accomplice. Especially if that lawman doesn't live. We'll say a gust of wind pushed the gate against him. But if that deputy saw you do it . . ."

"I didn't figure on causin' a killin'. I figured on stoppin' one." Trey felt as if his head weighed a hundred pounds. It kept trying to drop to his feet, and his stomach continued turning. "First time I ever saw a man shot. I didn't know it could happen so fast."

Abel Plunkett had come up after Kerbow. "I'll saddle your horse, Trey. How long'll it take to get your stuff together?"

"It's on the cot, what little there is."

Kerbow's strong hand was under Trey's arm, giving him support.

"You told me you want to learn the cattle business. You could learn a right smart, followin' a herd to Ellsworth."

Trey spat, trying to purge the sour taste of vomit from his mouth. "You're offerin' me a job?"

"With Jarrett lit out, I've got room for a willin' hand."

"But if I'm in trouble . . ."

"Get yourself up the trail forty or fifty miles. Make camp and wait for us. We'll catch up to you in five or six days."

Plunkett led the brown horse out, Trey's meager possessions tied on the saddle. "I hadn't agreed to pay you nothin' in cash 'til the drives commenced, but I feel like you've earned a bonus." He handed Trey a handful of silver dollars. There must have been seven or eight, by the feel. "Don't you ever tell the missus. She wouldn't approve of me bein' so free with my money."

Trey made it a point not to count the coins. That might have seemed mercenary. "I'm obliged to you." Plunkett could have afforded a lot more, as much work as Trey had done fixing up the barn and the corrals for the cattle season. The stableman would have played hell getting it done this cheaply by any of the regular carpenters around town.

Trey supposed there was a lesson for him in this. The man who knew how to hang on to his money was the one most likely to get rich and to stay that way.

Plunkett said, "If you meet anybody, tell them your name is Smith. You'll have kinfolks wherever you go."

Trey turned to Kerbow. "I hope I don't miss you when you come by."

"Miss fourteen hundred steers? You'd as likely miss Sherman's army." He held the brown horse while Trey mounted. "If you should run into Longacre, you'd best let him go his own way. I'd as soon sit under a lone tree in a lightnin' storm as to ride with him right now."

As Trey put the Trinity River behind him, he stopped and looked back, half expecting to see someone in pursuit. Nobody was, at least not yet. He had not originally intended to spend much time in Fort Worth, but he had remained a month or more. Now that he was leaving, virtually on a moment's notice, he wished he were not. He felt as if he were being driven out against his will, as Lige Connors in effect had driven him out of another town.

He had no food with him. All he carried was some coffee beans Plunkett had kept for a pot on the stable's little flat-topped stove.

"Many a time," Plunkett had said, "I've lived for days on nothin' but coffee and dust. It's a test of your manhood."

Trey had not been worried about his manhood, but he *was* concerned about his stomach.

The brown horse was well rested, having done little but eat for a month. Trey pushed him hard the first two or three miles. Then, seeing no sign that anyone was following, he slowed to an easy trot.

It was no challenge to find and follow the cattle trail. Though spring grass had risen, it could not hide the deep ruts which thousands of hooves had cut into the soil during past seasons. These crooked ruts were like a hundred tangled ribbons crisscrossing each other but bearing always in a northerly direction. He had been told that once a rut began to take form, cattle would follow it automatically, their hooves cutting it gradually deeper day by day, week by week. At the end of a long season many ruts would be inches deep and ground down to a powder ready to lift and drift in whatever direction the gentlest wind might blow. Like an old wagon road, such scars might take years to heal, if they ever did.

Ahead of him, near sundown, a line of small timber suggested a creek. The afternoon had warmed, and he had sweated under a spring sun only occasionally compromised by the passing of a white cumulus cloud. He looked forward to a cool drink of water.

The horse was his first priority. Trey loosened the girth and let the brown dip its nose into the creek. Holding the reins, he dropped to his stomach a yard upstream from the horse and cupped his hand so that it formed a tiny dam against the running water. He sipped, choking a little as water invaded his nostrils. When he had his fill he pushed to his knees.

Only then did he see the shadow on the other side of the stream, and the high-topped black boots. He blinked against the glare of the sinking sun. For a moment he could not make out the face, but he saw a pistol in the man's hand. His heart jumped.

The voice was familiar. "Damn it, punkin' roller, you're lucky I don't have a rifle. I might've shot you before you got close enough for me to see who you was."

"Jarrett?" Trey rubbed a sleeve across his mouth to soak up the water that clung to his chin. Surprise had set his pulse to racing. "I never expected to catch up to you."

"I kept seein' somebody behind me, and you kept on comin', so I naturally figured it was the law."

"Gault said you'd killed somebody."

"A bully. We had a fight, and I whipped him. He couldn't stand for that, so he came at me with a knife."

Longacre spoke of it as calmly as if it had been no more than a head-knocking wrestling match.

Trey said, "I couldn't be that casual about it if it was me."

"You think I go around lookin' for people to shoot?"

"You might've shot *me* if you hadn't seen who I was."

"Necessity. But I wouldn't have enjoyed it. You had enough water? We can still travel a good ways before we bed down for the night."

"I'm not goin' as far as you are. I'll be stoppin' a little farther on and waitin' for the herd."

"Don't build the cowboy life up too high, because it ain't all that much. Me, I always wished I could go to St. Louis or New Orleans and be a fireman."

Trey thought the fugitive was more likely to start fires than put them out.

Longacre mounted his horse. "If you're goin' with me, you'd best come on." He rode off half humming, half singing a profane barroom song, emphasizing those words that gave it its sinful flavor.

Trey considered Kerbow's admonition about letting the cowboy go his own way. But for the time being they were headed in the same direction anyhow. He saw no harm in their staying together. He spurred to catch up.

At dusk Longacre began eyeing the canvas bags hanging from Trey's saddle. "What you got in there to eat?"

"Just some coffee and a can to boil it in."

"You sure ain't well fixed for travelin'."

"I wasn't figurin' on leavin' so quick. Maybe we can find a farmhouse."

"I've got to be careful who sees me, at least 'til I cross into Indian Territory. The boys probably told the law I headed west, but some of them don't lie worth a damn."

They were about ready to make a dry camp in the dark when the cowboy spotted a tiny point of light. Trey had missed it.

Longacre said, "You better train yourself to watch for things, or you'll never see the gun that kills you." He reined toward the light. "They'll have a chicken house, at least, maybe even a smokehouse."

The dark shape of a farm dwelling loomed up ahead of them.

Trey felt the weight of the silver dollars Plunkett had given him. "I'll go buy us somethin'. You won't have to show yourself."

"Nobody'll see me. You stay here."

Trey protested that so long as he had money there was no need to steal, but Longacre disappeared into the darkness. A dog began to bark. A door opened, and a man stood framed in lamplight on a narrow front porch. Trey tensed, expecting Longacre to be caught. But the man shouted, "Shut up, dog!" and closed the door.

The dog quieted for a minute, then resumed barking. The people in the house ignored him a while, then the man stepped outside again. He picked up a stone from the front yard and hurled it toward the sound. The dog yelped in surprise, then ran away to a dark shed. Grumbling, the man returned to the house.

Probably no more than twenty minutes had passed, but it felt like an hour before Longacre returned. "There was a smokehouse, all right. How do you like ham?"

In the faint light of the stars, Trey could see that Longacre held a canvas-wrapped pork shoulder in front of him on the saddle. "I like it fine. But I can't eat it if it's not paid for." He rode toward the house.

Longacre shouted at him. "Where the hell you goin'?"

Trey did not reply. He fished one of the silver dollars from his pocket, decided it might not be enough and added a second. They made a ringing sound as he pitched them up onto the porch. He pulled away before the man had time to come out again.

An impatient voice demanded, "Dog, what're you up to now?"

Keeping himself in darkness, Trey hollered, "The money's on the porch."

"What money? Who are you?"

But Trey set the horse into a long trot, quickly putting the house behind him.

Longacre's voice was impatient. "There wasn't no need in you doin' that. He never would've missed one ham, as many as he had hangin' up."

"I want to be able to sleep at night."

"You'll sleep a lot better with a full belly. How much money did you throw at him?"

"Two silver dollars."

"The whole hog wasn't worth that much, squeal and all."

They stopped after a time, built a fire and roasted some of the ham on pointed sticks held over the flame. Trey thought it more elegant, even without beans or biscuits, than anything Mrs. Plunkett had fixed for him.

They came within sight of a settlement the next day. Longacre did not remember its name. "I do remember that they've got a crossroads store. Bought me some smokin' tobacco there last summer. How much money you got with you?"

Trey did a swift calculation. "A little over twenty dollars." He did not count the gold piece sewed into his boot.

"You'll need to keep that. Anyway, it ain't enough for where I'm goin'."

They made a wide circle around the little town. A mile or so beyond it, Longacre stopped. He pointed at a creek. "Why don't you get down and make us some coffee while I go back to town?"

"Thought you didn't want to show your face."

Longacre rode southward without answering. It was all-fired strenuous trying to understand him, and even harder to anticipate what he might do next. Trey kindled a small fire and set a can of water on it to heat. There had been no coffee in their dry camp last night or this morning, so he was ready for the bracing taste of it.

He had drunk most of a cupful when he heard a horse coming toward him in a run. He recognized the roan and the man leaning over its neck, spurring. Longacre began waving his hat.

"Come on, mount up!" he shouted. "Let's go!"

Trey held up the blackened can. "I've got coffee made."

"To hell with the coffee. Get on that horse and let's ride!"

Trey felt a chill of alarm. "What have you done?"

"I just got me a little road stake from that store."

"You robbed it?"

"I told him I'd send it back one of these days, when I get flush again. But that Dutch storekeeper wasn't about to make me a loan 'til I showed him my pistol. Him and a bunch of his farmer friends ain't far behind me."

"You go on. I didn't rob anybody."

"Suit yourself, but don't be surprised if them punkin' rollers decide otherwise. Adiós, farm boy." Longacre spurred away, the roan's hooves throwing up clods of dry earth.

Trey heard the sounds of pursuing horsemen. His pulse quickened as he recognized the potential danger in which Longacre had placed him. Too late, he began thinking it might have been smarter to ride on with Longacre, at least until they were in the clear.

He pondered again what Kerbow had told him about staying away from the cowboy. Why was it, he asked himself, that it seemed so easy to choose a wrong fork in the road and so hard to take good advice?

He counted seven horsemen, pushing hard. He tried to act calm as they reined up in a hostile circle around him. He lifted the blackened can in a gesture of goodwill. "Coffee?"

Trey instantly recognized one of the group as Simon Stark, the farmer whose family had spent a night in Plunkett's livery barn. His daughter had shown herself to be a crack shot with Trey's rifle. Trey remembered that she had said her father was even better. Stark was tall, lean, edging into middle age. He had big, rough hands seasoned by long years of gripping plow handles. He looked like the type who takes charge when the rest are trying to decide which way to jump.

His eyes pinched in quizzical study. "Seems to me like I know you."

"I'm Trey McLean. I was workin' in Mr. Plunkett's barn."

"I wish you was still there today."

A bareheaded, barrel-chested man with a small canvas apron tied around his thick waist gave Trey a look of cold rage. "This is not the man. But I bet by damn they work together."

Simon Stark grunted. "Charlie, you and Tom stay with him. We'll go see if we can catch that other one."

The storekeeper pointed a finger in Trey's face. "And Charlie, if this no-good says to you one wrong word, you shoot him, by damn."

They set off in a lope, following Longacre.

The farmer named Charlie, dressed in overalls, sat bareback on a big sorrel plow horse that might have weighed thirteen or fourteen hundred pounds and had feet that looked as big around as barrel heads. The animal was obviously too slow to continue the chase far. The shotgun the man carried across his lap seemed as big as a cannon when he pointed its muzzle at Trey. "Now, young feller, you set yourself down on the ground nice and easy, and don't you be movin' 'til we tell you."

Mouth dry, Trey said, "Yes, sir" and sank onto his rump.

The other man looked Trey over. "You got a gun?"

"A rifle on my saddle is all. I just use it for meat."

"And for holdin' up stores?"

"I never held up no store. I never held up anybody."

"You tryin' to make us believe you wasn't in league with that cowboy? Then how come him to ride right by where you were at?"

"This is the main road to Gainesville and the Red River, ain't it? Everybody rides by here."

"So you didn't know him?"

Trey had never been able to lie very well, but he lied now as if his life depended upon it. He had a hunch that it might. "Only time I ever saw him in my life."

Charlie gave Trey a long study. "I kind of want to believe him. He looks a little like my cousin's boy Jared."

"The one that's slow in the head?"

"Slow, yes, but there ain't no harm in him."

The two farmers drank up the rest of Trey's coffee while they waited. Trey got painfully tired, sitting on the ground, but that shotgun was not looking any smaller. By the time the rest of the men returned, he was so stiff he could barely push to his feet when ordered.

They had not caught Longacre. Trey tried not to show his relief.

The storekeeper punched a short, thick finger against Trey's chest hard enough to bring pain. "Now, *Verbrecher*, it gets tough with you if you don't tell where goes your partner."

"All I know is that he passed here headed north. And he's not my partner."

"He took from my store close to a hundred dollars, and some tobacco as well."

"He didn't leave none of it with me."

"You lie!" In a towering Teutonic rage the storekeeper's huge fist came up from below his waist and struck Trey a blow that snapped his head back. It felt as if it were exploding. Trey staggered, almost going to his knees. The merchant had a powerful arm from wrestling boxes, barrels and crates.

Trey braced himself for another blow.

Simon Stark stepped protectively in front of him. "Hold on, Max. You've got no call."

The farmer Charlie said, "Me and Tom, we've about decided he's an innocent bystander." He drew in close and examined Trey's face. "Looky there. You went and busted his lip."

Trey could taste blood and feel the burning as the lip swelled. He felt anger at the storekeeper, but he felt more anger at Jarrett Longacre for putting him in this position. "If you got robbed, mister, I'm sorry. But I had nothin' to do with it."

He sensed that by striking him Max had inadvertently aroused several of the other men to sympathy, including Simon Stark. A busted lip was better than a stretched neck. If it were left to the storekeeper, that neck-stretching would begin in short order.

Stark said, "You sure you're tellin' us the straight of it?"

"As straight as I can."

"You had a job in Fort Worth. What're you doin' here?"

Trey's mind raced, seeking a plausible answer. "I thought I might find me a better job up north. Mrs. Plunkett's cookin' was about to starve me out."

Stark accepted that. He knew Mrs. Plunkett. He turned to the storekeeper. "You didn't see him at the store, did you, Max?"

"No, but that don't mean . . ."

"It don't make sense that he'd stay here brewin' coffee and let us catch him if he had any part in the robbery, does it?"

"These young people today, they are no by damn good. I don't believe anymore half what they say."

"Looks to me like we owe this young man an apology. What did you say your name was?"

Trey told him again.

The tall farmer studied Trey's face intently. "My wife may have somethin' that'll help that lip. You in any hurry to be travelin'?"

Trey thought about the Fort Worth law. Maybe it wouldn't come this far just to find a material witness. "Not real big."

Max protested, "What about my money? What about that robber?"

Stark said, "I doubt the robber will stop this side of the Territory. You know how much chance we'd ever have of catchin' him there. Maybe some renegade Indian will lift his scalp."

"That don't by damn get my money back."

"Sometimes we have to be content with small blessings."

# FIVE

Trey found himself in a dilemma. If he revealed that he intended to join the trail herd when it passed by, Stark's next logical question would be why he was not already with it, why he had ridden north ahead of it. He could not afford to tell that he feared the Fort Worth law might be looking for him. As it was, the storekeeper was far from satisfied about Trey's innocence. Even as Trey rode away with Stark and three other farmers, Dutch Max was still shouting protests to anyone who would listen.

Trey thought it a good thing none of these men carried ropes on their saddles as the cowboys did. Max would gladly have put one of them to use.

Simon Stark looked critically at Trey's mouth. It burned, and when Trey touched it his fingers came away with a little blood. Stark said, "Max excites pretty easy. I hope he didn't bust any teeth."

Trey strained to see the storekeeper's side of it. "I reckon I'd've got excited too if somebody stuck a gun at me and took a hundred dollars."

That was about what he figured Lige Connors had robbed him of, but Connors had not used a gun. He had used a sheriff.

"I promised Max you'd stay at my place 'til the law has a chance to talk to you."

Trey was fairly confident he had crossed out of Tarrant County, but he wondered how much communication there might be between neighboring county sheriffs. It wouldn't take long for Fort Worth officials to make a connection between him and Jarrett Longacre.

Max might even yet have his satisfaction, though that would not get his hundred dollars back for him.

Stark said, "You didn't get those calluses on your hands behind a store counter. Farmer, ain't you?"

"From over in the blacklands. I came west hopin' someday to have some cattle and maybe some farmland of my own. No cotton, though. I'm done with cotton."

"Cotton's a good honest crop. But, then, I got no quarrel with cattle. Nothin' squares a man better against the day's good work than a skillet-fried steak drowned in gravy. Wish I didn't usually have to settle for hog."

Trey worried that he might miss seeing Kerbow's herd pass by. He was pleased to find that the trail lay only a mile or so to the west. "Don't those cattle overrun your field sometimes?"

"I keep a watermelon patch on the east side and tell the cowboys to help theirselves. They like melons too well to let their stock tromp them out."

Uncle Matthew might think of something like that, Trey told himself, but Pap never would. Pap would just raise hell.

The Stark farm looked somewhat like the one back home. Cotton plants were just rising up out of the rows. Corn stood about boot-top high, its green leaves bending to a warm spring wind. A low rail fence surrounded the field, most of its logs and posts a dark gray from years of aging in sun and rain. Here and there a new one provided a bright contrast, replacing one rotted or broken. The fence would be little barrier to any grazing animal that really wanted in, like those long-legged steers from South Texas. They could step across it and barely scratch their bellies.

The barn and sheds were of short logs, set upright and anchored in the ground rather than laid horizontally as most in East Texas were. Timber here was smaller, shorter and less abundant, so the picket style was more practical. The main house was of lumber, framed up in simple box-and-strip fashion. Behind it stood an older and smaller picket house, its roof sagging slightly like the weak back of an old plow horse. Trey guessed this had been the Starks' first dwelling, used now for storage or perhaps sleeping quarters for the boys of the family.

A thin gray wisp of smoke arose from a black stovepipe, which told Trey that the Starks had climbed high enough in the world to own a wood range; poor folks cooked on the hearth.

A porch fit in an *L* shape along the front of the house and its east side. A couple of rocking chairs stood idle. Hardworking people shunned them at this time of day, reserving them for quiet contemplation in the cool of the evening.

A couple of flop-eared hounds emerged from beneath the porch, trotting out to greet the riders with deep-throated baying. Trey's brown nervously stepped sideways, edging away from them. He had been wary of dogs since one had sunk its teeth into his left hind foot on the courthouse square back home. The brown's kick had left the dog's ribs stove in and precipitated a brief fistfight between its owner and Pap.

A young woman stepped out onto the porch in response to the commotion and shaded her eyes with her hand. The wind picked up her apron and waved it like a flag, though it barely ruffled the skirt of her drab gray housedress. The hem almost swept the plank floor. For the moment, she had Trey's full attention. He was sure he recognized her as the girl who had fired his rifle from the wagonyard door.

Stark confirmed his judgment. "My daughter Sarah."

Trey realized he was staring at her with his mouth open, and she was staring back. Tipping his hat, he felt his face warm. It was probably as red as fresh-cut beef.

If Stark noticed—and Trey did not see how he could have missed it—he betrayed no sign. "We'll water our horses and put them in the pen. Then I'll see how long it'll be 'til dinner."

The man called Charlie said, "If it's all the same to you, I'm behind on my plowin'. Unless you want us to stay and help you watch over this feller."

Nobody had openly articulated the notion that Trey was technically a prisoner, though Charlie's shotgun had given him a sense of it.

Stark shook his head. "This is an honorable young man. He won't leave until the sheriff talks to him."

That was a way of putting all the responsibility on Trey's shoulders. With his honor placed on the line like a stack of chips in the center of a poker table, he had no choice except to remain. They could not run him off now with a brace of Yankee muskets.

"I'm in no hurry to go anywhere."

He just hoped the herd did not get here before the sheriff.

Charlie and the other men rode away.

Mrs. Stark stepped out onto the porch, joining her daughter. She had more or less the same facial features as Sarah. She stood half a head taller, a little broader in hips and shoulders, though in her maturity she carried not a pound of extra weight that Trey could see. If anything, she tended toward the gaunt. The life of a farm woman in this developing country demanded long days of hard work that stretched into night.

"You was a long time at the settlement." Her tone of voice carried an implication that her husband had been expected home much sooner. A lot of chores were yet to be done before the day could be considered complete.

"Dutch Max got robbed. We made a long chase after the thief."

Her gaze settled harshly on Trey. "Is this him?"

"No, this young man just happens to be a material witness, is all. He'll be stayin' with us 'til the sheriff has a chance to talk to him."

Mrs. Stark appraised Trey like a trial judge looking down upon the accused. "Aren't you the boy we saw workin' in Mr. Plunkett's stable?" She turned back to her husband, not waiting for Trey's affirmative answer. "He looks strong. Maybe while he's here you can raise that hog shed you been figurin' on."

"He's a guest, Frieda."

Trey looked at Sarah again. She was dangerously close to smiling at him. He wondered if she was remembering how she had startled him with her unexpected marksmanship. He said, "I'll sure figure to earn my keep."

Mrs. Stark set her reservations aside but was probably leaving them within easy reach. Motioning for her daughter to lead the way back into the house, she paused to tell her husband that dinner would be ready by the time they watered and unsaddled their horses. "The sheriff might come at any time. You'd ought to start workin' on that shed."

A practical woman, Trey thought. He watched the girl until she disappeared within the house, then belatedly followed Stark around toward the pens. Chickens pecking amid old cow and horse droppings moved aside, one fluttering her wings and squawking in protest over the disturbance. Trey heard the loud grunting of a big sow, which snapped at one of the slower-moving chickens when it did not clear out of her way quickly enough. Several small shoats followed in her wake, squeaking and squealing.

The Stark family should not soon run out of ham or eggs, Trey thought.

He and Stark watered their horses in a creek that ran behind the house. The horse pen was crudely but solidly made of short logs stacked between pairs of posts and laced down with rawhide strips that had shrunk and dried to the consistency of steel. The gate was a single rail which Stark slid aside so they could enter, then slid back in place so the horses would not go out. Like the low fence around the field, it was heavily dependent upon faith. It would provide no challenge to a horse that truly wanted to leave.

Stark was liberal with the shelled oats he dipped from a bin and poured into a wooden trough. Trey decided no sensible horse would *want* out.

Sarah Stark went to a back window to watch her father with the tall young man she remembered from Fort Worth. "Mama, why do you suppose he left Mr. Plunkett's?"

"You'll have to ask him yourself. No, you ask your father. It's not fittin' for a young lady to be askin' questions of a stranger. Especially not one the sheriff wants to talk to." Mama arched her eyebrows. "And why would he be of any interest to you in the first place?"

"Just curious. He must be all right, else Papa wouldn't have brought him here."

"Your father would invite a stray dog into this house and never once think of askin' if it was all right with me. Why, he's even brought some of those heathen cowboys here. He has no judgment when it comes to character."

"The young man needs a shave and a bath, but otherwise I think he looks nice enough."

"He looked at you a lot, and I'm not sure he was *thinkin'* nice. You spend too much time readin' books. Men around here aren't like the ones in those books of yours."

Embarrassment brought heat to Sarah's face. "Mama . . ."

"You've reached an age where you'd better learn how men's minds work. You can't trust them if they get in arm's reach of you. And they're always tryin' to."

"You must not've felt that way about Papa."

"Yes, I did, and I always stayed a step ahead of him. Led him right to the preacher and never let him realize it 'til he was takin' his vows."

"Don't seem fair, settin' out to trick a man."

"It's the only way. They're bigger than us, but we can outthink them because they keep half their brain tied up with foolish notions. Now, let's set the table."

Sarah remembered, after she dwelled on it a while, that the young man's name was Trey McLean. *Trey*. Odd nickname. It teased her curiosity, but she respected her mother's admonition about not asking questions. She discovered that he had a voracious appetite for roast pork and red beans and biscuits. He mentioned that he had had nothing so far today except coffee.

Papa said, "A healthy appetite indicates a clean conscience."

She noticed that her mother's only visible reaction was a frown. But Frieda Stark had always been suspicious of strange men. Sarah was more inclined toward generosity, especially when the stranger was young like this one, and handsome despite his whiskers. He seemed not to have touched a razor to his face in two or three days, though this was commonplace among the men she knew. Few other than merchants made an effort to shave every day. She found herself wondering how it would feel to touch her hand to his freshly barbered cheek, or, even more deliciously wicked, how it would feel to have his cheek rub against her own.

At seventeen, Sarah was the next-oldest of the Stark offspring, second only to her brother Nathaniel. Her five younger brothers and sisters embarrassed her with their lack of manners at the table, but Trey did not seem to notice. It might be that he simply did not know the difference, but she preferred to believe he was too much the gentleman to betray any annoyance at their noise.

Frieda Stark asked some of the questions Sarah was too shy to ask, particularly about Trey's home and his future plans. She approved of his intent to acquire land someday, though she was less keen about his ambition to own cattle.

"Farmers are close to the soil," she said. "They toil for what they bring out of the earth. Herdsmen take the Lord's grass without labor and sit on their horses high and haughty."

It was to Trey's credit, Sarah thought, that he gave no sign he disagreed. "Yes ma'am," he said politely.

The sheriff was polite too, but firm, when he came the next day. He had followed the fugitive robber north as far as the county line without seeing anything except his tracks. Sarah listened from the front room while he questioned Trey on the porch. The lawman was of a suspicious nature like Sarah's mother, repeating his questions two or three times. McLean kept giving the same answers. Sarah could have told the sheriff that the young stranger was honest; she could see it in his eyes. The officer rode away knowing no more than when he came. Even less, perhaps, for he said Trey's description of the robber differed greatly from the storekeeper's.

Dutch Max was probably too excited to see straight, Simon Stark suggested.

Sarah's father had remained with Trey during the interrogation. "It's his duty to be thorough, son. But an innocent man has no reason to be fearful."

Trey seemed much relieved that it was over, even for an innocent man. He stood on the edge of the porch, looking eastward at the departing sheriff and southeastward in the direction of the cattle trail which led from Fort Worth past the farm. "First time I ever had anybody look a hole plumb through me that way. I was about ready to confess to anything he wanted me to, whether it was true or not."

Papa said, "We all have sins enough of our own. We don't need to take on anybody else's."

Sarah wondered what sins a man like Trey McLean might have left behind him. She had heard whispers about things that happened in wicked Fort Worth. She tried to picture him doing them, and herself being a part of it. Her body warmed at the thought.

She tried to push the image from her mind, for he would probably be scandalized if he had the faintest notion what her imagination conjured up. But the fantasies were persistent. They kept intruding whenever he walked into the house or she heard his voice. She could only hope he was not a clairvoyant, like crazy old Elijah Willet down the road claimed to be, for he might read her mind and think her wanton.

Many a young man, and a couple of older ones, had come calling the last couple of years. The only one who had stirred her to more than casual interest had been a temporary hired man Papa had taken on at harvest time. His name had been Andrew. He had been tall and muscular with a handsome face and strong hands that roamed where no decent girl was supposed to let them. Sarah had let them, a little, then had panicked and pulled away.

If Trey seemed a little nervous about sheriffs, he was not shy about hard work. He did most of the ditch-digging and the heavy ax work, trimming logs for the picket hog shed Simon Stark had been planning. He was particular about making the logs fit snugly together so they would turn winter's cold north winds and protect the young shoats from freezing. Even Sarah's mother began to admit to a certain respect for his perfectionism.

A while before supper, Papa came to the house to fetch the milk bucket. Trey remained at the new shed, where he had a couple of iron rods heating in a fire.

Papa told Mama, "Makes me wish we could afford a steady hired man. He'd be handy to keep around."

She gave her oldest daughter a critical study. "It's probably just as well that we can't."

He seemed to miss her point.

Sarah said, "I'll go gather the eggs."

She walked out the back door, a willow basket tucked under her arm. She headed toward the henhouse, then angled across to where the hog shed was nearing completion. Smoke curled from a log as McLean pushed a red-hot iron rod into it. It was a slow, laborious process, but a neighbor had borrowed the brace and bit and had not brought them back.

She said, "It's lookin' mighty nice."

He made a small smile. "*Nice* don't mean a lot to a hog."

"Papa says you and him'll have this finished tomorrow. You goin' to be ridin' on after that?"

"I don't like to wear out my welcome."

"You'd be welcome to stay here as long as you wanted to. We'd all be tickled . . . that is, Papa says . . ." She felt as if her tongue had gotten tangled up. It usually did when she tried to talk to a man, outside of family and a few neighbors. An exception was the bachelor schoolteacher, Mr. Craven, who had come calling several times from over on Boggy Creek. He had brought her several books by Sir Walter Scott and even some poetry. The books were romantic, but he was not. Folks said he was crowding forty.

She had heard Trey tell her father he was twenty-one-going-on-two. That, her mother warned, was a dangerous age around a girl of seventeen. The man knew enough to get her into trouble, while the girl didn't know enough to dodge his tricks.

Sarah wondered what kind of tricks Trey knew.

Trey said, "I like it here, but this ain't gettin' me anyplace. Soon as a cattle herd comes along I'll be seein' if I can sign on. They say there's opportunity in the cattle business for a man with enterprise."

She said, "You don't think there's opportunities around here?"

"This land's all got somebody's name on it. Farther west there's a lot that ain't yet."

"The cattle drives go north, not west."

"But they offer payin' work. Once I've earned me a stake, then I can go west."

"When you do, you'll be needin' a partner."

He stuck the rod back into the fire and took out another to continue burning through the log. "Pap and my uncle Matthew were partners once, a long time ago. They couldn't agree on much, so they had to split it all up."

"That's not the kind of partner I mean. You'll need a wife to help you."

"I suppose, eventually."

"You got a girl back where you come from?"

"Always had too much work to be lookin' for a girl. I figure when the time comes I can find me a wife without travelin' all that far."

"They're apt to be scarce out west."

Smoke quit coming from the hole in the log. He withdrew the rod and placed it back in the fire, then smiled at her. "You got any notion where I might find one?"

Her face warmed. "There's several eligible girls around here."

"Maybe I'll come lookin' . . . when it's time."

Two days later the morning wind from the east brought with it the faint smell of dust. Sarah stepped out onto the porch and shaded her eyes, looking into a sun that was an hour high. She made out distant horsemen, moving like ants along the horizon. From past experience she knew this meant a trail herd, headed north. And she knew, with a sinking of her heart, that it also meant Trey McLean would be leaving.

Her father seemed as excited as Trey. She had heard him say that if he were able to start life over again he would rather be a cowboy than a farmer. This always drew a rebuke from Mama.

At breakfast Papa said, "Trey, that's the first trail herd of the season. I expect you'll be ridin' off with it."

Trey looked across the table at Sarah. "If they're hirin'."

She blinked her burning eyes and said nothing.

He had been sleeping in the barn. Breakfast done, he walked out that way to pick up his few belongings and saddle his old brown horse. It was not Sarah's habit to gather eggs in the morning, but she took her basket, made a hasty check of the henhouse, then walked into the barn. Trey was tying his thin roll of blankets behind the cantle.

She said in a tentative voice, "I was afraid you might not come back by the house. I just wanted to tell you 'bye."

He finished a knot in a leather string and turned toward her. "It's been awful nice to know you, Miss Stark."

"Folks call me Sarah after they get to know me."

"I'm not sure I know you all that well."

"You could, if you stayed longer."

"Leavin' here ain't the easiest thing I ever done." He stared at her as if he had swallowed his tongue. Her own seemed to tie itself into a knot again. She thought of things she wanted to say, but none of them came out.

He moved a step closer. "Like I told you, I'm liable to come back this way again sometime."

"I expect I'll be here."

"I expect I'll find you."

He reached out for her and pulled her against him and kissed her on the mouth. She reacted first with surprise, for much as she had thought about it she had not really believed he would ever do it. Blood rushed to her cheeks. He started to pull away, but she clung to him. She initiated the second kiss, a longer one than the first.

She said as he pulled away at last, "You be *real* sure you come back here, Trey McLean."

# SIX

Trey had worried all along that Simon Stark would want to ride out to the herd with him, where somebody might give away Trey's prior acquaintanceship with the cowboy crew. Stark might then realize that Trey also knew the man who had robbed Max's store. He had not appreciated how heavy a burden a lie could become. Once told, it demanded continued protection and more lies to support it.

Fortunately, Stark decided that he and his sons would better spend their time cultivating the field, for spring rain had encouraged the weed crop as much as it had helped the corn.

Trey kept looking back over his shoulder toward the house. He had forgotten the injury Max had done to his lip, but he would be a long time forgetting the kiss Sarah had placed there . . . if he ever did. He still tingled from the passion of it. With a little more encouragement he might have stayed, dismissing his notion of finding a place for himself out west. But he had known Sarah for only a few days. His yearning for independence went back years.

The chuck wagon was moving ahead of the cattle so the cook would have time to whip up a meal before the cowboys overtook him at noon. Zack Lynch waved his hand at Trey.

"Howdy, farmer boy. Got any more of them Fort Worth cigars?"

"Sorry. I left town in kind of a hurry."

He found Ivan Kerbow in swing position toward the front of the herd, behind point rider Gil Atwater. The trail boss gave him a sober study. "I was afraid some sheriff had got you. Or worse, that you'd joined Jarrett Longacre."

Trey admitted that both things had happened to him, briefly. He told how he had encountered Longacre and about the robbery of the German merchant.

Kerbow grunted. "That boy'll get himself killed one of these days. And maybe whoever happens to be around him. You still wantin' a job?"

"I don't know much about drivin' cattle."

"There's not much to learn. Biggest thing is in knowin' when to stay out of their way." Kerbow glanced back over his shoulder. "A couple of the buttons quit me soon's we left Fort Worth. Got homesick for their mama's cookin'."

Trey gave voice to the question that had nagged him for days. "That lawman Gault . . . is he dead?"

"Wasn't when we left town. But if he pulls through he'll never be the man he was before. That bullet busted him up bad."

Trey felt a weight slip from his shoulders. Perhaps he was not an accomplice to a killing after all.

Kerbow frowned at the small blanket roll tied behind Trey's saddle and the war bag hanging off the side. "You don't look very well fixed for the trip, but you won't use that blanket much anyway. Nights are damned short in a drovers' camp." He motioned with his thumb. "Drop on back to the drags and help bring up the slow ones. First chance you get, stow your stuff in Pancho's hoodlum wagon." He noticed that Trey had no spurs. "You'll find some spare OK spurs in the wagon too. Cost me four bits a pair, but I can take that out of your pay."

Trey had never heard the term *drags,* but he soon figured out its meaning. The slowest, draggiest cattle inevitably fell to the rear. There the newest or the youngest men with the outfit had the dubious pleasure of eating the herd's dust while punching up the lame and the lazy.

He shared the drags with Johnny Fulton, who claimed to be eighteen but was probably closer to sixteen and away from home for the first time. When Trey had first encountered the outfit south of Fort Worth he had been struck by the extreme youth of most of the hands. He doubted that the boy had a razor with him; nor did he need one.

Trey recognized Lige Connors's cattle. They were larger-framed and had shorter horns than the rest of the herd. Most tended to drop back toward the drags, for they had not yet found their places in the order of dominance and had not become assimilated among the original members of the herd. Like people, cattle had their hierarchies, enforced by the sharp tips of their horns.

By the time Trey's end of the herd reached the chuck wagon and he had a chance for a tin plate of warmed-up beans and nearly cold biscuits, he sensed that driving cattle up the trail involved far more boredom than excitement.

Kerbow dropped back to the rear and took a long look southward, where the steers had left the scars of their several thousand hooves. Though this was only the first of many herds which would use the trail during the season, it had already grazed off or tromped down much of the newly risen green grass.

"Doin' all right, Trey?"

"We ain't lost a one."

Kerbow said, "Well, keep proddin' them. There's not a more important hand on the trail than the man that follows the drags."

Trey suspected Kerbow was trying to make him feel better about being stationed where the dust was thickest. Pap had always said the best place to learn about farming was from the south end of a plow mule heading north. The same principle probably applied to cattle.

The sheriff and the storekeeper Max showed up late in the afternoon as the lead cattle were being held up and the drags drifted in to the bed-ground Kerbow had chosen for the night. Trey tensed at sight of the lawman and the merchant sitting on a bedroll beside the chuck wagon, helping themselves to the contents of Zack Lynch's big black coffeepot.

Afraid they might make a connection between him and Longacre, Trey stalled. He remained with the herd while most of the hands went in for supper. He kept hoping the pair would leave. Finally Kerbow came, jerking his thumb toward the wagon.

"The longer you wait, the more suspicious they'll get. None of the boys has mentioned Longacre. No reason you should."

Neither the sheriff nor Max showed any surprise at seeing Trey. He suspected they had spotted him as they rode in. Suspicion lingered in the lawman's sharp eyes. "I was hopin' these cowboys might know somethin' about the man that robbed Max, but it appears he must've risen up out of a hole in the ground. I don't reckon you've remembered anything more you can tell me?"

"I already told you all I know. Maybe more."

The portly merchant's face was flushed. "I would put him in jail, Sheriff, and in the well I would drop the key."

Trey could read the dilemma in the sheriff's eyes. On the one hand he had no evidence that Trey knew the robber. On the other Trey was a transient, while Max was a voter and carried influence in the community.

The sheriff finished his coffee without relaxing his stern gaze. Once again Trey felt as if those eyes were boring a hole through him.

The officer said, "I'm givin' you the benefit of the doubt, and I'm givin' you a little advice. Been many a good man led astray by evil companions. Texas may be short of cash money, but it's got a-plenty of rope." He dropped his cup into the cook's wreck pan. "Much obliged for the coffee."

Max's fists knotted. "You don't put him in jail?" His angry eyes telegraphed the thought behind them. But Kerbow and the young cowboys moved into a protective semicircle around Trey. The skinny cook held a long iron pot hook in one big freckled hand. Max reconsidered.

The two men mounted their horses and disappeared southward into the dusk.

The cook's face twisted. "Now, farmer boy, I ain't askin' you no questions, but I hope you wasn't with Longacre when he made that wild sashay."

"I wasn't."

"Good. A thing like that can get a feller throwed out of his church."

Trey chafed to be across the county line and out of this sheriff's jurisdiction. There was no rushing the cattle, however. Gil Atwater was an experienced drover not many years younger than Kerbow. As point rider he set an easy pace that allowed them to graze as they walked. With any luck the steers would reach the railroad heavier than when they left South Texas.

Zack Lynch noted, "It's a mark of a well-run outfit when the cattle gain weight and the cowhands lose it."

Trey found it was true what Kerbow had said about not getting to wear out his blankets. The men took turns standing guard over the sleeping cattle at night, two at a time riding in a semicircle in opposite directions so that they met on first one side of the herd, then the other.

Kerbow cautioned, "Talk to them, sing to them, always let them know where you're at. Don't ever surprise them."

He explained that the herd had stampeded several times in its first days on the trail but had more or less settled down now to the routine. However, any loud and unexpected noise could bring the steers to their feet and set them to running in a blind panic. He dreaded spring storms with their thunder and lightning. For some reason, he said, those seemed worse in Indian Territory and Kansas than in Texas.

"Once we cross the Red, the Lord looks the other way. We're in the devil's hands."

For Trey, that dark thought was offset by the fact that no sheriff was likely to come looking for him north of the Red. He could put up with a stampede or two.

If sleep was at a premium for the cowboys, it was even scarcer for Ivan Kerbow. The trail boss kept a saddled horse staked a short distance from his bedroll and sometimes rode out to the herd two or three times during the night, quietly checking the guards and the cattle. Trey would occasionally awaken to see Kerbow sitting alone beside the glowing coals of the cook's fire, sipping coffee, staring off into the darkness. He seemed often to drift away into some melancholy world of his own and shut the door behind him so no one else could intrude.

The monotony of the drive allowed Trey's mind to roam. Often it took him home to the blacklands farm and reviewed the many things that had happened to him since he had set out on his own. It was futile to dwell upon Lige Connors and the way he had euchred Trey out of his four old cows. Yet the presence of the Connors steers kept pushing the greedy farmer into Trey's conscious thoughts in the daytime and into his dreams at night.

Trey devised a number of ingenious tortures, the most satisfying of which was to chain Connors to a stake, build a fire around him and see how much lard he would render through his pores.

When he tired of imaginary revenge, Trey would smother the fires of anger by walking a green meadow with Sarah Stark. He could remember in generous detail her unexpectedly warm good-bye and her plea for him to return. A creative memory expanded upon it, carrying it far beyond reality.

He might never see Lige Connors again, but he had every intention of revisiting Sarah. Sheriff or no sheriff.

The trail passed Gainesville, the last town before Red River Station. Only the cook and Pancho Martínez went in, taking the two wagons to pick up extra supplies. Some of the youngsters looked wistfully in the direction of the settlement, but towns of late had meant little except trouble for Trey. He could live without their pleasures awhile.

Kerbow hoped to cross the Red before nightfall, but the timing did not work out. He had to bed down the cattle a couple of miles south of the river. He kept watching a line of dark clouds building to the west. By dark, distant thunder rumbled, and lightning flickered to the west. Agitated, the trail boss kept walking beyond the firelight to stare at the building storm. He rode out to circle the herd and came back in no better mood. "They're like a fuse waitin' for a match."

Trey's night-herding tour began after midnight. By that time clouds had covered the stars so that the night seemed pitch black between lightning flashes. Though he could smell rain, he had not felt any. Some hands had slickers tied behind their saddles, but Trey did not own one. Pap had always said that anybody who did not have sense enough to get in out of the rain deserved a good soaking.

The lightning gave the air a sharpness that made Trey's nose tingle. He had heard stories about bolts melting the coins in men's pockets, burning holes in their shoes. He felt vulnerable but took some comfort in the thought that there were a dozen men and boys with the outfit. Even if lightning struck, he had better than a ten-to-one chance of survival.

He was not prepared for a sudden scream that raised the hair on the back of his neck.

Coming from somewhere out in the darkness, it sounded like a woman in desperate trouble. Trey's skin prickled. On the other side of the river lay Indian Territory. His first thought was that some unfortunate woman had fallen into hostile hands.

The scream came again. Trey had only a vague sense of its direction.

A flash of lightning revealed Ivan Kerbow riding toward him. Trey shouted, "Sounds like a woman out there."

Kerbow seemed criminally calm in the face of imminent tragedy. "It's just a panther. They scream like a woman bein' killed."

Kerbow's assurance brought only partial relief. Trey's nerves still tingled. "What do you reckon it wants?"

"Whatever it can find. They're especially partial to horseflesh."

Trey conjured up a mental picture of a panther springing on him in the darkness, killing his horse and himself as well. He would be unable to defend himself. His rifle was in the wagon.

Kerbow was irritatingly cool. "That cat is as scared of you as you are of him. But if it keeps up that racket it's liable to set the herd to runnin'. Now, *there's* somethin' to be scared about." He turned his horse and rode slowly the way he had come.

Trey smarted a little, fearing that his anxiety about the scream had branded him a greenhorn. He had a lot to learn. But he would. He would keep learning until he knew more than the teachers. If it took him twenty years, he would show Pap.

The panther's screams, on top of the thunder and lightning, had intensified the herd's nervousness. Many cattle had risen to their feet. They stood as if waiting for a signal.

The panther's third scream was much closer. The cattle created their own thunderclap. Those still lying down jumped to their feet, and those already on their feet broke into a sudden hard run.

Trey's horse was in the cattle's path. He was glad for the four-bit OK spurs, though he probably did not need them. The horse sensed danger as much as Trey did and set off in a hard run ahead of the cattle.

Behind him, barely audible over the rumble of hooves, he thought he heard the panther scream again. He turned in the saddle, shouting, slapping his hat against his leg. The cattle surged northward, toward the river. The best he could do was try to get out of their way. He urged the horse to the right, moving it from the immediate path of the stampede.

He was glad he was not riding his own brown. It probably could not have outrun anything except the cripples. Kerbow had assigned him this dun bronc, which perversely crow-hopped every time Trey got on him. He had wished for something punishing to befall the mount, like two broken legs. Now he hoped nothing would.

He thought at times he could hear other riders shouting somewhere behind him. He looked back during the lightning flashes, but the only horseman he could see was Kerbow, gradually closing the distance between them.

Trey never knew for sure what tripped the dun—a gully perhaps, or a stump. He knew only that he suddenly found himself being hurled forward, slamming against the ground and sliding. He looked back quickly, afraid the cattle would trample him. They kept stampeding past him with a clatter of hooves, spattering him with clods of mud.

The horse regained its feet. Trey, on his knees, reached desperately for the reins but could not grab them before the horse ran away. He turned, afraid he might be in the path of other cattle.

Kerbow rushed by, bending down to grab the loose reins and bring the horse to a stop. He led it back to Trey. "You hurt any?"

Trey knew from the burning that one side of his face was skinned. His shirt hung in shreds. "Don't reckon so."

Kerbow rode on after the cattle. Trey remounted and spurred hard to catch up with him.

If the herd had to run, he thought, at least it had chanced to do so in the right direction. Morning would find it closer to the river if not actually on its banks.

As the cattle began to tire, their panic subsided. Foam streamed from the leaders' tongues. Trey could only guess how far they had run—a mile certainly, probably more. One by one they slowed from a run to a trot and from a trot to a walk. Forward momentum finally stopped, and they milled aimlessly, exhausted.

Trey found his heart pounding hard. Now that the anxiety had passed, he felt exhilarated. It was as if fingers of electricity ran along his skin. He turned back to Kerbow, who had dismounted to tighten his saddle girth. "That was quite a run."

The trail boss replied without emotion, "Fair. I've seen them run all night and look for an excuse to start again."

Feeling a little let down, Trey realized it was better this way. Excitement sometimes exacted too high a price.

"What do we do now?"

"Hold what we've got and wait for the rest of the outfit to catch up to us in the mornin'."

A loud clap of thunder seemed to shake the earth, but the cattle had worn themselves out. Rain began in a blinding, wind-driven rush, cold with a feel of hail in it. The cattle stopped milling and turned their rumps toward the west wind. Kerbow donned the slicker he had carried tied behind his cantle. All Trey could do was hunch his shoulders and accept the soaking and the chill.

He heard a strange sound sweeping toward him from the west. It was like another stampede. A hailstorm began pelting him in the darkness. His hat afforded only limited protection. He felt as if someone were striking his head with a hammer.

Kerbow shouted, "Get under your saddle!"

The boss removed the saddle from his horse and drew it over his head and shoulders. Trey followed suit but almost lost the dun bronc, which jerked hard against the reins. Trey wrapped them around his wrist, accepting the risk of being dragged rather than let the horse break away and leave him afoot.

The cattle began drifting with the wind and the hail. Trey walked along with them, balancing the saddle over his head and retaining a firm hold on the reins. He saw several steers go to their knees, addled by large hailstones striking their heads.

The heavy hail ran its course, though the rain kept on. The cattle continued a slow drift. Trey stopped and saddled the horse, then swung up again, shivering uncontrollably. He wished he could build a fire, but even if he could find wood in the darkness it would be too wet.

Kerbow rode over to him. "You sure you're not hurt?"

Trey rubbed his hand against his face. The rain had washed the mud from it. "Nothin' that won't heal."

"When you signed on, you said you weren't sure you could handle this job."

"I'm still not sure."

Kerbow nodded approval. "For a green hand fresh off of the farm, you did good tonight."

Trey sensed that Kerbow was not inclined to be free with compliments. "You think I'll ever make a cattleman?"

"You just might."

Tired to the bone, the cattle halted their drifting. The rain slackened, then quit. The lightning moved eastward and allowed darkness to reenvelop the land. Trey lost touch with Kerbow until the boss sought him out.

"We'll stand our ground 'til daylight," Kerbow said. "Then we'll gather all the steers we can find and wait for the outfit to catch up."

Trey was thinking about Zack Lynch's warm campfire and the pot of hot coffee that must be steaming over it right now, if the rain had not drowned it or the hail knocked the pot to kingdom come. He shivered, chilled through.

Kerbow took off his slicker and handed it to him. "This'll keep the wind from cuttin' through those wet clothes."

"You need it yourself."

"I've stayed dry. Put it on before you come down with the ague."

Trey thanked him. Though his soaked clothing still clung, the windbreaking effect of the slicker eased the chill. "I hope I can pay you back someday."

"I hope I never get in a shape to where you have to."

It did little good to ride, for the night was so dark he could not see cattle more than a few feet away. He saw just enough to know that many exhausted steers were lying down despite the muddy ground and the cold of accumulated hailstones. He sat in the saddle, shoulders slumped. Without realizing it, he drifted off to sleep.

He awakened with a start and grabbed the horn as he was about to slide out of the saddle. His heart pounded. An early hint of daylight revealed the vague shapes of cattle bedded down thirty or forty yards away. Kerbow slouched in the saddle, sleeping as Trey had slept. Trey had observed how the more experienced men like Kerbow and Atwater could doze in the saddle without falling off, catching fleeting moments of sleep where and when they could. He felt an ache between his shoulder blades. He was still cold, and his stomach growled.

The morning remained cloudy, gray and chilly. Young cowboys started showing up, driving cattle northward, joining them to those Trey and Kerbow loose-herded. Trey was relieved to see them, but what he *really* wanted to see was the chuck wagon. It seemed in no hurry to appear.

Like Trey, some of the hands had been with the cattle all night and well into the day. A few, however, had been able to go back to the wagon and take breakfast. Johnny Fulton remarked that this morning's coffee had been the best he had drunk in all of his sixteen years.

Kerbow circled around all the cattle that had been brought together, taking a rough count. Then he rode northward to look at the river.

Trey's clothes dried on his back. To his joy, and that of the other hands who had not eaten since the previous night's supper, Zack Lynch showed up. The cook explained that the two wagons had had a hard time pulling through the mud. He made no apology. A wagon cook was above apologizing to cowhands. Fortunately he had enough dry wood stored in a rawhide cooney beneath the chuck wagon's belly to start a respectable fire.

While he waited for the biscuits to finish, Lynch cleaned Trey's facial scratches with whiskey that burned worse than if it had gone inside.

"Marks of the trade," he said. "You won't look like a real cowboy 'til you've got a crooked nose, a twisted leg and lose a couple of fingers between your rope and the saddle horn."

Trey asked, "How'd you get your bum leg?"

"Horse."

"And that busted nose . . . horse too?"

"No, I got that stickin' it into somebody else's business."

Trey munched on cold biscuits to smother the worst of his hunger while he waited for something hot. Lynch grinned at him. "There's times when cold biscuits taste like sweet ambrosia."

"I never tasted any ambrosia, but it'd have to go some to beat this."

The hands held the herd, funneling them down to single and double file as they passed between Kerbow and Atwater for counting. Kerbow tied a knot in a rawhide string for each hundred head. Atwater passed pebbles from his right hand to his left. When they were done, the two experienced cattlemen were only three head apart. Kerbow being the boss, his tally was official: fourteen hundred and forty-three.

"We're about seventy head short," he said. He detailed half the crew to fan out and hunt for them while the rest pushed the steers to the river.

Trey remained with the herd, which suited him fine. That kept him close to the chuck wagon.

The Red was on a rise, though not as high as Kerbow had feared, considering the ferocity of the night's storm. Clouds darkened again in the west. He decided it would be prudent to put the cattle across now, in the event the water came up more later.

The cook suggested that the hands remove their clothes and stow them in the wagon. "They'll be dry for you when you get to the other side."

Trey removed his boots and stripped down to his long underwear. The wind was too chilly, blowing across wet ground, for him to want to go buck naked.

The spotted lead steer had been up the trail before. Bell clanging, it plunged into the water just ahead of fifty or sixty steers Kerbow and the point man had cut off to make the start. The other cattle hesitated, but with prodding and shouting they fell into the wake of the lead steer. Trey and the remaining hands quickly brought up more cattle to keep the flow going.

The current was strong. Trey's horse was soon swimming. He saw the cook's logic in suggesting that he take off his clothes, for he had to slip out of the saddle to allow the horse freedom to swim. He clung to the horn and saddle strings.

The longer they swam, the wider the river looked. He felt himself tiring. He hoped the horse did not give out, for he probably could not fight the river's strong tow by himself. He sensed that the water's force was carrying him and the cattle downstream from their starting place.

The horse's feet found firm ground. Trey had been warned not to stop lest he fall into the grip of quicksand, so he swung into the saddle and urged the animal to keep moving. Shortly they were on the north bank. Many of the cattle, dripping water as they emerged, stopped to shake themselves like dogs.

Trey shivered, for a chill wind penetrated the wet underwear as if it had been fishing net. He looked back hopefully to see what progress the chuck wagon was making. His spirits sagged, for the wagon was back on the south bank. Its first effort at crossing had been aborted. He looked to the west, where the sun would be sinking now if its light could break through those black clouds. Darkness would be upon them soon, and the wagons were still on the wrong side of the river.

He was not much given to cursing; Pap held the family trophy on that. But at this moment Pap might have had to concede the contest.

He heard a voice from behind him.

"You boys sure are a pitiful sight!"

He turned in the saddle. Jarrett Longacre sat on Kerbow's roan horse, a smile lighting his bestubbled face. He looked disgustingly warm and dry and comfortable.

"I figured you boys'd be wet and cold comin' out of the river. I got a nice fire goin' up yonder on the high bank."

For the moment Trey put aside his resentment over the dangerous spot in which Longacre had left him after robbing Max's store. "I never figured we'd see you again."

"I've got to give Kerbow's horse back to him. I'm not a thief."

"No? What about the Dutchman's store?"

"I told the man I was just takin' that money as a loan."

Only three other hands had so far made it across the river, all of them younger than Trey. Atwater had turned back to assist Kerbow. Johnny Fulton looked especially miserable. He had not even kept his underwear on. His white skin looked almost blue. Trey and Scooter Willis stayed with the herd while Longacre led Johnny and another youngster to the fire. Trey met the oncoming cattle as they emerged from the river and hazed them gently toward those already across. The steers were drifting toward the higher banks and dropping their heads into the fresh grass.

At length the first two young hands warmed up and dried out. They returned to allow Trey and others to go to the fire as they came up out of the water. Johnny Fulton wore Longacre's slicker for some protection against the wind.

Trey found to his pleasure that Longacre had a pot of coffee going. He said, "You know that lawman Gault was still alive when Mr. Kerbow left Fort Worth?"

The news affected Longacre less than Trey had expected. "I ain't lost much sleep over him." Longacre grinned as he watched Trey caress a tin cup with his cold fingers and warm his innards with black coffee. "Just keep thinkin' about that Yankee whiskey at the end of the trail."

"I don't drink whiskey."

"A few more days like this and you will. Lost your ambition yet about bein' a cattle owner?"

"It won't be like this all the time."

"It's like this *enough* of the time. I'd still rather be a fireman."

Several animals were bogged in quicksand. It was up to Trey and the other hands to pull them out. Some were the big steers Lige Connors had thrown into the herd. Trey was tempted to leave them to drown, but his conscience was stirred by their desperate threshing. It was not the fault of these unfortunate critters that their owner was a son of a bitch.

The cattle finally made it across the river before full dark. The chuck wagon and the hoodlum wagon did not. Zack Lynch camped on the south bank. Three of the youngest hands, and the hungriest, swam their horses back across the river toward the firelight. Atwater, on the north bank now, counseled against taking the risk in the dark. Trey was resigned to a hungry night. At least he could warm himself beside the fire and take some strength from Longacre's coffee.

He considered butchering one of Connors's steers for beef. They could tell Connors that it had simply died. But he dismissed the notion. Jarrett Longacre had already turned him into a liar. He would not give Lige Connors the satisfaction of turning him into a thief.

The trail boss remained south of the river with the wagons, but the hands understood what was to be done and did it without his direction. Naked or in their underwear, they divided up the night guard. Those not on duty huddled around the fire. Those a-horseback wore Atwater's and Longacre's slickers against the night chill. Nobody got much sleep.

At daylight Trey saw the chuck wagon on the move. The cook and the hands who remained on the south side had tied logs to either side to aid in flotation. The teams from both wagons were hitched together for extra power. The river had dropped during the night so that the wheels should touch bottom most of the way across. Trey rode partway out into the water, ready to throw a rope to Lynch to tie to the wagon if it threatened to bog in the quicksand.

A cheer went up as the wagon pulled onto the north bank. Water streamed from between the boards that made up the wagon bed. Lynch took the wagon up to Longacre's fire. Trey found his shirt, britches and boots. He decided that at future river crossings he would keep his clothes on and take his chances.

Returning from an inspection of the herd, Kerbow stared at Longacre. "If I'd been you I wouldn't've stopped this side of the Platte. I'd go plumb to Montana, maybe even Canada."

"I knew you'd want your horse back. And you might need me."

"I could use your help. I just don't need the trouble you carry with you."

If Longacre felt any remorse, he did not show it. "I don't do it on purpose. Looks like I was born under an unlucky star."

"Unlucky for you and everybody around you."

---

It took about a month for the herd to cross Indian Territory in leisurely fashion, given plenty of time to graze along the way and put on weight. It crossed, each in its turn, Beaver Creek, the willow-lined Washita, the North Canadian, the Cimarron.

Hunting was good, allowing Lynch to vary the beef menu with

venison, prairie chicken and antelope. For the most part the traveling was pleasant, the weather warming and benign except for one electrical storm. Fearful of drawing lightning, the cowboys at Kerbow's suggestion took off their spurs and pistols and left them in the wagon. A bolt struck and killed two steers, setting the rest of the herd into a stampede similar to the one south of the Red.

Trey was disappointed that neither of the dead steers belonged to Lige Connors.

He derived some satisfaction, however, when a dozen Indians rode up one day from behind the herd. The first cowboys they encountered were Trey and Johnny Fulton, on the drags. Trey felt a numbing dread. He wished for the rifle he had left in the hoodlum wagon, though he wondered if he could have brought himself to use it.

One of the Indians held up his right hand and shouted, "How, John!"

Johnny blinked in surprise and pulled his horse in close to Trey's, putting Trey between him and the Indians.

The Indian began talking, though the only word Trey could decipher was "Wo-haw." He had been told that Indians often used this term for cattle. Much easier to understand were the signs the Indian made with his hands. He pointed to the herd and held up five fingers. Trey surmised he was asking for five steers.

Trey said, "You'll have to talk to Mr. Kerbow. That's him comin' yonder."

The trail boss approached at an easy lope, Gil Atwater beside him. Trey thought he saw recognition in the Indian's eyes. That was not surprising, for Kerbow had been up this trail several times. The Indian began talking both verbally and with his hands. Again he held up five fingers. Kerbow replied by raising one.

Kerbow's calm eased Trey's concern. He found himself fascinated, watching the two men bargain back and forth in sign language until they agreed upon a gift of two beeves.

Kerbow motioned for them to choose their own. They picked two of Connors's, which were the largest. Whooping and yelling, they chased the two animals away from the herd. Then one by one they loped up alongside the steers and drove arrows into them in the manner they would have killed buffalo. They jumped from their horses and began the skinning almost before the steers stopped kicking. Some ate the livers raw and warm.

Trey felt revulsion at the thought of biting into that quivering, bleeding flesh, but he could not turn away. These were the first Indians he had seen except for a few Choctaws who had drifted into Fort Worth to trade their winter catch of furs. The Choctaws had worn white-man clothes and talked a passable brand of English. These, eating the bleeding livers, were blanket Indians. Cheyennes, Kerbow said. It was not difficult to imagine them turning away from the two steers and coming after the cowboys. The notion made Trey shiver a little, though the wind was warm.

Atwater commented, "Ivan always let them take a toll for crossin' their country. It's only right. Besides, it's cheaper than havin' them come in the night and stampede the herd."

Young Johnny Fulton remained puzzled. "I never saw them Indians before, but they knew me."

Atwater's eyebrows went up. "Knew you?"

"The one that done the talkin', he said, 'How, John.' "

Atwater laughed aloud. "They call all white men John."

He was still laughing as he rode with Kerbow back toward the front of the herd. "How, John!"

---

Whatever latent wildness Jarrett Longacre carried within, the stolid routine of the trail kept it from bursting free. Trey had thought Longacre might challenge the Indians just for the hell of it and create a crisis for everybody, but he did not. On the contrary, the Indians seemed to arouse in him some feeling of kinship.

Watching the butchering of the beeves, Longacre told Trey, "Ever once in a while I get an urge to kill a buffalo or lift somebody's scalp. I've got a little Indian blood in me, you know. My folks didn't much like to talk about my grandmother."

It was more likely, Trey thought, that Longacre used the thought as an excuse to himself, if he needed one, for his occasional explosions of violence.

Trey received an object lesson in cowboy nicknames. From the day the Indians visited the herd, Johnny Fulton became known as How John. Everybody began calling him that except Scooter Willis. To Scooter, he remained Johnny.

Because "Trey" was itself a nickname, nobody saw fit to give him another.

A little south of the Kansas line the herd lost three steers and came near losing How John in the Salt Fork quicksands. The boy forgot the advice about not letting his horse stop and stand anywhere in the river. Suddenly he was yelling for help while his horse threshed in panic, bogging itself deeper into the river-bottom sand.

Sharing the drags with him, Trey was closest. His heart bobbed as he envisioned the horse drowning and carrying the youth with him. He rode to How John.

"Grab on to me!"

"I don't want to lose my saddle," the boy cried. "It's my daddy's."

Trey feared his own horse could become entrapped. "Damn it, forget the saddle. Grab on like I told you!"

How John lunged for him and missed. Trey grabbed the back of the boy's shirt. For a moment he felt that his horse was becoming stuck in the sand, that How John was going to get everybody drowned. But the mount pulled its feet free and surged forward, Trey pulling the boy's weight by his wet shirt. How John splashed and strangled, then grabbed Trey's arm in desperation. Trey's horse found firm footing and carried them up onto the bank. How John dropped to the wet ground, coughing up water.

Other riders rushed back into the river, led by Jarrett Longacre. He tossed a loop around the neck of the trapped horse and dallied the end of the rope around his saddle horn. Scooter Willis cast a second loop. Gaining firm footing near the edge of the river, they spurred hard, pulling against the ropes until it looked as if the horse would choke to death instead of drown. Its feet came clear of the gripping sand, and it pawed at the water. It went under once, then came up squealing and fighting. It reached the slippery bank and stood with its head down, coughing, choking, trembling.

The excitement was over by the time Kerbow got there. His eyes showed relief that the boy had survived, but he quickly covered up. "You know, boy, you damn near drowned a good horse?"

How John had no answer. He was still spewing up water.

When he regained breath, he thanked Scooter and Longacre for saving his horse and saddle. It never seemed to occur to him to thank Trey for saving his life.

Kerbow gave Trey a silent nod of approval that made up for the omission.

Longacre became moody as the distance to Ellsworth began to be measured in days. The younger hands stood in awe of his reputation and gave him breathing room. The outfit began encountering travelers on horseback, in wagons and buggies. Whenever a stranger approached, Longacre would disappear. He would show up later as if from nowhere.

At nightfall a day out of Ellsworth he took his blankets and a few other meager belongings from the two wagons along with a little coffee, flour and bacon.

"Leavin' us, Jarrett?" Trey asked.

"Already drawed my pay. Them John Laws in Fort Worth are smart enough to figure that I might hook back up with this outfit. I expect the Ellsworth sheriff'll meet the herd when it gets to town."

"If you could keep the hobbles on that wild streak, you wouldn't have all this trouble."

Longacre shrugged. "I have some Irish blood in me. My folks never talked much about my granddaddy."

He stood his tour of guard with the herd, then faded off into the night.

Gil Atwater's face furrowed as the next morning's conversation turned to the absent Longacre. "He reminds me of a pony I had once. As good a cow horse as ever I rode, when he behaved himself. But he'd bust in two at the worst possible time and throw me higher than a buzzard."

Zach Lynch declared, "I had a horse like that once. Finally shot him."

"I done better. I sold mine to a feller I didn't like. That was the last I saw of either one."

Ivan Kerbow's gray eyes seemed especially pinched. "With all his faults, Jarrett's a top hand. You don't come across the likes of him but few times in your life."

# EIGHT

Trey had been on the reception committee when the herd had approached Fort Worth. Now, as it neared Ellsworth, he found himself among those visited by the reception committee. Several merchants and bar operators rode out to give the Texans the town's official welcome. The saloonkeepers seemed mildly distressed when they saw how young most of the cowhands were.

"If we'd known these were mostly schoolboys," a merchant remarked, "we'd have brought some rock candy."

The saloon men lavished their main attention upon the older men like Kerbow, Atwater and Lynch, though these were seasoned enough not to be stampeded by the promise of a high time in town.

A saloonkeeper started to hand a cigar to Pancho Martínez, then changed his mind and turned back to Atwater. In Pancho's case, Trey surmised, the problem was not youth—he was as old as the point rider—but his skin's dark hue. A glint of suppressed resentment came into Pancho's eyes.

One of the whiskey merchants gave Trey a second look and decided he was old enough for at least a moment's attention. He handed Trey a couple of cigars. Trey stuck them in his pocket. He would give one to Pancho and one to Zack Lynch. Staying on the warm side of the cook could mean having a hot cup of coffee at some time when he needed it most, or having a cold biscuit or two hidden away to tide him through a long tour on night guard.

With the merchants and saloonkeepers came a man who wore a badge on his vest. He said little, but his eyes carefully appraised every man and boy in the outfit. Trey was the only one he approached directly.

"Mind telling me your name?"

"Trey McLean."

"Is that the name your folks gave you, or did you pick it yourself?"

"I've had it longer than I can remember."

"You look about the right age for somebody the Texas authorities wrote to me about. The name Longacre mean anything to you?"

"There was a feller named Longacre with the herd 'til it got to Fort Worth. He left."

Trey saw no need to volunteer that Longacre had rejoined the outfit later. If the sheriff didn't ask, it wasn't Trey's place to tell him.

The sheriff's eyes pinched down. "You look like a young man who's had a good Christian raising. I'm sure it'd pain your mama and daddy if you were to lie to me."

"I told you the gospel truth."

"If he was to show up now, I don't suppose you'd come and tell me?"

"No, sir, can't say I would."

"That's an honest answer. Well, if you *should* see him, tell him I don't really care much what he did in Texas, but I'd surely appreciate it if he wouldn't cause any trouble in Ellsworth. I'd be grateful if none of you did."

Kerbow rode back with the merchants to arrange for a place outside of town where the cattle could be loose-herded while he negotiated their sale. Because this was the first Texas outfit to hit town in the new season, he had every reason to expect a good price. Buyers liked good news to work its way back to Texas early. That would encourage other drovers to point their herds toward Ellsworth instead of Newton or some other shipping point. The last thing Ellsworth needed this soon in the year was for its cattle prices to look cheap and its merchandise to look high.

Most of the young cowboys were itching for a chance to go to town. Not since Fort Worth had they visited a settlement of any size or gotten away from the cattle. They had built up a fantasy of Kansas streets sparkling like gold, the women dazzlingly beautiful and the riverbank full of Kentucky whiskey.

Trey had stayed in Fort Worth long enough to know that any beauty was in the eyes of the beholders. He meant to hang on to most of his wages. However, he might be induced to squander four or five dollars on pleasure.

Camped within sight of Ellsworth's lamplights, Kerbow called together all the hands except for those who had drawn low cards and had to remain behind for night guard. As more or less the elders of the outfit, Kerbow and Atwater would also stay in camp to stand guard later in the night. So would Pancho, who carried a grudge and intended to leave Ellsworth none of his wages. Zack Lynch declared that he had already consumed enough whiskey for one lifetime. Though one or two drinks would be all right, he was waiting for reincarnation before he got drunk again.

Kerbow was not much for talking. He said, "Zack, tell them how it is."

The cook declared, "It's been a hard trip, and you boys've earned the right to crow a little. But remember that a crowin' rooster fetches the coyotes. When they've got you mumblin', fumblin', stumblin' drunk, they'll rob you blind. Then if you raise any fuss they'll throw you in the jailhouse.

"You're all too young to've been in the war. But you're from Texas, and to these folks that makes you Johnny Rebs. So stick together, watch yourselves and remember that we already lost one war."

The hands lined up to receive their pay. Most let Kerbow hold back part of their wages for safekeeping. Red-haired, freckle-faced Scooter Willis insisted on having it all. So did How John, who always did whatever he saw Scooter do.

Trey waited until last.

Kerbow eyed him critically. "You really goin' to be a cowman someday, or are you goin' to blow it in and work all your life for what somebody else is willin' to pay you?"

"I think I can get by on five dollars."

Kerbow and the cook exchanged pleased glances. The cook chuckled. "That kind of extravagance'll be the ruin of the country."

Trey said, "It'll take half of that, I expect, to buy me a slicker."

Kerbow nodded in satisfaction. "I wish I'd had that much judgment the first time I ever went to San Antone." He counted out five bills and added five extra.

Trey said, "That's more than I asked for."

"The second five is mine. It's worth that to me if you'll stay with the boys and herd them away from trouble. You're older and smarter than most of them. See they get back to the wagon."

The only stipulation Kerbow laid on the hands was that they not take guns to town. "I don't want to have to explain to any of your folks why I left their son buried in Kansas."

Trey was relieved. Some of these boys were careless enough cold sober. Drinking, they would be a danger to anyone within range.

He quickly realized that keeping up with this crowd was like trying to herd a covey of quail. Almost before they reached the first lamplighted street, he lost Scooter Willis. How John followed Scooter like a little dog following a big one. The two melted away into the darkness. Trey chided himself for not watching them more closely.

Of all the crew, aside from Longacre, he considered Scooter the most likely to seek out trouble. He was redheaded in temper as well as under his hat.

Most of the boys were eager to try the first saloon they came to. Trey would bet a dollar and a half some had never tasted whiskey in their lives, unless they had found a bottle belonging to some adult and had sneaked a drink behind the barn. Trey considered trying to talk them out of it, but it was a battle he would have to refight at the door of every such place in town. The best he could do was stall the boys a while.

"I need to buy me a slicker. Some of you've been sayin' you need one thing and another. Let's take care of the necessaries first. They won't drink up all the whiskey before we get there."

He managed to herd most of the bunch into a general store, though he lost Pete James, who would not wait. That left him four young drovers to oversee.

The merchant and a pair of clerks met them at the front door. In short order they sold two of the boys new outfits from the skin out. Wages melted like ice under a warm spring sun. Trey reasoned that the more they spent on clothes, the less they could spend on whiskey. Come daylight they would have something to show for the evening besides a community-sized headache. He herded what was left of his congregation into a barbershop for haircuts and a twenty-five-cent bath in a genuine cast-iron bathtub imported all the way from Chicago. A black porter even changed the water after three of the boys had used it.

When he could forestall the inevitable no longer, he followed them to a dramshop. He paused in the doorway to look out into the lamplighted street, hoping to see the wayward three who had eluded him, but they had disappeared.

He noticed that the bartender poured the whiskey out of a bottle that bore a Kentucky label, but he would bet its contents had never been within a thousand miles of that state. These boys would not recognize the difference anyway. A youngster known as Buckshot came near strangling, then remarked on its being prime stuff.

"Nothing but the best for you boys from Texas," the bartender declared. He noticed that Trey was not drinking and gestured at him with the bottle.

Trey shook his head. "I don't suppose you'd have any buttermilk?" He knew what the answer would be, but he was idly curious about the bartender's reaction.

The barman's jaw dropped. "You just brought a thousand cows up the trail, and you ask for *milk?*"

"They're steers. You ever try to milk a steer?"

"Not lately."

Trey placated the bartender by ordering a beer, which he could sip slowly with little effect upon sobriety.

After a time, the boys began talking loudly around a billiard table in the back of the room. Trey suspected they were influenced as much by their imaginations as by the watered liquor. After the bartender frowned darkly for the fourth or fifth time at his empty beer glass and one of the boys started pestering the others to lend him some money, Trey decided it was time to try edging the bunch back toward the wagon. Otherwise he might have to tie one or two to their saddles.

The bartender protested. "What are you, some kind of maiden aunt? These boys are old enough to decide for themselves when it's time to go to bed."

Buckshot lurched into a table where a group of locals were immersed in a game of poker. Chips and cards slid off onto the floor, the chips rolling in all directions.

A black-suited gambler lodged a protest with the bartender. "If you're going to turn this joint into a schoolhouse for sucklings, be damned if we won't find us a place that caters to grown men!"

The bartender decided his evening's take from the young Texans was not up to his standards and ordered them all out. Buckshot offered argument. Trey grabbed a handful of the youth's shirt and dragged him from the saloon in much the same manner as he had dragged How John out of the Salt Fork.

"Looks to me like we've had about all the hilarity we can stand for one evenin'," he declared. "We're goin' to the wagon."

He managed to herd the boys to their horses. He had to give a couple of them a boost up into their saddles. Buckshot fell off on the opposite side and had to be helped a second time before he found his seat. Trey got the hands started in the direction of camp when he heard someone holler. Pete James rode up in a lope and slid his horse to a stop.

"Trey! Scooter Willis is fixin' to get his head stove in, or worse. You better come get him."

Trey thought Willis deserved getting his head stove in, but the possibility of "worse" bothered him. "Damn him, where's he at?"

"Him and How John are over in Nauchville. They got theirselves throwed out of a parlor house. They're fixin' to try and fight their way back in."

Like an unwelcome relative, Nauchville kept a separate existence a few hundred yards east of Ellsworth proper. Its unsavory reputation had already found its way down the trail. Trey had heard about it before he ever crossed the Red River.

"You come and show me. The rest of you go back to the wagon and tell Mr. Kerbow."

Buckshot said thickly, "You're liable to need help."

"You're in no shape to be any. Now git!"

He had no clear idea what he could do. Perhaps some opportunity would present itself when he got there. He put his old brown horse into a lope. Pete James struggled to catch up.

Trey grumbled, "If you'd all stayed together like Mr. Kerbow said, there wouldn't nobody be in this fix."

James retorted, "You think we're a bunch of kids?"

"What the hell else?"

James pointed to a nondescript frame house. Lamplight shone dimly through shades in some of the upstairs windows. Other windows were dark. A lantern hung from the small overhang that passed for a front porch. It was not red, Trey noticed, but he thought it should be.

He could hear raucous voices from inside, and the scuffling sound of feet. Through the front door burst a burly man, holding Scooter Willis by his collar and the seat of his britches. He swung Scooter back, then forward, sending him tumbling down the steps and into the dirt. Next came the smaller How John, who landed on top of Scooter.

The big man shouted, "You yahoos try to come back in here a third time and I'll hand you your heads in a sack!"

Trey dismounted and led his horse up to where the two young cowboys struggled to untangle themselves from each other. "Wasn't the battle of Gettysburg bad enough? You tryin' to start the war all over again?"

The burly man came back out onto the porch, followed by a dark-haired woman who carried Scooter's hat. She was wearing some kind of flimsy black undergarment that started halfway down her large breasts and went only to about her knees. She wore nothing else that Trey could see, though he gave her a careful study. She sailed the hat toward Scooter. "You left this. I don't need none of your Texas lice."

Scooter's nose was bleeding, and his shirt was ripped as if he had fought his way through a briar thicket. He pointed. "That there woman, she taken my money but didn't give me nothin' for it, hardly. Five minutes, and she said I was through."

"You *were* through!" she shouted. "Come back someday when you've growed up to be a man!" She disappeared into the house, but the burly man remained, hands on his hips. Those hands looked strong enough to bend iron rails. The man breathed heavily. Disposing of Scooter and How John had caused him considerable exertion.

Scooter swayed to his feet. "Johnny, I think me and you can whip him this time. We've got him winded."

Trey realized that if the two made the effort again, he would have to try to rescue them. Nobody was likely to rescue *him*, certainly not Pete James. But he did not know what he could do short of shooting them, and that seemed a little drastic.

A horseman appeared out of the darkness, swinging a rope. Even in the poor light, Trey recognized Jarrett Longacre. Longacre dropped his loop over Scooter's shoulders, jerking up the slack as it settled around the young man's waist.

"Get their horses, farm boy, and let's go to the wagon."

Longacre dallied the end of the rope around the horn and set off in a trot. Scooter shouted something as the rope went taut and jerked him forward. He lost his feet a couple of times, and Longacre had to wait for him to find them. Scooter cursed him and threatened several varieties of fatal retribution. How John trudged along behind, trying to keep up, yelling for Longacre to slow down. But Longacre did not intend for Scooter to come up that rope after him, at least not until he had worn him to a nubbin, trotting all the way to camp.

Trey saw the dim shapes of two horsemen coming to meet him. Kerbow's voice demanded, "Who's that?"

"Us—Trey and Jarrett. We got some stragglers here."

Kerbow and Gil Atwater rode close enough that Trey could see their faces in the moonlight, and he reined to a stop. Longacre yielded slack in his rope. Scooter sank to his knees, gasping for breath. How John caught up.

Kerbow said, "I was afraid me and Gil might find you boys shot to pieces. Ellsworth can be bad enough, but *Nauchville*? How'd they find *that* hellhole?"

Trey gave Kerbow and Atwater a brief account of the situation in which he had found Scooter and How John.

Atwater said, "I've helped bury men killed over less."

Kerbow gave Longacre a nod of approval. "There've been times, Jarrett, when I've felt like beatin' you to death with a bois d'arc club. But I'm glad you turned up tonight."

Kerbow had a perfect face for poker, though so far as Trey knew he was not given to gambling except on cattle. The trail boss kept his true feelings masked beneath an expression that would have been proper for a funeral as prospective buyers came out one by one to inspect the herd and submit their bids.

The cook said the prices offered were higher than Kerbow had expected, but no one would have guessed it from watching the boss's face. He remained noncommittal until he was sure everyone who was likely to make an offer had done so. He sold the steers to a buyer with whom he had dealt before and whose draft on a Chicago bank he felt confident would be honored.

The hands had ample opportunity to visit town again in shifts, but the anticipatory glow of that first night was never quite repeated. In all, the first Texas visitation must have been a disappointment to the merchants and bar owners, Trey thought. However, they would have the whole season to make their pile as more and more herds arrived and older, thirstier, lustier cowboys came whooping and hollering into town.

It took the better part of a day to put all the cattle up the slanted loading chutes. Watching the train pull away, black coal smoke hovering over the line of wood-slatted cars, Trey felt a lingering pang of regret that his first real adventure was drawing to a close. However many others life might hold, this one would always remain special to him.

While Zack Lynch and Pancho loaded supplies on the two wagons for the return journey, Kerbow sold the extra horses. He kept only enough for the hands to ride back to Texas. Because all the mounts sold for one price, Trey took advantage of the opportunity to let the old brown go and keep a younger bay called Fox that had proven dependable on the trail.

The spotted lead steer would walk back to Texas tethered behind the hoodlum wagon. His services were too valuable to allow him to go for beef. Pancho Martínez fed him shelled corn from the palm of his hand, and the steer followed him like a dog.

Scooter Willis's grudge quickly faded after he visited a different fancy house. He came back wide-eyed and bewildered, as if in something of a trance. He invited Trey to go with him on a return visit, but Trey demurred.

A second herd arrived as the Kerbow outfit prepared to start south. Helping Zack Lynch break camp, Trey listened to six-shooters blazing into the air. The new bunch was riding into town, serving notice that it was primed, cocked and ready to fire.

The cook poured the leavings from the coffeepot into the hot ashes of his campfire and turned his best ear toward the racket. "A little older than our boys, but not a damn bit smarter. The barkeeps and the gamblers and the women'll smile tonight."

Trey looked toward Ivan Kerbow. The trail boss was shaking hands with the cattle buyer, who had ridden out to bid good-bye and express a hope that Kerbow would be back with another herd later in the year. The buyer took a pint bottle from a leather pouch on his saddle. He and Kerbow shared from it.

Trey said, "That's the only drink I've seen him take."

"A more sober man you'll not often find. He's had plenty of cause to drown himself in whiskey, but Ivan Kerbow tends to business."

Jarrett Longacre stood on the ground, holding his horse as he shook hands with the cowboys one by one. He came around in due time to Trey.

Trey said, "You're not goin' back with us?"

"The law'll probably meet this outfit soon as you-all cross the Red River. They'll be watchin' for me."

"Where'll you go?"

"Ain't sayin'. If you don't know, you won't have to lie to anybody."

Scooter Willis had gotten over his anger at Longacre for dragging him away from Nauchville. The red-haired cowboy and tag-along How John had spent all their wages in Ellsworth. Now they stood beside Longacre. Wherever he went, they were going with him. Kerbow had argued with them to no avail.

Longacre assured him, "I'll take care of them."

"You can't even take care of yourself. You'll get them shot, or maybe hung."

"We can take care of ourselves," Scooter declared.

Kerbow led the procession out across the first long hill. Zack Lynch hollered, and his team strained against the harness. Pancho Martínez followed, speaking to his mules in Spanish. Trey could not tell from his tone whether the words were profane or benign.

Pete James looked back over his shoulder at the town before topping the hill. "Damn it, Trey, I wish I could wrap up that little black-headed girl and take her home in my saddlebags."

"What would your mama say?"

"I wouldn't show her to Mama. I'd keep her hid out in the saddle shed and go see her every night."

Trey let himself wonder if he should have gone to one of the fancy houses despite his misgivings. After a time, however, Pete began to squirm in the saddle, scratching himself frequently. Trey decided curiosity unsatisfied was not necessarily a crippling ailment.

Travel with only the wagons was much faster than the trip northward with the plodding, grazing steers. A distance that had taken the herd two days was easily covered before sundown even with a late start. Nor was there any necessity for standing guard at night, for the horses could be picketed or hobbled. Trey found, nevertheless, that he kept waking up the first several nights at about the time he would have had to ride out to the herd. He would look up at the stars, listening to the pleasant sounds of the night, and feel content. He wasted little time or emotion on Lige Connors anymore. He found it far more pleasant to let his mind drift to Sarah Stark.

Every day they skirted around cattle herds bound for the railroad. Often Kerbow knew the bosses and some of the hands. He would stop for a brief shake and howdy, passing on information about the trail ahead, the market as he had found it, the reliability of the buyers. The young cowboys like Buckshot and Pete James would tell other cowhands about the wonders of Ellsworth night life. Their descriptions glowed with a brilliance that far surpassed Trey's recollections.

They encountered a few Indians as they moved down across the Territory, but these wasted little time with a southbound outfit that had no cattle to share. They concentrated upon exacting tolls from herds going north. Trey would study the bronzed faces, the dark and hungry eyes, trying to imagine himself looking at them over the sights of a rifle. The thought was troubling, for close-up they were individual human beings, not a vague and distant anonymous enemy.

He had given little thought to the Texas authorities in recent weeks. They came trooping across his mind as the procession reached the north bank of the Red River and he realized that the trees he could see on the far side of the wide, sandy-bottomed stream were rooted in Texas. It had been three months since Longacre had shot Officer Gault in Plunkett's corral. Trey did not like to wish hard luck upon others, but he hoped there had been enough shootings since that Gault's had paled in importance.

He was relieved that no reception committee of lawmen awaited on the other side. One lone officer came into camp, inquiring about Jarrett Longacre. He spoke of Longacre's having wounded a lawman in Fort Worth. By that, Trey assumed that Gault was still alive. All hands pleaded ignorance. Other officers had all they could handle checking cattle brands in northbound herds before allowing them to cross the river and move out of Texas jurisdiction. They showed no inclination to bother with an outfit heading home.

Trey took that as a positive omen.

South of Gainesville he made up his mind.

"Mr. Kerbow, there's some folks I want to stop off and see."

Kerbow frowned. "Seems to me like there's a storekeeper down there you *don't* want to see."

"I'll try to stay out of his way. But I'd like to visit the Stark family. I'll catch up before you get to Fort Worth."

"I know Mr. Stark and his watermelon patch. I seem to remember he's got a nice-lookin' daughter."

"Seems like I remember, too."

"Might be a good place to camp the night and treat the boys to watermelon." Kerbow's face wrinkled a little. "Sure you won't be stayin' there?"

"Just a visit was all I had in mind."

# NINE

Sarah Stark stood on the front porch watching Mr. Craven, the schoolteacher, ride off on his mule along the trail that led to Max's store and the crossroads schoolhouse. She sensed her mother leaning out the door behind her.

Frieda Stark demanded, "Didn't you invite Mr. Craven to stay for supper?"

"Said he had some lessons to prepare, so I didn't ask him."

Mama was eternally trying to get her interested in one eligible bachelor or another, those she thought had good financial prospects. She was especially insistent about Mr. Craven. She kept pointing out that he was an educated man. This region had been a frontier until recently, and large numbers of raw-raised children were deficient in reading, writing and totting up sums. A teacher of good reputation could count on finding a wage-paying position. Mr. Craven was a prime catch, and if Sarah did not grab him, some other unattached maiden surely would.

But Mama was not well versed in arithmetic herself, or she would have figured out that Mr. Craven was twice Sarah's age . . . almost as old as her father, in fact.

To Sarah, the teacher was too skinny by far, his legs too long for his trousers. He could eat a whole fried chicken by himself and keep putting away butter, gravy and biscuits after everybody else had finished. His conversation was always about books and things he had read in books. She enjoyed the books he brought her, but he was nothing like the characters in them. He was hardly the type to stir a girl to romantic notions, not like the hired man Andrew, and especially not like Trey McLean.

Andrew had rarely invaded her thoughts since she had met Trey. But Trey was always there, intruding at the oddest moments, insistent upon attention.

Mama contended that many things in married life were more important than romance, which tended to degenerate into something mechanical, inconvenient and even disgustingly messy.

Though she might have her shortcomings in figuring sums, Mama felt she had a pretty good eye for human nature. She had suspected all along that Sarah's easy dismissal of Mr. Craven and others who showed an interest was because she could not put that cowboy out of her mind. Mama never had been able to fathom other people's fascination with cowboys. She said they were a lusty, dusty, unwashed and unshaven lot, given to loud and profane talk and to reckless boasting. Most of them carried six-shooters they couldn't hit a barn with from the inside, though they were given to carelessly wounding one another by accident.

Granting that Trey had been quiet-spoken and had worked with diligence and skill in helping Papa put up a hog shed, he was probably no different from the rest when he fell back into cowboy company, Mama insisted. A mule might sometimes act like a horse, and at a distance even look like a horse, but it remained forever a mule.

To the east Sarah could see the dust of a trail herd beyond the field. They had been passing at a steady pace, from one to three or four a day, since Trey had left to join the first one. Now and then a rider or two or a chuck wagon would approach the house. She would feel her pulse begin to race, wondering if Trey might have returned. Then would come the moment of disappointment and the recurring admonition from her mother: "You're more apt to witness the second coming of Christ than to ever see that cowboy again. They are a footloose lot."

There were times when Sarah briefly considered giving in to her mother's constant pressure and showing Mr. Craven some serious encouragement. At least she would be free of Mama's nagging. It might even get her out of this overcrowded house. But any house she shared with Mr. Craven would probably seem crowded too, no matter how large it was. Because money was always scarce in the Stark family, she had often had to settle for something other than her first choice in the necessities of life. She did not want to follow that pattern in taking a husband.

She had been disappointed so many times that she allowed herself little hope the afternoon she saw two horsemen approaching from the northeast. She was at the barn, gathering eggs while her father patched a leather harness he had broken in the field. Her brothers were still out there afoot, hoeing weeds from the corn, continuing to work until Mama beat the supper call on an iron bar hanging at the corner of the porch.

"Riders comin', Papa. I expect they're here to see you." She returned to her chore, wishing some of the hens were less insistent on choosing out-of-the-way places to deposit their eggs. She was likely to take a bad fall someday, climbing up into the hayloft.

Simon Stark walked into the open and squinted. "I believe I recognize Mr. Kerbow." He seemed to have a slight chuckle in his voice. "The other one looks like the young man—what was his name?—who helped me build the hog shed."

Sarah nearly tipped the egg basket as she hurried out into the sunshine and shaded her eyes with her hand. "His name is Trey McLean!"

"Better go tell your mother we'll be havin' company for supper. I know she'll be tickled."

He knew she *wouldn't*, but Papa had a way of making little jokes by saying the opposite of what he meant. Sarah rushed to the house, leaving the back door swinging in her wake as she set the basket on the cabinet. "Mama, he's comin'." She hurried into the room she shared with her younger sisters and began to brush her hair.

Frieda Stark peered through the front window, then came to the door of her daughters' room, disapproval in her eyes. "Maybe it's for the best. Maybe this time he'll show his true face, and you'll realize what I've been trying to tell you."

"I've seen his true face, Mama. It's a right handsome face."

Sarah walked out onto the porch and watched the two horsemen approach. Papa strode from the barn to meet them, and Mr. Kerbow turned aside. Trey McLean kept coming, his gaze locked on Sarah as hers was locked on him. He took off his hat and made a little forward bow in the saddle.

"Miss Stark . . . Sarah. You're lookin' mighty pretty."

"So are you, Mr. McLean." She knew a man was not supposed to look pretty, but he did. His face was freshly shaven, his hair well combed. She suspected he had stopped at the creek to wet it so it would stay down.

He was perhaps a little thinner than she remembered, but she supposed that was a result of hard work and not always getting enough to eat on the trail. She would fix that if she could get him to stay around here a few days.

He dismounted and started toward her but stopped as Mama stepped out onto the porch. He bowed again, a little deeper this time. "How are you, Mrs. Stark?"

"Fair to middlin'. I suppose you'll be stayin' to supper?"

It was an invitation of sorts, but hardly a warm welcome. More like charity given with a grudging hand.

Simon Stark declared, "Of course they'll both be havin' supper with us. You remember Mr. Kerbow, don't you, Frieda?"

Sarah sensed that her father was trying to divert her mother's attention from Trey.

Papa said, "Mr. Kerbow traded us a hind quarter of beef for a bunch of watermelons last summer."

"I remember. Most of the cattle people just *take* them."

Sarah recalled that Mr. Kerbow had stopped by more than once on his drives or on his return. She had noted that he never seemed to smile. She had sensed something brooding and sad in his eyes, in his voice.

Kerbow said, "I'm afraid I have no beef to trade this time, but I'd be pleased if you'd let me buy my boys some melons. They're due a treat."

Papa said, "You just keep your money in your pocket and tell them to help theirselves."

Mama's voice sharpened. "I'm sure Mr. Kerbow would feel a lot better about it if we allowed him to pay for the melons. I'd say three dollars would be a fair price, and they could take all they want."

"Sold," Mr. Kerbow said. He moved his horse up close to the porch, stepped down and placed three silver dollars in Frieda's hand. "Me and the boys are much obliged." He pointed. "If it's all right with you, we'll put down out by the field."

Papa said, "No need in makin' a dry camp. There's a nice flat spot right yonder by the barn, in easy water-carryin' distance of the creek."

Sarah knew from Mama's expression that she and Papa would be having a discussion about this when they went to bed. Ever since Sarah could remember, Mama had done a lot of talking. Papa would nod politely, letting her have her say. Then he would go ahead and do what he had intended to in the first place.

But she would keep Mr. Kerbow's silver dollars.

Sarah and Trey stared at each other until Mama said, "Come on, Sarah. We'll be gettin' supper ready."

Sarah stopped inside the door and watched Trey ride away to fetch the chuck wagon and the rest of the crew. Mr. Kerbow led his horse to the corral. Papa walked beside him, asking questions about the trail and cattle prices at the railroad.

Mama opened the oven door to peer in at the biscuits baking there. "I don't know what gets into your father sometimes, invitin' those cowboys to camp at our doorstep. Surely he must know what an evil influence they can be on your brothers."

"Mr. Kerbow has always seemed like a gentleman."

"But he's an owner . . . he's not just a cowboy."

"Trey—Mr. McLean—says he intends to be an owner someday."

"The last time he was here, the sheriff was after him."

"Not *after* him, Mama. Just wanted to talk to him. Trey hadn't done anything."

"He hadn't been *caught* doin' anything. Mark what I tell you, child: He'll wind up in jail or on the end of a rope."

Sarah knew that arguing with her mother was as futile as chasing a hawk's shadow across a chicken yard. But she had to ask, "What did Grandma say about Papa the first time she saw him?"

"She said he'd be puttin' his shoes under a poor man's table as long as he lived."

"So Grandma was wrong."

"But your father's no fiddle-footed cowboy. He's done right decent by us . . . even if he *is* a poor judge of character."

Sarah wanted to go out and watch with her brothers as the lanky cook and his Mexican helper set up the chuck wagon camp near the barn. But she knew Mama would call her back and lecture her at length about the evil intentions of unprincipled young men.

Mr. Kerbow had said he had no beef to trade for watermelons, but he and Trey brought a venison hindquarter and backstrap from the wagon in gratitude for the invitation to supper. The trail boss said, "Trey jumped a nice fat doe this mornin'. Thought it might give you a little variety for your table."

Mama graciously thanked Kerbow but said nothing to Trey. Sarah made up for her mother's omission. "I hope you'll stay an extra day or two and help us eat it."

Trey looked to Kerbow. The trail boss said, "It's a handsome invitation, but there's people waitin' for their cattle money so they can settle debts and stop some interest."

Sarah's disappointment was like a long swallow of sour milk. Mama purposely set Trey at the far end of the table so he and Sarah could not conveniently watch each other while they ate. Sarah nevertheless leaned forward so she could sneak a look. She found Trey doing the same thing. Their eyes met and held. She could see regret in Trey's, and silent apology.

Mama asked Mr. Kerbow idle questions about the current fashions in Kansas and if they were much advanced over those in Fort Worth. Mr. Kerbow admitted that he had not paid much attention to that sort of thing. "You have to understand, Mrs. Stark, that Ellsworth is just a railroad shippin' town. It's a long ways from fancy places like St. Louis and New Orleans. Folks there are mainly interested in the newest ways to make money."

Papa put in, "I suppose they've got those pretty well refined, with gamblin' houses and such."

"*Sharpened* is more like it."

Mama gave Trey a narrow-eyed look. "I would imagine you had some experience with that kind of doin's, didn't you, Mr. McLean?"

Trey finished chewing a bite of biscuit. "Yes'm. Store up there charged me almost three dollars for a new slicker."

Sarah caught the disappointment in Mama's eyes. She doubted that Trey realized he had walked around a trap.

Mr. Kerbow knew. He said, "While we were in Ellsworth I asked Trey to watch out for the younger boys and make sure they didn't get into trouble. I found him most responsible."

Mama's voice was edged with irony. "That's nice to know." It wasn't, of course, from her point of view. Like Papa, she sometimes said one thing when she meant the opposite. You had to read the signs. She said no more while they sat at the table.

Papa and Mr. Kerbow talked a little about the late war. It was always one of Papa's favorite subjects, for he had been in the Confederate army. Mr. Kerbow was reluctant about his own experiences and did not allow himself to be drawn out far. Sarah sensed that he had taken emotional wounds whether he had suffered physical wounds or not.

She wondered if the rest of the Kerbow crew might be feeling slighted, eating their supper at the chuck wagon while Mr. Kerbow and Trey enjoyed a meal at the table . . . if indeed they *were* enjoying it. Her occasional glances at Trey found him ill at ease, pushing the food around on his plate and not really eating very much. Mr. Kerbow kept trying to shift the conversation to more pleasant subjects than the war.

After a while Papa and Mr. Kerbow sat in the rockers on the front porch, Papa taking his evening pipe. They talked about rain, or the lack of it, which was usually Papa's second favorite subject and one with which Mr. Kerbow seemed comfortable. Men who spent their lives outdoors, working with nature or fighting against her, seemed always preoccupied with the weather. It was a topic on which everyone from the richest landowner to the poorest sharecropper could find common ground for conversation. As Papa was fond of saying, of course, not one of them could do a damned thing about it.

Sarah's brothers slipped out of the house while Sarah and her mother were clearing the scant remains of supper from the table. They headed straight for the chuck wagon to mingle with the cowboys, reinforcing Mama's fears that her sons might be contaminated by exposure to an unwholesome element.

Mama said, "I don't know why your father doesn't go out there and bring them back."

Sarah volunteered, "I'll go fetch them." Trey had returned to the wagon after saying and then repeating his thank-yous.

"Better the boys be out there than you. I'll get them myself directly."

As the final light from sunset faded into dusk, Papa and Mr. Kerbow left the porch and strode toward the camp. Mama had gone down there a bit earlier to fetch her sons home, but they had slipped away again as soon as she returned to the house. The dishes washed and dried and put away, Sarah stepped out onto the porch and seated herself upon one of the rockers her father and the trail boss had vacated. She could see figures standing or squatted near the campfire, but she could not tell which might be Trey McLean. She knew better than to go down there. Mama would not let her hear the end of it for a month.

Trey's voice startled her. He appeared suddenly at the edge of the porch, a dark silhouette against the distant firelight. "Sarah?" He probably was unsure whether it was her or one of her younger sisters.

"I'm me . . . I mean, it's me."

"Be all right if I join you?"

"Mama's in the house."

"I didn't come to talk to your mama."

Sarah left the porch. "She wouldn't like it if she heard us talkin'. Let's walk a little."

They moved away from the house and away from the wagon camp where the firelight might betray them if Mama happened to look out the window. They walked a little apart at first, their steps slow and without particular direction. Trey took her hand.

She asked, "Anything special you want to talk about?"

He was slow to answer. "There's a lot I'd like to talk about, but I'm afraid it's not time yet. Later, maybe, when I've got somethin' to offer you."

"I'm not askin' you to offer me anything."

"But I want to, and someday I will . . . unless there's somebody else."

"There's not anybody else. And there won't be."

She stopped walking. He took another step, felt her hand pulling against him and turned toward her. She did not wait for him to make the move. She put her arms around him and kissed him. She felt a flush of warmth through her body. Her face burned as if she had taken too much sun.

Surprised, he quickly reacted by taking her in his arms and holding her so tightly that she almost choked for breath. They kissed as if it were the last kiss they would ever have. When he loosened his embrace she laid her forehead against his shoulder.

She murmured, "What do we do now?"

"Maybe we'd better not do anything. We don't have the right."

"We would have if we were married."

"But I don't have anything to give you. All I own is a horse and a saddle and a change of clothes. And my wages from the drive. Not a cow, not a plow, not nothin'."

She clung to him, wishing she had an answer.

He said, "I won't always be this way. Someday I'll have somethin', and I can ask you proper."

"Someday could be a long time comin'."

"A few years maybe."

"A lot of things can happen in a few years. Bad things."

"We won't let them."

"Then hold me while you can."

Morning always came early in the Stark house, but no earlier than in the chuck wagon camp. By the time Papa went out to the barn to milk, Sarah could see the campfire blazing and the young men stirring around.

She itched to go out there, to see Trey. But she could not hold him as she had held him in the dark last night, or say to him in front of others the things she had said when there was no one to overhear. She watched through a window and tried to pick out his silhouette from among the many moving in firelight. She had lain awake much of the night, aching with the knowledge that he would be going, that it might be months before she saw him again . . . if she ever did.

Fixing her father's and brothers' breakfast, she dropped an egg on the floor, spattering it and pieces of shell across part of the kitchen.

Mama shouted, "Clean that up before one of the boys steps in it! Where is your mind, anyway?"

Papa saw, but he said nothing. The way he looked at her, she had a feeling he understood. She turned away so neither he nor Mama could see the tears that welled in her eyes.

While the family was eating its breakfast in the house, the cowboys were eating theirs at the wagon. Sarah ate little. She cleaned off the table, sneaking glances out the window. Darkness was giving way to sunrise. The cowboys were loading their bedrolls onto the hoodlum wagon. Trey was helping the lanky Zack Lynch place his cooking utensils in the bed of the chuck wagon and hang a pot of beans on a hook beneath the chuck box. They had cooked over a slow fire all night and would need only heating at noon to make them ready for dinner.

She heard a knock on the front door. Mr. Kerbow stood on the porch, hat in his hand. Trey McLean waited on the ground, hands shoved deeply into his pockets, his face grave.

Sarah followed her mother and father outside. While Mr. Kerbow was saying his thank-yous, Sarah went down the steps to stand before Trey. He opened his mouth, but nothing came; nor could she bring out a word. They could only look at each other with eyes that reflected their pain. He reached out, and she took his hand, not to shake it but to grip it tightly.

Mr. Kerbow came down the steps. Trey turned quickly to follow him. Sarah sensed that he had to will himself to keep from looking back at her.

Mama said, "Sarah, we have work to do."

Sarah heard, but she could not reply. She watched as the wheels began to turn and the cowboys strung out beside and behind the wagons. Trey was the last. He gave up the struggle and turned in the saddle for a long look at Sarah as he moved away. She brought up her hand in a tentative wave.

"Sarah," Mama said.

Sarah walked around the corner of the house, out of sight, and leaned against the wall to cry.

---

At midmorning she could hear the sound of hammering from the blacksmith shed. She had been sleepwalking through her chores, unable to focus upon them. She walked out to the shed. As far back as she could remember, she had more easily carried her troubles to Papa than to Mama. Sometimes they did not even talk. What passed between them was felt more than spoken. Usually she sensed that he understood, and she felt a measure of relief even if the problem she brought to him remained unresolved.

Papa had a steel crowbar in the forge, heating its dulled end so he could hammer a sharp point back onto it. He nodded at her by way of greeting. When the bar glowed red he placed it on the anvil and beat upon it with a heavy iron hammer until the glow faded.

"You goin' to be all right, girl?"

Her throat was tight. "I wanted to go with him."

He dropped the end of the bar into a bucket of water, where it sizzled, and steam arose. "I know. I could see it in your eyes, and I hurt with you."

"There's a hundred things could happen, Papa, things that might keep him from ever comin' back."

"The only thing sure about this life is that there ain't nothin' certain."

"Was it ever like this with you and Mama?"

He paused, remembering. "It was. We was brought up in Georgia, you know. I was fixin' to come to Texas to try and find me a place of my own. We knew there was a big chance we'd never see each other again. So we eloped. Run off in a hay wagon and got married at the county seat. Time her folks caught up to us, the knot was too tight to undo."

"Mama never told me about that."

"Didn't want you gettin' any notions." He placed his hand on her arm and looked into her eyes. His own eyes were sad. "Are you gettin' a notion?"

"I am, Papa."

"I'd be a hypocrite to tell you not to do what we done. But are you sure in your mind? When you're young it's awful easy to let your feelin's get the best of your common sense."

"I'm sure, Papa. Would you come chasin' after me? Would you let Mama?"

The sadness deepened in his eyes. "You've always been my girl, but you're not my *little* girl anymore. You're of an age to decide for yourself."

She kissed him. "Think you could spare that old gray horse?"

"He'd give out on you, I'm afraid. I'll put your mother's sidesaddle on Dunny."

She hurried back to the house. She found an old carpetbag her mother had let her and her sisters use on the family's few wagon trips to Fort Worth. She began packing her clothes into it; there were not many.

Mama's eyes widened as she came to the door.

"Sarah! What in the world . . ."

"No use tryin' to stop me, Mama. I'm goin' after him."

"That cowboy? But what about Mr. Craven . . . Think what you're doin', girl."

"I *am* thinkin'. If I don't go now I may never have another chance."

She had feared she might have to fight her way past her mother, but Frieda stood back and watched, her face dark with misgivings. She dabbed a handkerchief to her eyes, then went into the bedroom she shared with Papa. When she returned she held a small velvet purse.

She said, "Ever since you were small, I've been savin' back a penny here, a penny there, puttin' them away so you'd have a little bit of a dowry when the day came. Only, I never thought the day was goin' to come sudden like this." She handed the purse to Sarah. "There's maybe fifty-sixty dollars in here. It's not much, but it's more than your father and me had."

Sarah hugged her, both crying.

Sarah closed the carpetbag. Mama followed her to the door and out onto the porch. She cautioned, "This wasn't the cowboy's idea, was it?"

"It's mine, Mama."

"He may send you back."

"I won't let him."

Papa brought up the dun horse. He embraced his daughter, then gave her a boost onto the saddle and tied the bag behind her. Mama brought out a rolled quilt that Sarah had helped to make on the quilting frame that hung from the parlor ceiling. Papa tied it atop the bag. He said, "You write us, now, you hear?"

"Every chance I get."

Mama stood beside Papa as Sarah put the horse into a trot and picked up the wagon tracks. She turned once and waved.

# TEN

Trey tried to think ahead instead of back, but Sarah's image lingered like the warm glow of a waning campfire. Leaving his own home had been less painful than leaving the Stark farm. Pete James rode ahead of him, speculating gleefully upon the beauty of the girls he and the others would be seeing in Fort Worth. Ellsworth had awakened new appetites in Pete, opened new doors for his passage into manhood . . . if the word *manhood* applied to a boy not yet out of his teens.

His cheerfulness made Trey grit his teeth.

Trey sensed that Zack Lynch was looking at him from the seat of the chuck wagon. Trey pulled his horse in close to the front wheel.

Lynch said, "Pete's just a colt that's found the gate open. He's runnin' and kickin' up his heels."

"I reckon he's got a right."

"He may outgrow it, and he may not. I've seen old men with gray beards still runnin' after whiskey and women. It's like chasin' a rainbow; they never can find where it begins or ends. And even if they found it, they wouldn't know what to do with it.

"Boys like him'll be followin' somebody else's cows all their lives, but you're cut out of different cloth. I knew a girl once like that one back yonder. If I'd grabbed on to her when I could have, I wouldn't be a dried-out old bachelor today."

"I haven't got anything to give her."

"At your age, who does? At your age, and hers, it don't take much."

"Maybe in two or three years."

"That's what *I* thought."

The cook had told Kerbow they had better go by the Dutchman's crossroads store and pick up enough flour to get them to Fort Worth. Maybe some coffee too.

They came to the creek where Trey had brewed coffee while Jarrett Longacre robbed Max's store. The memory chilled him.

Kerbow drew up beside Trey. "You'll do well to take roundance on that settlement. Meet us a mile or so south."

Trey did not want another confrontation with the storekeeper. He bypassed the village, cutting back into the trail on the other side. He dismounted and loosened his cinch to let the bay horse rest while he waited for the outfit. To the south he could see another herd moving slowly toward him, its point rider out in front. Already, seeking fresh grass, the herds were traveling a line farther west than the Kerbow outfit had done earlier in the season. Even more than before, the trail was a broad jumble of interlaced dusty grooves, beaten out by thousands upon thousands of plodding hooves. The grass that remained in its center would not feed a jackrabbit.

Kerbow would be coming back this way himself in a few weeks. While he had been on the trail to Kansas he had a representative traveling through South Texas, finding owners who wanted to send steers up the trail. Kerbow's cowboys would accompany the rep back over his route, throwing the cattle together for a second drive of the season. Given any kind of luck, he should deliver his herd to the railroad ahead of fall's first frost. The biggest problem would be in finding decent grazing along the way. Summer's blistering heat would dry the grass to a brittle brown. Moreover, hundreds of herds would have preceded his up the same trail, competing for every bite of forage.

Trey saw the two Kerbow wagons coming from the settlement, the crew strung out before and behind them. Kerbow loped up ahead. The look on his face disturbed Trey. His first thought was of the storekeeper Max. "Trouble?"

"That depends." Kerbow pointed with his chin. "We picked up another rider."

Trey almost choked. Sarah rode alongside Lynch's wagon, on a dun horse he had seen in her father's corral. "How . . ." He broke off.

"The *how* is easy, and the *why*. The real question is *what next?* Logical thing would be to send her home. But I don't think she's in any mood right now to be logical. Are you?"

"I don't know."

Trey was acutely conscious of all the cowboys' eyes upon him as Sarah rode up to him and stopped. His mind raced in circles. He had no idea of the right thing to do or say under the circumstances. He realized how empty his first words to her sounded. "Sarah, what're you doin' here?"

"I came to be with you." She extended her arms, asking him to help her down from the horse. But he stood awkwardly shifting his weight from one foot to the other and wondering what to do with his hands.

"But I've got a job. I've got no place to put you."

"You don't have to put me anywhere. I'll go where you go."

The arguments seemed to stick in his throat. He glanced toward Kerbow, but the trail boss's gaze was studiously focused elsewhere. Zack Lynch offered no aid. Trey suspected that even if the two men voiced their opinions, their advice would conflict.

Pete James declared jauntily, "If you don't want her, I'll take her."

Frowning, Gil Atwater poked Pete's arm so hard the cowboy hollered.

Kerbow drew his horse up beside Sarah's. "How old are you, Miss Stark?"

"Seventeen. Be eighteen just before Christmas."

"Do your daddy and mother know what you've done?"

"I didn't run away, if that's what you're askin'."

"I can't imagine they're happy about this." He waved his hand toward the gathering of cowhands. "You're an unmarried young woman, and you're askin' to go along with a bunch of unmarried men. Can't you see how that looks?"

Sarah's soft eyes went to Trey. "I figured we'd be married by the first minister we find."

"What afterwards? This chuck wagon is all the home Trey's got."

"As long as I can be with him, it's all right."

Kerbow looked again at the cowboys. They were watching with lively interest . . . much too lively. "But a woman in a wagon camp . . ."

Trey could see that Sarah was not going to turn back. The longer he looked at her, the less he wanted her to. "I guess I'll have to give up my job, Mr. Kerbow. I'll find one that'll let me stay put."

"Where?"

"On a farm someplace. Or maybe in Abel Plunkett's livery stable if he hasn't hired anybody permanent."

Kerbow shifted his gaze from Trey to Sarah and back again. "He wouldn't pay you enough to support a wife."

"I'm not goin' home," Sarah declared.

Kerbow shrugged. He nodded at the cook and set his horse into motion. Trey tightened his cinch, taking his time to let the others move ahead before he remounted.

Sarah's eyes reflected apprehension but no sign of defeat. "You're mad at me."

"Just confused. I don't know what we're goin' to do."

"The first thing, we'll get married." She reached to touch his arm. "Papa says the Lord always provides. He never shuts one door without openin' another."

"What if that door opens over a deep pit?" Trey said.

He purposely trailed behind the procession, not wanting to subject Sarah, or himself, to the speculative stares of the young hands. He could guess the images they were conjuring up. Pete James and Buckshot made it particularly obvious what they were thinking.

By the time they made camp for the night, most of the young men had accommodated to Sarah's being with them. Trey realized that some of their initial bawdy response had been caused by shyness and embarrassment, from not knowing how to react to her unexpected arrival. Even Pete modified his behavior, tipping his hat before offering to help Sarah down from the saddle. His action took Trey by surprise. He realized he should have made that offer first.

Like most of the others, he still struggled with his own coming of age, trying to determine his proper role. Half the time he did not know what to say to her, or how to act. His body was telling him what he wanted to do. His mind was telling him he should not.

He regarded Kerbow and Lynch and Atwater with a bit of envy. They were old enough to have put this awkward stage behind them, to have found comfortable ground. At least he hoped so.

Sarah offered to help Zack Lynch prepare supper. He received the suggestion with both appreciation and skepticism. "Cookin' in Dutch ovens over an open fire is a right smart different from a kitchen," he said. "But if you'd like to peel some spuds . . ."

He set Pancho Martínez to other chores, like dragging up more wood than would possibly be needed. Peeling potatoes would ordinarily have been one of Pancho's swamper jobs. But Trey could see that the cook enjoyed being close to Sarah. He supposed a man never got *too* old, though he was confident Lynch would shove both feet into his own fire rather than do anything that would cause her embarrassment or harm.

Kerbow dragged his bedroll away from the hoodlum wagon but did not untie it. He seated himself upon it and beckoned Trey to join him. He stared a while toward Sarah. "You know the best thing would be to send her back to her folks."

Trey nodded, but he saw how prettily Sarah smiled as the cook made some sort of joke with her. "What's the next best thing?"

"She can't follow you all over south Texas gatherin' stock, and she sure can't go up the trail. You couldn't want that kind of life for a woman."

"Like I said, I'll find me a job where I can stand hitched."

"You wouldn't be satisfied long with just a job." Kerbow stared at Sarah. "I've been hatchin' on an idea. I'd intended to give you more seasonin' first, but that girl has forced my hand."

Trey had been yielding Kerbow only part of his attention, concentrating the rest on Sarah. Now he sat up straight and listened.

Kerbow said, "This may smell like a rose, but it's got thorns hidden in it. Don't say yes 'til you've thought it through, you and that girl both." His frown indicated deep misgivings. "I've got a place out beyond Fort Griffin, north and west of the Clear Fork. Put my claim on it after I got back from the war. Figured to build me a big herd of my own. But things happened . . ." His face took on a dark, brooding look Trey had seen come over him before.

"I've kept the place for the time when I quit drovin'. I go there every fall to brand my calf crop and fix what's broke. But I know a lot of my calves wind up with somebody else's brand because I'm not there to take care of them. And I've got a field layin' fallow because I'm not around to tend to it."

"You're offerin' me a job there?"

"Not just a job. A share of the calves you brand and of whatever crops you raise."

Trey thought he should feel elated, but doubt nagged him. "Are you sure I'm the man for it? I'm still awful green."

"I watched you all the way up the trail. You've faced up to responsibility every time you've been challenged. You've got the makin's."

"I'll take the job."

Kerbow shook his head. "Ain't told you about the thorns yet." He looked again at Sarah, working beside the chuck box. "That girl's never been away from her folks before. Neighbors are scarce, and some that's there, you wouldn't want to know. As to Fort Griffin, the devil would be ashamed to claim it. I don't think you'll need to worry about Indians anymore, but there's the isolation. From a woman's standpoint, that may be the worst thing of all. It's already killed one woman out there."

His eyes pinched.

Trey said, "I'll bet the only thing she'll ask is how do we find it."

"I almost wish I hadn't brought up the subject. You might be better off at Plunkett's livery stable. I'm sure that girl would be."

---

Sarah had no bedding except for the rolled quilt she and her mother had laboriously pieced together for her hope chest. Several cowboys offered to give her their own bedrolls and sleep on their saddle blankets. Trey said, "It's my place to do that."

Lynch and Pancho used a wagon sheet to rig a crude lean-to, more screen than shelter. The cook told her, "I wish we had a tent for you. There's times a lady needs her privacy."

She was flattered and a little fluttery over so much unaccustomed attention. "This will do just fine, thank you. I didn't intend to be any trouble."

Ivan Kerbow said, "The trouble hasn't even begun yet."

Trey lay awake far into the night, thinking about the prospect of marrying Sarah . . . studying on Kerbow's proposition . . . and wondering if the authorities in Fort Worth might be waiting to question him about how that wagonyard gate happened to swing up against the lawman Gault at the worst possible moment.

Trey steeled himself for the worst as the outfit crossed over the Trinity River bridge, turning toward Plunkett's barn. He recognized the deputy marshal who had stood at Gault's side that day. The man was leaning against a hitching rack in front of a dramshop, watching riders and horses pass. For a moment his gaze touched on Trey, and Trey's breath came short. But the deputy gave him scant attention. Instead, he focused on Sarah. Trey let a pent-up breath escape.

Just before the procession reached Plunkett's, a familiar figure waddled out into the street. Lige Connors waylaid Ivan Kerbow. "I believe, Mr. Kerbow, that you and I have some business to discuss."

Kerbow made no pretense. He disliked Connors and showed it. But business was business. "In due time, Mr. Connors. But first I have arrangements to make with Abel Plunkett."

Connors started to follow Kerbow into the livery barn, but Plunkett appeared in the wide doorway. He took a stern stance, feet apart, big hands on his hips. "I've told you, Lige, this is *my* place. You stay out of it."

Face scarlet, Connors told Kerbow in a voice unnaturally shrill, "I'll meet you at the bank." He stomped away.

Plunkett shook hands with Kerbow but did not pull his angry eyes away from Connors until the farmer had disappeared around the corner. "Lige's been in town for a week, waitin' for you to show up with his money. Last two-three days he's been tellin' everybody you probably ran off to Chicago or someplace with it."

"I've never cheated any man out of his rightful due."

"But Lige has, every chance he got. That's why he can't trust anybody else." He noticed Sarah for the first time. "Ain't that Simon Stark's daughter?"

"It is. Her name's goin' to be McLean if she and Trey don't do the sensible thing and back out."

Plunkett's big mustache lifted at the ends. "Well, I'll swun. Reckon I'd best take her over to our house. The missus'll be right glad to see her."

The cowboys unsaddled their horses and turned them into a large corral, then helped Zack Lynch and Pancho unhitch the wagon teams. Kerbow and Plunkett shared a drink from a bottle Plunkett kept in a desk drawer. Plunkett picked up the bag containing Sarah's few belongings and escorted the girl toward his house.

Watching her go, Trey was disturbed by a feeling that he himself was being watched. From the deep shadows of the barn, the lawman Gault materialized like a malevolent ghost. He bore himself stiffly, as if his shoulders were bound. His appearance surprised Kerbow as much as it surprised Trey. Gault's dark eyes seemed sunk back deeply into his head. His skin had the sallow, drained look of a man who has spent a long time indoors, ill. His gaze touched Trey, moved over the rest of the cowboys, then returned to Trey.

"Where is Jarrett Longacre?"

Trey's throat was so tight he could not answer.

Kerbow replied, "He's not with us."

"So I see. But where is he?"

"Who knows? Maybe in Kansas. Maybe in heaven or hell."

"Not in heaven, if I am any judge." Gault's eyes never left Trey. "Everybody claimed it was a gust of wind that pushed the gate against me."

Trey made no effort at a reply.

Gault said, "I did not feel any wind. But I saw you back there."

Trey tried to think of an answer but was grateful for the silent message in Kerbow's eyes: *Keep quiet.*

Kerbow said, "If you have any complaint against this young man, I suggest you file a charge. But close to a dozen witnesses will say you're wrong."

Gault frowned. "This town is short of many things, but it has never lacked for godless men who would bear false witness." He took a couple of steps toward the street and stopped. "As you can see, my left arm is impaired now. But sooner or later I will find Jarrett Longacre, and my good right arm will deal with him. Him and any other sinner who would take his side." He gave Trey another hard study, then moved away. Trey shuddered.

Kerbow said, "You'd best not stay in this town a day longer than you have to."

"I hadn't figured on it."

"Right now I'll need you to go to the bank with me."

Trey could not remember that he had ever been in a bank before. He had never had enough money at one time to require a bank's services or collateral enough to borrow on. The interior struck him as Spartan and dark, almost as oppressive as Sheriff Micah Bracken's jail had been. His acceptance of it was not helped by the sight of an impatient Lige Connors, who followed him and Kerbow through the door. Connors carried a canvas satchel. Trey assumed it was for the money.

Connors gave Trey a hostile scrutiny. "Mr. Kerbow, you are not very discriminating in the employees you hire. This young man once stole four cows from me . . . or tried to."

"Seems to me like you've got that backwards. You stole the cows from *him*," the drover said.

"The young man is not only a thief but a liar."

Kerbow's jaw tightened. "I'll sign a draft for you. Then you can be on your way."

"I do not accept drafts, sir. For me, cash is the only legal tender." One puffy hand patted the canvas bag for emphasis.

Stiffly Kerbow said, "The bank will accept my draft, and it will provide you with cash." He laid out his account book, showing the number of steers Connors had turned over to him and the price paid in Ellsworth. He prorated the herd's head-count loss, which had come to five percent. Connors's share of that loss was ten steers.

Connors protested. "Did you count my steers separately? Can you make an affydavy that you actually lost ten of them?"

"They were mixed with the others. The only fair way is for all owners to accept five percent as their share of the loss."

Trey feared the two men might come to blows. But the set of Kerbow's jaw indicated that he would stand his ground from now until snowfall. Connors let off steam like an idling locomotive. "You will never handle any of my cattle again!"

Kerbow's voice was cold. "I've already made that promise to myself."

Connors scrutinized the draft and again began to steam. "What's this? You've deducted another hundred dollars."

"I figure a hundred dollars is a fair round sum to pay Trey for his four cows, with a little allowance for interest."

"This is an outrage! I won't stand for it."

"Then sue me. But you'll have to come to San Antonio to do it. I'm leavin' here soon as I finish my business."

Connors fumed and foamed but collected his cash from the banker, whose manner made it clear that his distaste for the man was on a par with Trey's and Kerbow's. Connors stalked out, his bulk requiring so much of the doorway that he bumped the bulging satchel against the jamb.

The banker growled, "He's a fool, toting that money around. There are twenty men in town who would gladly shoot him for half of what he is carrying."

One, Trey thought, would be tempted do it for nothing.

Kerbow paid Trey for his labor on the drive and added a fifty-dollar bonus. That, on top of the hundred dollars for his four cows, made Trey feel rich as a European prince he had read about.

"Thanks for makin' Connors pay up. I wouldn't have asked you to lean out over the edge for me that way."

"I enjoyed the show. He probably sweated off twenty pounds right in front of our eyes."

Trey had never thought much about marriage. He had assumed he would live the bachelor life until he was thirty or so. By then he expected to be a well-fixed cattleman. There would be time enough to select the right woman to share all that luxury.

Instead, he found himself standing in silent terror before an amiable minister he had never met until today, in a white frame church he had never entered before. Through the west windows the late-afternoon sun cast a golden glow across the pulpit and out upon the Kerbow crew, Abel Plunkett and his wife. When the minister asked who was to give this woman in marriage, Zack Lynch replied, "Me, Parson."

The ceremony completed, Trey stood beside Sarah, his knees shaky, receiving congratulations and feeling more than a little bewildered by the speed of it all. Mrs. Plunkett was hugging Sarah and calling her a poor girl. As she walked toward the door she declared loudly enough for everyone to hear, "She doesn't know what she's done, marrying a cowboy. Mark what I tell you, she'll be barefooted before the summer is out. And with child."

Plunkett tried to quiet her, but her voice continued to trail behind her as she walked out the door, down the steps and into the dirt street.

The cowboys crowded around, taking advantage of the opportunity to kiss a pretty bride. Lynch kissed her first, then kissed her again when all the others had finished their turn. He said, "Ain't often I get a second helpin' of anything."

Walking out of the church with Sarah on his arm, Trey felt a glow that hovered somewhere between pleasure and desperation. The glow chilled when he saw Gault standing beside the steps, dressed in a long black coat despite the warmth of the summer day.

Trey felt riveted by the lawman's dark eyes. Gault's voice was one of a minister preaching hellfire and brimstone. "Would you begin a new life with the burden of a troubled conscience?"

Trey tried to form some sort of answer but could not. Gault shifted his gaze momentarily to Sarah, touching his fingers to the brim of his black derby hat. "I hope, young lady, that you can help this confused young man find the way."

Sarah watched him walk down the street. She turned to Trey. "The way to what?"

Trey fumbled for words. "The way to Fort Griffin, I guess."

As a wedding gift, Kerbow paid for a two-dollar hotel room. He said, "It's not fittin' for newlyweds to spend their weddin' night in a wagonyard. No tellin' what may come to the two of you later, but at least I want to see you off to a good start."

Trey sensed a troubled soul behind the trail boss's forced smile. It challenged his own anemic confidence. He said, "Thanks. And don't you worry about us, Mr. Kerbow. We'll do just fine."

Kerbow treated his crew and the newlyweds to supper in the hotel dining room. It seemed strange to Trey, eating off a white tablecloth with a black waiter serving food from the kitchen and saying "sir." It was a world away from the wagon camps of recent months. Even at home he had not been used to such refinements as tablecloths, much less the idea of anyone serving him. He saw Pete James and Buckshot bending down to sneak swigs from a bottle they hid beneath the long table. At this point he would not have minded having a drink himself.

Even when the food was removed from the table and the coffee got cold, the cowboys seemed in no hurry to leave. Zack Lynch finally asked Kerbow what time it was.

Kerbow looked at his pocket watch, then lifted his gaze to Trey and Sarah. "It's late. We'd better be gettin' along." He turned toward Pete. "*All* of us." He pushed his chair back and arose from the table. "Trey, we've got to buy supplies for you to take to the ranch. I'll meet you in the lobby about eight o'clock in the mornin'." He reconsidered, looking at Sarah. "No, nine o'clock is early enough."

The cowboys filed out of the dining room, most of them looking back wistfully at the young couple. Zack Lynch paused as if he had something to say. Whatever it was, he changed his mind and kept it to himself. Kerbow said, "Zack, I'll buy you and Gil a drink before we go to camp."

Lynch replied with a grin, "You're the boss. I guess we've got no choice."

Trey and Sarah sat alone in the dining room except for the black waiter, who gathered plates and cups from the table. The waiter smiled pleasantly. "You young folks stay just as long as you want to. You ain't botherin' me a particle."

Trey stared uneasily at Sarah and found his discomfort mirrored in her eyes. His skin prickled with impatience to take her upstairs, yet fear made supper lie heavily on his stomach. He knew very well what tradition demanded of the wedding night. Yet, how could he do such a coarse thing to her? She was so fresh and young and innocent. . . . He found her hand trembling.

Trey said, "I suppose we ought to go so they can finish cleanin' up in here."

Her lips were pinched, her voice unnatural. "I suppose."

He pushed out his chair a little more forcefully than he intended. It tipped over backward, clattering loudly against the pine floor. She made a nervous little laugh and arose as he righted the chair. Trey took her arm and moved toward the door, acutely aware of the waiter's effort not to grin.

They walked across the small lobby and started up the stairs. Looking back, Trey saw the waiter standing in the dining room door, his gaze following them. The night clerk leaned his elbows upon the registration desk. He was watching too.

Sarah whispered, "Reckon they know we just got married?"

"I don't see how they could, unless somebody mentioned it at supper."

At the door, he fumbled with the key. He had had little experience with locks. Nobody except storekeepers and the bank had them back home . . . they and the jail. He held the door open and waited for Sarah to go in. She hesitated.

"Aren't you supposed to do somethin' now?" she asked.

His mind raced ahead. He felt his face flush warm. "We don't have to be in a hurry about it."

She said, "You're supposed to carry me through the door."

"Oh."

He picked her up clumsily. She put her arms around his neck and leaned her head against his shoulder. Mrs. Plunkett had washed her long hair, and it still smelled faintly of perfumed soap. The warmth he had felt in his face seemed now to rush through his whole body as they clung to each other. He kissed her soft cheek. She lifted her head, turning her face toward him. He kissed her again, on the lips. Her arms tightened around him.

Presently she said, "I wouldn't mind if you held me this way all night, but I'm afraid you'd get tired and drop me."

He set her down but kept his arms around her. "You don't weigh as much, hardly, as a dogie calf."

She made a tiny laugh. The tension eased. "I don't believe anybody ever told me a thing like that before."

"I meant it good."

"I know." She pressed snugly against him. "Mr. Craven used to read pretty poetry to me, but I'd rather have you compare me to a dogie calf."

The only light in the room came by reflection from the hallway. Trey lighted a lamp before closing the door.

"It's a nice room," Sarah said, clutching his arm. "Somethin' we can always remember."

Kerbow had made it a point to get them a room that fronted onto a balcony, facing out upon the street. Its furnishings were modest: a washstand with a large porcelain basin and a pitcher; a dresser with a large oval mirror; a chifforobe in which Sarah had hung the few clothes she had brought along. Against one wall stood a four-poster bed, covered by a handmade quilt. Trey's eyes were drawn to it, though he tried to pretend it was not there. Sarah looked at it, then at him, her cheeks coloring.

From outside he heard a racket, men shouting, singing. He heard his name. He walked out the door onto the balcony, where a soft breeze touched his face. Down on the street he could see several Kerbow cowboys on horseback. Somewhere Pete had picked up a tin pan, and he was beating against it with a stick. His horse shied from one side to the other, spooked by the noise.

Sarah joined Trey and placed one arm around him. "What in the world?"

"Shivaree. Wishin' us good luck."

"Does it have to be so loud?"

"Wouldn't be any point to it if it wasn't."

Seeing them standing together, the hands cheered. Pete shouted something Trey could not make out. Coming from Pete, it was just as well, he thought. That boy had learned too much too fast.

Some of the boys were inviting the couple to come down. At the end of the balcony, a set of steps led down the side of the hotel. But Trey had no intention of using them.

Presently a peace officer came along. Trey could not see his badge, but he recognized the deputy city marshal who had been at the wagonyard the day Gault was shot.

The cowboys quieted while the officer talked to them. Trey could not hear the words, but he saw the man point in the direction of Plunkett's wagonyard. Reluctantly Pete and the rest gave in to the voice of authority and began pulling away, hollering their good-byes. The lawman stood alone, looking up at the balcony. He grinned with a knowing air.

"They're gone," he called. "Now you can go to bed." He walked away chuckling.

Sarah leaned back into Trey's arms, covering his hands with her own. "He's right. Or don't you want to?"

"I suppose there's nothin' else left to do."

Trey closed the door behind them and pulled down the window shade. He started to blow out the lamp. She caught his hand. "Don't. I can't see you in the dark."

She had been married in a dress her mother had made for her to wear to church. It buttoned in the back, and she asked Trey to help her undo it. He fumbled, his hands shaking.

She smiled. "Haven't you ever helped a woman with her buttons before?"

"First time I ever did *any* of this."

"It's the first time a man ever helped me. We'll just have to learn together."

Sarah slipped out of the dress and draped it over the back of a chair. She let down her long, straight hair, which cascaded almost to her waist. She turned to face him in a white cotton shift that clung snugly to her bosom. He had to stare. He touched his hand to the side of her face and moved it slowly down her neck, over her shoulder and partway along her arm. He yearned to touch her breasts but could not summon the courage.

"You're beautiful."

"And you were goin' to blow out the lamp."

He turned away, undressing with his back to her. When he was done he found she was already in bed, a sheet pulled up almost to her shoulders. He wondered how he must look to her, standing there in his long underwear. Awkward, certainly, for that was how he felt. His body ached to crawl into bed with her. On the other hand, he had a wild urge to grab his britches and run. He was unsure which compulsion was strongest.

She lifted the cover on his side of the bed, silently inviting him to join her. Sliding between the sheets, he felt an electric shock as he touched her. He jerked away. She grasped his hand, pulling it to her lips, kissing his fingers.

"It's all right," she whispered.

"This whole thing takes some gettin' used to."

"We have all the time in the world," she said, and drew her body up close against him, encircling him with her arms. He tensed at first. He felt as if he had taken a long drink of whiskey. She held tightly, kissing him, pressing her stomach against his, dissolving his fears in her warmth.

He returned her kiss, on her soft lips first, then on her cheek, her neck. As inhibitions melted away, he pulled down the shift and kissed her breast. She trembled, and he wondered if he was moving too quickly. He tried to pull away, but she did not let him go.

Her breath was hot in his ear. "There's nothin' for us to be afraid of, or ashamed of."

He wondered a little at first about the thinness of the walls, the thought that the sounds they made might carry to other rooms. That concern was soon shunted aside in the urgency of the moment. He felt as if he were drawn into an undertow, slowly drowning.

It did not matter. If this resembled drowning, he thought, then drowning must be a pleasant way to die.

They clung fiercely together, coming down from the crest of the tide as he had seen cattle tire of running and drop to a walk, then finally to a standstill.

He wanted to talk. He wanted to tell her how beautiful she was, but words seemed too small for the grandness of what he felt. He lay on his elbow, his arm beneath her neck, so he could look down into her face in the glow of lamplight and watch her eyes smile as he kissed her.

# ELEVEN

The road west from Fort Worth was well worn and easy to follow, for it had been used by the military, by settlers, by freighters and mail carriers. Beyond Fort Griffin, to the west and northwest, it would be dimmer and might well fade away entirely before they reached Ivan Kerbow's place. But that was days out in front. Trey would worry about that when and if he had to. For now, he was enjoying the pleasantness of the day, the easy plodding of the sturdy team, the warm closeness of Sarah beside him on the seat of the farm wagon Abel Plunkett had taken in on a horse trade and had sold to Kerbow.

At last he had Sarah truly alone. Even in their hotel room, he had been nervously aware that other people lay in their own beds a few feet away, that thin walls were no assurance of true privacy. She leaned against him, her hand gripping his leg.

Behind them in the bed of the wagon, covered by a heavy tarp, were supplies Kerbow had bought for their use on the trail and at the ranch: flour, salt, bacon, coffee, some rope, medicines to treat the ailments of man or horse. There was a well-used rifle Trey had bought so Sarah would always have a weapon within reach when he was away from the house. "Just in case coyotes get into your chickens, or somethin' . . ."

He left the "or something" hanging like a broken limb.

In a pair of crude willow cages rode a rooster and several hens. Even in the wilderness, Sarah said, she wanted to hear a rooster crow every morning and have eggs to cook with.

Kerbow had told Trey, "I haven't been to the place since winter, so I don't know what kind of shape you'll find it in. It's got a good stone cabin that the first settler built. I put an iron stove in it, if some thief hasn't packed it away."

An iron stove would be a luxury on the frontier. Well, Trey thought, they could cook on the hearth if they had to. Most people did, out past the settlements.

Kerbow had given Sarah a long, lingering look which spoke of misgivings, of regret that he was sending her to such a faraway place. His parting words to Trey had been, "You keep a good watch on that girl, and don't you hesitate to get her away from there anytime things don't look right."

"What kind of things?"

"That's hard to say. It's still a raw country. And a damned lonesome one."

Trey's bay horse Fox walked behind the wagon at the end of a long tether, with Sarah's Dunny and a stocking-footed black Kerbow had sent along as an extra mount. He had left a couple more horses at the ranch after using them last winter, but he could not be sure they would still be there. They might have strayed away, either on their own or with two-legged help.

Also tied behind the wagon was a sorrel mare Plunkett had given to Sarah as a wedding present. A colt trotted behind her. Plunkett had said the mare was safely in foal again. "You're startin' off toward a fortune in the horse business," he said.

The leave-taking had been marred only by the ominous presence of the lawman Gault, watching with dark eyes from across the street.

Sarah noticed him. "That man starin' at us so hard . . . who is he, anyway?"

"Peace officer. Name of Gault."

"If that's the kind of officers they have around here, I'd hate to see what the outlaws look like."

In the first miles out of Fort Worth the road led through and over open, grassy hills, past a number of farmsteads and small ranches. The nature of the vegetation told Trey that rainfall here was not as liberal as in the cotton-growing blacklands where he had grown up. The farther west he went, the chancier farming would be. He saw much more evidence of livestock-raising here than of the plow. He had no quarrel with that.

They stopped for noon in the shade of a small grove. There would be time enough tonight to cook a hot meal. For now they would eat from a sack of leftover cold biscuits, sausage and boiled eggs the hotel's smiling black waiter had brought to the newlyweds at their departure.

Sitting on the edge of a canvas spread upon the grass, Trey noticed that Sarah was staring at the trail that led over a distant hill and disappeared to the west. He thought he saw apprehension in her eyes.

"Scared?" he asked.

"It's just the newness of everything. A new land. A new life, not knowin' quite what to expect out yonder."

"You'll get used to it. *We* will."

"We've already made it past the first lesson." She took his hand and brought his fingers to her lips. "We'll learn the rest of it together too."

He drew her close and held her.

Soon he became aware of hoofbeats. He pulled away from her,

frustrated. "Wasn't lookin' for any company," he grumbled.

Face flushed, Sarah straightened her dress. "I guess the Lord meant some things to wait for the dark."

Two riders approached from the direction of Fort Worth. A buggy trailed behind them, pulled by one big horse. Its lone occupant sat in the center of the seat, the vehicle sagging under his weight. Trey groaned.

"Trouble comin'." He motioned for Sarah to remain behind him as he took a few steps forward. His first thought was that Lige Connors had brought the law out to harass him about the payment for his four cows. His rifle was in the wagon, but he did not move toward it. He intended to give the law no trouble.

As the riders neared, he decided they were not lawmen. They looked more like some of the toughs he had seen loafing on the streets of Fort Worth, making their living at whatever kind of devilment came to hand so long as it did not involve sweat or heavy lifting. He had second thoughts about the rifle but still made no move toward it. Fighting had never been in his nature except as a last resort, and gunfighting certainly was not. To him, a gun had only one legitimate purpose: to provide meat for the table.

The men did not look friendly, so he offered no greeting. Hands on his hips, he uneasily watched them rein up almost within spitting distance. To ask their business would be idle. They would tell him soon enough, or Connors would. The two men dismounted, one glancing back at Connors, closing the distance in the buggy.

The taller man asked, "You-all havin' dinner?"

It was a useless question, for the food was in plain sight on the canvas. The man was making conversation to hold Trey's attention until Connors could catch up.

Trey said, "Help yourselves if you're hungry." He did not feel generous, but he was stalling, just as the two horsemen were. Connors pulled up, swaying precariously as he struggled to climb down from the buggy. Trey was disappointed that he managed not to fall.

Connors's voice was belligerent. "Well, young fellow, thought you'd got clean away, didn't you?"

"I had nothin' to get away from."

"You took money that belongs to me. I am here to recover it. And I have brought these gentlemen to give you a stern lesson in the wages of sin." He jerked his head at the two toughs. "Find my money."

They were upon Trey in an instant, pushing him back against the wagon. Sarah made a cry of protest and began pummeling first one of the men, then the other, with her fists. They paid no attention to her. One socked Trey on the jaw, stunning him. They went through his pockets and felt his waist, looking for a money belt.

Connors said, "It's probably in the wagon."

The shorter of the men climbed up and threw off the tarp that covered the supplies while the taller one held the struggling Sarah at arm's length. Disturbed, the caged hens began fluttering and making frightened noises. The short man untied the bedroll and cast the blankets out onto the ground one at a time. He dumped the contents of Trey's war bag and the bag in which Sarah had her extra clothes. He opened a canvas sack and turned triumphantly toward Connors.

"Got it!"

It was the bag in which Trey had placed the money for the cows, his earnings from the trail drive and a couple of hundred dollars Kerbow had provided to pay whatever ranch expenses might arise between now and fall.

"That's my money, mine and Mr. Kerbow's!" Trey shouted. He made a grab at the bag as the man in the wagon pitched it to Connors. The second man's fist came at Trey in a blur of speed, striking him like a hickory club, driving him back against the wagon.

Connors made a quick count and grinned. "Looks like I got back what you taken from me and some interest besides." He looked up, the grin gone. "Now, teach him a lesson."

Trey's head spun. Lights reeled before his eyes, but he tried again to grab the canvas bag. Though he saw the blow coming, he could not move to avoid it. It drove the breath out of him. He collapsed beside a wagon wheel. Sarah knelt beside him, sobbing.

The man in the wagon found something else. "This looks like a lady's purse." He pulled back the drawstring and shoved one hand inside. "Some more money in here."

Sarah jumped to her feet and made a run at him. "That's mine. My mother gave it to me."

The man pitched it to Connors. Sarah rushed toward the farmer, reaching for the purse. He slapped her with the flat of his hand. "Back off, missy, if you don't want to get hurt."

She struggled for the bag, and he struck her again, this time with his big fist. She fell to the ground.

The mood of the two toughs changed suddenly from exuberance to a deep chill. The man on the ground stepped between Connors and the girl. He grabbed a handful of Connors's shirt.

"Hit her again and I'll bust your arm."

Connors sputtered.

The man declared, "We come here to help you get your money. We didn't come to beat up on no woman. That can get a man horse-whipped. Even hung."

The other thug jumped down from the wagon. He took Sarah's hands and helped her to her feet. He turned to Connors and yanked the purse from him, giving it to Sarah.

Trey took hold of the wagon wheel with both hands and pulled himself up. He and Sarah put their arms around each other.

Connors was first surprised, then outraged. "I'm payin' you men for a job of work."

The taller tough leaned down, his nose almost touching Connors's. "All of a sudden it comes to me that we've just heard you talk. We ain't seen no pay yet."

"And you won't if you don't do what I tell you to."

The tough turned to his companion. "Jasper, go out to the buggy yonder and see what he's got in that satchel. He's been settin' on it like a mother hen."

Connors's anger turned to alarm. "That's mine!" He turned toward the buggy. The tall tough stuck out his foot. The farmer fell on his stomach and took a mouthful of dirt.

Jasper shouted from the buggy, "Money! Lots of money!"

It was the proceeds from the sale of Connors's steers.

Connors spat dirt. "I'll have the law on you!"

The tall man snickered. "You goin' to tell them you hired us to rob this boy and beat up on him?" He waited for an answer but received none. "If you go runnin' to the law, *we'll* tell them. Like as not we'd all wind up in a cell together. Now, wouldn't that be cozy?"

He motioned toward the canvas bag that belonged to Trey. "I'd put that back in the wagon if I was you, boy." He unhitched the horse from the buggy and told Connors, "We'll take him up the trail a couple miles and turn him loose. Time you catch him and get back to town, you'll run off a right smart of that lard."

The two men mounted up and started eastward toward Fort Worth. Jasper triumphantly carried Connors's satchel. The tall man led the buggy horse.

Connors's round shoulders slumped as he watched them. Trey picked up the canvas bag that contained his own money and put it back into the wagon. His jaw ached, and one eye burned. He knew it was swelling shut. But he could still see well enough to spot the rifles lying beneath the seat. He picked up one and started toward Connors.

Fear leaped into the farmer's face. He raised both hands protectively. "You stay away from me! Stay away, I say!"

Coldly Trey said, "You know I could shoot you where you stand. I could bury you out behind that thicket and burn your buggy. Those two ginks goin' yonder, they wouldn't talk. Nobody would ever know what went with you, and I doubt there's many would give a damn."

Connors' flabby jaw dropped. "You wouldn't!"

"Why wouldn't I? You're a long way from your pet sheriff."

Connors looked at Sarah. "Girl, I never meant you no harm. Talk to him, won't you?"

Sarah's eyes narrowed. "Shoot him, Trey."

Connors gave a yelp and turned to run. His legs were heavy as nail kegs, but he managed more speed than Trey would have expected. Trey aimed just to Connors's left and squeezed off a shot. It kicked up dust near the farmer's feet and improved his pace.

Trey turned back to Sarah. "You all right?"

She rushed into his arms, trembling. He decided her emotion was as much of outrage as of fright. He said, "They won't bother us anymore."

"I was afraid they would hurt you bad."

"They might've if you hadn't pitched in." He carefully touched fingers to her chin, where Connors had struck her with his fist. The blow had left a red mark. "Maybe I ought to shoot him after all." Connors was still within rifle range.

She said, "Mine'll heal quicker than yours. Let him go."

He managed to smile at her, though the effort made his jaw hurt. "They busted up our dinner. You want any more to eat?"

"I've lost my appetite."

"Then let's load up. Time Connors comes back for his buggy, we'll be way down the road."

He shook out the blankets and rolled them while Sarah gathered up the leavings of their interrupted meal. The hens had settled down.

He said, "You sounded kind of cold-blooded when you told me to shoot him. Did you really mean it?"

"I think I did, right that minute."

"Remind me to never let you get mad at me. Not even for a minute."

Trey searched Connors's buggy. Finding a shotgun, he smashed the stock against the hub of a wheel. The farmer would not consider using the weapon now, at least until he had a new stock fitted to it. Trey was fairly certain Connors did not carry a sidearm. As tight as his clothes were, he had nowhere to hide one.

They kept traveling until almost dark, then pulled out of the ruts and around the back side of a hill so their campfire could not be seen from the trail.

Sarah looked behind them. "You don't think he'd follow us after what-all he went through?"

"Not likely, but it doesn't hurt to give ourselves a little edge. Anyway, we'll have our privacy if anybody happens to come down the road."

She kissed him on his swollen cheek. He winced.

She asked, "Does that hurt?"

"Some. But it's worth the price."

---

Kerbow had told him the wagon trip to Fort Griffin should take about a week. From there to the ranch would require more than a day, probably closer to two. It had not sounded like much, but on the ground a mile was a mile, and there were a lot of them. Trey followed the well-marked road to the small town of Weatherford, then a cut-across to Fort Belknap, bypassing Fort Richardson and Jacksboro. Belknap in its time had hosted Union, then Texas Confederate, then Union troops again. From Belknap the trail dropped southwestward toward the crooked course of the Clear Fork of the Brazos.

Along the way Trey and Sarah passed slower-moving freight wagons hauling supplies and grain to the military posts. Trey found the freighters mostly congenial in manner if profane in speech, an occupational hazard for men who dealt daily with the natural recalcitrance of oxen and mules. They were curious about the young couple, intrigued by the fresh prettiness of the bride. They offered to share their campgrounds and give her their protection, but at this early point in their marriage, Trey and Sarah preferred being alone. Nevertheless, a couple of nights they made their fire within rock-throwing distance of freight outfits, just to be on the safe side.

Kerbow had told him Fort Griffin was a raw place, long on violence and short on law. The freighters confirmed the trail boss's judgment.

"You'd better look poor and talk poor," one warned him. "There's two things them high-binders on the Flat can't stand: law officers and the thought of somebody else havin' money. If they take a notion you've got somethin' worth stealin', they're liable to come callin' on you."

"They wouldn't get much."

"Some don't ask for much. There was one a while back killed a peddler for a pair of boots."

"Just a pair of boots?"

"He didn't set his sights very high. Some of the town folks invited him to a party down on the river and decorated a tree with him. But that didn't do the peddler much good."

Trey glanced uncomfortably toward Sarah, stirring a squirrel stew over glowing coals. "I'm not lookin' for any trouble. I'm just goin' to take care of Mr. Kerbow's cattle and try to build a herd of my own."

"Well, you'll find some good people out yonder, and you'll find some double-rectified scoundrels. Ain't always easy to tell them apart on first acquaintance."

By freighters' descriptions, Trey was only a short distance from Fort Griffin when he saw two riders spurring toward him from the west. One was a couple of hundred yards out in front. The man trailing was using his quirt. His gray horse seemed to be struggling. The leader reined up in front of the wagon and drew a pistol from his belt. He was a tall man with heavy black whiskers and black eyes wide and wild. Trey did not need a long acquaintanceship to class him as one of the scoundrels the freighter had warned him about.

The man focused his attention on the horses tied behind. "That bay," he shouted, "does he run pretty good?"

Trey did not answer. He knew the man intended to take the horse in any case. He looked down at the rifles beneath the wagon seat, but the rider had the look of a rattlesnake coiled to strike.

Without leaving his saddle, the newcomer untied the bay Fox as the other rider pulled up on the tired gray. "Fresh horse, Bill. Catch up to me." Without waiting, he jabbed spurs to his own mount and loped away, anxiously looking back over his shoulder as if the devil and all his minions were chasing him.

The man called Bill hardly took his eyes from Trey as he switched his bridle and saddle to the bay. "I'm swappin' horses. Ain't got time to argy price." He spurred after his partner, who was almost out of sight.

Sarah said in resignation, "At least he left you his horse."

"Probably stolen." Trey clenched his fist in helpless anger. "Hell of a country I've brought you to."

If the gray *was* stolen, Trey did not want to be seen with it. He set the team into motion. The gray decided to join the horses tied behind the wagon. Trey got down and tried to chase the animal away. It trotted off a short distance but, when the wagon moved again, turned and trailed after it.

Trey wondered if anyone had ever been hanged as a horse thief because a horse followed him home.

The gray favored its right forefoot a little. Its right knee was skinned. It had probably stumbled and fallen, laming itself.

The men's desperate manner had indicated that they were being pursued. Their pursuers soon swept into view. Trey counted seven riders pushing hard toward him on the trail from the west. He wished even more strongly that the gray horse had stayed behind.

The riders reined up in a swirl of dust. Their grim faces made questions seem superfluous.

One of the men pointed to the gray. "Ain't that the one Greasy Bill Hartley was ridin'?"

"Sure looks like him," declared a man with a badge on his vest. His eyes burned into Trey's. "How'd you come by him, young feller?"

Trey explained about the theft of his bay. He half expected that they would disbelieve him, as some had the time Jarrett Longacre had robbed the Dutchman's store.

A tall posseman drew his horse in close to Sarah's side of the wagon. He studied her intently. "Is that the way it was, young lady?"

Her voice was higher pitched than usual. "That's what happened."

Trey thought he had seen the man before, but that seemed unlikely. He had never been in this part of the country.

The man said to the sheriff, "She wouldn't lie to us. You can tell by lookin' at her, she's too nice for that."

The sheriff demanded, "What would you know about a *nice* lady, Mead?"

*Mead.* Trey remembered. This was the rancher who had rented a buggy from Abel Plunkett to take one of Fort Worth's soiled doves for a ride. *What was his last name? Overman? No, Overstreet. That was it, Overstreet.*

To Trey's relief the lawman seemed to accept the explanation once Sarah had endorsed it.

"How far ahead of us are they?" he asked Trey.

"Maybe a mile. The thief that took my horse was a ways behind the other one."

"You stay in Griffin. Maybe we'll get your horse back for you." The riders were quickly gone, using their spurs and their quirts. Overstreet looked back a couple of times. Trey was sure he was looking at Sarah, not at him. When the horsemen passed out of sight, he set the wagon into motion.

Sarah asked, "What do you suppose they're chasin' those men for?"

Trey shrugged. "Not for singin' too loud in church. I wonder if Griffin has even *got* a church."

In a sense, Fort Griffin was two places, not one. The military post stood on a tall hill, proud and aloof. As he pushed across the ford at the Clear Fork, Trey could see the flag waving on its pole atop a considerable prominence. The town of Fort Griffin, known as "the Flat," lay along Collins Creek beneath the post, neither aloof nor with much reason for pride. It stretched haphazardly northward along a street that led from the foot of the hill down to the bank of the tree-lined river. It was the westernmost trading center for venturesome ranchers, farmers and hunters in this relatively undeveloped section of Texas. They could buy supplies here without having to travel the long distance eastward to Fort Worth or Denison. Not for two hundred miles or more to the west, and that in New Mexico, was there another town. Between here and there, a traveler risked losing his scalp to free-roaming Comanche and Kiowa who still considered the high plains their own, even though they seemed to have given up this region below the caprock.

Freighters had told Trey that the Flat had a new two-story frame hotel run by a German and his wife, but he was not in a mood to waste his limited resources on that kind of luxury. The wagon men had a campground near the river where it was easy to lead their teams of mules and oxen to water. Trey had found most freighters to be good company, even if their language must sometimes burn Sarah's ears. She seemed not to notice, but he figured she hid her embarrassment to save him concern. Or, having been brought up in a sheltering family, she might simply not realize what some of the terms meant. He preferred to believe that was the case.

Griffin was as yet too far west to enjoy the trail-drive business that enlivened Fort Worth, but people were saying its time would come. The settlement was beginning to see some buffalo-hunter traffic, drifting down from the north because the Kansas herds were rapidly thinning.

For now, the squalid little town on the flat below Government Hill concentrated heavily on peddling whiskey and sin to the soldiers, to cowboys and freighters and to meat hunters who salted down buffalo tongues and humps for sale in cities to the east. It was home to a variety of human driftwood who worried little about the future, men too busy taking care of today, making hay while there was sunshine and trying to reap more than they sowed.

He had finished watering the animals and staking them on grass when the posse returned. The gray had followed him all the way to town. Though Trey did not stake him, the horse stayed close by the others, acting as if he had found his family.

Trey recognized his bay horse Fox as the riders neared his camp. The man who had stolen him was still astride, shoulders slumped in despair, hands tied behind his back. Blood had dried on one side of his shirt. A sleeve had been torn away and wrapped around a wounded arm.

Two of the possemen peeled off from the others and came into camp. They tipped their hats to Sarah, who was reheating beans in an iron pot for the second day. One was the man who had spoken to her earlier. He concentrated his attention on Sarah. "My name is Mead Overstreet. I am at your service, ma'am."

He was well dressed for a place like this, as if he had had a bath this very morning and a change of clothes. Sarah stared at him in a way that vaguely troubled Trey. The man was strikingly handsome. Trey wondered if she was comparing him to her husband. When it came to looks, Trey knew he must come out second best.

She said, "I'm Sarah McLean. That's my husband Trey."

Overstreet gave Trey only a quick glance. "It's a pleasure, ma'am, to make your acquaintance."

Trey said, "We already met once. I was workin' in the wagonyard in Fort Worth last spring."

He sensed that Overstreet did not remember him. Most people would not pay much attention to a swamper in a wagonyard. And

Overstreet's mind had been on women at the time. The way he looked at Sarah, it still was.

The other posseman told Trey, "We'll bring your horse back later. You better not ever bet on him in a race. Greasy Bill found out he's a little too slow."

"What about the second man?"

"His brother, Jonas. Flat outran us."

"How come you chasin' them?"

"Murder. They stove in a card sharp's head and lit out with his money. Folks here don't stand still for that kind of doin's." He jerked his head. "Comin', Overstreet?"

Mead Overstreet touched fingers to his hat. "Duty calls, ma'am. But perhaps we shall meet again."

Trey decided Fort Griffin had little to offer that he wanted. Come daylight, he and Sarah would pull out.

The smell of cooking drew a hungry-looking hound whose ribs showed through his tan-colored hide. He ventured up close to Sarah's fire before Trey made a run at him.

"Git!"

The dog trotted off, tail between its legs, and stopped twenty feet from the fire to look back.

Sarah said, "Poor dickens probably hasn't had anything to eat all day."

"If he belongs to somebody, let *them* feed him. If he doesn't, let him go catch a rabbit. We don't need his fleas in camp."

The dog sat on its haunches, eyes begging. Sarah broke off a piece of cold biscuit and tossed it toward him. Jumping to its feet, the dog caught it in midair. Sarah threw him another piece, which he downed in a gulp.

"You'll never get rid of him now," Trey warned.

During daytime the town seemed devoted to conventional business. Trey and Sarah watched freight wagons coming and going, cowboys riding in and out, soldiers skirting the edge of town as they came in from patrol or whatever other duty had taken them away from the post. Late in the afternoon several Indians came by, the men riding horseback, their women following afoot. They showed no sign of hostility, but Sarah moved close to Trey.

"I'd guess they're Tonkawas," he said. "Freighters told me the army uses some of them as scouts. They're blood enemies of the Comanches."

She clutched his arm. "I'm glad they're not *our* enemies."

"They won't do us any harm. But if I was that dog, I'd be nervous."

"They'd eat a dog?"

"I hear they eat *people.* Their enemies, anyway. That's why all the other Indians are down on them."

At sunset he and Sarah heard a cannon as the flag was lowered on the parade ground atop the hill. The distant sound of a bugle came in fragments, much of it lost on the wind.

Nightfall masked the town's crude appearance and awakened a different mood. With darkness came the music, the shouting, the laughter. It reminded Trey a little of Ellsworth. Half a dozen cowboys loped their mounts in from the crossing and fired pistols into the air as they hit the street. Trey looked quickly to the staked horses, afraid the noise might spook them into jerking the pins out of the ground and running away. The colt ran off a short distance toward the river but whinnied and came back to its mother after the momentary scare had run its course.

The gray horse paid little attention to the shooting. Its calm manner seemed to reassure the others, for none of them broke loose. The dog had hung around camp, warily watching Trey but wagging its tail each time Sarah came near. It trotted off after the cowboys, barked and came back. Its pleased attitude seemed to say, *I chased them away for you.*

Trey kept wondering when—and if—the possemen would bring the bay back to him. He had hoped it would be tonight, for he wanted to start west immediately after breakfast. He was about to give up and prepare for bed when he heard the sound of hooves. In the gloom he could see four horseback riders and perhaps a dozen men on foot, moving toward his camp. One of the horsemen seemed to be crying.

Mead Overstreet came to the dying campfire. He spoke to Trey, but his eyes went to Sarah and remained with her. "We didn't forget about your horse. We'll bring him to you soon's we finish with him."

Trey thought he recognized Fox just beyond the range of firelight. A man was slumped in the saddle, making a whimpering sound. Trey guessed he was Greasy Bill, the posse's prisoner.

The men disappeared in darkness, moving up the river.

Sarah clutched Trey's arm. "What do you suppose they're fixin' to do?"

The night was pleasant, even a bit warm, but Trey felt a chill that made him shiver all the way down to his feet. "I don't think you'd want me to tell you."

In the distance, he heard a muffled cry, suddenly choked off. Cold, he walked to the campfire. "You reckon we've got any of that coffee left?"

Shortly he saw men straggling back toward town. Most avoided the firelight as if ashamed to be seen. Overstreet and another man returned, leading the bay horse. It was saddled but had no rider.

Overstreet looked at Sarah first. "My compliments, ma'am." He turned to Trey. "We're done with your horse."

"What about the saddle?"

The other posseman said, "Keep it. A man never knows when he may need another saddle."

"That gray horse followed us to town. I figured he was probably stolen."

The posseman replied, "If so, it was someplace else. Greasy Bill was ridin' him when he showed up here. Looks like you've got yourself a new horse to go with the saddle. A man never knows when he may need another horse."

Sarah stared at Overstreet in the dim firelight. "You hanged that fellow."

Overstreet said, "He and his brother did murder."

"But I thought everybody was entitled to have a trial."

"He had one, by the vigilance committee. They found him guilty."

The two men disappeared into darkness. Shuddering, Sarah turned into Trey's arms. But he could offer no warmth against her chill. He was cold himself.

He regretted now that he had brought her here, but he could not tell her so. Acknowledgment of his doubts might make her fearful. He would hide his feelings and hope for the best.

# TWELVE

Sarah had counted the men who went down to the river, and she counted again when they returned. One had not come back. She did not sleep much, for no one had to tell her that a man's life had been choked out of him beyond the camp, and that he remained there, alone in the darkness, suspended from a limb. She spent a cold night, clinging to Trey until the first pale light of dawn. He did not sleep much either. It was the first night since their wedding that they had not made love.

Trey stirred the banked coals of last night's fire and coaxed a new blaze to life, then hung the coffeepot from an iron bar over the flames. It swung back and forth. Sarah shuddered, picturing Greasy Bill swinging the same way after the horse was led from under him.

Trey reached down to stabilize the pot. Sarah turned away, putting a butcher knife to a slab of bacon they had bought in Fort Worth. Her hands trembled, and she lacerated the bacon more than sliced it. She pitched a couple of rough pieces to the dog, whose presence in camp Trey had come to tolerate, more out of resignation than of choice. She found herself thinking of home, wishing she were there.

It had seemed grandly romantic at first, like a heroine in a novel, trailing after the handsome cowboy who had aroused the woman in her. And, from the relative safety of Fort Worth, the idea of pioneering westward had seemed equally grand and romantic. But long, lonesome days on the trail, seeing hardly anyone except her new husband and some gruff, dusty, sunburned teamsters, had sobered her. Each new mile had added to her concern about the sparsely settled land and about herself, forcing her to confront the deep chasm that existed between fancy and fact, between dreams and reality.

Growing up in a small and stable farming community that was no longer part of the frontier, she had been dimly aware that conditions were rougher and law more elemental farther west. But she had not been prepared for what she had witnessed here. She knew Trey's upbringing had been somewhat like her own, though he had been seasoned by a trip up the cattle trail and was better conditioned to accept the violence and rough justice of this mean outpost.

She wondered if she would ever become the strong woman she aspired to be, or if she would shrink back and fall short. She asked herself and found no answer. She hoped Trey did not sense her feeling. She could only try to keep up a brave face and never let him know.

She was glad they would not need to stay in Griffin to replenish their supplies. Kerbow had seen to it that they left Fort Worth with everything they needed. He had said freighting costs made prices higher in Griffin.

As they left camp, the newly risen sun at their backs, she made a strong effort not to look toward the trees. But some morbid compulsion drew her gaze in that direction, and she glimpsed the still form hanging there. She tore her eyes away and leaned against Trey. She avoided looking back at Griffin.

The dog trotted alongside the wagon. It had adopted them—her, anyway. She called it Ulysses, after President Grant.

Trey pointed out that Grant was a Union man. "I guess it's all right to name a dog after a Yankee general, but I wouldn't name a good horse after one."

The trail from Griffin northwestward was less pronounced but easily followed at first. For the present they did not have to recross the Clear Fork, though Kerbow had said its wide meanderings would place it in their path again on their way to his land. Far yonder, beyond sight of Griffin, lay the Double Mountains and the broken edge of the caprock. Past that stretched the high, mysterious plains which only the Comanches and the Kiowas knew well. The military only now had begun to explore and map that region, to search out its secret canyons, its hidden watering places, the sanctuaries to which war-painted raiders until recently had fled after violent forays into the settlements.

To the southwest, according to the crude map Kerbow had drawn, lay silent Fort Phantom Hill, an ill-fated predecessor to Fort Griffin. A teamster had told Sarah and Trey the soldiers hated the forlorn post so much that on the night after its abandonment, several sneaked back and set it afire.

Kerbow's ranch lay to the northwest of Griffin, along a small creek beyond their second crossing of the Clear Fork. Trey kept referring to the map, watching for scanty landmarks in the pitch and roll of a sandy terrain broken at intervals by timbered creeks, draws and dry washes. He could only guess at the miles. He left the main trail and followed the wanderings of a much weaker one, losing it a couple of times. He saddled the bay horse and rode in wide circles to avoid having to take the wagon over the bumpy ground in his search. The afternoon of the second day, he reread Kerbow's scribbled notes for the twentieth time and studied the shape of a rise to the northwest. To people who knew mountains, this would be only a modest hill. To

Sarah, having grown up in the gently rolling country north of Fort Worth, it was a mountain.

Trey said, "That looks like what Mr. Kerbow described. We're almost home."

Sarah took some relief from the thought that the grinding wagon trip was nearly over, yet she was apprehensive. As they had traveled, she had been able to hold on, at least tentatively, to some wishful fantasies about what awaited them. Shortly she would have to confront the realities, whatever they were.

They had passed only a couple of settlers' houses since leaving those clustered near Fort Griffin. She could only guess how far it might be to her nearest neighbor.

Three cows appeared to one side of the dim wagon trace, two followed by spotted calves. Trey squinted, trying to read their brands. The dog, which had trotted in the shade of the wagon during the heat of the day, moved out to investigate the cattle. Trey called roughly to him.

"Useless! You come back here."

"His name is Ulysses," Sarah chided.

"Useless fits him better."

Trey pointed out a K Bar brand on a cow's hip. "That's Mr. Kerbow's. House ought not to be far now."

The calves were not earmarked or branded. They had been born since Kerbow had left here last winter. Trey said that as soon as he and Sarah got settled in, he would take care of that chore.

She saw the top of the stone chimney first as the trail led up a mild, sandy slope. She felt partially reassured, for she had nursed a hidden fear that they would find the house burned or fallen in. In a wild country like this, one could not be sure of anything. She had dreaded the thought that they might have to live out of the wagon until they threw up some kind of rude shelter like the rough picket houses she had seen around Griffin, mud plugging the open spaces between the upright logs that formed the walls. Back home, people had outgrown such pioneer structures and considered them good enough only to shelter livestock, like the hog shed Trey had helped Papa to build.

Trey seemed buoyed by sight of the stone cabin. "There she stands. Bet you were worried that somebody might've burned the place down."

"I knew all along we'd find everything all right."

Her voice sounded hollow. She hoped he would not notice. He appeared so sure of himself that she did not want to shake his confidence.

She felt an initial pang of disappointment in the cabin. It was small, yet it looked solid, built of stones cut to sharp corners and shaped for a tight fit. Kerbow had said some squatter—he did not know who—had raised it before the war and had broken out a small field alongside a spring-fed creek that ran behind the house. Perhaps the first settler had gone off to fight for the Confederacy and had never returned. Perhaps the Indians had gotten him, or their threat had driven him to give up and move away.

During the war, when many fighting-age men left to serve their country, the Indians were quick to recognize the weakness of the remaining defense. They sharply increased their pressure against scattered homesteads and small settlements. Families who remained on the West Texas frontier had often withdrawn into makeshift enclaves for mutual protection in places such as the Hubbard Settlement and the civilian fort known as Davis, east of present Griffin on the Clear Fork. "Forting up," they had called it. From these crude outposts the men ventured forth in armed groups to work their cattle and tend their fields, seeking strength in whatever numbers they could muster.

Some became disheartened and abandoned the frontier. For a time during the war the western fringe of white expansion had retreated eastward. For that time, the Indians prevailed. Now the line pressed westward again, farther than before. Now everyone said the

Indians were no longer a threat, at least here beneath the caprock.

Sarah saw something move, or thought she did, and her fingers dug into Trey's arm.

"What is it?" he demanded.

"There." She pointed. "Only, I don't see it now."

Trey brought the team to a stop and stared for a minute or two. Nothing moved.

"Could've been a coyote," he said. "First thing I've got to do is to build a good high roost for those hens of yours. We'll be lucky if they live long enough to give us a dozen eggs."

Perhaps she had not seen anything. Perhaps it had existed only in her mind, for she was in an unsettled mood that could convert any deep shadow into some kind of booger. Her chill persisted, but she was determined not to let Trey know. She could not have him thinking he had married a timid woman.

Beyond the stone cabin stood a smaller structure built in picket style. She assumed it was a bunkhouse for whatever hands came to spend the winter with Kerbow and help him work his cow herd.

Trey pulled up short of the cabin. He reached down for his rifle, then climbed over the wheel. "Stay put 'til I look around." He studied the ground warily as he walked up to the wooden door, made of rough one-by-twelve planks. He pushed the door inward and waited a moment, then moved up on the thick stone slab that served as a front step. He leaned forward cautiously, hesitating before he went inside. In a moment he was back in the doorway.

"Wasn't sure what I might find inside—a rattlesnake, or maybe a wolf."

She knew better. He had feared he might find somebody in there, an Indian perhaps, or a fugitive like the one hanged at the edge of Griffin.

He helped her down from the wagon. "House looks all right. Got an iron stove like Mr. Kerbow said."

The dog sniffed at the open door and would have gone inside had

Trey not hollered, "Useless, git back out of there!" It retreated beneath the wagon and sat on its haunches.

Sarah preceded Trey into the cabin. Everything in it was covered by a thin layer of sand and fine dust. The cast-iron stove was smaller than her mother's back home but large enough to cook a decent meal. Against one wall in the single room was a plain handmade table and in one corner a bed large enough for two people if they were fond of each other. On open shelves of plain planks lay a set of tin plates and cups and a few cooking utensils.

Trey said, "Everything we need, looks like."

He sounded more cheerful than she felt. Spartan though the cabin appeared, at least it was better than some picket shack. She said, "It'll do fine. Just needs cleanin' up."

A skillet sat on the stove's flat top. Dried, curled-up leavings of meat were stuck in congealed grease. On the table were an unwashed plate and a bent tin cup, a knife and a fork. Some drifter had used the place but had not expended the effort to clean it up. A poor way to repay hospitality, she thought.

Trey said, "I'll start unloadin' our stuff from the wagon."

"Not yet. I want to give this place a scrubbin' first."

"Right now?"

"The sooner it's clean, the sooner we can move in. Fetch me a bucket of water." She reconsidered the way she had couched the order, sounding too much like her mother. "Please."

She found a broom and swept down the stone walls, knocking loose a couple of dirt-dauber nests. Next she scrubbed the flagstone floor. Somebody had taken pains to cut the flat rocks in such a way that they fitted snugly together. Their once-rough surfaces had been smoothed somewhat by years of treading. Someone had thoughtfully left dry firewood in a box beside the stove. She kindled a blaze and set a pan of water on to heat so she could wash all the tinware before she used it. She mopped even the slab of rock that served as a stepping stone outside the door.

While she was busy at that, Trey watered the horses and staked them on grass. He said he did not want to turn them loose until he had time to give the whole place a good looking over. That was going to be his first priority.

He stood in the doorway and peered into the house, not risking dusty boots upon her wet floor. He looked concerned. "We may have neighbors closer than we thought. I've found tracks."

She felt that chill again. "Indians?"

"No, boot prints. And tracks of a shod horse out at the pens. Somebody's been here lately."

Sarah pondered the significance. Having neighbors might be good news, or it might be the worst. The discomforting image of Fort Griffin flashed into her mind.

Trey said, "I found somethin' else. You'd best come and see."

She did not like the somber look in his eyes. She joined him outside, where clouds were beginning to build, gray and threatening. The dog looked up at her, wagging its tail. Trey pointed to a small stone structure a couple of hundred yards away, at the upper end of a gentle slope. As they neared it, she realized it was a fence made of rocks stacked about three feet high. Inside stood a marble slab.

The even cut of the letters showed that the marker had been carved by a professional stonecutter, possibly in Fort Worth or San Antonio, and brought here for placement. It said: MARTHA KERBOW 1846–1872.

"His wife?"

Trey put his arm around Sarah. "He had his doubts about sendin' you out here. Told me this place had already killed one woman, but he never explained what he meant. Now I guess we know."

"Do you suppose Indians . . ."

"I don't know what to suppose. But I'm startin' to wonder if I did right to bring you here."

She leaned against him. "I told the preacher I took you for better or for worse."

"We didn't figure on the worse comin' so quick. Doesn't this place scare you a little?"

It did, but she did not want to admit it. "I promised to go where you go and stay where you stay. Like Ruth in the Bible."

"Maybe Ruth's husband didn't take her to such a gone-yonder country, way out past the settlements."

"She'd have stayed with him wherever he went."

She heard a distant rumble. Thunder. To the west, the clouds were darkening.

Trey said, "Fixin' to come up a storm. I'll get the wagon under the shed. And the coops. First thing in the mornin', I'm goin' to build a safe roost for those chickens."

"You'd better chop some more wood too, and fetch it into the house while it's still dry. I'll get supper started."

They had been lucky so far. It had not rained on them once during the trip west. Now it wouldn't matter. They had a roof over their heads . . . if it didn't leak.

The cabin looked less formidable since she had scrubbed it out and fetched in their belongings. She had put their own blankets on the bed. She topped them with her star-pattern quilt, the result of many long sessions with needle, thread and scraps of cotton cloth. On the mantle over the fireplace she set a photograph of her mother and father, stiff and stern in their best Sunday go-to-meeting clothes. She hoped that would give her some feeling of home. She wished she had been able to bring her books. She had packed only her Bible. She would miss Sir Walter Scott.

The wind played around the eaves, probing at the small windows, a harbinger of the coming storm. Sarah was kneading dough for biscuits when a strange sound stopped her abruptly. She thought for a moment she heard a woman crying. Nerves tingling, she listened intently. It came again, this time slightly different. Following it to its source, she discovered that the wind had found a cracked windowpane and was moaning through the tiny opening.

She felt foolish. Yet, the grave and the sound reminded her that another woman had once lived in this house, and presumably had died here. It was easy to imagine that something of her spirit remained.

She would not tell Trey. He might take it as a stronger indication that she truly did not belong here. He was her husband, and she belonged with him.

The rain began just at dark. The dog barked persistently, then retreated to the shed where Trey had placed the wagon. Sarah watched the roof, expecting to see water start dripping through. Only one leak developed, just in front of the fireplace. She set a pan on the floor to catch the water. Trey climbed up on a chair to see where the rain was finding its way in.

"First thing in the mornin', I'm goin' to patch that."

They pulled two chairs close together and sat a while holding hands, listening to the rain on the roof, the roll of distant thunder. Sarah managed to push some of her doubts aside and feel reasonably content.

They went to bed tired, but not too tired for lovemaking. The thunder built and the lightning crackled, reaching a peak about the time Sarah and Trey did. The stone walls vibrated with the ferocity of the storm.

The door swung open. Someone stood there, a black silhouette against a blinding flash of lightning.

Sarah screamed.

As quickly as it had opened, the door closed. The figure was gone. Trey jumped from the bed and grabbed a rifle from its pegs over the mantle. He threw the door open and shouted out into the storm. "Who are you?"

The only sound was the thunder and the pounding rain. He called a couple more times, to no avail. Finally he turned, closing the door. He placed the rifle back on its pegs.

"First thing in the mornin', I'm goin' to cut a bar for that door."

He came back to bed and embraced her, for she was trembling.

Sarah remembered the sound of the crying woman. That had been just the wind, but this had been real, for Trey had seen it too. Trey's strong arms held her firmly against his warm body. But the chill remained with her as she lay wide-eyed and sleepless all night. She still saw the figure in the lightning flash long after the storm ebbed away.

With daylight, Trey went outside to look for sign but came back shortly, pausing on the step to wipe mud from his boots. "No sign of a track. Rain washed everything clean. Wonder we didn't hear the dog bark."

"Too much thunder."

The figure had been wearing a hat. Sarah said, "I don't think he was an Indian."

"Probably just somebody lookin' for shelter from the rain. He didn't expect to find anybody here."

"Why did he run away?"

"I'd've run too if you'd screamed like that at *me*."

"I was surprised, that's all, him standin' there. I wasn't really scared." She had been, but Trey might argue for sending her back home if he knew. She did not want to quarrel with him over it. They had not been married long enough for a fight. That would come in due time—it had occasionally with her mother and father—but there was no point in starting sooner than necessary.

Trey had vowed to do so many things first that he had to reconsider his priorities. He decided it did not seem likely to rain again for a while, so the roof could wait. The chickens had been fed in their coops all the way from Fort Worth, so they could tolerate that confinement a little longer. He cut a branch from a cedar tree and shaved it down to proper size with the chopping ax, making a bar to fit within two iron frames the cabin's builder had set between the stones on either side of the door.

"It'd take a batterin' ram to get through when that bar is in place," he declared.

Sarah wondered who would want in that badly, and why. She choked down her doubts and fears so Trey would not know. She had always regarded herself a strong woman, and she was determined that he see her that way.

After breakfast Trey explored some more. He fetched Sarah to show her what he had found, a small rock house protectively built over the bubbling spring which fed the little creek. Barely tall enough for her to stand in, it had been roofed with rough-cut shingles. Hooks set into the cedar rafters were meant for hanging meat. Cool, clear water ran through a trough of stone and mortar.

"Milk cooler," Trey said. "But we've got no milk cow."

"I guess we don't really need one right now. But we will, sooner or later, when nature takes its course."

He said, "You don't reckon it's already happened?"

"It's had plenty of chances." She took his hand.

He looked at her stomach as if he expected to see something already. "Let me know when. I'll find us a milk cow somewhere."

She kissed him on the cheek. "Not yet a while. But we'll keep on trying."

# THIRTEEN

Trey backed off and looked with a critical eye at the chicken pen he had built. Now Sarah could confine her hens at night and perhaps foil nocturnal predators. He had trimmed small tree branches into pickets and spaced them tightly together. He assumed coyotes were likely to be the main threat to his having an egg or two for breakfast. This should turn them back unless they were hungry enough to dig under. It might not thwart a good climber such as a raccoon, but everything which lived in this wild country—animal, fowl or human—had to take its chances.

Inside the pen he had built a crude roost with a modified brush-arbor covering that would provide some protection from the elements. When he had time after meeting more pressing concerns he might build something more substantial, but this would do for now. He did not intend to invest more labor in these clucking, dirt-scratching hens until he was satisfied that they could survive and multiply.

What would a chicken know about fancy fixings, anyway?

He knew the hens were important to Sarah because they were like a little bit of the home she had left behind. They would help her make the adjustment to a new place, a new life.

Kerbow's cattle were Trey's primary concern, beyond getting Sarah comfortably settled in what was to be their home. He rode out in a wide circle, seeing how many he could find bearing the K Bar brand. Kerbow had told him there should be close to two hundred and fifty mother cows. In two days of searching, Trey found fewer than half that many. It stood to reason that some had drifted beyond the range over which he had ridden. There were no fences to hold them back. It also stood to reason that some might have been helped along on their journey by men who had little respect for others' property.

Actually, he was exploring the land as much as searching for cattle. He wanted to learn as quickly as possible the sandy hills and the valleys, the springs and the creeks, the open flats and the timbered draws. Kerbow owned only a few hundred acres on paper, but the unwritten custom of the country gave him free use of many times more until someone established legal claim to specific portions by purchase from the state of Texas. Only relatively small blocks were deeded as yet. No one paid for the use of the rest. This was too far from Austin for officials to come collecting. They would wait for the early squatters to make it safe; then they would venture west and impose their will and the authority of the state upon those intrepid trailblazers who had made settlement possible.

In the main the region was made up of long, rolling hills, most often based on sand but sometimes rocky where outcrops broke through. Broad open grasslands were interspersed by lowlands timbered with elm, hackberry, a scattering of mesquite and cedar. Pecan trees grew tall along many watercourses, and briars were sometimes thick enough that Trey had to pick his way through with care.

Now and then, far to the west, he could dimly see the blue edges of the caprock that marked the broken eastern rim of the great uplift.

The high plains remained largely Comanche and Kiowa country, though determined buffalo hunters had invaded it, eager for the money the shaggy hides would bring. As yet it remained unchallenged by land-seeking settlers. A man might forfeit his life trying to sink a plow point into that prairie sod.

Between here and the caprock, rough breaks marked the transition between the rolling plains of the Brazos River watershed and the plateau that lay beyond. Erosion had carved long, crooked fingers all the way down to red clay and gray-green hardpan. There, cedar and other hardy vegetation clung where soil was deep enough to sustain them, but their hold seemed precarious.

In his searching Trey found many unbranded, slick-eared calves following K Bar mothers. He intended at first to catch and brand each one wherever he found it, but that meant he had to rope them before he could bring them to hand. He soon decided he needed much practice before he could put any faith in the rawhide lariat tied to his saddle. He chased a calf around and around in a circle until it stopped in exhaustion, body humped, its tongue streaming saliva. He felt almost as weary himself, having cast a dozen loops without catching anything except dust.

He realized that the only practical way to brand these calves would be to drive them into a pen and wrestle them down by hand. So he gathered a dozen he came across on his third morning's venture and began pushing them toward the cabin. Though he brought the cows along, even momentary separation set off anxious bawling by mothers and calves.

Some kept trying to turn back. He became so absorbed in not losing any of them, and in picking up a few more he came across, that he did not see the two horsemen until they were almost at his side. Their sudden appearance jolted him. Had they been Indians, he might have been bristling with arrows before he was aware that they had overtaken him.

He made no move toward the rifle beneath his leg.

"Mornin', men," he offered in a tentative voice, hoping they were friendly.

If they were, they hid it well. Trey concentrated his attention on a broad-shouldered, middle-aged man with several days' growth of black whiskers. The rider slouched, shifting his considerable weight to one side of his saddle. Trey suspected that was so he could reach his pistol more easily. Gray eyes pierced Trey with silent accusation. "Where do you think you're takin' them cattle, young feller?" As he spoke, a gold tooth caught the sunlight.

"I'm takin' them in to brand the calves."

"The cows bear Ivan Kerbow's brand. You are not Ivan Kerbow."

"I'm workin' for Mr. Kerbow. He sent me here."

Keen eyes appraised him. Doubt remained strong.

"You got any way to prove that?"

"Got a letter at the house. Mr. Kerbow wrote it to whoever it might concern." He searched the faces for sign of belief.

The second rider had his hand on the butt of a pistol strapped on his hip. He looked like a younger version of the older man; his whiskers were boyishly soft, his face freckled and his body forty or fifty pounds lighter. Trey surmised that he was the older man's son. "Anybody could've wrote a letter. How do we know it's in Mr. Kerbow's hand?"

Trey did not know how to answer that. "All I can do is tell you."

The older man's sun-burnished face creased into a deep frown. "Don't recollect I've seen you around here before."

"We only came a few days ago."

"We?"

"Sarah—my wife—and me."

The gray eyes flickered with surprise. "You brought a woman out here?" The man's stiff shoulders eased, and the sharpness left his voice. "That puts a whole different complexion on the matter. Ain't likely you'd bring a wife if you was here to steal cattle." He glanced at his son, nodding that everything appeared to be all right. "We'll help you drive these critters to the pens." His frown melted into a smile that showed the gold tooth in all its splendor. He extended his hand. "Blackman's my name, George Blackman. Boy with all the freckles is my son Adam."

Relieved but still shaken, Trey gripped each man's hand. "Pleased to meet you. Ain't had time to hunt up my neighbors."

"We heard the cattle bawlin' and decided to hunt *you* up. From time to time we get some reckless folks driftin' through, takin' stock that don't belong to them."

"If I'd been one, what would you do?"

"Take you to Fort Griffin. If you were lucky, you'd stand trial. But they got a vigilance committee over there that ain't famous for patience."

A small chill passed between Trey's shoulder blades. "I saw a samplin'."

"The law is a little loose sometimes. It lets people wiggle out of payin' up. But I never saw a lawyer slick enough to talk one of them outlaws back out of the grave."

Blackman revealed that he knew Ivan Kerbow, but not well, for Kerbow spent no longer here than was necessary to work his calves and gather any long-age steers he judged ready to make the drive to the railroad.

Trey inquired about Kerbow's wife, and the grave. Blackman shook his head. "Happened before I came here. I heard some idle gossip, but I don't give credit to such as that."

The dog came to meet the cattle, barking until Trey rode ahead and scolded him smartly. Sarah moved out onto the stone step, calling the dog to her side. She watched as Trey and the two neighbors pushed the little bunch of cows and calves through an opening and into the pen. Young Adam Blackman stepped down to slide three long, thin logs into place and close the pen opening. The calves could have slipped through but stayed close by their mothers.

The elder Blackman stared across the yard at Sarah. "If we'd

nown about your young lady, we'd've been waitin' here to welcome
ou."

"Somebody was, almost." Swinging down and tying his bay horse
o the fence, Trey told about the visitor who opened the door during
he storm their first night here, then disappeared.

Blackman frowned. "Dodgin' the law, more than likely. There's
enerally a few of them owlhoots camped in the thickets up towards
he caprock."

Sarah stood in front of the cabin, waiting to meet the visitors.
Jneasily Trey asked, "Reckon they're any danger to her?"

Blackman shook his head. "There's some would kill *you* for that
orse and never blink an eye, but they ain't apt to hurt a woman. The
igilance committee would hunt them to the hottest corner of hell,
nd they know it."

"I'm still wonderin' if I ought to've brought her so far out here."

"Aside from the long chance of Indians, I don't think you need to
vorry much about people doin' her harm. But lonesome, now . . . the
onesome out here is a woman's worst enemy."

"*I'm* with her."

"You ain't been married long. Sooner or later she'll get to talkin'
o the walls and wishin' for the company of other women. There ain't
ny, hardly."

"What about *your* wife?"

"The lonesome got too much for her, so I built her a cabin at the
dge of Fort Griffin. Me and Adam, we're batchin' it 'til the country
ettles up more."

Sarah grasped Trey's arm as she greeted the visitors. Blackman
ntroduced himself and his son.

She smiled. "I'm real tickled to find out we've got some neighbors, Mr. Blackman. Be nice now and again to have a woman to talk
o."

Blackman shook his head. "Call me George. I'm right sorry to tell
ou, but as far as I know there ain't another woman within twenty-

thirty miles. Well, there's Katy Rice, but you don't want to know *her*.

"Why not?"

George struggled with the answer. "I can tell you're quality folks and Katy . . . well, she ain't the sort that fits in your kind of company.

Sarah seemed to understand.

"The scarcity of good women is why me and this ill-mannered son of mine are so taken with you. That's not to say we wouldn't be taken with you anyhow. We'd stare at *you* even if there was a whole crowd of women around."

The compliment brought back Sarah's smile. "Don't you-all be in any hurry to leave. I'll fix us some dinner."

"You'd have to chase us away with a stick, ma'am. We'll help your husband with the brandin'."

In anticipation of the need, Trey had stacked a pile of dead timber in a corner of the pen. He built a fire and fetched a set of blacksmith-hammered irons he had found stored beneath the shed. He placed the stamp ends atop the burning wood to heat. He had helped brand some cattle back home, though livestock had been less important to the McLean family than cotton or corn.

Adam Blackman said, "The big outfits rope the calves and drag them to the irons. It's a lot more fun that way."

His father replied, "Ain't supposed to be fun. It's supposed to be toil and travail. The Book says you earn your bread by the sweat of your brow." He silently counted the sixteen calves. "You young fellers can grab them and wrestle them down."

Trey said, "I tried ropin'. I couldn't catch anything."

"What I know, I learned from some Mexican hands. They been ropin' since the Creation, almost. I'll try and teach you a couple of loops."

The irons gradually turned red. Adam Blackman walked out among the calves, grappling with one until he threw it to the ground. Trey jumped on with him to hold it down. George found a ragged old piece of canvas beneath the shed and wrapped it around his hand so he could hold the hot iron. It took two, one for the letter K and a straight edge for the bar beneath it. The branding done, he whetted a pocketknife against his leg, then notched the calf's ear with the swallow-fork mark Trey had seen on the Kerbow cows.

The calf's bellowing brought its mother to the defense, lowering her head, tossing her horns in threat. George slapped her across the nose with his hat, and she turned back.

"You got to watch these old heifers," he said. "They can do a man some damage."

Indeed, Trey had already found range cattle to be far less tractable than the farm stock he had known. They had a will of their own and the sharp horns to enforce it.

The branding took a while, for the irons had to be reheated frequently. When the calves all carried the new brand and the young bulls had been converted into steers, George said, "I'd let them stay in the pen 'til after dinner; give the calves a chance to settle down and get a bellyful of milk before you turn them out. They'll forget the rough treatment and be gentler next time you go to work them."

A rough bench stood near the front door with a bucket of water, a tin pan and a bar of lye soap. The men washed their hands and faces and dried on a towel Sarah brought to them.

She had baked a batch of biscuits and fried up venison from a deer Trey had shot. She had made a big pot of beans the day before, expecting them to last through several reheatings. The visitors went through most of the pot at one sitting, along with all the meat and biscuits. Making up for lost time, Trey thought. He remembered his mother commenting once that she had seldom seen a fat bachelor. George was nowhere nearly so fat as Lige Connors, but he was solidly built. He would have pulled down a cotton scale to the two-hundred-pound level or thereabouts.

Trey was comforted by the thought of having friendly neighbors. Moreover, their holdings lay in a southwesterly direction. They should serve as a buffer of sorts against the human flotsam who took refuge in the breaks and canyons beneath the ragged caprock that lay just beyond sight.

Fort Griffin had left a bitter taste in his mouth. These visitors helped sweeten the flavor.

"You-all are welcome here anytime."

Sarah added, "And always figure to stay for dinner."

George's gold tooth gleamed. "You can bet on that."

---

The vastness of the land evoked an awe in Trey, a sense of challenge and unrealized potential. It was so big, so wild . . . Back home, he had been constrained most of the time by the narrow boundaries of the family farm. Here, where he could see for miles, the only constraint was his own occasional question about his adequacy to meet the challenge.

He could almost imagine, though he knew it was not true, that he was the first man other than Indians to skirt along the untracked fringes of the timbered creeks, to break the brooding silence in the long, brushy draws. Aside from the presence of cattle, a white man's innovation, the land bore little sign that it was anything other than what it had forever been, a hunting ground. He frequently watched deer bound away into the protective timber. Occasionally he encountered a few buffalo grazing or lounging in the grass, chewing cud. He might ride for hours without seeing a house, a corral, any tangible mark of the invader's hand.

Now and then he came unexpectedly upon signs of previous tenants: old campgrounds where smoke-blackened stones lay in circles around dead fire pits, where broken and imperfect arrowheads lay discarded, testifying to some past artisan's demanding pride. Turning his ear to the wind, he could imagine he heard the lingering voices of those who so recently had fought with full heart rather than yield to new conquerors. When he allowed his mind to drift in that direction he felt sorrow for them, mitigated by the knowledge that it had always been so.

The Comanche himself had come as an invader, wresting these grounds by force from those who had conquered it earlier. Conquest had been the way of the world, not simply of the West. Hungry invaders enjoyed the spoils for the length of their season, then lost to some new interloper who came with greater strength, a more unyielding hunger.

Those who came to this land now would have the use of it a while, but always they would have to watch over their shoulders, for others would come with needs of their own and want it as much. The soldier dispossessed the Indian and opened the way for the hunter and trapper, to be succeeded by the cattleman, who then gave way to the farmer.

Trey wondered who would come in the wake of the farmer, but he did not dwell long on the question. His concerns were focused on the present. To avoid cutting into Kerbow's cattle herd for meat, he brought home game—venison, squirrels, prairie chickens. When he could make time, he fished in the creek below the cabin. To butcher a beef for him and Sarah alone would be wasteful, for much of the meat would spoil before they could eat it. In more settled areas it was customary for neighbors to pool, taking turns butchering, dividing the beef in portions that would allow full consumption. In time, when there were more neighbors, perhaps such a system could be developed here.

Once he had branded all the calves within a half-day's radius of the cabin, he began venturing farther out. This stretched his days, for often it was dark before he made his way home. Sarah would hang a lighted lantern on a corner of the shed to guide him. To avoid having to drive a handful of cows and calves all the way to the house pens each time, he constructed a couple of hasty brush corrals at strategic points. He carried an iron ring tied to his saddle strings. He could heat it anywhere, clamp it between a pair of sticks and use it to make the K Bar brand. It was less neat than one done with the stamp irons, but those irons were awkward and heavy to carry on horseback.

To many people, a running iron or a blackened cinch ring was regarded with suspicion, for these were common tools of the rustler. Trey began carrying Kerbow's letter of authorization in his shirt pocket as a precaution, should he come upon someone who did not know him.

One day he penned five calves in a brush corral several miles west of the cabin, leaving their bawling mothers outside. While he was in the midst of running a K Bar on the calves' hides with the heated ring, a tall man rode up carrying a rifle across the crook of his arm. He pointed the muzzle at Trey.

"Friend, you raise your hands while I take a look at those cows and calves!"

Trey obeyed quickly, dropping the ring into the sand along with the sticks that held it.

The man rode closer, trying to see the cattle without taking his eyes from Trey. Trey realized this was Mead Overstreet, whom he had first met in Fort Worth and had seen again riding with the posse that chased the Hartley brothers. Overstreet had returned Trey's bay horse after the hanging—and had paid special attention to Sarah.

Overstreet lowered the rifle but left it pointed in Trey's general direction. "Good thing there wasn't none of *my* cows standin' out here bawlin'. That's Kerbow's brand. How come you puttin' it on those calves?"

"I'm workin' for Kerbow." Trey started to reach for the letter in his shirt pocket but stopped abruptly as the rifle's muzzle moved back up. He raised both hands higher. "I've got a letter here."

The man squinted, looking closer at him. "I've seen you. In Griffin a while back, wasn't it? Had a young lady with you."

"My wife, Sarah."

Overstreet lowered the rifle to his lap. The threat drained from his dark eyes. "I remember her . . . and you. Had no idea you-all were comin' out this way."

Trey wiped sweat onto his sleeve and found his hand trembling. He doubted that he could ever get used to people pointing weapons at him. "This is the most suspicious country I've ever been in."

"You the one built this pen?"

"I just threw it up in a hurry. It's not much for pretty, but it's good enough for what I need."

"Been watchin' it for several days. It looked like a rustler job." Overstreet extended his hand as it were an afterthought, as if friendliness was something he had to work at. "Mead Overstreet. My ranch is mostly yonderway." He pointed in a westerly direction, then swung his finger to the south. He claimed a lot of country.

"Trey McLean."

"I suppose you're livin' at Kerbow's place. I'll drop by one day soon and pay my respects to your wife."

Trey remembered what Plunkett had told him about Overstreet sometimes bringing a prostitute out to stay with him a while. "I take it you're not married."

"Never felt the urge. When a man needs a woman he can hire one. Cheaper than a lifetime mortgage and not near as sticky." He made a knowing smile as if sharing a shady joke.

Trey guessed Overstreet to be in his thirties. With men who spent their lives outdoors, facing sun and wind, extremes of heat and cold, age was often hard to judge. He was about the size and general build of the almost forgotten Jarrett Longacre.

Trey said, "Do you know of any women around here that Sarah could get acquainted with?"

"Just Katy Rice." Overstreet's face twisted. "You wouldn't want your wife to associate with Katy. And your wife wouldn't want *you* to associate with her."

George Blackman had mentioned that name. Trey's curiosity was aroused. "Where does Katy Rice live?"

Overstreet's disdain was evident. "One place and another, wherever she wants to. Right now she's somewhere off yonderway, in the breaks." He jerked his thumb northwestward.

"She got a family?"

"Katy changes men to suit her fancy and don't bother haulin' them to a preacher. They're cow thieves, mostly. Sooner or later we'll catch them in the act, and there won't be any more Katy."

Trey remembered what had happened to Greasy Bill Hartley. Overstreet had taken a hand in that. He had a handsome face, in much the same way that Jarrett Longacre did. But Trey saw something in his eyes that made him glad when Overstreet left him.

---

Twice, bawling cattle had drawn the attention of others to Trey. Now that same sound caught Trey's interest as he circled several miles northwest of the cabin. Riding the gray horse he had inherited from the luckless Greasy Bill, he followed it until he came upon a lone rider driving half a dozen cows in an easterly direction. The horseman did not see Trey at first. Trey reined into a stand of hackberry trees and waited for the small procession to reach him. All the cows bore Kerbow's K Bar brand.

The broad, drooping brim of a weathered old hat hid the rider's face. The saddle sported conchas made of silver dollars that hinted at easy money . . . if the proceeds from stealing cattle were easy money. To Trey, rustling looked like hard work, akin to any other phase of the cowboy trade, though perhaps it compensated for its extra risks by paying better . . . while it lasted.

He laid the rifle across the pommel of his saddle, then rode out into plain sight. The rider's hand dropped to a pistol and stopped there, for Trey had the drop.

Trey had almost grown accustomed to confrontations, but most had been aimed against him. It was different this time. "What're you doin' with those Kerbow cows?"

"Where the hell did you come from?" The voice sounded like a woman's. Trey took the rider for a boy not yet full-grown.

"I'm workin' for Mr. Kerbow."

The rider gave him a moment's guarded study. "Well, then, I'm turnin' them over to you. They strayed onto my grass. I was just pushin' them back to where they belong."

That was plausible enough, though Trey suspected it fell short of the whole story. "Where are their calves?"

"I never saw no calves. These are dry cows."

Trey made no claim to being an experienced cattleman, but he could see that some of the cows' teats were slick and clean. They had been suckled, and not long ago. A couple of the udders were stretched with milk. Every so often a cow would look back and bawl.

He decided it was prudent not to voice his suspicion. The shooting in Plunkett's corral was never far from his mind. He had no wish to start one of his own. He rode closer for a better look.

"You're a woman!"

"Been one for years."

The hat and the shadow beneath it had obscured her face, and a loose-fitting shirt had disguised her shape. She wore a man's work trousers made of plain blue ducking. Now that he could see her features, he thought them pleasant enough, though her eyes were not friendly.

He said, "You'd be Katy Rice."

"Now, how is that any of your business?"

"I've heard of you. My name's Trey McLean."

"Never heard of *you.*"

"Only been here about three weeks."

"You want these cows or not?"

"I'll take them off your hands."

Trey expected a lecture about keeping K Bar cattle away from other people's grass, but she seemed eager to be on her way. She demanded, "You got anything else you want to say?"

"Pleased to meet you, is all."

"Damned few people *are.*" She turned away abruptly. Trey watched her while she remained in sight, which was not long. She disappeared into a thicket.

He turned his attention to the cows. One, bawling, started back in the direction from which she had come. Trey circled around to stop her. "Whoa, old sis. Let's don't be overtakin' the lady. She's already in a bad enough mood."

He held the cows a while, then pulled back and let them go. One took the lead and struck a strong walk along the tracks she and the others had just made. The rest strung out behind her. Trey followed at a respectful distance, not wanting to distract the cows from their course. He had learned that a cow separated from her calf will instinctively try to return to the place she left it.

He put the rifle back into its scabbard. Even if he encountered Katy Rice again, she would recognize the rifle as an empty threat. He could not imagine himself squeezing the trigger against a woman.

After a couple of miles the cow in the lead hastened her step, breaking finally into a trot and bawling. Trey sensed that she was nearing her calf. Somewhere ahead, a calf replied to its mother's call.

In a sandy, brushy draw Trey rode unexpectedly upon a haphazard corral loosely constructed of dry deadfall timber. It was well hidden, visible only when he came within twenty yards. The cows had bunched next to the rough fence. Inside, six bawling calves were imprisoned in a space no more than fifteen feet across. They appeared to be winter calves, old enough for weaning and making their own way.

He realized that was the reason they had been penned here and their mothers driven off. Once they were weaned, it would be safe to put someone else's brand on them, for they would no longer follow K Bar cows.

He remembered something George Blackman had told him: "Once an unbranded calf don't follow its mammy anymore, it's fair game for whoever slaps a brand on it. There's lots of ways to wean one before its time, and a good cow thief knows them all."

*It's a damned wonder Mr. Kerbow has any calves left,* Trey thought.

Several bundles of feed had been placed inside the enclosure to keep the calves from starving. They had barely touched it so far. They would, when they became desperately hungry.

His first thought was to get the calves away from here. But seeing no sign that anyone was around, he decided to put the Kerbow brand on them as quickly as possible to prevent their falling back into the wrong hands. He gathered dry wood, built a small fire and laid the iron ring among the reddening coals. He wrestled down each calf in its turn, tying its feet, then earmarking it, castrating the males and running the K Bar brand. When he was done, he dropped the ring into the sand to cool. He threw back the branches that barred the opening, letting the calves out to rejoin their mothers. As an afterthought he built up the fire and kicked the coals against the fence in several places. The deadfall timber smoked, then burst into flame.

To himself he declared, "There won't anybody pen K Bar calves here again, not without they put out some sweat rebuildin' the corral."

He had sweated some himself, partly from exertion, partly from apprehension that someone might ride in on him. It seemed improbable that Katy Rice was working without an accomplice or two. Now that the cattle had paired up, he pushed them eastward in the direction of their home range. He thought it likely that the smoke would bring the woman to investigate. He frequently looked over his shoulder as he trailed the reunited pairs, but he saw no sign of her.

It was for the best, he thought. He didn't see that they had much to talk about.

# FOURTEEN

Katy Rice appeared suddenly out of the timber, so close Trey could almost have touched her. A black-whiskered man rode alongside. Caught off guard, Trey jerked the gray horse to a sudden stop. At first she glared at him, but the harsh expression softened as she looked at the calves, safely carrying the K Bar brand and plodding along with their mothers. She shrugged in resignation, like a poker player who has found himself outbluffed.

She said, "Smart son of a bitch, ain't you?"

"If I was, I wouldn't've let you slip up on me this way."

She wore a big pistol on her hip—it looked like a Navy Colt.

Her companion held a six-shooter, however, and his black eyes carried a heavy threat. Trey was startled to recognize Jonas Hartley. This was the murderer who had stolen the bay horse east of Griffin, then had abandoned his brother to the posse that pursued them.

Hartley declared, "I know you. And I know that horse you're ridin'. He belonged to Ol' Bill."

"He left him when he took my bay."

"Damned poor trade, it was. That bay couldn't outrun a three-legged turtle." He looked at Katy Rice. "I say we shoot him and take back these calves."

"They've got a brand now. You want to get caught with them?"

"At least we ought to take Bill's gray and let this horse thief walk home."

She pointed westward. "Shut up, Jonas. Go back yonder a ways and wait on me."

Hartley's dark eyes crackled, but she spoke with an authority too strong to defy. He started to rein his horse around, then looked back accusingly at Trey. "Was you with the mob that hung poor Ol' Bill?"

"I wasn't there."

He considered adding, *Neither were you. You ran away*. But better judgment prevailed. Hartley still held the pistol.

Katy watched Hartley ride away. "So you're workin' for Ivan Kerbow."

"You know him?"

"I know him."

"I'm also workin' for myself. I'm drawin' a percentage."

"Slow pickin', ain't it? Like pullin' bolls in somebody else's cotton patch."

"I've got plenty of time."

"Nobody ever knows how much time he's got. The sand may be runnin' through the glass faster than you think."

"I never expected to get rich quick."

"Doesn't have to take a lifetime. How long 'til Kerbow comes back?"

"This fall, when the trailin' season is over."

"I'll bet he don't even know how many cows he's got."

"He has a pretty fair idea. Of course, with him bein' away so much, there's been a good many strayed."

She nodded knowingly. "Been some of them helped along. Between now and fall that whole herd could stray all the way to Wyoming or Montana. An ambitious young feller could improve his percentage a whole lot."

She was pressing the conversation in a direction he did not want to go. "It's my job to see that they don't."

"Could be a more dangerous job than you think." She rested her right hand on the Colt. "How long you been off of the farm?"

It still surprised him the way everyone seemed to know. "Long enough to get the cotton lint out of my ears."

"But not so long, I hope, that you won't take a little friendly advice."

She turned her head suddenly. Trey caught the sound of horses. His first thought was that she and Hartley were being reinforced, but Hartley pulled farther away, losing himself in a nearby thicket.

George Blackman and Mead Overstreet rode up. Overstreet rode tall and straight in the saddle. George slouched, hardly a graceful figure. He seemed disturbed, but he was saying nothing, which in itself was enough to give Trey cause for worry.

Overstreet studied Katy Rice with eyes dark and hostile. He had drawn his rifle. "Well, Katy, looks like this boy has caught you in the act."

Trey was close enough now to see that her eyes were hazel in color. Apprehension had risen in them. He said, "She was just bringin' some K Bar stock back to where they belong."

"I'll *bet!*" Irony was strong in Overstreet's voice. "We'll take her to Fort Griffin. You can file charges on her, and that'll be the end of Katy's rustlin'."

Katy's jaw was set in silent defiance.

Trey said, "There wasn't nothin' rustled. She even helped me brand these calves." He wondered at the ease with which he could lie anymore; he owed that to Jarrett Longacre.

Surprise flickered in her eyes, but she covered it quickly.

Overstreet tried to stare Trey down, but Trey held his ground better than he would have expected.

Overstreet growled, "Well, Katy, I thought sure as hell we had you this time. But I *will* catch you one of these days."

She found voice. "You'll have to get up awful early in the mornin'."

"If I have to, I'll stay up all night. Just because you're a woman don't mean your neck can't be stretched." Overstreet roughly shoved his rifle back into its scabbard. "You comin', George?"

"No, I reckon I'll ride along with Trey for a ways." As Overstreet rode off, George muttered, "Didn't care to ride with Mead in the first place. He's damned poor company." Eyes narrowed, he shifted his gaze to Katy. "You ain't picked *your* company too well either, Trey."

Katy said, "Don't worry. I'm fixin' to go home. Mind if I talk to the farm boy alone for a minute, George?"

George grunted. "Best thing about this country is that it's free. I'll be followin' your cows, Trey." He set his horse into a slow walk. *Slow* seemed to fit his style.

Trey found Katy staring at him, puzzled.

He said, "Looks like your friend Hartley ran off and left you. Like he did his brother."

"He's not much for nerve, but you can't fault him for good sense. They'd hang him if they ever got him to Griffin. How come you lied for me?"

"I wouldn't want to see them hang *you.*"

"Nobody's goin' to hang me. Least of all that son of a bitch Overstreet."

"That's probably what Hartley's brother thought."

"George Blackman is all right. Mead, though, he's a four-flusher and a damned sight bigger cow thief than I'll ever be. If the vigilantes *really* wanted to hang somebody, he'd be a good one for them to start on." She looked off in the direction he had taken. "I owe you a favor."

"Best favor you can do me is to leave Mr. Kerbow's cattle alone."

"Fair enough, but I can't speak for anybody else." She slowly worked up to a smile. "You're a nice feller. If your wife ever throws you out of the house, come see me."

"How did you know I'm married?"

"Jonas. He said she screams good and loud."

"That was him we saw in our door the first night?"

"He didn't know there was anybody in Kerbow's cabin. It don't take much to booger him since they hung his brother."

Trey considered. "Sarah's been used to havin' a big family around her. She hasn't talked to a woman since we left Fort Worth. She'd enjoy visitin' with you."

Katy's eyes laughed. "Farm girl, I'll bet, another punkin' roller like you. I doubt that me and her have got anything in common."

"You're a woman."

"There's some would argue with you about that. Take care of yourself, cotton farmer."

She disappeared into the thicket that had swallowed Jonas Hartley. Trey caught up to George and the plodding cow-calf pairs.

He expected rebuke. The rancher said, "Taken all in all, Katy's not a bad-lookin' woman."

"Hard to tell, her dressin' like a man."

"I've seen her when she wanted to look like a woman, and she did. But she ain't as pretty as that girl you've got at home."

Trey sensed that George's imagination was carrying him down a false trail. "I've got no interest in Katy Rice, nor any other woman except Sarah."

"I hope you'll remember that. Katy's turned some good men's heads when she felt like it. How else do you think she's stayed out of jail, or worse?"

"I never thought before about a woman rustlin' cattle."

"Life can be cruel hard on a single woman tryin' to survive out here. She don't find many doors open except to a bedroom."

Trey and George released the cows and calves on the creek below the cabin. By then the animals were more than ready for a drink. They spread out along the bank, dropping their muzzles into the water.

George said, "You'd best keep an eye on these old hussies. They'll drift again." He turned his attention to Sarah, who was working in the garden Trey had plowed and planted for her soon after their arrival. She wore a slat bonnet which extended well forward of her face and shaded her eyes. Nevertheless, she raised her hand to her forehead for better vision against the sun's glare. Even at the distance, Trey thought he could see her smile.

The rancher said, "I wonder if you know how lucky you are."

Defensively Trey replied, "I told you before, I've got no interest in Katy Rice."

"I never said nothin' to the contrary."

"I just didn't want any part in makin' trouble for a woman."

"Katy don't need help from me or you for that. She's always run with a wild bunch. I wouldn't give two bits for her chances of gettin' old. If the law don't kill her, some outlaw will."

Trey cringed.

George continued, "I've got nothin' against her, aside from the fact that I'd bet you a good mule she's slapped her brand on some of my calves. If I wasn't a married man I'd probably be tryin' to get into her bed." His eyes danced as he indulged in a moment of fantasy. "But I *am* married. Anyway, she'd likely shoot me if I tried it. And my wife'd shoot me if she knew I'd thought about it."

Sarah came to the garden fence. Her smile was mostly for Trey, but she shared a bit of it with George. "Get down and rest yourself. I'll be fixin' supper in a little while."

"Much as I'd like to, I'd best be gettin' home and makin' sure Adam don't burn the house down. Boy means well, but he needs a heap of watchin'." He stared at her with open admiration. "The sight of you makes me wish I had the missus out here."

"Why don't you go and fetch her? She and I could visit when we commence to feelin' lonesome."

"I'll proposition her, next time I go to Griffin for coffee and flour." His eyes met Trey's. Trey could not tell whether the look was of playful mischief or was dead serious. "We *did* see another woman today. Get Trey to tell you about Katy Rice."

He put his horse into a gentle trot.

Sarah turned to Trey. "Who is Katy Rice?"

Trey's face reddened. He had not convinced George that his only interest in Katy had been concern about keeping her out of the law's clutches, or the vigilantes'. He told Sarah he had encountered the woman driving Kerbow cows off what she claimed as her share of the range.

Sarah said, "Take me to her place sometime. I'd like to meet her."

"They say she's an outlaw."

"A woman outlaw? I never heard of such a thing."

"Anyway, you wouldn't like the company she keeps." He told her about Jonas Hartley.

"Maybe she just feels sorry for him."

More likely, he thought, Katy kept Hartley around because she needed a man's help in her cattle-stealing operation. But he said, "That's probably it; she's probably got a big heart."

---

The gray horse had been gone for a while before Trey missed it. He had planted a crop of corn in Kerbow's small field, knowing the odds were against him but gambling that fall's first frost would be late enough to allow the crop to mature. He found it necessary to plow out the weeds before they took up the scarce moisture and starved the corn. For three days he had not saddled up to ride out and see after the cattle, so he did not realize the gray was missing until he saw the bay Fox come up to the pens by himself. The two horses had struck up a friendship. Wherever one grazed, the other was usually with it.

Trey's first thought was that a homing instinct might have headed the gray back toward Fort Griffin. But that seemed unlikely; it had made itself at home here, especially since partnering up with Fox.

Sarah was feeding her chickens when he told her of his suspicions. "I think somebody came and stole him." He remembered that Katy Rice had intervened when Jonas Hartley had wanted to take the gray and leave Trey afoot.

"You goin' after him?"

"He's the best horse I've got. He knows more about workin' cattle than I do."

"You might have to fight. You think one horse is worth it?"

He did not relish the idea. If it came to the use of guns, he stood a strong chance of coming out second best. But he had a responsibility. "We can't let people get the notion they can come and take whatever they want. Next time they might steal the rest of the horses. Or all of Mr. Kerbow's cattle."

"What about the law in Fort Griffin?"

Justice as he had seen it administered in Griffin had a deadly finality. And if vigilantes found Katy in Hartley's company, they might dispense double justice on the spot. He did not want to see another man hanging from a tree, much less with a woman beside him.

"Our claim on that gray ain't any too strong if the law mixes in. Like as not, Greasy Bill stole that horse."

"All the more reason to forget about it. Let the rightful owner tangle with the horse thief if he wants that gray bad enough." She threw a handful of maize so hard that the startled hens squawked and fluttered.

In the few weeks of their marriage, Trey and Sarah had not had an argument worthy of the name. He did not want to start now, but he also did not want to give up the horse without making an effort at recovery.

He put his arms around her. "If I don't go, I'll always wonder: Did I hold back because you wanted me to, or because I was afraid?"

Her eyes filled with tears. "Then be careful. It's lonesome enough out here when there's the two of us. There wouldn't be anything left for me if you got yourself killed."

Trey looked back several times as he left the cabin. He wished he had a good excuse for not going, a solid reason that would not dog his conscience and make him question his courage. Sarah was right; if this mission got him killed, she could not stay here by herself. A raw country like this was not kind to any woman, least of all a widow.

He had only a general idea where Katy Rice's place was, somewhere to the northwest in the breaks that approached the ragged edges of the caprock. There he should find Jonas Hartley, unless the outlaw had decided to put this part of the country behind him.

Fear began to chill him as he pushed the bay into a trot. He hoped it might be easier when the cabin was no longer in sight behind him, but it was not. With each mile, he grew colder inside. He wanted to turn back, but he had invested too much pride. He began to hope that when he found Katy's place, Hartley would be gone. That would salvage his self-respect, for he was not skilled enough to track the man down. He would have a valid reason to give up the search.

He did not expect to find the cabin out in the open; Overstreet had indicated that it would be hidden. That seemed logical, given Katy Rice's reputed line of business. If she was allowing Hartley to stay, it was probable she had harbored other fugitives before him. For all Trey knew, several men of Hartley's caliber might be around the place now.

Several false trails led him nowhere, ruts beaten out by cattle or perhaps buffalo, trails he thought might lead to water. It stood to reason that wherever Katy lived, there had to be fresh water.

Eventually he came upon a dim pair of twin tracks that only wagon wheels could have made. Reaching down, he touched his hand to the stock of the rifle.

The cabin appeared as he broke into a small clearing. It was of crude cedar picket construction, like others he had seen in this western edge of settlement. It looked as if it had been thrown up in haste by someone who doubted he would be here long. Trey could not judge its age. Built mostly of natural materials found close at hand, this type of structure began looking old as soon as sun and rain darkened the ax cuts. Once abandoned, it soon would slump back to the ground from which it had come, dissolving with little tangible trace beyond the stones of the fireplace and shards of bluing glass from the small windowpanes.

Beyond the cabin stood a small barn, built in the same manner as the house. In one of the brush corrals he saw the gray horse. The bay perked its ears as the gray nickered.

Jonas Hartley's bearded face bobbed up over the top of a fence, mouth open in surprise. Trey drew the rifle from its scabbard. Hartley disappeared, then reappeared at a gate.

"What you doin' here, boy?"

Trey's throat tightened, and he had trouble bringing out the words. "I came for my horse."

"Ain't no horse here belongs to you."

The gray shoved its head over the fence and nickered again at Fox.

A second figure appeared beside the gate. Katy Rice wore the same plain, dusty working clothes as the other time Trey had seen her. Calves moved behind her in the small corral. Gray woodsmoke lifted above the top of the fence and disappeared against the open sky. She and Hartley had been branding calves. Trey saw no cows. The pair had probably weaned these the way they had tried to wean the K Bars he had found a few days ago. Whomever the mothers might belong to, these calves would belong to Katy Rice when the branding was finished.

Trey's palms sweated. The rifle felt slippery in his hands. "I don't want any trouble. But I came for that gray horse."

"Back away, boy." Hartley's hand was on the butt of a six-shooter holstered against his hip. He shoved aside a waist-level tree branch that served as one of three bars across the gateway. The remaining two bars were at knee and shin level, well below his line of fire if he drew the pistol.

Katy hurried up behind Hartley. She wore the same Navy Colt Trey had seen her carrying before. "Let him have the horse, Jonas. A shootin' would fetch the law out here. One horse ain't worth it."

Sarah had said the same thing.

Hartley scowled. "That was my brother's horse. Took him off of a dead Indian. Ain't nobody havin' that horse but me." He jerked his head. "Clear out of here, boy, if you don't want a bullet in the belly."

Trey's throat felt as if a strong hand held a strangling grip. He had no voice. The only answer he could give was to hold his ground in silence.

He saw murder in Hartley's dark eyes as the man's hand came up with the pistol. Trey whipped the rifle to his shoulder. He saw fire spit from the pistol as he jerked the rifle's trigger.

A blinding flash was followed by a searing pain. His head seemed to explode. The startled horse moved from beneath him. Trey knew he was falling, but he never felt the impact when he struck the ground.

---

He had no idea how long he had been unconscious. His head throbbed as if someone were pounding it with an ax handle. He could see little except a random series of flashes, like lightning in a wild spring storm. Moving his hand, he felt earth beneath him, but his senses told him he was not lying in the sun. Someone had dragged him to the shade.

Something wet trickled down the side of his head. His fingers found a soaked cloth spread across his forehead.

Katy Rice sounded angry. "I was afraid your brains might seep out. But anybody who'd get in a gunfight over one damned horse ain't got many brains to start with."

He knew a moment of panic. "I can't see you."

"You sure you got your eyes open?"

He did, but he saw little except a dazzling light, augmented by intermittent flashes. "I think I'm blind." He heard fear in his voice.

"Jonas's bullet put a new crease in your hair. Probably did somethin' to your eyes. Lucky you ain't deader than a post."

"Where's he at?"

"He's layin' out yonder where he fell."

"Dead?"

"I'd say he's halfway to hell already."

"But how . . ."

"You and him fired at the same time."

"I killed him?"

"You intended to, didn't you? Ain't no sense shootin' at somebody without you mean to kill him."

Trey had never been angry enough at anyone actually to kill. He had toyed with the notion in Lige Connors's case, but he had known he could never bring himself to do it. Now he had killed a man he was not especially mad at; he had just wanted to get his horse back. Despair washed over him.

She misunderstood his reaction. "Don't worry. You'll live. Your sight'll probably come back when the shock wears off."

"I never killed anybody in my life."

"He was just a sneak thief, and not much good a one. It was a question of time 'til he caught a bullet or stretched a rope."

"Then why did you let him stay out here?"

"All he asked for was a place to hide out from the law and the vigilance committee. And I needed some help with my cattle."

"You can't just leave him layin' out there. What're you goin' to do with him?"

"Right now the big question is what I'm goin' to do with *you*. If I don't get you home, people'll start lookin' for you. Reason I picked this place so far from anywhere is that I don't fancy havin' a lot of company."

He could understand that. Visitors might find some freshly branded calves and start wondering where the cows were. There was no telling what else they might find.

She said, "I've got a wagon out yonder. You lay still 'til I come back."

He did not know much else he could do. He tried to raise himself onto his elbows, but his head hurt too much. He gave up the effort. When Katy moved, he saw a vague shape but nothing more. Perhaps she was right; perhaps the sight would come back after a time. But for now he felt helpless as a baby lost in the dark of the piney woods back home in East Texas.

After a time he heard the jingle of trace chains and the rumble of wagon wheels. A bulky shape moved past him. He knew it was a team of horses or mules. Katy's voice called, "Whoa!" and in a moment she knelt beside him. "If you're strong enough, you can sit on the seat with me. If you're not, you'll have to lay in the wagon bed alongside Hartley."

"Where're you takin' him?"

"I got little choice but to haul him to the sheriff in Fort Griffin. Soon's word got out that there was a shootin', the law'd be out here."

The thought of lying beside Hartley's body made Trey's stomach turn over. "I think I'll try sittin' up."

She removed the wet cloth and wrapped a dry bandage around

his head, then took his hands and brought him to his feet. He swayed at first, having trouble standing. She led him to the wagon. He felt for the spring seat and climbed up over the wheel. His head threatened to burst, but he made himself sit. The alternative was too grisly to contemplate.

She climbed up on the other side and put the team into motion.

Trey asked, "What about my horses?"

"I tied them on behind."

"The gray too?"

Her voice was sharp. "Him especially. Last thing I need around here is a horse that there's been a killin' over."

The path was rough, which intensified the pounding in his head. He held to the edge of the seat as nausea threatened his balance. "Hartley's liable to be pretty game time you get him all the way to town."

"He didn't smell too good when he was alive."

She was right about Trey's sight coming back, though improvement was gradual. He began seeing well enough to know that the team was horses, not mules. He looked behind him, trying not to see Hartley's body. Katy had covered it with a tarp. Trey's two horses trotted along peacefully, tied behind just as she had told him.

Aware of her anger, he said, "You can't blame me for this."

"Hell yes I can, you and Jonas both. I told him to leave your damned horse alone, told him he'd cause the law to come pokin' around. Law has never meant nothin' to me but trouble."

"I didn't figure on killin' him."

"You thought you'd just ride in here and he'd let you take that horse, pretty as you please? You're greener than a gourd."

"Nobody knew Hartley was out here except me and you. We could bury him and say nothin'."

"You couldn't keep it a secret. It'd eat on you 'til you had to tell somebody. Best we show our hand right off. If I take him to town, maybe the law'll figure it's not worth the long ride back out here."

Trey hung his head. He was acutely conscious of the body lying behind him. "I'm glad I didn't see him die."

"Don't feel sorry for him. He wasn't worth it." She considered for a moment. "You didn't see nothin' after his bullet nicked you?"

"Nothin'. All I can remember is thinkin' he'd shoot me again and finish me off."

"He would've. Be glad he's dead."

There was no trail worthy of the name, just a faint trace, for little wagon traffic had passed through this sparsely settled section. When Trey's headache showed signs of easing, the rough ground and the frequent jolting brought it back with a vengeance. Little by little, however, his vision began to return. He could see the team with some clarity, though in twin images that he could not quite bring together.

He kept his eyes closed much of the time, hoping that might hasten recovery. He opened them when Katy said in a gritty voice, "Uh-oh! We got company comin'."

Two riders approached rapidly from the direction of his cabin. Not until he recognized George Blackman's voice was he sure who they were. George rode up close, frowning at the bandage wrapped around Trey's head. Mead Overstreet followed.

"Trey! Sarah told us you'd gone after a horse thief. We was afraid we'd find you layin' dead someplace."

"Came awful close."

The blood scent from under the tarp made George's horse snort and draw back. George became aware of Hartley's covered body. He gave Trey a look of disbelief.

Trey blurted, "I didn't want to kill him. I never wanted to kill anybody!"

Overstreet drew his horse up close to Katy Rice. His voice was severe. "What's your part in this?"

She did not answer. Trey said, "I came up on this man a ways west of here, with my horse. Katy heard the shootin'."

Overstreet drew back the tarp to see the dead man's face. "Jonas Hartley!" His voice darkened with threat. "We chased him all over hell. You been protectin' him, haven't you, Katy?"

Katy was defiant. "Hartley? Who the hell is Hartley?"

George was more concerned about the living than the dead. "I sent my boy Adam to Griffin to fetch the law. Probably be sometime tomorrow before it gets here." He dismounted and stepped up to the wagon for a closer look at the dead man.

"I've seen this feller in Griffin. Bad medicine." He gave Trey a long study. "You bit off a big chunk, takin' on a rattlesnake like this. I told Adam to try and bring a preacher along with the sheriff if he could find one. Figured you'd need a Christian burial."

"I don't know myself how I managed. I'm not proud of it."

"A killin' ain't to brag about. But survivin' against the likes of this one ain't no small thing either, not for a farm boy." He nodded at Overstreet and turned toward his horse. "I'll lope on ahead and let Sarah know he's all right. She's half sick, worryin'."

Overstreet cut him off. "I'll go. I expect the young lady'll be mighty relieved."

He galloped away. George frowned. "I'd rather been the one that went." He remounted slowly and stiffly while Katy set the team to moving.

Katy looked back before she said in a low voice, "Thanks. You're a good liar, cotton farmer."

"That's somethin' else I'm not proud of."

"You could've told them you found Hartley at my place, and I'd've been in Dutch up to my ears. That's twice now you've lied for me."

"You've already set yourself up for trouble enough. I didn't want to cause you any more."

"What trouble are you talkin' about?"

"If they ever rounded up your herd, I expect they'd find a lot more calves than cows."

She made a little grunt that might have been meant for a laugh; he was not sure. "You could be right."

The dog's barking brought Sarah running out of the cabin. She lifted her hand to her forehead to shade her eyes against the late-afternoon sun, then hurried toward the wagon, shouting at the dog to hush.

"Trey!" she called. "Trey!"

The flaring of her long skirt startled one of the horses in the team, and it attempted to jump over the wagon tongue. Sarah did not realize the driver was a woman until she heard the female voice scolding her. "Your husband's already been shot. You want him in a wagon wreck to boot?"

As Mead Overstreet had told her, Trey wore a bandage wrapped around his head. He extended his hands toward her.

"Trey, I was never so scared in my life."

The woman said, "You came damned near losin' him. You ought to've kept him here."

"He had his mind made up to go."

"A woman's got ways to keep a man at home. Especially when she's young and good-lookin' like you."

Sarah found strength in Trey's hands and felt reassured.

His voice was deep and troubled. "I killed a man."

She did not allow herself to look in the bed of the wagon. "Mr. Overstreet told me. It's all right."

"It's not all right. A horse ain't worth a man's life."

The woman said, "Been many a thief hung over nothin' more."

Sarah looked at her more closely. This was the Katy Rice she had heard about. The woman's nondescript work clothes covered whatever feminine shape she had. The face, half hidden under the sagging brim of a man's hat, was brown from long days in sun and wind, but the features were pleasant. Sarah could imagine that men might consider Katy moderately pretty, especially if they weren't used to seeing many women. She wondered what Trey thought, then chided herself for even a momentary flirtation with jealousy. After all, she owed Katy Rice at least some gratitude for tending his wound and bringing him home.

Katy moved the wagon up in front of the stone cabin and said, "You-all better help him down, else he's liable to fall."

George Blackman stepped in front of Sarah. Without wasting conversation, he helped Trey negotiate the wheel. Standing on the ground, Trey swayed and reached out to steady himself against the wagon. Sarah threw her arms around him and squeezed him so hard that he groaned.

She asked worriedly, "Do you see me all right?"

He made a weak effort at smiling. "I see two of you. I can't tell for sure which one is real."

Katy said, "Two wives for the price of one. Many an old boy would give all he owns for a bargain like that."

Sarah took Trey's arm. "I'll help you into the house."

"The horses . . ."

George said, "I'll take care of the horses. Then I'll have me a little coffee and be headin' home." He turned to Overstreet, who stood in the open door, a cup in his hand. George said, "I expect you'll be anxious to be gettin' home too, won't you, Mead?"

Overstreet did not answer. His eyes were on Sarah. She had been so grateful for the news he brought that she had hugged him. His arms had been strong, and he had seemed more than willing to offer her the comfort she needed at that moment.

George continued, "Katy'd best stay here with you. Sheriff'll be wantin' to talk to her." He turned to the woman. "I expect you'd rather talk to him here than at your place."

Sarah said, "She'll be welcome to put up with us."

Katy nodded. "Much obliged," then jerked her head in the direction of the shed. "We'd ought to be puttin' this horse thief under cover. Might rain tonight."

The thought of picking up the tarp-covered body and moving it from its place in the wagon bed was unsettling to Sarah. "Move our wagon out and put yours in," she said as she guided Trey to the door.

Trey's expression was bleak. She wondered how much was to be blamed on his wound and how much to his brooding over the death of the man under the tarp.

She said, "It could've been you layin' in the wagon. I'd've cried over you. I don't imagine anybody'll cry over *him.*"

"I already have."

It would take time, she thought, to help him work through the remorse and find peace with himself. "Mopin' about it won't bring him back. And if it did, he'd probably try to shoot you."

After Overstreet had brought the news, she had prepared a pot of coffee to be ready for the men. She placed a cup in Trey's hands. "You'll feel better after you get this down. I'll be startin' supper. You're probably starved half to death."

"Ain't even thought about eatin'."

"Maybe that's part of what's wrong with you."

In a fleeting moment of gallantry, George let Katy Rice enter the cabin ahead of him. "I believe I smell coffee."

"It's been ready for a while. Hope it's not too strong," Sarah said.

"It ain't too strong 'til you have to start cuttin' it with a saw." George poured a cup for Katy. "You've had a nasty job saddled on you today. Maybe this'll bring you back to life."

The woman sipped a little and looked across the cup at Sarah. "My heart'd pump better if you put a little whiskey in this."

"Sorry. We haven't got a bottle in the house."

Katy shook her head. "They say the meek'll inherit the earth someday. I don't think I want to be here."

George said, "Don't worry. It ain't fixin' to happen right away."

Ever since Overstreet had arrived, his eyes had followed Sarah. Now she became aware that they were boring into Katy Rice with an enmity so strong it almost crackled.

George unwrapped the bandage and looked critically at Trey's wound. It was swollen, but the blood had dried. "An eyelash farther in and you'd be layin' out there with that horse thief. Do you see any better?"

"I still see two of you, but you're startin' to pull closer together," Trey said wearily.

"Don't you be frettin' over what you done today. Like as not, you saved the county the expense of a trial. Or at least saved the vigilance committee a night's sleep." George moved to the door, jerking his head at Overstreet. "We'd best be goin', Mead."

Overstreet turned to Sarah. He took both her hands in a solid grip. "I'm glad I was able to bring you good news. If there is ever anything I can do for you . . . anything . . ."

Sarah said, "You mentioned that you have some books. I'm starved for somethin' to read."

"I'll bring them one day soon."

George said impatiently, "You comin', Mead?"

The tone of voice seemed out of character for him, and Sarah sensed that neither man had much liking for the other.

George left, then returned to the open doorway. "When Adam gets here with the sheriff, don't you let him hang around too long. Tell him I got work for him to do."

Katy Rice appeared relieved to see them all go. Sarah said, "George is a good neighbor. But I guess you know that."

"We don't see each other much."

"And Mr. Overstreet was awful kind to lope ahead and let me know about Trey."

The woman's voice hardened. "Kind? Mead Overstreet? I can think of a lot of words for him, but *kind* ain't one of them."

Sarah wondered what that meant but felt it might be imprudent to ask. "Livin' by yourself, you must get fearful lonesome. *I* do, and I've got Trey for company."

"There's worse things than bein' by yourself. I spent a lot of my life with *too many* people around, too much . . ." The woman's face twisted as if the coffee had gone bitter.

Sarah busied herself fixing the supper she had promised Trey. She had prepared the biscuit dough earlier and let it rise. She shoved the pan into the small oven and moved a pot of beans closer to the hot end of the stove. She sliced off several thick strips of bacon and laid them into a heating skillet. "It won't be fancy, but it'll be fillin'."

The woman gave her a thin smile. "I've had fancy, and I've had fillin'. Give me fillin' every time."

Sarah had reserved judgment about Katy Rice. That fleeting smile settled her doubt. In spite of her strangeness, or perhaps because of it, Sarah decided to like her. At least she was company, and there had been painfully little of it around here. At times when Trey was gone she had let herself break down and cry out her homesickness, her desperate feeling of isolation.

She stole glances at the woman, fascinated by her contradictions. People said Katy Rice was a cattle thief. Sarah had pictured her as hard-bitten, evil-eyed, breathing fire and brimstone. Yet she looked like any number of hardworking young farm women Sarah had known. She could have gained that weathered look following a plow and a mule, or working a large garden to feed a family. It challenged Sarah's imagination to picture the womam living up to her outlaw reputation.

She considered her words before she spoke. "You know, I suppose, the stories people tell about you?"

"Some of them are halfway true."

"I don't believe them at all. You could've left Trey out there to fend for himself. You could've pretended you hadn't seen or heard anything."

"Like I told him, you'd sooner or later have searchin' parties huntin' all over my place. I don't want a bunch of lawmen aggravatin' my life."

"Don't you need a man out there to help you?"

"Only now and then, when I got some heavy work to do. How come everybody thinks a woman has got to have a man, anyway? You can't depend on them, you can't trust them. They help you a little, then they think you owe them somethin' extra. They get notions, and first thing you know you've got to run them off like an egg-suckin' hound."

"You have a poor opinion of men."

"You would too if you'd seen as many as I have, and from *where* I have."

"What do you mean?"

"You know what a crib is?"

"Somethin' to put a baby in."

The woman gave her a look of mild exasperation. "You're as green as that husband of yours. Maybe I'll tell you sometime, when you're older."

Sarah invited her to spend the night in the cabin. She figured

Trey was too ill for lovemaking, so privacy was little issue. But Katy declined the offer. "The bunkhouse'll do fine for me. It's close to the shed, so I can hear if the wolves catch scent of that horse thief."

"The dog'll set up a racket if wolves go to prowlin'."

"I got little more trust in dogs than I have in men."

Sarah watched Katy carry her blanket roll into the picket bunkhouse. The thought of her spending the night close to the corpse of Jonas Hartley made her squeamish, but it seemed not to bother Katy. Sarah could only imagine what worse experiences she had endured.

The woman had met her concern with perverse amusement. "Dead men can't hurt you. It's the live ones you got to worry about. I'll bet Mead Overstreet was glad to offer you comfort."

"He was real nice."

"And handsome too?"

"I never thought of him quite like that." She *had* noticed, but it didn't seem a thing for a married woman to talk about.

Katy said, "There was a time I thought he was handsome too, and sweeter than honey. But if you go to harvest the bee tree, you'd better figure on gettin' stung."

Sarah could not rest for thinking about Hartley. She lay on her side with her arm across Trey in silent invitation. He squeezed her hand but made no other response. He must still be hurting, for usually it took only the most oblique signal to arouse him. Tonight she would have been more than willing, for she was grateful he was alive, warm and breathing here beside her.

She relived for a while the fear that had gripped her when Trey had ridden away to retrieve his horse. There had been times when she had felt angry at him for bringing her to this far place where she spent most of her days alone. Indeed, for much of the day he rode out she had alternated between anxiety for his safety and resentment for his putting their future in jeopardy. She visualized how barren life would suddenly have become if something had happened to him, how desperately more lonely than it already was. She moved his hand to her breast and pressed it there. He was still awake. She asked, "Are you still hurtin'?"

"Feels like somebody clubbin' me with a singletree."

Gently she rubbed her hand over his forehead. The bandage was gone and the wound cleaned, but she could feel that there had been some swelling. "I wish I could make it better."

He squeezed her fingers. "You have."

She knew some of his pain had nothing to do with the wound, and nothing she could do would help that pain much. She was silent a long time, clasping his hand. From his breathing, she knew he was not asleep.

She asked, "What do you think about Katy Rice?"

"She did me a good turn. But she's a cattle rustler."

"She's kind of pretty, though. Isn't she?"

"For an older woman."

"She's not much older than you are. Maybe no older at all."

"She's done a lot more livin'. You can see it in her eyes."

Obviously Trey had looked at her eyes. The thought bothered Sarah a little. "I've heard that some men are drawn to women who seem a little bit dangerous."

"I'd as soon hold a lightnin' rod in my hand and walk out in a thunderstorm. I'm glad there's nothin' dangerous about you."

"There *could* be." She kissed him but received little reaction. She waited a while, then turned onto her other side.

⊱—o—⊰

The dog's barking alerted Sarah to the approach of three horsemen a midmorning. She walked onto the stone slab that served as a fron step and called back to Katy Rice in the kitchen. "I see Adam Blackman. Must be the sheriff with him."

Katy joined her. "I can't remember a time when a John Law meant good news to me."

Trey walked out from the horse pen to meet the visitors. He was bareheaded—the swollen wound made it too painful for him to wear a hat—and Sarah joined him, sympathetically placing her arm around his waist. Katy remained on the step, watching.

To Trey, Sarah said, "I hope you're not goin' to tell the sheriff anything that'd get Katy in trouble."

"And maybe sic the vigilance committee onto her? I'm here to mind Mr. Kerbow's business, and ours, but nobody else's."

Adam Blackman spurred ahead. Grinning, he stepped down and grasped Trey's hand. "I'm tickled to see you standin' on your own two feet. We brought a preacher. Figured we'd come for a buryin'."

Trey's voice was solemn. "You have, but not mine."

Sarah recognized the man wearing a star on his shirt. He had led the posse pursuing the fugitive Hartley brothers just before she and Trey reached Fort Griffin. She had not seen him with the group who hanged Greasy Bill, but she figured it would have been improper for a duly commissioned officer to be a party to such an extralegal event. The third rider had to be the minister.

The sheriff gave a moment's surprised attention to Katy Rice, standing beside the cabin. He dismounted in front of Trey and said, "I see you got your horse back." The gray stretched its neck across the top of the corral fence and pointed its ears toward the newly arrived horses. "Any trouble?"

Trey touched his hand to the side of his head. "Some. Come with me and I'll show you."

The sheriff handed his reins to Adam. He and the minister followed Trey to the shed which sheltered the woman's wagon. Sarah held back.

Trey lifted the tarp but turned his head so he did not have to look beneath it. The sheriff recoiled. "How the hell did you ever get the drop on Jonas Hartley?"

"I didn't. You could call it a draw, except I was a little luckier."

The sheriff walked back to Katy. "What did you have to do with all this?"

Trey answered for her. "She heard the shootin'. She's the one brought me home."

The sheriff still looked at Katy, not at Trey. "And where'd this take place?"

Trey said, "A ways northwest of here."

The sheriff demanded, "That how it happened, Katy?"

She nodded dully. "There's nothin' else I can tell you."

The sheriff's expression indicated that he was not convinced. "Main thing is that Hartley's dead. I won't have to hang him. You can be proud of yourself."

"I'm not. I wish I'd let him keep the horse."

"Think of it like killin' a snake, except that a snake has an excuse. It just does what nature meant it to."

Katy said, "I guess you'll want my wagon to take the dead man to town."

"He's fixin' to get a little ripe. We'll haul him out yonder someplace and bury him. I expect he's already half roasted by now." He looked at the minister. "Not even a deep-water Baptist can pull him back out of Lucifer's clutches."

Adam pointed toward the little rock enclosure where Kerbow's wife was buried. "There's a graveyard up yonder."

The sheriff shook his head. "That's holy ground. We wouldn't want to contaminate it." He turned to Trey. "If we can borrow a shovel, we'll take him down the creek a ways, out of sight."

Sarah said, "Time you-all get back, I'll have dinner fixed."

The sheriff glanced at Katy. "You care to come along and see him buried?"

"He don't mean nothin' to me."

The sheriff and Adam rode their horses while Trey hunched beside the minister on the wagon seat. Sarah knew he had rather take a beating than go, but he felt responsible for seeing Hartley put away.

Katy said, "I doubt they'll be long. The sheriff'll find a place where the diggin' is soft. I'll help you with dinner."

The sheriff and the minister did not tarry long after putting away a generous feed. Burying Hartley had no more adverse effect upon their appetites than if they had ridden out here to deliver the mail. Adam headed west, obeying the instructions his father had left for him to come home.

Sarah asked Trey, "Did you-all put up any kind of stone?"

Trey's mood was dark. "I'll fix one. But I won't need any marker to remember where that grave is at."

Katy looked southeastward, where the two horsemen were fading from sight. "Now that the law's finished with us, I can tell you how it really was."

Trey blinked. "How it was?"

"You missed Jonas Hartley. I had to shoot him myself."

Trey stood immobile as a fence post. "I didn't kill him?"

"You were layin' on the ground, knocked out cold. He was fixin' to finish you off. I begged him not to, but he was bound and determined. So I shot the son of a bitch."

Trey seemed to have fallen into a trance. Sarah demanded, "Why did you let him think he'd done it? Why didn't you tell us before?"

"The sheriff would've figured out that I was helpin' Hartley stay clear of the law. He probably suspects it anyway, but he's got no proof. It makes him happy to think Trey did the killin', and I like to see a sheriff happy as long as it's not costin' me nothin'."

Trey burst out laughing, a wild laugh born of relief, not of humor. Sarah sensed that he could as easily have cried. She put her arms around him.

A troublesome thought intruded. She said, "What if Hartley had friends that might take it in their heads to get even?"

Katy dismissed the notion. "He wasn't the kind that had many friends. Even Greasy Bill wouldn't've put up with him if they hadn't been brothers." She gave Trey a thoughtful study. "If you'll think about it, you'll see I done you *two* favors. From now on you've got a reputation. Thieves'll think hard before they bother anything that belongs to you and Kerbow."

Sarah asked, "Do you know Mr. Kerbow?"

"I know him, a little."

"Did you know Mrs. Kerbow?"

"Her too."

"He never told Trey what happened to her."

"He'll tell you, if he wants you to know."

Katy walked to her wagon, where the team was still hitched and waiting. Sarah hurried to catch up. "Katy, wait."

Katy untied the reins from the brake and climbed up onto the seat. "I got things to do."

"Thank you for savin' my husband."

"I couldn't let him get killed on my place. There'd've been no end to the trouble."

"Is that all it was?"

The woman gave her a thin smile. "You've got a decent man there. See that you take care of him."

"I do the best I can."

"Too bad Martha Kerbow couldn't do the same for her man." She raised the reins to start the team, then lowered them. "Do you know how to shoot?"

Puzzled, Sarah said, "I'm a pretty good shot."

"Any time Mead Overstreet comes to your house, make sure you stay close to a gun." Katy clucked at the team and moved away with the wagon.

Sarah returned to Trey. "You goin' to be all right?"

This time he did not pull away when she put her arm around

him. He raised a hand to his head. "All of a sudden I'm not hurtin' much anymore. And I'm seein' better."

She hugged him as if he had just returned from a long journey. "You still need a lot of rest. Come on in the house. We can rest together."

# SIXTEEN

Trey was not in a cheerful mood. He was spattered with mud, one britches leg ripped by the horn of a cow that had no gratitude after he had pulled her struggling calf from the unforgiving embrace of a bog hole. In the late afternoon, he rode to the cabin and saw Sarah standing on the front step, looking apprehensive.

Instead of first riding to the corral to unsaddle the gray horse, his usual routine, Trey rode directly to her. "Somethin' the matter?"

She looked off toward a low hill that bowed the horizon line to the northeast. "This place can get scary sometimes when you're not here." She pointed. "There's a man out yonder. Been there for maybe two hours. He doesn't come any closer. Just stays out there and watches the house."

Trey squinted, trying to see. It had taken a week for his vision to return to normal. The man stood at the edge of a mixed-brush motte, holding his horse.

Sarah asked, "Reckon he's an Indian?"

"Looks to me like he's got a hat on. May be some friend of Katy

Rice's, huntin' a place where the law won't bother him. He might not know just how to find Katy's." He started to remount. "Maybe I ought to go out there and talk to him."

She took his hand. "No, don't. He might be a friend of Hartley's, come for revenge. I've got a loaded rifle standin' just inside the door."

That told him how uneasy she really had been. "I doubt anybody thought that much of him."

By the time Trey turned the gray loose and placed his saddle on a rack beneath the shed, the watching man was riding in on a black horse. Trey drew his saddle gun from its scabbard and carried it toward the cabin. He had to force himself to walk slowly. He did not want the visitor to think he was afraid, though he was, a little. He turned in the doorway and leaned against the jamb, the saddle gun in his hand. Sarah retreated inside, picking up the rifle.

Trey sensed something familiar in the way the horseman held himself, the way he sat in the saddle. With recognition he said sourly, "It's Gault!"

Though the weather was warm, bordering on hot, Gault wore a long black coat.

Sarah said, "He looks like a preacher. Or an undertaker."

"He's an undertaker's friend."

The man drew rein twenty feet from the door and stared morosely at Trey. For any other visitor, Trey would have extended an invitation to get down and visit a spell. For Gault he had nothing to say. The silence stood solid as a wall until Gault spoke.

"You're hard to find, Mr. McLean. Even the good Lord has probably lost track of you."

"If I'd known you were huntin' me I'd've put up signs."

Gault slowly swung down from the horse. He held his arm and shoulder stiffly, a result of the bullet Jarrett Longacre had put in him. "You're climbing in the world. The first time I saw you, you were swamping out a stable."

"It was honest work. So is this."

"Maybe you never were quite the innocent swamper you were made out to be. I hear in Griffin that you've acquired a reputation as a man-killer. What did you do, hit him with a gate?"

*He knows.* The thought gave Trey a chill.

"What do you want here, Gault?" He did not even use the *Mr.* that he gave most other men.

"Who do you have inside?"

"Just my wife. There's nobody else here."

Gault dropped the reins. His horse stood still as if tethered. The man strode up to the front step, eyes fixed sternly, brushed past Trey and entered the cabin. He stared a moment at the startled Sarah. "You can put the rifle down, young lady. I'm not here for your husband. Not today, at least."

Trey demanded, "What *are* you here for?"

Gault looked around the room as if he suspected that someone might be hiding beneath the bed or behind the stove. "How long has it been since you saw your friend Longacre?"

"Last time was at Ellsworth, when we delivered Mr. Kerbow's herd. If you want him, I reckon you'll have to go to Kansas."

"He seems to have worn out his welcome up there. The authorities are offering a substantial reward for his capture, or for proof that he is dead. I believe they would prefer the latter."

"And so would you, I expect."

"Do you fault me?" Gault raised his crippled arm as far as it would go. "I would like nothing better than to see him laid out on a board with pennies on his eyes. I would gladly furnish the pennies."

"What did he do in Kansas?"

"Three cowboys held up a bank. There was some shooting, and a teller was badly wounded."

Three cowboys. Trey's skin prickled. Jarrett, Scooter Willis and the boy nicknamed How John had remained behind in Ellsworth. "What makes them think it was Jarrett Longacre?"

"Someone knew him by sight. He has a way of being remembered wherever he goes." Gault touched his bad arm.

"Why would he come here?"

"This part of the country is a well-known haven for fugitives. It is my understanding that this place belongs to Kerbow. It seems logical that Longacre would know where it is, and you are a friend of his."

"He'd have no way of knowin' I'm here."

"If you're hiding him somewhere, I'll find him." He turned to Sarah. "You look like a God-fearing young lady who would not bear false witness. Have you seen Jarrett Longacre?"

Sarah had watched and listened with her mouth open in confusion. "I never knew any Jarrett Longacre."

Sternly Trey said, "Leave her alone. She doesn't know what you're talkin' about."

Gault cut his gaze back to Trey. "But you do. If Longacre isn't already here he'll *be* here, and I'll get him. I would advise you not to interfere. I am sure the Lord would not want this young lady to find herself a widow." He backed toward the door.

Resentfully Trey said, "For a man who makes his livin' with a gun, you talk a lot about what the Lord wants."

"I was for a time a man of the cloth. I carried God's message to those who knew Him not. But I found that many of those who needed it most would not listen. The only way I could bring them to Jesus was to smite them hip and thigh."

He moved outside and paused beside his horse, his eyes fixed firmly on Trey as if to reinforce his message. He mounted and rode away in a slow walk.

*Giving me time for a change of heart,* Trey thought.

Sarah laid down her rifle. She clenched her fists in anxiety. "Who is that man? And what has any of this got to do with you?"

He had never told her about Longacre or the incident in Plunkett's wagonyard. At first he had feared trouble with the law. Later he had seen no reason to awaken an unpleasant subject that had finally seemed at rest. Watching Gault move off into the distance, he knew it was time to tell her.

She listened, nodding gravely. "I remember the way that man looked at us in Fort Worth. He gave me a chill."

"He meant for it to. He knew what I did to him."

"You were tryin' to keep him from murderin' your friend."

"To him it wasn't murder. It would've been an execution, like that vigilance committee in Fort Griffin."

She cringed at the memory of the hanging. "It was your friend that robbed Dutch Max's store, wasn't it?"

"I didn't know he was fixin' to do it."

"So he rode off and left you to face the law all by yourself. Some friend."

"He told me I'd better run with him, but that would've made me a part of it. So I stayed and took my chances."

"You never told us about that."

"Would you have believed me then? Your mother had me figured for an outlaw. You would've too, more than likely."

"I always thought you had an honest face."

"You need one when you have to lie your way out of trouble."

"Doesn't sound to me like your friend was worth lyin' for."

"I wasn't lyin' for him. I was lyin' for me."

---

Gault did not reappear, but over the following days Trey had an eerie sense of the man's presence, of being observed wherever he rode. He realized the feeling probably grew out of an overactive imagination, but it haunted him nevertheless. He found himself watching for the lawman, expecting to see him hiding in the edge of every motte, behind every hill. The sight of a coyote slinking through the curing tall grass made Trey turn quickly in the saddle. A hawk suddenly flapping its wings and rising up from its nest startled him into reaching for the saddle gun. The hawk made a keening cry, attempting to draw him away from her young.

If Gault was trying to worry him half to death, he was succeeding. He was probably biding his time in Fort Griffin, taking advantage of whatever comforts that frontier village offered while he waited for some indication that Longacre was in the country. But Trey could not help imagining that the man stalked him like some dark gray wolf.

*Damn you, Gault,* he thought. *And damn you too, Jarrett Longacre.*

He was eventually able to shove Gault to a back corner of his mind and concentrate on his chores: drifting cattle back from the imaginary outside line, hauling in deadfall timber to build up the depleted woodpile, working the field, branding the occasional newly born calves. These summer calves were the hardest to raise because they came at the hottest time of the year when the grass was suffering and cows' milk-producing ability was severely tested. But he had no practical way to fence the bulls away from the cows and control the breeding season. The best he could do was to push the new mothers and their offspring to those places where the forage was best.

To protect against thievery, he put the K Bar brand on baby calves as quickly as he found them. Though Katy Rice had promised to leave the Kerbow cattle alone, this broad expanse between Fort Griffin and the caprock was home to independent-minded operators who swung a wide loop and would not give a damn what Katy Rice had said.

Often he did not reach home until after dark, too tired to do more than eat a little supper and kiss Sarah good night. She would be full of the pent-up talk she had saved all day, but he would drift into the deep sleep of exhaustion even while she was speaking to him. Occasionally he would awaken to find her lying with her back turned to him, sobbing quietly.

Dodging rain showers one afternoon, he hazed a cow and her wobbly-legged, newly branded calf toward the creek. He practiced with his rawhide reata, catching their heels, then letting them kick free. He was at last acquiring some mastery of the catch rope. George Blackman had shown him a quick, quiet, wrist-twisting loop he could throw without stirring the cattle unduly, dropping it like a snare in front of their hind feet so that they stepped into it. Trey had found it useful for catching calves on the range without having to drive them several miles to a pen for branding.

The rattling, chain-jingling sound of a vehicle caught his attention. Gault flashed into his mind, but he reasoned that the lawman was unlikely to handicap his mobility by using a wagon or buggy. Recoiling the rawhide rope, Trey left the cow and calf on the bank of the creek and rode toward the noise.

He found George Blackman driving a wagon, slouching on its seat the same way he slouched in a saddle. The load was covered by a tarp spread over hoops to protect it from rain. Tied behind, a milk cow plodded along, her sides bulging, her udder starting to swell. It would not be long before a new calf discovered the world. Trey spurred up, hailing the rancher. "George! You won't make it halfway home before dark. Come on up to the house and stay the night."

The rancher waved his hand. "Figured on it."

"What you want a milk cow for? You won't ever milk her. Your hands don't fit the teats."

"Ain't mine. She's yours. You're goin' to be the one milks her, so when I drop by for one of Sarah's good dinners I can have butter to smear on my biscuits."

"I hope she didn't cost much."

"Dirt cheap. Feller was quittin' the country and wanted to be shed of her. Call it a Christmas gift to you and Sarah."

"It's a long time 'til Christmas."

"The man that thinks ahead is the one that *gets* ahead. Tie on behind and ride up here with me."

George took up a good part of the wagon seat, but he moved over as far as he could to make room.

Trey said, "We'll pay you for the cow."

"I'll take it out in biscuits and butter."

They talked idly of rain and cows and kindred concerns while the wagon bumped along the road. George asked if Trey had ever gotten a good count on the Kerbow cows. Because he had never rounded up the entire herd at one time, Trey's figure was more an educated guess than an actual tally. "There's a pretty good chance I've counted some cows two or three times. Ain't learned to tell most of them apart."

"When you get to the point that you give them names, you've quit bein' a rancher and started bein' a stock farmer." George's face went serious as he broached a new subject. "There's a right smart of talk in town about you shootin' Jonas Hartley. You've got yourself a reputation, son."

Trey grimaced. Reputation! The truth was a heavy burden upon his conscience. He wished he could shed that burden by telling everybody that a woman had killed Jonas Hartley. But for Katy's sake, he couldn't.

George said, "It ain't necessarily a bad thing. It's apt to make the highbinders take roundance on this outfit from now on. There was several people askin' me about you."

"I'll bet one of them was named Gault."

"Preacher-mouthed feller? He was by my place the other day. Questioned me like I was on the witness stand in court. He suspicioned I know somethin' about Jarrett Longacre."

"Do you?"

"I got acquainted when he was here with Kerbow last winter. Likable enough, but no sense of caution." George grinned, remembering. "Him and Mead Overstreet had a hell of a fight. Mead brought a crib girl out to stay with him, and Longacre got to sneakin' over to see her when Mead was gone."

Trey did not want to talk much about Longacre. He suspected George, like Mead Overstreet, might have some connection with the Fort Griffin vigilance committee. Many of the respectable citizens belonged or at least approved the committee's adminstration of justice. If Jarrett *did* come, he faced trouble enough with Gault. He did not need the vigilantes too.

Nearing the cabin, Trey saw a saddled sorrel horse tied to the corral fence. His stomach knotted as he thought of Gault. The lawman had been riding a black horse on his last visit, but there was no reason he might not have an extra mount.

George said something sharp under his breath. "I believe that's Mead Overstreet's horse."

"Good. I thought Gault was here again."

George frowned at him. "You don't know Mead very well."

Trey shook his head. "He brought Sarah some books a while back."

"The better you know him, the less you'll like him."

The dog came to meet the wagon, barking, making the team nervous. Trey shouted, "Useless! Git!" The dog paid no attention. "I'd shoot that fool dog, but Sarah's fond of him. Helps keep her from bein' lonely."

George grunted. "The lonesome can sure eat on a woman out here . . . make her do things she ordinarily wouldn't consider."

"Like what?"

Overstreet came out and stood on the front slab.

George said, "Like lettin' the wrong people into her house."

Trey glanced at him sharply. "You sayin' Mead . . ."

"I ain't sayin' nothin'. Just whisperin' in your ear, is all."

Sarah walked out to meet the wagon. She gave Trey and the rancher a broad smile. Occasional company always brought a shine to her eyes. "Pleased to see you, George. Where'd you find the milk cow?"

He lied jovially, "Runnin' loose on the town section. Looked like she needed a better home."

"Supper'll be on the table time you turn the stock loose."

"Best news I've heard all day."

Overstreet untied his horse and led him to where Sarah stood watching George and Trey unhitch George's team. He tipped his hat. "I thank you for the coffee, Sarah, and the visit. You make this old place sparkle."

She smiled. "I do appreciate the books, Mr. Overstreet."

"Mr. Overstreet was my father. I'm just Mead to you." He nodded at George and Trey. "I'd like to stay, but I'll have to ride hard to be home by dark."

George's voice was flat. "If you'd left an hour ago you wouldn't have to be so tough on your horse."

When the animals were fed, Trey and George trooped to the cabin. Sarah was at the stove, working on their supper. Trey kissed her, though he was a little shy about it in the rancher's presence.

George said, "What did Mead want?"

Sarah dipped strips of venison in flour. "Nothin'. Just said he was close by and stopped for a visit."

The older man's brow wrinkled as he studied her. "Days must get awful long here when Trey leaves you by yourself."

Sarah glanced at Trey. "They can. And yet, sometimes when he's gone it's . . . well, I was tellin' Mr. Overstreet it's almost like there's somebody in the house with me. It's like I can hear somebody breathin', somebody talkin'."

George's eyes narrowed. "Like maybe the ghost of Martha Kerbow? Thing like that'd make my hair stand on end."

"No, it's a friendly feelin', like there's somebody here who understands."

It had not occurred to Trey that she harbored such feelings in silence. "You never told me."

"You'd just say it's my imagination, and I already know that. It's the way the wind plays through a crack in the windowpane."

"First time I go to Griffin I'll see if I can find a glass to fix that with."

"No need. It's like havin' company."

"Sounds crazy to me."

"When I was a little girl I used to imagine I had a playmate. Nobody could see her but me. It was a comfort, because I didn't have another girl my age around."

"You're too grown-up for a make-believe playmate."

"I know it's just the wind. But it feels nice to imagine there is somebody."

George said, "*Imaginary* company can't do her any hurt."

Trey realized George was trying to tell him something without putting it directly into words. If Overstreet had done or said anything untoward, Sarah would surely tell him when the two of them were alone. He would not even have to ask her. But her face was untroubled, her eyes content.

He decided George was exaggerating about Overstreet.

After supper, when the sun was near to setting over the caprock and the day's heat had largely dissipated, Trey dragged two chairs out to the yard. He set them in the long, deep shade of the cabin.

George stuffed a black pipe with tobacco and lighted it, eyes showing pleasure in the first long puffs. "Always admired this place. Wisht I'd seen it before Ivan Kerbow."

Trey nodded. "I wish it was mine."

"You're young. You've got plenty of time to get one of your own, yours and Sarah's. From things I've heard, I gather that this ain't always been a happy place."

"What have you heard?"

"Just gossip." George puffed on his pipe. "Seen Katy Rice?"

"Not lately. Ain't been lookin' for her."

"I'm afraid she'll come to a bad end one of these days. First time somebody really catches her stealin' . . ."

"What would they do to her?"

"Whatever it takes." George took the pipe from his mouth and stared idly at it. "I used to have a little mare, prettiest filly ever I saw. But she was outlaw to the core. Done all I could to break her from pitchin', but she was just as bad the last time I rode her as she was the first. Finally bucked into a fence and broke her leg. I hated to shoot her, but there wasn't nothin' else left."

"Katy's not a horse."

"But she's an outlaw."

George slept in the picket bunkhouse. After an early breakfast, he went out to hitch his team. Sarah prepared a little lunch for him to carry along, for in the slow-moving wagon he would be most of the day in getting home. She took it to him, then leaned against the corral fence to admire the new milk cow and speculate on how long it would be before she freshened.

The rancher said, "Trey, I took it for granted that you know how to milk."

Sarah said, "Anytime he can't, I can. I milked when Papa and the boys were busy in the fields."

Trey was not keen on the prospect of adding that chore to his others.

George smiled at Sarah. "You'll be needin' that cow sooner or later. Just as well be prepared."

Trey rode out in a different direction than yesterday, searching for any new additions to the herd. He watched young calves jump and play while older calves followed their longhorned mothers' example and tended to the business at hand, grazing the summer grass, putting on flesh to stand them through the winter. He found no calves he had not already branded.

A woman's voice shouted from behind him. "Hey, cotton farmer!" Before he turned, Trey knew it was Katy's.

She rode her horse out of a brush thicket. Trey suspected she had hidden there until she was sure who he was. As on the previous times he had seen her, a floppy hat shaded her face, and she wore a man's loose-fitting clothes.

He touched the dusty brim of his hat. "Katy. It's been a spell."

"For a fact. How's Sarah?"

"Fine. Just fine."

"She pregnant yet?"

Trey's face warmed. "Not that she's told me."

"Maybe you're not tryin' hard enough."

Trey struggled for an appropriate reply but found none. "She'd be tickled if you'd come over for a visit. You're the only woman she's seen."

"I'll study on it."

Trey had been stewing about what George had been trying to tell him. He asked her, "How long have you known Mead Overstreet?"

The warmth went out of her hazel eyes. "Why? People been tellin' you stories?"

"He was at our house yesterday when George and I rode in. George didn't say much, but he didn't like it."

"George is a smart feller."

"What can I tell Sarah about Overstreet?"

"That she'd just as well pet a rattlesnake. Ever see a rattlesnake charm a rabbit?"

"Nope."

"In the end, it always bites the rabbit." She leaned toward him, her eyes intense. "You love that girl?"

"More than anything in this world."

"Then hold her tight. And don't let any rattlesnakes in the house."

# SEVENTEEN

Ulysses barked, and a hen squawked in startled response. Sarah lifted the rifle from its pegs and walked outside, her thumb on the hammer. Constant vigilance was the price for keeping her chickens alive. Many predators fancied them, and they had managed to harvest a couple. Trey persisted in calling the dog Useless, for more than once it had noisily stood guard in the open gate and turned back cattle he was trying to pen. But it had taken a proprietary interest in the handful of chickens and made life difficult for anything that tried to get close, even a possum or a rabbit.

At first she saw nothing amiss. The hens were scratching the ground and pecking at whatever they stirred up. But the dog was making the kind of noise that indicated a coyote might be trying a sneak attack.

She saw the horseman and knew he was Gault. The dog went out to meet him, nipping at the heels of the lawman's black horse. Gault rode up near enough that his shadow reached almost to the cabin. "Call off your dog, young lady, before I am forced to shoot him."

Sarah pointed toward the shed. "Ulysses, git!"

The dog responded to either name, Ulysses or Useless, or ignored it, depending upon its attitude at the moment.

Gault said, "I hope you do not intend to use that rifle."

She had almost forgotten she had it in her hands. "I thought you were a coyote."

"I have been accused of worse." He looked around cautiously. "Is your husband here?"

She knew who Gault was looking for. Trey had told her more about Jarrett Longacre than she really wanted to know. "Trey's out seein' after the cattle. There's nobody here but me."

Gault dismounted, holding his stiff arm close to his body. "I prefer to look for myself." He moved toward the cabin.

Ordinarily it would not have mattered, but Gault's manner implied that she was lying. She stepped in front of the door, holding the rifle in both hands. "This is my house, sir."

Trey's angry voice startled her. "Gault! Back away!"

She had not seen him ride into the corrals, but she felt joy at seeing him now. He strode up past the bunkhouse and took a stand at her side. He was not armed, but his determined manner told her the only way Gault could move him would be to shoot him.

Gault declared, "You know I am still looking for Jarrett Longacre."

Firmly Trey replied, "He's not here. For all we know, he's in Canada or Mexico. Nobody's seen him."

"So you say."

"So I say."

Trey stood firm, matching Gault's steely determination. Sarah was surprised and pleased. Experiences of recent weeks had toughened Trey more than she had realized.

Gault surrendered in a silent contest of wills. "I am told a woman named Rice gives aid and comfort to fugitives."

"I wouldn't know about that."

"I have no interest in what she has done in the past. But if she should be hiding Longacre . . ." He left the rest unstated. "Where is her place?"

"Yonderway." Trey made only the vaguest sign.

"Where yonderway?"

"Go find it yourself."

"I will." Remounting, Gault faced Sarah and Trey. "I would like to regard you as a God-fearing, Christian couple. I would be most disappointed if I find out you've lied to me." He reined the horse around the cabin. The dog, emboldened, trotted out to bark the lawman on his way. Sarah started to call it back but reconsidered. Ulysses gave Gault a send-off.

Trey said, "There's some people ought to never be given a badge."

"You think he might hurt Katy?"

"She's handled her share of bad ones. Anyway, Gault's got no reason to do her harm. If Jarrett was anywhere around, he'd come here."

"I hope he never does. Sounds to me like trouble follows him wherever he goes."

"It doesn't follow. He carries it with him like a pocket watch."

She turned to the doorway, for the rifle seemed uncomfortably heavy in her hands. "I didn't know you were back."

"I saw Gault comin' and tried to beat him here. I thought he was Mead Overstreet."

"Why would you hurry for Mr. Overstreet?"

He did not explain. "I've got to go unsaddle my horse."

---

From the front door, she saw two strangers sitting on horseback at the edge of the timber, looking toward the cabin. As a precaution she fetched her rifle down from its pegs and took a stand on the stone slab. The men put their mounts into motion, leading a packhorse.

Northeast was not a normal direction for people coming from Fort Griffin. Most followed the wagon trace, angling up to the Kerbow ranch from the southeast. She suspected these men had purposely avoided the settlement, and that alone was reason enough to be suspicious.

It had been a week since Gault had ridden by here and then on to Katy Rice's. He had returned for another look at the Kerbow place on his way back to town. He claimed he had found the woman's cabin but had not seen her.

Trey had said that was because Katy had seen him first.

The two riders had the look of cowboys. They stopped fifty yards out to study the place again, then proceeded cautiously, one riding a little ahead of the other. He reined up his sorrel horse ten yards short of Sarah. The second rider quit farther out, poised to turn and run. Sarah was not accustomed to people being afraid of her. She lowered the rifle.

The first horseman sat straight in the saddle. He appeared young, probably shy of thirty, though she could only guess what his face would be like without its whiskers and a dark look of distrust. He declared, "Didn't expect to find anybody here, least of all a woman. Who are you?"

She put no welcome into her voice. "I'm Sarah McLean. I'm guessin' you might be Jarrett Longacre."

The distrust deepened. "How would you come to guess that? Somebody been lookin' for me?"

"A man named Gault."

Longacre grimaced. "I figured some owlhoot would've killed him by now."

"He looked healthy enough a few days ago. He seemed awful anxious to see you."

She hoped to discourage Longacre enough that he would ride on to somewhere else . . . somewhere far from here.

Longacre edged his horse closer. "This is Ivan Kerbow's place. How come you here?"

"My husband's Trey McLean. He works for Mr. Kerbow."

"That farmer boy? He didn't have no wife."

"He has now."

A smile slowly overrode Longacre's distrust. "So the punkin' roller got himself married. I suppose you came off of the farm too. Where's he at?"

"Out scoutin' for strays and newborn calves."

The other rider cautiously moved up. He was red-haired, still in his teens, his whiskers soft and uneven. His nervous eyes searched restlessly, as if he expected law officers to jump up from a dozen hiding places.

Longacre said, "This nervous lad is Scooter Willis."

Sarah looked beyond him. "I thought there were supposed to be three of you."

The two riders exchanged quick glances. "There's just us."

"I don't know when Trey'll be back. You-all will want to water your horses before you move on."

Longacre stepped down from the saddle. He appeared tired. "If it's all the same, we'll wait."

"There's no tellin' when Gault may show up. We never know he's comin' 'til he's on the doorstep."

"If he comes, it'll be his own fault. Git down, Scooter, and go water the horses." He handed his reins to the youngster. "You got any coffee, ma'am? We run clean out."

The coffee was left from breakfast and had become strong enough to kill ants, but Longacre sipped it with relish. Sarah could feel his gaze following her as he sat at the table. His attention made her uneasy yet at the same time aroused and pleased some sense of vanity she had suppressed, living out here so far from other people. She had experienced the same feeling when Overstreet visited her.

She said sternly, "You had me worried, sittin' off yonder watchin' the place. You might've been outlaws come to take revenge on my husband."

"Who would want revenge against the farmer?"

"A horse thief was killed a while back. The word's gone around that Trey did it."

Longacre snorted in disbelief. "He wouldn't stomp a centipede, hardly, much less kill a man."

"Folks think he did. That's why I met you with the rifle."

"Can you really shoot that thing?"

"You bet I can."

Longacre's tone turned apologetic. "We didn't mean to scare you, but we didn't expect to find anybody here. At the best we figured you for squatters. At the worst we were afraid we might be fallin' into a den of thieves."

Thieves? In a better mood, Sarah might have laughed at the irony.

Willis stopped in the doorway, repeatedly looking behind him. "Horses been watered. What we fixin' to do now?"

"Unsaddle them. We're stayin' a while."

The boy eyed Sarah with misgivings. "Who's this lady?"

Sarah took pleasure in the fact that he referred to her as *lady*, not *girl*.

"Trey McLean went and got himself married."

Willis did not remove his hat until Longacre prompted him. "Ma'am." He looked up at the ceiling as if he found it strange. She suspected he had not spent much time under a roof lately. His gaunt appearance stirred her to sympathy.

"How long since you-all had anything to eat?"

Longacre replied for both. "We split a prairie chicken for supper last night."

"Then I'll be fixin' you somethin'. Trey wouldn't like to see you leave here on an empty stomach."

"We'd be much obliged. But as to leavin', we been needin' to rest our horses a while."

"With Gault lookin' for you?"

"Hadn't figured on Gault. But life is always throwin' surprises at you. You ride them out the best you can."

The boy went back to turn the horses loose in a pen and feed them. Longacre watched Sarah kneading biscuit dough. "Must've been kind of sudden with you and the farm boy."

She explained that her father had brought Trey to their farm after Dutch Max had accused him of complicity in the robbery of his store. She purposely put a barb into her voice. "That was after you ran off and left him there to face the trouble all by himself."

"I told him he'd better go with me."

"If it hadn't been for Papa, they would've dragged Trey off to jail."

"His choice, not mine. He figured he could talk his way out of it. I reckon he must've, or he wouldn't be here."

"No, he'd be in the penitentiary for somethin' you did."

"Look at the other side. If it hadn't been for that, you and him wouldn't've got together. You'd still be sewin' for your hope chest and wishin' for a man to come along."

She flared. "I never had any shortage of suitors."

"I don't doubt that. But a green farm boy just out of the cotton patch?"

"That farm boy wasn't too green to save your life when Gault tried to shoot you."

Her rebuke silenced him for a minute. "I didn't go to make you mad, and I take back what I said about Trey. I still owe him for that."

"The best way you can pay him is to keep on movin'. You'll bring trouble on him if you stay here."

"I don't go around huntin' for trouble, but every time I look over my shoulder it's gainin' ground."

"Have you ever tried to outrun it?"

"I've never run from anything in my life."

"Maybe you should. Mr. Gault has got a hangman's eyes."

"Our horses are give out. So are we. Anyhow, it'd be poor manners to go without even sayin' howdy to Trey."

"I'd call it bad manners holdin' up Dutch Max's store, or that bank in Kansas."

"We didn't go into that bank to rob it. I asked them for a loan, but they wanted collateral. All I had was my six-shooter. As for your ill-mannered Dutchman, I sent him back his money from up in Kansas."

"What about the bank teller you shot?"

"I paid him by not plumb killin' him. Wasn't no call for him to pull a gun on me."

She marveled at the easy way he justified himself. His reasoning had holes big enough to drive a freight wagon through, but he seemed unaware of them. He probably regarded himself as honest, after his own fashion. She began to understand how Trey had liked him despite his off-center way of looking at the world as an apple tree ripe for picking.

The men ate hungrily, though Willis got up a couple of times and went to the door, eating a biscuit while he scanned the horizon. "I don't like it here, Jarrett."

"It'll grow on you."

Longacre thanked Sarah for the meal. "It's been some days since I've had a shave or a bath. If you'll excuse me, ma'am, I'll be goin' down to the creek. Come on, Scooter. A little water won't melt you either."

Sarah, feeling slightly wicked for it, went to the door once and leaned out cautiously to look toward the creek. The only grown man she had ever seen naked was Trey, and even he was shy about letting her see him that way. She did not see Longacre or Willis. They had discreetly gone where they were screened by timber.

The two came back after the better part of an hour. Both wore clean though wrinkled clothes out of their pack. Gone were Longacre's whiskers, and his face was pleasant. She found herself staring like a schoolgirl with a crush. He was almost as good-looking as Mead Overstreet.

Longacre grinned. "I hope we're not as scary anymore."

"You've improved considerable."

The boy stopped in the door. He looked behind him. "Don't you reckon one of us ought to be keepin' watch? Ain't no tellin' who might come."

"Do that. Go find a place where you can see all around."

Longacre filled his coffee cup from the pot on the stove and sat down at the table. He rolled and lighted a cigarette, spilling some tobacco on the floor without seeming to notice. *Not used to house manners*, Sarah thought. Some woman would have a lot to teach him, if he lived long enough.

She washed the plates and cooking utensils and began putting them away. She was acutely conscious that Longacre's gaze followed her. She suspected he had not been around women much, at least since he had been on the dodge.

He asked, "You ever sit down?"

"Very little durin' the daytime. There's the cookin' and the cleanin'. There's the garden and the chickens. Always somethin' to be done."

"It'll make you old before your time."

"Everybody gets old."

"Not me. There'll be somethin' or somebody get me before my hair ever turns gray."

"You shouldn't say such things. Keep talkin' about somethin' and it's liable to happen. The way you've been livin' . . ."

"Ain't much I'd want to change . . . just a little more time sleepin' in a real bed, eatin' at a real table, havin' a nice woman to talk to."

She saw loneliness in his eyes, hiding behind a forced smile. She could relate easily to that. "If you'd square yourself with the law and settle someplace, you could have those things."

Longacre finished his coffee and went back outside. Shortly she walked to the door, wishing for Trey to come home. She saw Longacre brushing off the sorrel he had been riding. Willis sat on the low milk-house roof with his legs dangling off. Suddenly he pointed and jumped down. He and Longacre quickly caught up their horses and led them into the concealing timber along the creek. Sarah stepped out into the yard to see what had alarmed them. Probably just Trey, she thought.

A horseman approached from the west, ramrod-straight in the saddle. He was not Trey; she could always recognize her husband by the way he sat in the saddle. She knew also that this was not George Blackman, for George had a distinctive way of sitting a little off center, first to one side and then the other. She had always wondered if this posture did not tire his horse by throwing it off balance.

Mead Overstreet reined up, his warm smile showing a fine, even row of white teeth. "Hello, Sarah. Just passin', thought I'd stop."

Sarah tried not to look toward the creek where the fugitives had gone. Normally, any visitor would be welcome, breaking the monotony of her isolation. Overstreet in particular had a charming way about him, an easy smile that always touched a responsive chord. He reminded her of a hero in one of the novels he had brought to her. Secretly she had admitted to herself that he was more handsome than her husband, though on no account would she ever admit that to anybody else.

She just wished he had not come today. But to deny him hospitality might arouse suspicion. She said, "I'm sorry Trey's not here," hoping he would accept the hint and ride on.

"That's too bad," he said, but he did not really seem disappointed. He looped the bridle reins around a post.

She hoped he would not perceive her nervousness. Overstreet had been one of the vigilantes she had seen lead Greasy Bill to his final appointment. At first that had been a troubling contradiction to the pleasant face he always presented to her. But she had become reconciled to the notion that a tough country sometimes demanded tough measures. Most of the men she had known were uncomplicated, easy to figure out. The contrast lent Overstreet an air of mystery that intrigued her.

Because of his tie to the vigilance committee, she feared what he might do if he found out Jarrett Longacre was here.

Before she thought better of it, she said, "I've got some dried-apple cobbler." She knew a moment of near panic before she remembered that she had cleared away the tableware Longacre and Scooter Willis had used. She brought Overstreet a cup of coffee and scooped some cobbler into an extra saucer.

He exhibited the warm smile that always pleased her. "There is no substitute for a woman's hand at the cookstove." He attacked her pie with a gusto that ordinarily would have stirred her pride as a cook had she not been uneasy about the outlaws nearby. She stole a quick glance through the door toward the timber where they had disappeared. They would just have to stay out there a spell.

She became aware of the tobacco Jarrett Longacre had spilled on the floor. She moved her foot to try to push it under the table but realized she would probably only call attention to it.

He talked at first about cattle and rain and the high cost of flour. His gaze was fastened upon her in a way that told her his mind was moving in one direction and his idle words in another. He suddenly switched the subject. "I've been wonderin' about somethin'. Your hair . . ."

"What about my hair?"

"I've never seen it any way but rolled up. I'll bet it's long and pretty when you let it down."

"I roll it up durin' the day to keep it out of my way."

"I'd love to see it down. I'll bet it goes to your waist."

"Almost." She hesitated, wondering about propriety, then unpinned the bun and shook her head to let the hair fall freely.

He said, "That long hair is your glory. You ought to never roll it up again." He stared with eyes that spoke of a hunger which coffee and cobbler would not satisfy. He seemed to look right through her clothes.

This man badly needed a woman of his own, she thought. She tried to direct his attention to something else . . . anything else. She went to the stove. "Would you like me to fix some more coffee? I'll need it for Trey anyhow."

He arose from the table and came up behind her. She felt his arms close around her waist, drawing her back against him. "I don't need any more coffee. You're what I need."

In shock, she was unable at first to move, locked in the strength of his arms. She felt his breath warm on her neck, heard his heavy breathing in her ear. She felt herself melting into confused submission. Heat flashed into her face as he turned her around and leaned down to press his mouth against hers. She trembled in an electric tingle that seemed to run all the way down to her legs.

He kissed her again. She tensed, wanting to push him back or draw away but at the same time *not* wanting to. She could not move her feet. His overpowering embrace threatened to crush her ribs.

"Please," she managed, fighting for breath. "This is wrong."

He did not reply. He held her all the tighter.

"Trey might come back anytime."

"You know he won't. He leaves you by yourself all day. If you were mine, you wouldn't have to listen to voices in a broken windowpane for company. I'd love you the way you need to be loved."

She wanted to pull away from him but was paralyzed by conflicting reactions. He began unbuttoning the top of her dress, exploring inside. Her skin seemed to burn beneath his firm hand. She realized that if she did not stop him now, there might be no stopping for either of them. She managed to twist out of his arms. She pointed toward the door.

"Leave, Mr. Overstreet. Leave now!"

His face was flushed, as Trey's flushed when they made love.

Frustration coarsened his voice. "You don't really want me to go."

"I do. Please, go."

"You were likin' it. I could see it in your eyes."

"I'm a married woman."

"Married to a green farm boy. All he knows about women is what he learned behind a barn."

"He knows enough for me. Now go, before he comes home."

"The color in your face says I've lit a fire in you."

She knew by his eyes that he was toying with the idea of grabbing her again. She edged toward the woodbox and gripped a piece of dry mesquite.

Overstreet shrugged. "I'll go, but you'll wake up at night with that boy layin' there beside you and wonder what it would be like with a real man. I'll let you study and fret over it awhile 'til you're ready to find out."

She backed away to give him room. He picked up his hat where he had dropped it earlier. He paused in the door. "Just keep thinkin' about it."

When he was gone she dropped the chunk of wood on the floor. She fumbled with the buttons on the dress, then slumped at the table and laid her head in her arms.

But even as she cried, she was already wondering. What *would* it have been like if she had not freed herself, if he had taken her as he intended? She tried to force the image away, but it was like a spreading stain that seeped deeply and darkly into the fabric of her mind.

---

Longacre and Willis allowed Overstreet plenty of time to get out of sight. That gave Sarah a chance to regain her composure, at least superficially.

"That was Mead Overstreet, wasn't it?" Longacre asked as he walked into the cabin. The boy remained outside, on watch.

She tried to sound calm. "He's one of our neighbors."

Longacre stared at her. Anger building in his eyes said he was guessing what had happened. "I had a run-in with him when I was workin' here." He looked at her more closely. "You been cryin'."

"No, of course not." She became aware that she had rebuttoned the dress crookedly.

Longacre's fists clenched. "I can still catch up to him." He turned toward the door.

"No, please. Wasn't much happened, not worth bringin' more trouble down on you."

"I wouldn't kill him. I'd just fix him to where he'd never bother a woman ever again. I owe that to Trey."

"I don't want Trey to hear about this. Please, don't tell him anything." She remembered how Trey had gone after the man who stole his gray horse. He would be far more determined to go after a man who had forced himself upon his wife. He might lose, as he would have lost to Jonas Hartley had Katy Rice not intervened.

Longacre was reluctant. "All right, but Overstreet had better not touch you again." He examined the chunk of firewood she had dropped on the floor. "I don't see any blood on this."

"He backed away."

Longacre pitched the mesquite into the woodbox. "Next time, you'd better hit him with it, hard enough to kill him."

# EIGHTEEN

As was her custom on those many days when Trey did not return until long after dark, Sarah had hung a lantern outside the cabin door to help him find his way. He had ridden far today and worked late. The quarter moon yielded pitifully little light. He guided himself mostly by instinct until he saw the lantern's welcome yellow glow and heard Useless bark.

He was hungry. Sarah had probably fixed his supper hours ago and it had long since gone cold. He saw her standing in the cabin door and thought he could not blame her if he found her a little sulky.

She came, carrying the lantern out to the corral to meet him. She appeared agitated. "You've got company," she said.

Trey saw two strange horses in the corral and made a wild guess. "Jarrett Longacre?"

"In the bunkhouse. Him and a cowboy named Scooter."

Trey wondered. "There's supposed to be three of them."

"There's just the two. Sooner you get them away from here, the better for them *and* us."

"Jarrett's a friend of mine."

"Friend enough to die for? It could come to that if Gault finds him here. You'll be lookin' back over your shoulder as long as he stays."

"Been doin' that anyway." He tried to throw her off the subject. "You got anything in there to eat?"

"It'll be ready time you turn your horse loose."

Trey took the lantern. He unsaddled Fox and poured a little grain into a trough. It cost too much to waste. He gave his horses only enough for a bribe so they would willingly come into the corrals when he whistled. They had to depend on grass for most of their sustenance. Perhaps he would make a crop of hay and corn this year if he received enough rain, if the first frost held off until late, if . . . Farming was beset with more *ifs* than five-card stud.

He knew the voice before he turned to see the face. "Howdy, farmer boy. Do you work all night? Seems like you've got more call for a lantern than for a bed."

Hard work had given Trey a crushing grip. His handshake caused Longacre to wince. "Damn it, Trey, I'm glad you didn't have ahold of my neck."

"From what I'm hearin', a bunch of people are lookin' to put a rope around it."

"They ain't come close."

"You know there's a bloodhound on your trail, name of Gault?"

Longacre's voice took on gravel. "He'd better hope he never catches up to me. He'll wish he'd stayed in San Antonio, jailin' drunks."

"He's crippled from that bullet you put in him at Plunkett's wagonyard."

"His fault. He had it in his mind to kill me. I wish I'd finished him when I had the chance."

Trey did not like the tone of voice, but he could understand the feeling behind it. "If it was just me, you'd be welcome to stay as long as you want to. But you've got my wife awful nervous."

"Can't blame her for bein' nervous, spendin' so much time out here all by herself."

"There's a lot of work to be done . . ."

"You never know who or what might show up while you're gone."

"Been a long time since Indians came around, but Gault's been here, and he'll come back. You'd better move on in the mornin'."

"I'm about out of places to run to."

"They wouldn't know you in New Mexico. It's not too far if you strike out over the caprock."

"The Comanches and Kiowas still have a notion the high plains country belongs to them."

"I thought you've got Indian blood in you."

"Not enough, and it's not Comanche. They don't rate other tribes much higher than they rate the white man."

Trey could not see that he was gaining any ground. "Bet you were surprised to find me with a wife."

"Even a blind hog finds an acorn once in a while. If I had your luck, maybe trouble wouldn't dog me all the time."

"The kind of trouble you have, luck ain't no part of."

Scooter Willis came out of the bunkhouse and shook Trey's hand. He had a hangdog look, like a colt whipped over the head with a rope one time too many. He remained a couple of steps behind, his eyes downcast, as Trey and Longacre proceeded to the cabin.

Trey ventured, "I thought How John Fulton was with you."

Willis looked away. Longacre said, "Not anymore."

"Surely you didn't go off and leave him someplace? He's too green to make it on his own."

"Nothin's ever goin' to bother How John again."

The finality of Longacre's tone indicated that this was as much as he wanted to say.

Trey could not remember when he had eaten a meal in a more awkward silence. Sarah puttered around the stove, but her mind seemed somewhere else, far away. A dozen questions hung suspended in the air like smoke on a still evening. They remained unspoken and unanswered, but Trey was acutely aware of them. The others seemed aware too.

His gaze kept returning to the red-haired cowboy slumped in a wooden chair, twisting his hat in his hands, shaping and reshaping the crown. Trey sensed that Scooter was nervous enough to wet his britches, wanting to say something but not feeling free.

At length Longacre said, "Scooter, we've rode a far piece today. Time we crawled into the soogans."

Willis gave Trey a silent look Trey could not quite read. "I want to look around a little first, make sure there ain't somebody out there."

Longacre stood up. "There ain't, but if it'll make you feel better . . ." He gave Sarah a moment's frowning study, then walked out. The sound of his spurs followed him toward the bunkhouse. Willis's eyes were intense as he listened.

Trey said, "Now, Scooter, what about How John?"

The boy was near tears. "Johnny's dead."

Trey felt a tug of sadness, though the news did not surprise him. He had sensed it from Scooter's and Longacre's manner. "Want to tell us what happened?"

The story tumbled out. The youngster's voice gained speed as if he feared Longacre might come back and stop him before he could finish. "It was that holdup. We didn't have no idee Jarrett was goin' to rob that bank. He said he wanted me to go in with him to ask for a loan. Left Johnny outside to hold the horses. Jarrett taken all the money he could see. When the teller pulled a gun out of a drawer, Jarrett shot him.

"There was several people come a-runnin' and shootin'. We didn't know Johnny was hit, not 'til he fell off of his horse a ways from town. Jarrett told me to get him back into the saddle while he taken care of the bunch that was after us. He turned around and charged them, shootin' like a wild man. Scattered them like a covey of quail.

"We never seen any more posse. Johnny died that night. We didn't have nothin' to dig a grave with. Best we could do was pile up brush so the coyotes wouldn't get him."

He cried uncontrollably. Sarah put an arm around him and talked quietly, trying to ease the pain of his remorse.

Trey felt like crying too, remembering the boy he had rescued from the Salt Fork quicksand.

Willis blurted, "I didn't want none of this, and neither did Johnny. All I want is to go home."

Trey asked, "Why don't you?"

"Jarrett's afraid I'll talk too much."

From the doorway came Jarrett's accusing voice. "You've already talked too much."

Trey went to Scooter's defense. "He didn't tell us much we hadn't already heard from Gault. He's lookin' for you and two others. People up there must not know they killed Johnny Fulton."

Longacre's voice softened. "The boy was dumber than dirt but good-hearted. There wasn't no use in them shootin' him."

"There wasn't any use in you holdin' up that bank."

"We was broke. What you supposed to do when you're broke and there ain't no work except holdin' on to a plow handle?"

"Then you hold on to a plow handle."

Trey listened with sadness to the footsteps as the two went together to the bunkhouse. "I ought not to've let Scooter and Johnny stay behind in Ellsworth."

"How could you make them come if they didn't want to?"

"I could've drug them out of there like I drug Johnny out of the quicksand. I could've tied them in a wagon. Now Jarrett's got one boy killed. Scooter's liable to be next."

Her face showed worry, perhaps even fear. He said, "They're my problem, not yours. You've got nothin' to be frettin' about."

He was surprised and pleased by the way she came to him in bed after she blew out the lamp. She made love with an intensity that startled him, as if she feared this might be the last time. But it wouldn't. He figured on this sort of thing lasting at least fifty or sixty years.

Longacre was the first to enter the cabin at daylight. He spoke to Sarah, then to Trey. "Me and Scooter, we had us a long talk. His horse is a good one, but it's about wore out. Reckon you could trade him one of yours?"

"You-all leavin'?" Trey said, hope in his voice.

"Scooter is. He just wants to go home."

"Don't you?"

There was sadness in Longacre's eyes. "I wish to God I could, but they're bound to have paper out on me. There was that scrape in San Antonio, and the one up north. Them folks in Kansas know who I am. Scooter and How John were just 'parties unknown.' Long as Scooter keeps his mouth shut, he'll be all right."

"Do you think he will?"

"He's just a big, awkward kid. Them home folks ain't goin' to turn him in."

"What'll *you* do?"

"I'll let my horse rest a few days while I make up my mind."

"Gault may not give you a few days."

Sarah sacked up some grub, a little flour, a little coffee, a good-sized chunk of bacon, some leftover breakfast biscuits. Trey traded Scooter a black horse Kerbow had left behind. He didn't think Kerbow would mind. Willis's weary, sore-footed mount looked like its equal or better. All it needed was a few days' rest and good grazing.

Trey gave Scooter a little advice. "I'd make a circle around Fort Griffin if I was you. It's a good place to get into trouble."

"I've *been* in trouble. I don't want no more of it."

"Cut in south of Griffin and strike the military road. They say it goes down to Fort Concho, then on to San Antonio. You'll know the way home from there."

Longacre advised, "Keep quiet and there's no reason for anybody to know you ever got mixed up in anything. All anybody knows about you and How John is that you were cowboys. There's cowboys behind every bush."

"What should I say about Johnny?"

"He was an orphan boy. Nobody's apt to ask. If they do, just say that the last time you saw him was in Kansas."

"That'd be a fact." Solemnly Willis stuck out his rough hand. Longacre took it, then Trey did. The boy looked toward Sarah and took off his hat.

Trey watched him set the black horse into a solid trot. He wanted to think Scooter would reach home safely and live a long, quiet life, free of the trouble that had bedeviled him. But the hapless kid was short on judgment and easily led. Chances were that he would fall under the influence of the next Jarrett Longacre who came along and be swept into some ill-conceived adventure that might kill him as the one in Kansas had killed How John.

*At least we've given him a chance,* he thought. *That's all I know how to do.*

Longacre's melancholy look told Trey how much Jarrett wished he could ride south with Scooter. But the cowboy had cut himself away from his home country. It struck Trey that not all punishment required a stay in jail. In its own way, exile was a harsher sentence.

The dog began barking and trotted westward along the wagon trace that led from George Blackman's place. One moment, Longacre was two rows away from Trey, helping him hoe weeds from the corn. The next, he disappeared as if he had dropped into a hole. Even at three hundred yards, Trey recognized the oncoming horseman by his style of riding. He muttered under his breath.

Longacre had gone to his belly, hiding himself amid the green cornstalks that whispered in a gentle wind like schoolgirls sharing secrets. Trey said quietly, "Gault's comin' yonder."

Longacre's voice barely rose above the rustling of the corn. "I doubt he seen me. But if he comes too close, don't get between me and him. I don't want to shoot you by mistake."

"I don't want you shootin' me *or* him. You just stay low. I'll go lie to him."

Perhaps Gault's visit would serve a useful purpose. It should demonstrate to Longacre that remaining here was too risky. If the dilemma were Trey's, he might well head west across the high plains, choosing the Comanches as a lesser hazard.

He walked down to the end of the row rather than cut across and risk breaking down some of the stalks. It was tough enough making a decent crop against the vagaries of weather without damaging it himself. He laid the hoe against the rail fence and climbed over. He wondered how Gault could wear a black coat in this hot weather.

Gault had been riding for the cabin but altered his course, angling toward the field. Trey wiped sweat from his face onto his sleeve. "Back again, are you?" It was an empty question and only marginally civil.

"And for the same purpose as before. I am still seeking Jarrett Longacre."

Trey started to say Longacre had not been around, but he offered a different reply that technically was not a falsehood. "You won't find him here."

He hoped not, anyway.

"If he were here, you would not tell me."

"No, I wouldn't."

"Which is why I keep coming back to see for myself."

The dog was making the black horse nervous. Because its barking had warned of Gault's approach, Trey scratched its ears. "Good dog, Ulysses."

Gault said sourly, "A barking dog is an abomination."

"Depends on what he barks at."

Trey followed as Gault turned the black and rode to the cabin. The dog made a low growling sound deep in its throat but stopped its noise when Trey pointed a finger.

Sarah had come out onto the front step to see what had disturbed Ulysses. Though she managed not to show it, Trey knew she was probably tingling with apprehension for Longacre, and for Trey himself if shooting should erupt. But Trey was beginning to lose some of his own uneasiness. Surely Longacre was prudent enough to remain concealed, and Gault was unlikely to ride through the corn.

Gault nodded at Sarah but did not tip his derby or even bring his hand to the brim. It remained near the butt of the pistol on his hip. "Young lady, I'll not invade your house if you will give me your word that Jarrett Longacre is not hiding inside."

"He's not, but you're welcome to come in if you'd like to."

Gault glanced toward the corrals. "I did happen to notice that new calf out yonder, so I take it that your milk cow has freshened. If you could spare me a cup of milk, I would be much obliged to you."

"You can have all you want. Trey, how about goin' down to the springhouse and fetchin' a bucket of last night's milk? It ought to be nice and cool."

Trey was impatient for Gault to leave, but he realized Sarah was trying to allay the man's suspicions. Skin prickling, he went to the small stone building. Cloth-covered jars containing yesterday's and today's milk stood in a trough beneath the bubbling spring. The cool water coursed through the trough and around the jars on its way down to the creek. He stole a look toward the field as he returned to the cabin. Longacre was keeping his head down.

Sarah broke the skim at the top of the jar and poured a cup almost full. Gault spoke his thanks and drank the milk as if it were the last on earth. Sarah asked with her eyes, he nodded, and she refilled the cup. He drank half of it, then stared with pleasure at the rest. For the moment the grim cast was gone from his face. "This country . . ." he said with a sigh, "so many cows and so little milk. I've never understood why men lose their heads over whiskey. Milk is by far the better choice."

He sipped slowly at what was left as others might sip at wine. "When I was a boy in Pennsylvania, we had a farm. It was my daily chore to milk six cows. There was nothing I loved better on a cold day than to tip up the bucket with the milk still steaming and drink my fill, foam and all. What a wonderful time it was."

Sarah asked, "How'd you come to be in Texas, doin' what you're doin'?"

"The war. I thought I would serve the Lord by carrying His word to the soldiers. But somehow the Word was lost amid the blood and mud and misery, and I was drawn into the killing myself. By the time the war ended, I was serving God with a gun instead of the Book. At least the men I now kill deserve it."

Trey said, "There's a lot worse ones out there than Jarrett Longacre."

"I'll get to them. But I have personal business with Longacre." He touched his stiff arm.

Ulysses began barking again. Trey felt the hair bristle on his neck. He feared Longacre had left concealment and aroused the dog.

Gault started for the door. "I hope that barking does not cause my horse to break loose."

Trey cut in front of him. "Just enjoy your milk. I'll go hush up that fool dog."

He saw nothing of Longacre, but the dog was trotting toward a wagon that slowly made its way up the trace from the direction of Fort Griffin. He knew the team.

Stepping back into the cabin, he told Sarah, "Katy's comin'."

Gault set down the cup. "Katy Rice? Twice I have found her place, but I have not yet laid eyes on her."

Trey thought, *You wouldn't now if she knew you were here.*

It was too late to wave her away. In any case, Gault had nothing on Katy, so he saw no harm in their meeting face to face.

Sarah walked out in front of Trey, careful not to booger Katy's team as she had done before. Trey did not permit himself to glance toward the cornfield, for Gault watched from the doorway. He wondered what Longacre must be thinking about all this company. The tension had to be eating on him like a swarm of hungry ants.

Sarah greeted Katy as a long-lost friend. "Get down, get down. Trey'll take care of your wagon and team. You'll stay all night with us, won't you?"

"Guess so. It's a long ways home, slow as this wagon travels." Katy climbed down. Her gaze, full of suspicion, went to Gault. She wore the usual man's clothing, though her brown hair tumbled past her shoulders when she removed her hat and slapped it against her leg.

Quietly she said, "Feller over yonder, he's been to my place. Lawman, ain't he?"

Trey took the reins from her hands and wrapped them around the brake. "That's Gault. I expect you've heard about him."

"Are you in trouble?"

"No, he's lookin' for Jarrett Longacre."

"Anybody who can stir up a lawman like that has got to be worth knowin'."

Gault moved out of the doorway and down from the front slab. "So you're the elusive Katy Rice. I've tried twice to see you."

"I saw *you.*"

"I hear you have given sanctuary at times to men who had reason not to be found. You would not by chance be harboring a fugitive named Longacre?"

"I never met nobody by that name." She jerked her thumb toward the wagon. "But go look under the tarp if you want to. Anybody you find there, you're welcome to."

Gault made no move toward the wagon. She was obviously baiting him.

He turned to Sarah. "I heard you invite this young woman to spend the night. I don't suppose that invitation would apply as well to me?"

Sarah looked at Trey. Trey said, "No, sir, it don't."

Gault did not seem to take offense. "I thought not." He nodded at Sarah. "I am much obliged to you for the milk." He mounted the black horse and rode away in a walk, the dog seeing him off but remaining beyond range of the horse's hind feet.

Katy raised an eyebrow. "Milk? Strychnine might be more fittin'."

Sarah said, "You wouldn't think it, but he's an old farm boy, kind of like Trey. Life has not been good to him."

"Ain't apt to get any better, the way he's goin' about it."

Trey climbed into the wagon and moved it up beside the shed. Katy had fetched supplies from Fort Griffin. The sky showed no sign of a cloud, so he saw no need to put the wagon beneath the shed. A tarp afforded all the protection the load would need. He unhitched the team, led it into a corral and removed the harness. A stealthy movement past the shed told him Longacre had worked up nerve to leave the cornfield.

Longacre kept the shed between him and the cabin. He complained, "I've seen whole towns where there wasn't this many people movin' around." By Trey's unhitching the team, Longacre could see that the wagon's owner did not plan on leaving today. "Looks like I've got to sleep in the brush tonight."

"It's just Katy Rice. She'd as soon cut off her arm as give somebody away to the law."

"I heard about her when I was workin' here for Kerbow, but I never seen her. Bet she's as ugly as a mud fence."

"You can judge for yourself. Help me feed her team, then I'll take you up and introduce you."

"I'm in no hurry. You sure Gault ain't comin' back?"

"I'm not sure about anything, except that you lead too interestin' a life for me."

Longacre studied the wagon trace and the horizon line long and hard before he allowed himself to venture beyond the protection of the shed. "I don't trust Gault not to double back and stand watch on the place."

But after a bit he felt confident enough to troop up to the cabin beside Trey. Sarah and Katy Rice sat in chairs pulled back from the table. Trey nodded his head toward Longacre. "Katy, you said you'd like to know Jarrett Longacre. Well, this is him."

Her hazel eyes brightened. She looked Longacre up and down as if she considered buying him. "I expected to see horns and a tail. You look damn near normal."

Longacre appeared as surprised as she did, and pleasantly so. "You look a lot more normal than I thought too. If you had a dress on instead of them britches . . . at least everybody would know you're a woman."

"When it made any difference, they always seemed to figure it out all right. In this country I'd be better off most of the time if everybody did think I was a man."

After a time, Trey and Longacre returned to the field to continue hoeing the corn. Longacre worked awhile, then leaned on his hoe and looked toward the cabin. "What you reckon them two are talkin' about up there?"

Trey shrugged. "I don't guess it matters much. Main thing is that Sarah's got a woman to visit with for a change. Even if that woman is Katy Rice."

"Why do you say *even if*? Katy looks all right to me. From what

I've heard, she just travels her own road and don't ask anybody's opinion."

"Like somebody else I know."

"I learned a long time ago not to ask permission. Nobody gets to tell me no."

As suppertime approached, Longacre paused for a long look around before he stepped up onto the cabin's stone slab. Trey entered ahead of him and stopped in surprise.

He had never seen Katy Rice in a dress. Now she wore one of Sarah's. Her long brown hair was brushed out and past her shoulders, though it was not so long as Sarah's. Trey could only stare. He had not considered Katy a particularly pretty woman, but he revised his opinion.

Sarah showed Katy off as if she were a work of art. "What do you think?"

"I think you hid the real Katy Rice under the bed or someplace."

The woman seemed a bit embarrassed. "Sarah's idea. I don't see no purpose in it myself."

Entering the room, Longacre stopped in midstride. His mouth dropped open, but no words came out.

Sarah said, "I told you, Katy. Put you in a dress and you'd have all the men's attention."

"That's the kind of attention got me into my first trouble. I've been tryin' to get along without it."

The four of them sat in the enveloping dusk, talking of home, of childhood, of old dreams fallen aside. Trey enjoyed the glow in Sarah's eyes. It was brighter than he had seen it in a long time.

Katy apologized for yawning and attributed it to her long trip to Griffin. "Been puttin' it off as long as I could. I hate that town. But I'd run out of just about everything."

Sarah said, "You'll stay in the cabin tonight. Trey can sleep in the bunkhouse with Jarrett."

The idea was not to Trey's liking, though he would not speak against it. Longacre said, "Katy can have the bunkhouse. I'm not used to a roof anyway."

The woman smiled. "You're a gentleman, Mr. Longacre."

"A failin' I keep tryin' to get over."

At daylight, Trey went out to call Katy and Longacre to breakfast. He expected to find Longacre's bedroll under or near the shed, but he did not. He called, and Longacre came out of the bunkhouse. Then Katy also came out, wearing Sarah's dress.

The warm look that passed between the two told Trey all he needed to know. He supposed he ought to feel shocked, but he was not. He had seen a lot since leaving the farm. But he couldn't tell Sarah. Given her sheltered upbringing, he felt that she *would* be shocked.

Trey hoped Longacre would go with Katy to her place. That would at least get him away from the Kerbow ranch and put him where Gault was less likely to trap him.

Trey and Longacre hitched Katy's team to the wagon, and Trey waited with increasing anxiety to see Longacre saddle his horse. But he was disappointed.

Longacre took Katy's arm and gave her a boost up into the wagon, then held on to her hand considerably longer than necessary. The two smiled at each other. Katy was back in her accustomed man's clothes. She said, "I told you how to find my place if you take a notion to visit."

Longacre's smile widened. "Gettin' acquainted with you has given me a lot of notions."

Sarah told her, "You come back real soon."

Katy put the team into motion. Trey watched as she pulled away, then turned to Longacre. "I thought maybe you'd go with her. Katy could probably use your help over there."

"It ain't that it didn't cross my mind. Me and her, we talked about it. She told me some things." Longacre's gaze went to Sarah, who had started back toward the cabin. "We both decided you need my help more than she does."

"I've been doin' right good by myself."

"Maybe not as good as you think. You need to be able to stay closer to the house. A lot closer."

"What about Gault?"

"Mr. Gault'll just have to watch out for himself."

# NINETEEN

Sarah knew why Jarrett Longacre had not gone home with Katy. After breakfast, while the men were at the corral hitching the team, Katy had told her the two had considered it. However, they had agreed he should stay here to help Trey shoulder some of the work burden and keep him closer to home. They suspected that sooner or later—probably sooner—Mead Overstreet would come back to find out if Sarah had weakened. Sarah had confided in Katy about her experience with the rancher.

Sarah begged Katy, as she had begged Longacre, not to tell Trey.

Katy had warned, "Mead does all his thinkin' from the belt down. He's a hound when it comes to women, sniffin' around hopin' to find one in heat. He found one here once."

"Martha Kerbow?"

"At least your husband comes home of a night. Hers was sometimes gone for weeks at a time. He ought to've known how lonesome a woman can get."

"Don't you ever get lonesome, Katy?"

"Not often. One good thing about bein' by yourself is that you never have to listen to foolish talk, unless it's your own."

Sarah suspected that Katy and Longacre had been together through the night. Both had a glow about them that left little doubt. She hoped Trey did not notice, however. He would probably be shocked. "You seem to like Jarrett Longacre's company."

A smile lighted the woman's hazel eyes. "He knows how to make me feel good." She caught herself and forced the smile down. "But I got along without him up to yesterday. I can get along without him now."

Sarah watched Katy's wagon so long as it remained in sight, the sense of loneliness pressing down like a heavy burden as the woman disappeared in the distance. She had to resist an urge to run after Katy and beg her to stay a little longer. She turned back toward her husband and Jarrett Longacre. Their presence should offset the feeling, but she knew they would saddle up shortly and ride off someplace. As usual, she would be left alone.

She was perfectly capable of riding sidesaddle, but Trey had never invited her to accompany him out onto the range. The thought probably never occurred to him. Without stating it in so many words, he had no quarrel with the common notion that such work was for men, and the woman's responsibility was tending to home, garden and chickens.

She wished the sound of the wind in the broken window glass really *was* the ghost of Martha Kerbow. At least it would provide her some company.

She never heard Overstreet's approach. Either the dog was asleep or it had strayed off somewhere. It spent a lot of time down on the creek trying to scare up a rabbit or something else it could chase. She was standing at the stove, poking wood into the firebox, attention fixed on a pot of beans simmering beside the steaming teakettle. The fare was plain most of the time, but Trey and Longacre never complained so long as they had red beans and hot biscuits at every meal.

The first she knew of Overstreet's presence was his arms, suddenly clasped around her waist from behind. She gasped in surprise, thinking for a second or two it was Trey, come home much earlier than expected. But the arms were not Trey's, nor the groping hands.

The voice was quiet, barely more than a whisper. "I've waited long enough for you to think about it."

She was stunned at first, too much in shock to react. Then she tried to twist from his grasp, but his arms were too strong. He lowered his head to kiss her on the neck. His breath was warm as he rubbed his face in her long hair.

"That beautiful hair," he said. "Just the smell of it is like a double shot of whiskey." He touched his cheek to hers. It was smooth.

"I shaved fresh this mornin', just for you."

Shock began giving way to a melding of anger and fear—anger that he would even try taking advantage of her, fear that if he was determined enough, he was strong enough.

The last time, she had reacted in confusion, torn between wanting him to stop and wanting him to go ahead. Now she suffered no such conflicting emotions. "Turn me loose. Turn me loose right now!"

His right hand clamped over her left breast. She tried to pry his fingers apart but found his strength greater than her own. He began unbuttoning her dress, as he had done before. He slid his hand inside against her skin. The other time, his touch had warmed her blood. Now it only fired resentment.

He said, "Fight, if it'll ease your conscience. But you know you've been thinkin' about it. You've been waitin' for me to come back."

She screamed, "Trey!"

"I watched him and whoever was with him ride away. No tellin' when they're liable to be back." He began pulling her toward the bed.

She grabbed the corner of the table, but he pried her hand free. Anger boiled within her like the water in the teakettle. She beat her fists against him, without apparent effect. His face reddened with excitement as he pushed her backward onto the bed, breathing hot in her face. She felt that he would crush the breath from her lungs as he brought his full weight down upon her. He lay there, holding her immobile, kissing her forehead, her eyes, her cheeks, hungrily seeking her lips while she fought to turn her face away. His hands explored her bosom, then her thighs, and tugged at the hem of her long skirt.

He turned, dropping his gun belt off the far side of the bed. In that instant she managed to slide from beneath him and jump to her feet. Her eyes sought out the rifle on its pegs over the fireplace, but he seemed to outguess her. He sprang from the bed and sprinted across the room, placing himself between her and the weapon. She turned back, looking desperately for something she could use to defend herself.

She thought of the woodbox, a stick of firewood again. But the stove was closer, and the teakettle. She grabbed its handle and swung it around. It burned her fingers, but she hardly felt the pain. As Overstreet rushed toward her, she swung the kettle in an arc that brought a stream of hot water pouring from the spout. Some of it splashed against her hand and arm, but much of it went into Overstreet's face. He squalled and cursed in surprise and pain.

She swung the kettle a second time and scalded him again. He stopped, bringing his hands to his blistered face. She darted around him, dropping the kettle as she reached for the rifle. The vessel clanged upon the flagstone. Steaming hot water spilled onto the floor.

Sarah drew back the hammer with her thumb and brought the muzzle to bear upon Overstreet's belly just as Trey burst through the door. Jarrett Longacre was only a step behind him.

Trey shouted, "You son of a bitch!" He delivered a fist into Overstreet's face with all the strength of a man who had spent his life bending his back and exercising his arms at hard labor, and all the fury of a husband who had found his wife violated. Overstreet stumbled backward, catching himself with his arm against the hot stove.

He pushed quickly away from the searing heat, crying out.

Sarah smelled burned fabric, burned flesh.

Longacre stood just inside the door, a pistol in his hand pointed toward the ceiling.

The passion which had aroused Overstreet in his pursuit of Sarah now shifted to fury in his fight with Trey. Bellowing, he rushed with his head low, his fists knotted. A red welt was rising on the side of his hand and another across his face. But rage overrode whatever pain the burns had imposed. He sent Trey reeling backward into the stone facing of the cold fireplace. Still holding the rifle, Sarah stepped aside so they would not knock her down.

She looked toward Longacre, silently asking with her eyes that he do something to help Trey. Just as silently, Longacre shook his head and gave her a look that said this was Trey's fight. To interfere would deny him his right as a husband, and as a man, to defend his own.

The fight seemed to drag on for an hour, though she knew it lasted only minutes. Each man gave as much as he got, one advancing and driving the other back, then retreating, on the receiving end. Both went down several times, each time a little slower to rise to his feet and resume the battle. The fight spilled out the open front door, across the stone slab and into the dirt of the open yard.

Overstreet's startled horse drew back against the rein tied hard to a post. The leather snapped. The animal wheeled and trotted off to join Trey's and Longacre's horses that had not been tied.

Sarah wanted to stop the fight but did not know how. She dismissed a transient impulse to shoot Overstreet. Surely no one could seriously blame her after what he had tried to do, and in light of the fact that her husband stood in real danger of being hurt. But she could not pull the trigger. She wondered if she could have done it even earlier, when she had brought the rifle down to defend herself.

The two men moved more and more slowly until each lay on the ground, wheezing and puffing, trying in vain to rise. Trey's clothes were torn, his face bloodied and beginning to swell. Overstreet looked no better. Trey pushed himself painfully to hands and knees and tried to crawl toward Overstreet but collapsed onto his stomach.

Calmly Longacre said, "Looks to me like you two have brought this thing to a draw." He walked to Overstreet, who lay on his side. He kicked the man in the rump. "Get up from there. Get up or I'll blow a hole in you and tell God you just died."

Overstreet fought for breath, coughing, gasping in an effort to fill his lungs. His bloodied nose appeared broken. A front tooth was gone. The hot water had left an angry red splotch across his face. Never again would he be handsome as he had been before. He managed to get to hands and knees. Longacre caught his horse, tied a knot in the broken rein as a temporary repair, and led the animal over to him.

"You better leave while you can. In about three minutes I'm declarin' open season." He took a hold beneath Overstreet's armpits and helped the man struggle to his feet. Overstreet managed to lift his left foot to the stirrup but was unable to swing into the saddle until Longacre gave him a boost up.

Longacre mounted his own horse and shook down his rope. "Let's see how fast you can get away from here. I'm fixin' to whip you off of this place."

Overstreet's words were slurred, but Sarah could understand them. He gave Longacre a look that was pure black hatred. "Gault's been lookin' for you."

Longacre swung his rope. "Get movin'." He lashed the doubled rope across Overstreet's shoulders. Overstreet's horse, all too used to the sting of a quirt, bounded forward at the singing of the rope and the sound of it striking the rider. Overstreet grabbed the horn to keep from falling from the saddle. His horse broke into a run. Longacre followed closely, whipping Overstreet across the shoulders.

Sarah dropped to her knees beside Trey. She helped him to his feet, but he managed only to reach the front step. There he slumped upon the stone, staring blankly at his battered and blood-smeared knuckles. Sarah felt like weeping but thought it would be an unseemly display of weakness after what Trey had gone through for her. She went to the washstand and wet the cloth she always kept draped beside the water bucket there. She touched it gingerly to Trey's face. He flinched at the sting.

She said, "I can wash away the dirt and the blood, but I'm afraid there's not much I can do about the swellin'."

"It'll heal." He took her hand and attempted to squeeze but had to turn loose, wincing. "Jarrett told me Overstreet has bothered you before. Why didn't *you* tell me?"

"I was afraid you might try to kill him and get yourself killed instead."

"You didn't think I could beat him?"

"You *didn't* beat him. Like Jarrett said, it was a draw. But at least I've still got you, alive."

"If I was dead I wouldn't hurt so damned much, in so damned many places." He tried to focus upon her face but seemed to have trouble with his eyes. One was darkening and swelling almost shut. "There was already somethin' wrong with him before I ever hit him. What did you do?"

She became aware that her dress was still partly unbuttoned. She quickly fastened it, for she saw Longacre returning, coiling his rope. "I scalded him. Poured teakettle water on him."

He grunted. "Good thing you already took some of the wind out of him, else he'd've whipped me, like as not. Then I *would* be a sorry-lookin' sight."

"You look like Ivanhoe to me, and all those other knights I've read about. Right now you're the handsomest man in the world."

Longacre dismounted. He dropped the reins and walked to the couple on the doorstep. He gave Trey a critical study. "You appear like you'd been drug on the end of a rope."

"I never done much fightin'. Always seemed like there had to be a better way to fix things."

"It was a piece of good luck that he didn't have a pistol on. He might've shot you before you ever got in the first lick." Longacre looked at Sarah. "Or maybe not. You had the rifle in your hands. You wouldn't've given him a chance to shoot Trey, would you?"

"I don't know. I don't know if I could've pulled the trigger."

"Anytime you pick up a gun, you'd better be ready and able to shoot it. The other feller will be."

He took the rifle from her hands and opened the breech. "You might've knocked him in the head with it, but you wouldn't've shot him. Damned thing's empty."

"Empty?" Sarah felt as if her breakfast would come up.

Trey took the wet cloth from her hands and held it to his bruised, torn knuckles, frowning against the pain and the burning. He asked Longacre, "How long did you keep whippin' him?"

"Couple hundred yards. Maybe three. Didn't want him to be forgettin' about it."

"He won't. He knows who you are. He'll go tell Gault."

A troubled look came into Longacre's face. "I reckon he will. Kind of wish now I'd killed him last winter."

"You can't stay here anymore."

"I reckon not. There's no profit in killin' Gault."

Sarah suggested, "You could go to Katy Rice. She knows places where a whole army would have trouble findin' you."

Longacre offered no argument. "I've heard worse ideas." He stared at Sarah, then at Trey. "But what about Sarah? Anytime you go off and leave her alone, Overstreet might show up again."

"I'll kill him if he does."

"Killin' is easy talked about, and all too easy done. But it's hell to live with afterwards."

Sarah offered hopefully, "You don't have to leave me by myself. When you go out and see after the cattle, I can ride with you."

Trey was silent a moment. "I could use the help."

"I've just been waitin' for you to ask me."

Longacre nodded in satisfaction. "Then I'll throw my stuff together. There ain't much of it."

If Trey harbored any thought of riding that day or the next, aches and pains from the fight forced him to change his mind. His legs and arms were sore, his knees and elbows almost too stiff to bend. One eye was black and puffed so badly that he could not see out of it. The other was only a little discolored but watered as if he were in mourning. His hands were cut and swollen enough that he was unable even to milk the cow that evening; he yielded the chore to Sarah.

She applied wet cloths to his raw face and rubbed bacon grease into his wounds.

He said, "I've seen them butcher beeves on the trail that wasn't cut up this bad."

"You've never looked better to me than you do right now. You know what was fixin' to happen if you hadn't showed up just when you did."

"Jarrett and me, we saw Overstreet sneakin' in to the place like a chicken thief."

"I don't much think he'll try anything again. Time folks hear what he did, he'll have a hard time stayin' in this country."

"Who's to spread the word? Jarrett can't."

"Tell George. It'll get around."

"We'll ride over to his place tomorrow."

The next day Trey was in no condition to ride anywhere, but he did not have to. George Blackman showed up on his own. Sarah saw him approaching as she fed her little flock of hens. Anxiety touched her until his off-center slouch in the saddle satisfied her that he was not Overstreet. As he eased from his horse, she wondered how much of the creaking came from the leather and how much from his weary joints. She knew he must have left home long before daylight to reach here this early.

He showed none of his usual easygoing nature. His eyes searched quickly over the place. "I gather that you folks had a ruckus here."

"Wasn't anybody killed. How'd you hear about it?"

"Ran into Mead Overstreet yesterday, headed for town. He looked like he'd tangled with a den of bobcats."

"Trey doesn't look any better. He was barely able to crawl out of bed this mornin'. He didn't stay up long."

George's face furrowed like a rutted road. "Mead gave me his version of what caused the fight. I'm makin' a wild guess that he left out the main part."

A little of yesterday's anger and humiliation returned to her. "I imagine you're guessin' pretty close to the truth."

"Did that son of a . . . did he . . ."

Though none of it had been her fault, she could not help feeling a touch of shame. She looked at the ground. "He didn't quite get it done."

George cursed beneath his breath. "Been men hung for less."

"I wouldn't want it to come to that. They hung a man while we were in Fort Griffin. It was ugly."

"It sure does get their attention, though. Whatever they've done, they never do it again." He tied his horse and followed her into the house. He looked down balefully at Trey, lying on the bed. Trey extended his battered hand, but George declined to take it.

"Don't want to hurt you. I'll shake with you double someday when you've got well." He looked around as if he expected to see someone else. "Mead was on his way to fetch Gault. Said you been aidin' and abettin' a criminal. Tried to make me think that was what the fight was about, but I know him better than that."

"Jarrett Longacre. Gault has told you about him."

"More than once." He looked toward the door. "I don't reckon he's still around here."

Sarah said, "He left after the fight." She did not say where he had gone, and she hoped George would not ask.

"Like as not I won't be the only company you have today. I'll stay around if you'd like."

Trey smiled, though the effort hurt. "We'd be tickled."

Sarah said, "Bet you're hungry, George. I'll fix you somethin' to eat."

"I'd be obliged. I did leave a long time before breakfast." He went to the door. "Any chores need doin'?"

Sarah shook her head. "Everything needful, I've already done."

George nodded with satisfaction. "I don't know what Kerbow is payin' you-all, but it ain't enough."

Trey dragged himself to the table and sat while George put away a day's work for Sarah's hens, along with a generous amount of salt pork and most of a pan of biscuits. George's conversation drifted from one subject to another but kept coming back to Gault. "The man don't seem like he knows for sure who he's workin' for. He'll talk a while about God and heaven, then first thing you know he's talkin' about sendin' a bunch of men to hell."

After visiting a while, George walked out into the front yard, then down to the barn and corrals. After a long time he was back. "Never talk about somebody you don't want to see because they're liable to show up."

Sarah felt cold. "Gault?"

"And Mead Overstreet's with him."

Trey arose painfully from the bed and paused at the fireplace, reaching for the rifle on its pegs above the mantle.

George said, "Best way to keep from havin' a shootin' is to not be carryin' any guns."

To Sarah's relief, Trey stepped back without the rifle.

The ranchman grunted. "Mead ain't worth it anyway. He may not know it, but he's about done in these parts."

The three of them stepped outside, just beyond the stone slab, and waited for the two riders who came up the wagon trail from the direction of Fort Griffin. As they drew near enough, Sarah could see that Overstreet's face was as puffed and discolored as Trey's. It occurred to her that Katy Rice would probably enjoy this sight. She would bet that Overstreet was not doing all his thinking from below the belt today.

As the men drew rein, Trey's gaze was locked on Overstreet, but he spoke to the older man. "You're in poor company, Mr. Gault."

"I am aware of that, but in the service of Lord or law, one does not always have the privilege of choosing." He gave Trey's face a long study. "I believe the two of you must have been dragged by the same horse."

Trey made no reply. Gault spoke a pleasant-enough howdy to George, then looked at Sarah in a way that made her uncomfortable. "I regret to say, Mrs. McLean, that I am disappointed in you and your husband. I had come to regard you as good, honest Christian folk. But you lied to me. You told me Jarrett Longacre was not here."

"He wasn't," she replied. "He showed up after your last visit."

"And I would assume that he is no longer here?"

"He's not. You're welcome to come in and look around."

"I don't believe that is necessary. I would guess that he left soon after the fight."

Trey said, "He did."

"And I don't suppose you would care to tell me where he was going?"

"No, sir, I don't believe we would."

"An honest answer. I expected no more. I'll find him for myself if he is to be found." He glanced up toward the sun. "It is getting toward midday, and we have had nothing today except some coffee. I would be willing to pay what it is worth if we might stay for dinner."

Sarah said, "You'd be welcome, Mr. Gault, and we wouldn't think of takin' your money. But Mr. Overstreet will not set foot in this house." She was surprised by the hardness of her own voice. "If he does not turn around right now and leave, I'll fetch a gun and shoot him."

Gault was taken aback. "I would never have expected to hear such a threat from the lips of a gentlewoman."

"It's not a threat. It's a promise. Mr. Overstreet knows why."

"I can imagine the reason." Gault turned in the saddle. "Mr. Overstreet, I can dispense with your services now. I would advise you to take to heart what the young lady says."

Overstreet glared at Trey and Sarah, then started to turn his horse around. George shouted at him, "Just a minute, Mead." He walked out halfway toward the man and took a challenging stance, his feet well apart. "If I was you, I'd settle my affairs and leave this part of the country before everybody finds out what you did. Else the whippin' you took yesterday is goin' to look like a birthday party."

Overstreet said something Sarah could not hear, then declared, "Go to hell, George. You can all go to hell." He finished his turn and rode away.

The others watched him go, but Gault kept his eyes on Sarah and Trey as he dismounted. "It would seem we have all been guilty of being in bad company. But the man was of use to me. Even the devil has his purposes."

Gault led his horse down to the creek, loosened the girth and let the animal water. Then he tied it to a corral fence and returned. He asked Sarah, "Have you seen Katy Rice of late?"

"Not in a while."

"Were I a wagering man, which I am not, I would be willing to risk a hundred dollars that Mr. Longacre has seen her, that in fact he is with her now."

Sarah hoped her eyes did not betray the truth, though she doubted it would make much difference. Gault would go to Katy's in any case. Surely Katy and Longacre must expect that. Longacre was probably miles away from that place, safely camped in some hidden canyon. But Gault's probing gaze left her uncomfortable. She said, "I'll go in and start dinner."

"I regret that I may be placing a burden on you."

"Mr. Gault, you've done that since the first time ever I set eyes on you."

The men soon followed her into the house. They pulled chairs out from the table. Trey slumped, still hurting.

George said to Gault, "There's a lot worse men in the country than Jarrett Longacre, with a lot bigger price on their heads. Don't you think you'd be doin' better to hunt them?"

"My quarrel with Mr. Longacre goes beyond the question of reward." He raised his stiff arm.

"And if you was to kill him, would your arm get any better?"

"Perhaps not. But I would sleep better if I saw Mr. Longacre bleed as he has caused others to bleed."

Sarah called upon her memory of Scripture. " 'Vengeance is mine, sayeth the Lord.' "

"But sometimes He needs men's help in getting it," Gault said. "I offered Him my services a long time ago."

# TWENTY

Trey knew the question was idle, but he asked it anyway after Gault left. "Headed toward Katy's place, didn't he?"

George and Sarah had watched the lawman leave. Sarah said, "Jarrett's too cagey to stay around there and get caught. And Katy's too smart to let him."

The rancher said, "If you see him again, tell him I hear the climate's good in New Mexico. It's even better in California. Wouldn't be bad for Katy's health, either."

"I already told him," Trey said. "He wasn't listenin'."

"You ain't goin' to be up to much work for a while yet. I'll send Adam over to stay and watch after things for a few days."

"It ain't necessary, George. We'll manage."

"But I wouldn't sleep for worryin' about you two, and an old man needs his rest."

Sarah said, "You're a great friend, George. I don't know what we'd do without you."

"As long as you keep fixin' them good biscuits, you ain't goin' to find out."

By the time they saw Gault again, most of Trey's bruises had faded, the swelling had left his face and he was able to see through both eyes. Gault appeared weary, and his horse was looking gaunt. Trey did not have to ask if he had had any luck in finding Jarrett Longacre.

Sarah invited Gault to stay for dinner. He wolfed his food as if it was the first he had had in four or five days, which Trey suspected was not far from the truth. Gault said as he refilled his plate, "I am afraid old age is overtaking me. I used to be able to live like a coyote for weeks at a time. I must have ridden out every canyon and searched every brush thicket from here to the caprock."

"Maybe Jarrett skipped the country."

"No, he is still out there somewhere. I could feel him watching me time and again. I believe that boy must have Indian blood in him."

"He claims he does. And maybe some wolf, too."

"Indians . . . wolves . . . they are kindred spirits."

"You givin' up and goin' back to town?" Trey could hear the hope in his own voice.

"For now. I have used up what few supplies I carried. I have worn out my horse, and also myself."

Trey wondered if the law allowed Gault to commandeer supplies and perhaps a horse. He did not ask, for it might give the man ideas.

Gault said, "Should you happen to see your friend Longacre, tell him I have not given up. He had just as well come in and surrender, for I shall hound him until I catch him or he dies."

Trey had forgotten how pretty a figure Sarah cut, riding sidesaddle. Spotting a cow with a calf shaded up beneath a hackberry tree, she rode forward for a closer look. "It's a little heifer, and it's not branded yet."

Sensing trouble, the cow rose to her feet and began moving away, the calf dutifully trotting along beside her. Trey shook down his rawhide rope and circled around them. The cow turned back but saw Sarah behind her and stopped, confused. Trey approached the calf in a walk and dropped his loop quietly around the small neck. Feeling the noose draw tight, the calf ran for its mother. Trey eased his bay horse forward so the calf would not hit the end of the rope too hard and choke itself. He dismounted, walked down the rope and flanked the heifer, tying its feet so it could not get up. Frightened, it bawled for its mother and kicked futilely against the leather string that bound it.

"See if you can keep that old hussy from puttin' a horn in me," Trey said. Sarah moved forward, positioning her horse between the calf and the fretful cow. Trey gathered some scattered sticks of dead wood, stuffed several handfuls of fall-dried grass among them, then shielded a match from the cool north wind while he started a small fire. When it had built up enough heat, he laid a short S-shaped piece of iron rod among the coals. A blacksmith had curved the ends of the rod for a wagon cook to hang pots over a campfire. Trey had found it served well as a running iron. It was easier to use than the cinch ring he had first employed for burning brands on the open range, where it was unhandy to carry long-handled stamp irons.

When the iron began to glow, he removed it from the fire, a heavy leather glove shielding his hand from the worst of the heat. He ran a K Bar brand on the calf's left side, keeping it small. The brand would become larger as the calf grew. He notched the right ear, then untied the leather string. The heifer scrambled to its feet and ran for its mother, both bawling for each other. The cow sniffed anxiously at her offspring, perhaps uncertain about the strange odor of burned hair. The two trotted away side by side. Trey coiled and tied his rope, then took a small tally book from his pocket. He made a mark on a page where he had written *Heffer cfs brandded.*

"Another for Mr. Kerbow," he said, coiling his rope.

"And for us. He promised us a share of the calf crop."

In the days she had been riding with him, he had found Sarah taking a healthy interest in the cattle and in the range itself. He was a little surprised. He had assumed that because she was a woman she would be interested in little that went on beyond the house, the yard and her garden. He had been afraid every time he saw her push her horse into a lope, expecting to see her take a fall. But she stuck to the sidesaddle as if she had been tied on. She was a better horsewoman than he would have imagined.

She became animated whenever she saw deer dart for the cover of nearby timber, and he could remember few times he had seen her more excited than the morning they rode up on a dozen or so buffalo. The black, shaggy animals broke into a lumbering lope when Sarah pressed them too closely. Trey felt compelled to call her back, afraid the horse might run away with her. It had never seen buffalo before. Neither had Sarah.

Her voice was high-pitched with emotion. "Where'd they come from?"

The animals were putting on their heavy winter hair. "Down off of the caprock. They drift south with the geese."

"They're beautiful, in an ugly kind of way."

He did not know how to reconcile *beautiful* and *ugly*. "But they aren't worth much in dollars, not as much as cattle. Up north, people are huntin' them just for their hides, and sometimes the tongues. The rest goes to waste."

"Seems a shame."

"But buffalo on the range means there's less grass for cattle, and farmers can't keep them out of their crops. Sooner or later the buffalo'll have to go."

"It still seems a shame."

He could not argue the point. He remembered his own first sighting of buffalo as the Kerbow trail herd had moved across Kansas.

"The Indians . . . the buffalo . . . they've got to make way for the new time comin'."

"The new time is us. But what happens to us someday when we're the old time, and there's a *new* new time? What do we do when they come to push *us* out of the way?"

Trey had no answer.

They came to a creek and dismounted to let their horses drink. Her eyes glowed with reverence as her gaze swept the horizon. "When we first came out past Fort Griffin, I was fearful scared of this country. I didn't know if I could ever learn to fit in. But now it's like I was waitin' all my life just to come here."

"Even if it gets a little lonesome sometimes?"

"I guess I've gotten used to that. I don't hear voices in the house anymore. It just sounds like the wind, whistlin' through the broken window glass. It's a beautiful country, Trey, beautiful." She put her arms around him and kissed him on the mouth. "Thank you for bringin' me to it."

They let go of the bridle reins. The horses would not stray away, no matter how long they stayed here. Arms around each other's waists, Trey and Sarah walked up the creekbank and sank down together upon the grass.

---

He had long since come to depend upon a horse's keen eyesight and instincts to alert him to things he might miss, the gray horse in particular. Anytime the animal's ears suddenly pointed forward, Trey knew it had seen something: a cow, a deer, another horse. In this case it was a dozen or so horses. All had riders.

Though he had come to take it for granted that Indian trouble was a thing of the past, the sight of so many horsemen aroused his cautionary instincts. "Let's pull back into that timber yonder," he said. "Maybe they haven't seen us yet."

Sarah asked no questions, though his reaction had disturbed her. She reined around and put her mount into a thicket just ahead of him.

He squinted, trying to focus better on the horsemen. "There's a couple of Indians, but the rest of them are soldiers. I wonder what . . ."

There was but one way to find out. He left the thicket and moved toward the riders. Sarah pressed to catch up with him. One of the soldiers signaled, and the group changed direction. Trey reasoned that the two Indians were scouts, probably some of the Tonkawas who lived just outside of Fort Griffin. He knew little about army rank, but he assumed that one of the soldiers whose uniform looked better than the others was an officer.

The officer commanded the detail to halt. He gave Sarah more attention than Trey. "How far from home are you?"

Trey pointed with his thumb. "Three, maybe four miles."

"I would strongly recommend that you return there. We have had a report of an Indian raiding party."

Trey felt alarm for Sarah. He saw her eyes widen. "I thought they had quit comin' down from the high plains."

"The only thing certain about Indians is that you cannot predict what they are going to do."

"Where are they at?"

"The report was vague. We are not sure where it came from. We were simply advised that someone had seen a war party to the west of Fort Griffin. We are out now looking for sign."

"We've got some neighbors who ought to be warned."

"That would have to be up to you. I do not know where you settlers live."

Trey wished Sarah were not with him. They would be vulnerable if caught out here in the open. But to send her home by herself was unthinkable. "It's not too far over yonderway to George's place."

"What about Katy and Jarrett?"

"I'll leave you with George and Adam and go to Katy's place myself."

The officer asked, "What kind of house do you have?"

"Stone."

"Good. It should be easier to defend than most of the flimsy picket shacks I have seen around here. I would suggest you gather your neighbors and fort up within its walls." He motioned with his hand, and the detail rode on.

Trey took a long look around, wondering what his reaction would be if he actually saw a Comanche war party. The only Indians he had ever seen were a few Choctaws trading in Fort Worth and some Cheyennes asking for beeves from Kerbow's trail herd. He had been told that a Comanche raiding party in full cry could curdle a man's blood and turn his knees to water.

"We'd just better hope we find George to home."

They did. George was leaning against the outside of a corral fence, shouting advice to his son Adam, who rode a crow-hopping young bronc around and around inside. The old ranchman stared in surprise at Sarah riding sidesaddle. He did not even look around when the boy lost his seat on the bronc and struck the soft sand with a dull thud.

"Well, I'll swun, Sarah. Didn't know you could ride anything except a wagon seat. I'm tickled that you-all've come to visit."

Trey said, "I'm afraid you won't be tickled at what we came to tell you."

George's broad smile died as Trey related the officer's message. Adam Blackman, picking himself up from the ground, had heard enough to capture his full attention. Trey looked past the corral at the cedar-picket home and remembered what the officer had said about the superiority of stone walls.

"George, I wish you and Adam would take Sarah home and barricade yourselves inside our house. I'll go warn Katy and Jarrett. If Jarrett's still there."

Sarah asked, "What about Mead Overstreet?"

Trey frowned. "What about him?"

"He ought to be told."

"Let the son of a bitch find out for himself."

"He'll never be a deacon in the church, but you can't just leave him at the mercy of the Indians. You've got to warn him."

Acceptance was like swallowing a dead rat, but Trey forced himself. "All right, I'll go by his place on the way to Katy's." He turned to George. "You-all take care of Sarah."

Sarah said, "You take care of yourself. Keep your eyes open."

He kissed her and spurred away toward Overstreet's.

He found Overstreet at home and fiercely suspicious. The man met him at the front door with a pistol in his hand. Like Trey, he had lost most sign of the bruises, but a deep knuckle cut still showed red on his cheekbone. When he opened his mouth, Trey could see a gap where one of his front teeth had been broken off. "If you've come over for some more fight, I'll be happy to accommodate you."

"Another time. You pick it to suit yourself. But we may have a different kind of fight on our hands." Trey explained what the officer had told him. "I'm tellin' the others to gather at our place. The Indians would have a hard time comin' through those walls."

"You said you'd kill me if ever I set foot there again."

"Afterwards, that'll still go. But right now you need us and we need you."

"All right, but I ain't ridin' with you. I wouldn't want a bullet in my back."

"I wouldn't do that. Anyway, I'm goin' from here to Katy's."

"The country'd be better off if you let the Indians get her."

"I expect that's what she'd say about you."

He did not wait to see Overstreet leave. He struck out toward the rough blue edge of caprock, his senses alert to everything that moved or made a noise. He fancied he saw Indians in every thicket, in every red-clay gash that runoff water had carved across the eastward-slanting plain.

He was shouting for Katy before he broke through the last stand of timber and came into view of her half-hidden picket shack. She met him at the door, holding a rifle. "What the hell is the hollerin' about?"

Her brow furrowed as he told her and she contemplated the possibilities. "It's risky for Jarrett to show himself. What chance would he have if Gault was to find him?"

"What chance would he have if the Comanches did?"

"Hold on to your horse." She fired the rifle into the air three times. The gray horse jerked back against the reins, and Trey almost lost him. Katy went into the shack, shouting over her shoulder, "Saddle my horse for me, would you? I'll gather up some stuff."

It was perhaps fifteen or twenty minutes before Jarrett rode out of a thicket, ready for war. He carried a rifle pointed in Trey's direction, lowering it upon recognition.

"I thought the vigilance committee had laid siege on Katy's place. You've strayed off your range, ain't you, farm boy?"

Katy came out of the shack as Trey explained. Jarrett asked, "Who-all you reckon'll be there?"

"George Blackman and his boy Adam. You and Katy and me and Sarah. And Mead Overstreet. That's all I know about."

"I reckon I'll be safe enough, then, as long as I don't turn my back on Overstreet."

Katy's voice was critical. "You warned Mead? The country'd be better off if you let the Indians get him."

Trey felt more secure, traveling with Jarrett and Katy, but he did not relax his vigilance. He made it a point as much as possible to skirt well around brush mottes and thickets where a raiding party might hide in ambush. Though Jarrett tried not to show concern, Trey sensed that he was extremely watchful, placing himself between Katy and any potential source of attack. He supposed watchfulness had become second nature to Jarrett, given his high popularity with officers of the law.

He kept looking back at the sinking sun, wishing it would stand still a while. He did not relish riding in darkness, not being able to see what might be waiting for them. It was dusk but not yet full dark when the three approached the stone house. Sarah had not yet lighted the lantern she had gotten in the habit of hanging out for him when he was late. It might not be prudent tonight anyway. She hurried out to meet them when they rode up to the corral. She threw her arms around Trey as he stepped down from his tired horse.

"I was startin' to worry somethin' fierce."

"It was a long circle. Did Mead Overstreet show up?"

"He's been keepin' watch by the barn. George won't hardly let him come in the house."

"George is a good judge of character."

"I think Overstreet's a little ashamed of what he did."

Katy declared, "Only thing he's ashamed of is that he didn't finish doin' what he meant to. Give him half a chance and he'll try you again."

Overstreet's voice came sharply from the darkness of the shed that adjoined the barn. "What would you know about shame? I found you in a Fort Worth whorehouse."

"At least *I* changed."

"Damned little, except that maybe you don't take pay for it anymore."

Jarrett yelled, "Damn your big mouth, Overstreet!" He started toward the dark figure which had stepped to the edge of the shadow.

Trey caught his arm. "Not now, Jarrett. We can cut cards for him when this is all over."

"You had *your* chance at him. You're just not mean enough. Next time I whip him, there won't be nothin' left but a wad of hair and a spot of grease." But Jarrett backed away, unsaddling his horse. He said, "Comanches are the best horse thieves in the world. Wouldn't take much for them to come in the night and set us all afoot."

Trey said, "We'll tie the gates shut. That'll slow them down a little. And we'll take turn about standin' guard." He hoped the dog might be of some help too. It usually barked when anyone approached, including Trey himself. But lately Trey had gone back to calling him Useless instead of Ulysses. The dog had taken to straying away at night, answering the distant siren call of the coyotes. It would return at daylight, weary and footsore from fruitless wanderings but no wiser than the day before.

Trey did not sleep much after standing his midnight watch. He dozed fitfully on a raw bunk in the picket bunkhouse. The men had left the stone house to the two women, who slept behind a barred door. Trey heard Sarah's rooster crow. He assumed that heralded daybreak, though sometimes the fool rooster decided to crow when it was still pitch dark. Its intelligence was several notches below even that of the dog.

In the gloom of the closed bunkhouse Trey could see Jarrett Longacre sitting on the edge of a cot, awake. Mead Overstreet lay on a cot in a corner, as far from the others as he could get. The only sound Trey heard was George Blackman's heavy breathing. He still slept. His son Adam was outside. He had taken the night's final watch.

"Mornin'," Jarrett said quietly. "Looks like we've all still got our scalps."

"I hope we've still got our horses."

Trey had slept in his clothes, but he had removed his boots. He pulled them on, then opened the door. It faced east, and he could see the beginnings of dawn outlining the tops of the trees. He poked his head out the door, looking toward the corral. The horses were safe.

He smelled woodsmoke and knew Sarah was up, for she had kindled a fire in the stove. She would be starting breakfast soon. He wondered where George's son had stationed himself. He stepped farther out into the open, searching. In a minute Jarrett Longacre followed him, strapping his gun belt around his waist.

"Lose somethin', Trey?"

"Adam. I don't see him anyplace."

He heard a voice that was not Adam's. "I am afraid the young man fell asleep on duty. I have him here."

Trey knew before he turned on his heel.

Gault!

The lawman stood at the corner of the bunkhouse, holding a horse's reins and training a pistol on Longacre. "Jarrett Longacre, you are under arrest. You will unbuckle that belt and drop it to the ground. Carefully, or you will find yourself facing your Lord before the sun rises."

Adam Blackman stood sheepishly to one side, his head bowed. "I'm sorry, Trey. I didn't sleep all night, worryin' about them Indians. Then when I came out to stand my guard, everything was so quiet . . ."

The dog must have been asleep too, or more likely gone off somewhere hunting for the coyotes.

Gault said, "I would be obliged, Mr. McLean, if you would call the other gentlemen out of the bunkhouse. And tell them to bring no guns."

"We'll all be needin' our guns if the Indians show up."

"There are no Indians. I started that rumor myself to see if it would smoke out Mr. Longacre. Now, call the others."

Trey went to the bunkhouse door. He took another long look at Gault before he obeyed the directions. He saw in the man's stern face a determination that would not yield to argument. George was the first to come out. He saw in a glance what had happened. He said nothing, but his eyes bespoke sympathy and regret for Longacre.

Overstreet emerged, gun belt dangling from his hand. "What's this about no guns?" He saw Gault and Longacre, and his mouth cut into a grim smile. "Well, I'll be damned. Finally caught you, didn't he, Longacre? I was hopin' to shoot you myself."

Gault was all business. "Your gun, Mr. Overstreet. Drop it."

"You think I'd do anything to help that outlaw? I'm here to help you, Mr. Gault."

"You can help me best by dropping that pistol to the ground."

"You're liable to need me and this pistol. These others, they're all against you. But I'm with you. I want to see Longacre get everything that's comin' to him." He strapped the belt around his waist.

Gault jammed the muzzle of his pistol against Overstreet's stomach. "I said drop it!"

Overstreet dropped it. Anger flashed in his eyes. "You wasn't too proud to let me help you before. I'm the one told you Longacre had come here, remember?"

"I had use for you then. I have no use for you now."

"Goddamn you, you Bible-spoutin' old bastard."

Gault gave Overstreet a withering look. "Put a rein on your blasphemy. The Lord may send a thunderbolt to strike you down, and I do not want to be standing at your side." He turned to Trey. "It will be a long ride to Fort Griffin. I do not believe your young lady would want Mr. Longacre and me to travel hungry."

Trey gave Jarrett an apologetic look. Jarrett appeared resigned. "It ain't your fault. Ain't nobody's fault except maybe mine. I don't even blame Gault. I made a mistake not sleepin' in the brush."

Gault said, "You made a mistake the first time you went afoul of the law. Now, Mr. McLean, if you please . . ." He made a tiny motion with the muzzle of his pistol.

Trey tapped his knuckles against the wooden door. "Sarah!"

He heard the bar sliding out of place. The door opened inward. Sarah stood just inside. "Is everything all right?"

"Not exactly."

She saw Gault and realized immediately what was happening. He motioned for everyone to enter the cabin ahead of him. He had the pistol in Jarrett's back as he moved through the door.

"Now, everyone except Mrs. McLean will please stand in that corner so I can keep a watch on you. Young lady, I would be much in your debt if you might prepare a little breakfast for Mr. Longacre and me."

Katy came forward and put her arms around Longacre. Gault seemed inclined to separate the pair, then thought better of it and left the couple alone. "I am afraid, Miss Rice, that you have misplaced your affections."

Overstreet snickered. "It ain't the first time. She used to do it for money."

Gault's voice was impatient. "Mr. Overstreet, your loose tongue offends me."

"I'm just sayin' they make a good pair. Him a wanted outlaw, her a—"

Katy shouted at him, "Shut your foul mouth, Mead! You're a hell of a one to talk about other people. Mr. Gault, you really want to know what kind of a man he is?"

"I already know, and I intend to have nothing more to do with him."

"I'll tell you anyway. First time ever I saw him, I was workin' in a Fort Worth parlor house. He offered to pay me to come out here and stay at his ranch with him. I thought it had to be better than what I was doin', but it was worse. Soon as the new wore off he turned mean, beatin' on me 'til one day I bent a rifle barrel over his head, took a horse and left."

Overstreet growled, "She always was a thief."

"Thief? If I was, I learned from the best of them." She turned to George Blackman. "I'll bet the vigilance committee'd be real interested in how he started that herd of his. He stole cattle from you and everybody around him, especially Kerbow. It was easy with Kerbow because he was gone most of the time on business. But cattle wasn't all he stole from Kerbow. There was Martha."

Overstreet warned, "You're lettin' your mouth run loose, Katy."

"He taken advantage of her like he tried to take advantage of Sarah, only Martha let him. Kerbow was off on a long cattle drive, and she was lonely. Sarah, you asked me once how Martha died. She killed herself. Kerbow never knew why, just figured it was the lonesome drove her out of her mind. But she left a note. I found it and burned it."

Overstreet's face had gone scarlet. "She's a damned liar. Don't listen to her."

"Kerbow'll listen when he gets back, because I intend to tell him. He'll kill you deader than a skinned mule, if the vigilance committee don't beat him to it. You got her pregnant and then turned your back on her. She didn't see any way she could tell Kerbow, so she walked down to the creek and shot herself."

"I told you . . ." Overstreet swung his fist and knocked Katy staggering.

Jarrett roared in rage and charged at him. He slammed Overstreet against the wall. Katy barely had time to step out of the way, blood trickling from the corner of her mouth. Overstreet cried out as Jarrett's knuckles smashed his nose. He rushed forward, nearly bowling Jarrett over. The two men knocked the table aside as they scrambled for position.

Gault stepped around them, waving his pistol. "Stop it, you men. Stop it, I say!"

If they heard him, they gave no sign. Gault seemed about to wade in between them but reconsidered and moved back, giving them room. Nothing he could have done, short of shooting them, would stop the fight anyway.

Sarah and Katy moved together. Katy's eyes were wide with apprehension for Jarrett.

Trey looked at the rifle on its pegs over the mantle. He had made it a point to see that it was loaded since the day of his own fight with Overstreet. He considered his chances of reaching it and decided they were poor. He suspected Gault would shoot him if he had to.

The fight was savage but short. Overstreet struck a blow that sent Jarrett to his knees, then made two long strides toward the fireplace. Even as Trey shouted a warning, the rifle was in Overstreet's hands. He brought the muzzle down toward Jarrett.

Gault's age and old injuries did not prevent him from being quick on his feet. He stepped protectively in front of Jarrett, the pistol pointed toward Overstreet.

"This man is my prisoner. Drop the rifle."

Trey would always wonder whether Overstreet was trying to hit Gault or to shoot past him and hit Jarrett. Flame spat from the barrel. The walls seemed to tremble from the noise and force of the shot. Powder smoke blossomed white and spread across the room.

Gault stumbled, falling back against Jarrett Longacre. By reflex the lawman jerked the pistol's trigger. The bullet ricocheted from the flagstone and sang through the open door. Jarrett caught Gault in his arms and eased him down.

Overstreet stared in shock at the rifle, then at the gasping lawman. He appeared suddenly staggered by the enormity of what he had done, of the punishment that surely awaited him.

He regained composure enough to drop the empty rifle and grab the pistol from Gault's trembling hand. "Don't nobody move." He backed toward the cabin door. "First one tries to come out, I'll kill him!"

As quickly as Overstreet cleared the stone step, Trey reached for the rifle. He jacked the spent cartridge from the chamber and shoved in another from several lying on the mantel. He rushed out the door.

Overstreet grabbed Gault's saddled horse, mounted hurriedly and hammered his heels against the black's sides.

He would make a perfect target, riding away. Trey lifted the rifle to his shoulder, steadied the barrel and brought the sights into line with Overstreet's back. He tried to squeeze the trigger, but his finger would not respond. Sweat began to roll down into his eyes and burned them.

He lowered the rifle. "I just can't do it."

Jarrett stepped out beside him. His voice was raw. "By God, I can!" He took the rifle from Trey, set it firmly against his shoulder and fired.

Overstreet's hands went up over over his head, flinging Gault's pistol away. He tumbled to the ground.

Jarrett lowered the smoking rifle. "Somebody ought to've done that years ago." He handed the weapon back to Trey. "Like I told you, you're not mean enough for this country." He turned back into the cabin.

George had come out, his face long in shock. He stared toward Overstreet, who lay with one leg doubled beneath him, the other extended awkwardly, just as he had landed. George said, "He's wrong, Trey. You're the kind this country needs. Maybe someday *it* won't be so mean." He moved down from the stone slab. "I reckon we better go see about Mead."

"I reckon."

Gault's horse had run a short distance and stopped. It came back, nostrils extended, ears poked forward as it made a skittish circle around Overstreet's body. Trey saw the blood-rimmed hole the bullet had made almost squarely between the shoulder blades. George knelt to examine the man.

"Dead?" Trey asked.

George nodded. "Better than facin' the vigilance committee. He probably never knowed what hit him."

Trey shuddered. "I'm glad it wasn't me that done it." He remembered something Jarrett had told him. Killing a man was easy. Living with the killing was hard.

They returned to the cabin and found Gault lying on the bed, his shirt ripped away. His face was the color of cold ashes. The wound was in his shoulder, near the ragged scar of the one Jarrett had placed there months ago. Jarrett was bent over him, and Katy cleaned the wound with a rough-torn piece of cotton cloth. Sarah stood behind her, holding a pan of steaming water.

Gault looked up at Jarrett. He rasped, "I suppose you'll take advantage of my situation. You'll run again."

"I'd be a fool to stay around 'til you heal up and come after me."

"When will you ever stop running?"

"When you give up chasin' me."

Gault sucked a sharp breath between his teeth as Katy probed the edges of the wound. "Twice in the same place. Why has the Lord afflicted me so?"

Sarah said, "Maybe He's tellin' you to go back to your true callin'."

"I was called to be His avenging right arm."

"You know about vengeance, but you've forgot what the Lord said about forgiveness. If you'd been carryin' the Book instead of a gun . . ."

Frowning, Jarrett explored the wound. "Got to dig in there and take that bullet out. I don't reckon there's a drop of whiskey in the house?"

Trey said, "There's not."

Gault looked up apprehensively at Jarrett. "Surely you are not the one to do it."

"I've had a little experience along these lines."

"You could let your hand slip and kill me. No one could ever prove you did it on purpose."

"Yes, sir, I could do that. Now, Mr. Gault, this is fixin' to hurt like hell. You can pray or you can cuss, whichever helps the most."

Gault did some of both, until he fell unconscious. The bullet came out. Jarrett dropped it into the wash pan and wiped cold sweat from his forehead onto his sleeve.

A flock of geese flying south caught Trey's attention. He reined the gray horse to a stop and looked up, listening to the honking sounds they were making. These were stragglers, for he could already feel the first breath of winter in the early chill of the fall mornings.

As the sound of the geese faded, another sound came to him, the jingling of trace chains, the rattle of wagons. He rode down toward the town trail and saw them. In the lead he recognized George Blackman's. George had come by two days earlier on his way to Griffin to lay in supplies for the winter. Behind him came a chuck wagon and a hoodlum wagon, four horsemen trailing them.

Kerbow!

Trey spurred down to meet them. He came to George's wagon first. Sitting beside George was a middle-aged woman wearing a slat bonnet and a friendly smile. George raised his hand in greeting and sawed on the lines to stop his team.

"Trey, I want you to meet my wife. I talked her into comin' out and stayin', now that she's got Sarah for a neighbor."

Trey tipped his hat. "Mighty pleased to meet you, Mrs. Blackman."

"It's Thelma. And I'm mighty anxious to meet your little lady."

"You will, just over the hill yonder. Sarah'll be real tickled to see you."

Wagon cook Zack Lynch pulled his chuck wagon up behind George's vehicle and stopped, shouting a howdy at Trey. Pancho Martínez gave a holler from the hoodlum wagon. Kerbow pushed forward on horseback, followed by the three other riders. Two were strangers, but Trey knew by their look that they were cowboys. The third was Pete James.

Trey shook hands with Kerbow, then with each of the others in turn. Kerbow asked, "Everything all right here?"

"Couldn't be much better. Got a feed crop ready to cut. And we had some fall rain, so we're goin' into the winter in pretty good shape for grass."

He realized he sounded like George Blackman. George had taught him how to rope and how to read a cow's mind, and how to think like a cattleman as well as a farmer. What George might lack in style a-horseback, he made up for in results.

Kerbow said, "I went to services while we were in Griffin. You wouldn't guess who was preachin'."

"Mr. Gault?"

"George says this time Jarrett dug a bullet out of Gault's shoulder instead of puttin' one in. I suppose Gault has given up huntin' him."

"He said he'd take up the search soon as he got healed. But I think he just wanted Jarrett to leave here and try for a fresh start where nobody knows him."

"It had better be a long way off."

"Katy Rice sold her cattle to George. Her and Jarrett headed west."

"She's a strong woman. Maybe she can cool down the wild streak in him. If she can't, at least she's one who can keep up with him." Kerbow motioned toward the other three riders. "We've come to brand the calf crop."

"They're done branded. I been catchin' them soon as I could find them." Trey took the tally book from his pocket and thumbed to the pages where he had kept track of the branding. He passed it to Kerbow.

Kerbow eyes lighted with satisfaction as he counted the marks. "To tell you the truth, I did a lot of worryin' afterwards about sendin' you and that girl out here, a couple of green farm kids. But you've made a good hand. Just the kind of workin' partner I need to take care of this place."

"Partner?"

"I haven't got time to stay around here much." Kerbow frowned.

"But only if it's all right with that young lady of yours. I saw the loneliness here drive another woman to her death."

Trey, Sarah and George had agreed that with Overstreet dead and Katy gone, there was no reason anyone should ever tell Kerbow the real reason his wife had killed herself.

"It's not as lonesome as it used to be. George's wife has come to stay, and there's a young couple out of Weatherford took up the place Mead Overstreet was squattin' on. Country's startin' to settle up pretty good."

Kerbow seemed pleased. "Then I reckon the boys and me can turn around and go on to south Texas. I've got to start linin' up cattle for next spring's drive."

"You can stay and help me cut the feed crop."

"These are cowboys. That's farmer work."

Sarah's milk cow was grazing near the wagon road. Kerbow looked at her in puzzlement. "I don't remember leavin' a milk cow here."

"A gift from George. Said he figured we'd be needin' one sooner or later. And from what Sarah told me the other evenin', he was right."

Kerbow came near letting one of his rare smiles escape. "Whenever you see a milk cow, it's time for the cowboys to make room. The punkin' rollers are movin' in."

Trey loped on ahead of the wagons to tell Sarah that company was coming.